Ellen Elizabeth Frewer, David-Léon Cahun

The Adventures of Captain Mago

Or a Phoenician Expedition, B. C. 1000

Ellen Elizabeth Frewer, David-Léon Cahun

The Adventures of Captain Mago
Or a Phoenician Expedition, B. C. 1000

ISBN/EAN: 9783337077525

Printed in Europe, USA, Canada, Australia, Japan

Cover: Foto ©Andreas Hilbeck / pixelio.de

More available books at **www.hansebooks.com**

THE ADVENTURES

OF

CAPTAIN MAGO

OR

A Phœnician Expedition

B. C. 1000

BY

LÉON CAHUN

*ILLUSTRATED BY P. PHILIPPOTEAUX, AND TRANSLATED FROM
THE FRENCH BY ELLEN E. FREWER*

NEW YORK
CHARLES SCRIBNER'S SONS
1889

PREFACE.

THE following pages pretend to no original or scientific research. It is their object to present, in a popular form, a picture of the world as it was a thousand years before the Christian Era, and to exhibit, mainly for the young, a summary of that varied information which is contained in books, many of which by their high price and exclusively technical character are generally unattainable.

It would only have encumbered the fictitious narrative, which is the vehicle for conveying the instruction that is designed, to crowd every page with references ; but it may be alleged, once for all, that for every statement which relates to the history of the period, and especially to the history of the Phœnicians, ample authority might be quoted from some one or other of the valuable books which have been consulted.

Of the most important of these a list is here appended :—

1. F. C. MOVERS. Das Phönizische Alterthum.
2. RENAN. Mission en Phenicie.
3. DAUX. Recherches sur les Emporia phéniciens dans le Zeugis et le Byzacium.

4. NATHAN DAVIS. Carthage and her Remains.
5. WILKINSON. Manners and Customs of Ancient Egyptians.
6. HŒCKH. Kreta.
7. GROTE. History of Greece.
8. MOMMSEN. Geschichte der Römischen Republik (Introduction and Chap. 1.).
9. BOURGUIGNAT. Monuments mégalithiques du nord de l'Afrique.
10. FERGUSSON. Rude Stone Monuments.
11. BROCA and A. BERTRAND. Celtes, Gaulois et Francs.
12. ABBÉ BARGÈS. Interprétation d'une inscription phénicienne trouvée à Marseille.
13. LAYARD. Nineveh and its Remains.
14. BOTTA. Fouilles de Babylone.
15. REUSS. New translation of the Bible, in course of publication.

A few foot-notes are subjoined by way of illustration of what might have been carried on throughout the volume; and an Appendix will be found at the end, containing some explanation of topics which the continuity of the fiction necessarily left somewhat obscure.

CONTENTS.

vi   CONTENTS.

LIST OF FULL PAGE ILLUSTRATIONS.

And Thirty-six smaller Text Illustrations.

THE ADVENTURES OF CAPTAIN MAGO

CHAPTER I.

WHY BODMILCAR, THE TYRIAN SAILOR, HATES HANNO, THE SIDONIAN SCRIBE.

I AM Captain Mago, and Hiram,[1] King of Tyre, was well aware that my experience as a sailor was very great. It was in the third year of his reign that he summoned me to his presence from Sidon,[2] the city of fishermen, and the metropolis of the Phœnicians. He had already been told of my long voyages; how I had visited Malta; how I had traded to Bozrah,[3] the city founded by the Sidonians, but now called Carthada[4] by the Tyrians; and how I had reached the remote Gades in the land of Tarshish.[5]

The star of Sidon was now on the wane. The ships of Tyre were fast occupying the sea, and her caravans were covering the land. A monarchy had been established by the Tyrians, and their king, with the *suffects*[6] as his coadjutors, was holding sway over all the other cities of Phœnicia. The fortunes of Tyre were thus in the ascendant: sailors and merchants from Sidon, Gebal, Arvad and Byblos were continually enlisting themselves in the service of her powerful corporations.

[1] Hiram I. reigned from 980 to 947 B.C.
[2] Sidon, or Zidon, in the Phœnician tongue means "fishery."
[3] Bostra, or Bozrah; hence Byrsa, the citadel.
[4] Carthage, or Kart-Khadecht, the new city.
[5] Tarshish, the Tartessus of the Greeks, Spain.
[6] Suffect, or *chophet* (plural *chophettim*), the Hebrew and Phœnician magistrates preceding the monarchy.

B

When I had made my obeisance to King Hiram, he informed me that his friend and ally, David, King of the Jews, was collecting materials for the erection of a temple to his god Adonai (or *our Lord*) in the city of Jerusalem, and that he was desirous of making his own royal contribution to assist him. Accordingly he submitted to me that at his expense I should fit out a sufficient fleet, and should undertake a voyage to Tarshish, in order to procure a supply of silver, and any other rare or valuable commodity which that land could yield, to provide embellishment for the sumptuous edifice.

Anxious as I was already to revisit Tarshish and the ands of the West, I entered most eagerly into the proposal of the King, assuring him that I should require no longer time for preparation than what was absolutely necessary to equip the ships and collect the crews.

It was still two months before the Feast of Spring, an annual festival that marked the re-opening of navigation. This was an interval sufficient for my purpose, for as the King directed me to call first at Joppa, and to proceed thence to Jerusalem to receive King David's instructions, I had no need for the present to concern myself about anything further than my ships and sailors, knowing that I could safely trust to the fertile and martial land of Judæa to provide me with provisions and soldiers.

The King was highly gratified at my ready acquiescence in his proposition. He instructed his treasurer to hand over to me at once a thousand silver shekels[1] to meet preliminary expenses, and gave orders to the authorities at the arsenal to allow me to select whatever wood, hemp, or copper I might require.

I took my leave of the King and rejoined Hanno my scribe and Himilco my pilot, the latter of whom had been my constant associate on my previous voyages. They were sitting on the side-bench at the great gate of the palace,

---

[1] The silver shekel was the standard money of the Phœnicians, and was worth about 2*s.* It was a tenth part of a shekel of gold.

and had been impatiently awaiting my return, mutually
speculating upon the reason that had induced the King to
send for us from Sidon, and naturally conjecturing that it
must relate to some future enterprise and adventure. At
the first glimpse of my excited countenance, revealing my
delight, Hanno exclaimed :

" Welcome back, master ; surely the King has granted
you some eager longing of your heart ! "

" True ; and what do you suppose it is ? " I asked.

" Perhaps a new ship to replace the one you lost in the
Great Syrtes ; and perhaps a good freight into the bargain.
No son of Sidon could covet more than this."

" Yes, Hanno ; this, and more beside," I answered. " But
our good fortune at once demands our vows ; let us hasten
to the temple of Ashtoreth,[1] and there let us render our
thanks to the goddess, and sue for her protection and her
favour to guard our vessels as we sail to Joppa. To Joppa
we go ; and onwards thence to Tarshish ! "

" Tarshish ! " echoed the voice of Himilco, with a cry of
ecstasy : and as he spoke he raised up his sole remaining
eye towards the skies ; he had lost the other in a naval
fight. " Tarshish," he said again : " O ye gods, that rule
the destinies of ships ! ye stars,[2] that so oft have fixed my
gaze in my weary watch on deck ! here I offer to you six
shekels on the spot ; 'tis all my means allow. But take
me to Tarshish, and vouchsafe that I may come across the
villain whose lance took out my eye, so that I may make
him feel the point of my Chalcidian sword below his ribs,
and I vow that I will offer you in sacrifice an ox, a noble
ox, finer than Apis, the god of the idiot Egyptians."

Hanno was less demonstrative. " For my part," he said,
" I shall be satisfied if I can barter enough of the vile wine of
Judæa, and the cheap ware of Sidon, to get a good return

---

[1] Astarte. The Aphrodite of the Greeks ; the goddess of navigation, and
the national deity of the Sidonians.

[2] The stars in the constellation of Ursa Major were also tutelary deities of
navigation ; the pole-star by the Greeks being called "the Phœnician."

of pure white silver. I shall only be too pleased to build myself a mansion upon the sea-shore where I can enjoy my pleasure-boat as it glides along with its purple sails, and so to pass my days in ease and luxury."

"Remember, however," I replied, "that before you can get your lordly mansion, we shall again and again have to sleep under the open sky of the cheerless West ; and before you arrive at all your luxury, you will have to put up with many a coarse and meagre meal."

"All the more pleasant will be the retrospect," rejoined Hanno ; "and when we come to recline upon our costly couches it will be a double joy to dwell upon our adventures, and relate them to our listening guests."

Conversation of this character engaged us till we reached the cypress-grove, from which the temple of Ashtoreth upreared its silver-plated roof. The setting sun was all aglow, and cast its slanting rays upon the fabric, illuminating alike the heavy gilding and the radiant colours of the supporting pillars. Flocks of consecrated doves fluttered in the sacred grove, alighting ever and again upon the gilded rods that connected one pillar with another. Groups of girls were frequently met, dressed in white, embroidered with purple and silver, either hastening, pomegranates in their hands, to make a votive offering at the shrine, or sauntering leisurely in the sacred gardens. Ever and again, as the temple-doors were opened, there was caught the distant melody of the sistra, flutes, and tambourines, upon which the priests and priestesses were celebrating the honour of their goddess. Such were the sounds, the modulated measures of the music mingled with the soft cooings of the doves and the joyous laughter of the heedless maidens, that combined to make a mysterious murmur that could not fail to impress the minds of such as us, rough mariners unaccustomed to anything more harmonious than the groanings of the waves, the creaking of our ships, and the howling of the wind.

I went with Himilco to consult the tariff of the sacrifices, which was exhibited, engraven on a tablet and affixed to the feet of a huge marble dove at the right-hand entrance to the precincts of the temple. As my own offering, I selected some fruit and cakes, the value of which did not exceed a shekel, and was just turning back to call Hanno, when I encountered a man in a dirty and thread-bare sailor's coat, who was hurrying along, muttering bitter curses as he went.

"Help me, Baal Chamaïm, Lord of the heavens!" I involuntarily exclaimed; "is not this Bodmilcar, the Tyrian?"

The man paused, and recognised me in a moment; and we exchanged the warmest greetings.

Bodmilcar, whom I had thus unexpectedly met, had been one of my oldest associates. Many a time, alike in expeditions of war and commerce, he had commanded a vessel by my side. He was likewise already acquainted with Himilco, who consequently shared my surprise and regret at meeting him in so miserable a plight.

"What ill fate has brought you to this?" was my impatient inquiry. "At Tyre you used to be the owner of a couple of gaouls[1] and four good galleys; what has happened? What has brought it about that you should be here in nothing better than a ragged kitonet?"[2]

"Moloch's[3] heaviest curses be upon the Chaldeans!" ejaculated Bodmilcar. "May their cock-head Nergal[4] torture and burn and roast them all! My story is soon told. I had a cargo of slaves. A finer cargo was never under weigh. The hold of my Tyrian gaoul carried Caucasian men as strong as oxen, and Grecian girls as lissome as reeds; there were Syrians who could cook, or play, or dress the hair; there were peasants from Judæa

---

[1] Gaoul, a round ship, employed in merchant service.
[2] Kitonet, a short tunic, worn by Phœnician sailors.
[3] Baal Moloch, the sun god.
[4] Nergal, the Chaldean god of fire and war, always represented with a cock's head.

who could train the vine or cultivate the field.   Their value was untold."

"And tell me, friend Bodmilcar," I inquired, "where are they now?   Did they not yield you the countless shekels on which you reckoned?"

"Now! where are they now?" shrieked out the excited man; "they are every one upon their way to some cursed city of the Chaldeans, on the other side of Rehoboth.   Instead of shekels I have got plenty of kicks and plenty of bruises, of which I shall carry the marks on my body for a long time to come.   The naval suffect gave me a few zeraas,[1] just to relieve my distress, and had it not been for that, I should not have had a morsel of bread to keep life in me.   It is now three days since I arrived in Tyre, and to get here I have been continually walking, till my feet are so swollen I can hardly move."

"You mean you have walked here?" said Himilco, compassionately.   "But surely you might have found a boat of some sort to bring you?"

"Boat!" growled Bodmilcar, almost angrily; "when did boats begin to journey overland?   Did I not tell you I came from Rehoboth in the land of those cursed Chaldeans?   But hear me out, and you will sympathise with my misfortune.   I started first of all along the coast, buying slaves from the Philistines, and corn and oil from the Jews.   I went across to Greece, and made some profitable dealings there.   I chanced upon a few wretched little Ionian barques, and secured some plunder so.   Then I conceived the project of going through the straits, and I succeeded beyond my hopes in getting iron, and, what is more, in getting slaves from Caucasus.   My fortune was made.   I was proceeding home, when just as we neared the Phasis, on the Chalybean coast, some alien gods—for sure I am that neither Melkarth nor Moloch would so have dealt with a Tyrian sailor—some alien gods, I say, sent down a frightful storm.   With the utmost peril I contrived to save

---

[1] Zeraas, small copper coin.

my crew and all my human cargo; but the bulk of my
goods was gone, and my poor vessels were shattered
hopelessly. There was but one resource; I had no alternative but to convey my salvage in the best way I
could across Armenia and Chaldea by land, consoling
myself with the expectation of finding a market for the
slaves along the road. But once again the gods were
cruelly adverse. We were attacked by a troop of Chaldeans; fifty armed men could not protect a gang of four
hundred slaves, who, miserable wretches as they were,
could not be induced by blows or prayers to lift up a hand
in their own defence. The result was that we were very
soon overpowered, and that, together with all my party, I
was made a prisoner. The Chaldeans proposed to sell us
to the King of Nineveh, and I had the pleasure of finding
myself part and parcel of my own cargo."

"But, anyhow, here you are. How did you contrive to
get out of your dilemma?" I asked my old comrade.

Bodmilcar raised the skirt of his patched and greasy
kitonet, and displayed a long knife with an ivory handle
hanging from his belt.

"They forgot to search me," he said, "and omitted to
bind me. The very first night on which there was no
moonlight I was entertaining a couple of rascals who had
charge of me, by telling them wonderful tales about Libyan
serpents, and about the men of Tarshish who had mouths
in the middle of their chests, and eyes at the tips of their
fingers; openmouthed, they were lost in amazement at the
lies I was pouring into their ears, and were entirely off their
guard. I seized my opportunity; and having first thrust
my knife into the belly of one of them, I cut the throat of
the other and made my escape. I took to my heels, and,
Moloch be praised! the rascals failed to find a trace of me.
But now that I am here, the gods only know what is to
become of me. If I fail to get service as a pilot, I must
enter as a common sailor in some Tyrian ship."

"No need of that, Bodmilcar," I exclaimed; "you have

made your appearance just at a lucky moment. All praise to Ashtoreth! you are just the man I want. I have a commission from the King to fit out ships for Tarshish; I am captain of the expedition, and here at once I can appoint you my second in command. My pilot is Himilco; and here is Hanno, my scribe; we are on our way to the temple of the goddess, and are going in her presence to draw up the covenants."

"Joy, joy, dear Mago!" ejaculated Bodmilcar; "may the gods be gracious to you, and repay your goodness! I shall not regret my disaster at the hands of the Chaldeans, if it ends in a voyage to Tarshish with you. Only let Melkarth vouchsafe us a good ship, and with Himilco to guide our course, we cannot fail to prosper, even though our voyage be to the remotest confines of the world."

Hanno, who meanwhile had joined us, took out from his girdle some ink and some reeds, with a little stone to sharpen them, and having seated himself upon the temple steps, proceeded to draw up the articles which appointed me admiral of the expedition, Bodmilcar vice-admiral, and Himilco pilot-in-chief. Himilco and myself both affixed our seals to the document, and Bodmilcar was proceeding to do so likewise, feeling mechanically for his seal, which he remembered afterwards that the Chaldeans had stolen. I gave him twenty shekels to buy another, and to provide him with a new outfit of clothes. Then, with Himilco, I proceeded to make my oblation of fruits and cakes to Ashtoreth; and in the highest spirits we made our way to the harbour, where our light vessel, the *Gadita*, was awaiting us.

Early next morning we set vigorously to work. I drew out the plans of my vessels upon papyrus sheets. My own *Gadita* was to be kept as a light vessel; but I resolved to have a large *gaoul* constructed as a transport to carry the merchandise, and two barques to act as tenders to the gaoul, which would draw too much water to approach very near the shore. As an escorting convoy I chose two large

HANNO PROCEEDED TO DRAW UP THE ARTICLES.

H. Philimore

To face Page 8.

double-decked galleys,[1] manned by fifty oarsmen, similar to those recently invented at Sidon. At this period, the Tyrians had three of these galleys in port ; they were very rapid in their course, and drew very little water ; they were armed with strong beaks at the prow ; were worked both by oars and sails, and were adapted either for war or commerce.

I determined to use cedar for the keel and sides of my vessel, and oak from Bashan, in Judæa, for the masts and yards. I discarded the ancient method of making my sails of Galilean reeds or papyrus-fibre, preferring to have them woven out of our excellent Phœnician hemp, which the people of Arvad and Tyre are skilful in twisting into a very substantial texture. It was of the same material that I resolved to make my ropes.

As I was going through the arsenal, and wondering at the accumulated mass of copper, I espied a little store of the beautiful white tin obtained from the Celts in the distant islands of the far north-west. Previously to my own voyage those islands had been all but unknown, and I believe that I may say that my own investigation of them has conferred as great a benefit upon the Phœnicians as they had reaped two hundred years before by the discovery of the silver mines of Tarshish.

The sight of the copper determined me upon carrying out a plan which I had for some time been contemplating. It occurred to me that if the keel and flanks under water were protected with copper in the same way as the prows had hitherto been, the solidity of the vessel would be greatly increased, and the wood would be far less liable to decay. Accordingly, I made up my mind to protect the prows of the galleys with a hard alloy of copper and tin, and to sheathe the keels and flanks of all the four vessels with plates of wrought copper. The copper of Cyprus I rejected as being too soft and spongy for my purpose, and that

[1] For details of the construction of these galleys, see notes at the end of the Volume.

of Libanus as far too brittle ; but the firm yet ductile Cilician metal suited me admirably, and Kheleshbaai, the renowned Tyrian founder, set to work at once to forge me some large sheets, three cubits[1] long by two wide.

The King had placed 200 workmen at my disposal ; and, in order that I might better superintend their operations, I took a lodging with my three friends in a house at the corner of the Street of Caulkers, just opposite the arsenal, and there from my window upon the fourth floor I could well overlook the men working in the docks below.   I directed Hanno to make out a list of the goods we should require for barter, and he and Himilco chiefly busied themselves in collecting the things together ; whilst Bodmilcar, with two of my sailors, kept perambulating the neighbourhood of the harbour, succeeding tolerably well in securing recruits for my crew from amongst the seamen who were loitering about the quays, with tilted hats, looking out for employment.

On the first day of the month Nisan,[2] just four weeks after I had undertaken my commission, I returned home for my evening meal, and found my companions in hot dispute.

" How now ! " I cried, on entering the room ; " what's this ? What is the meaning of this angry contention ? "

" I am telling Bodmilcar," said Hanno, " that he has about as much brains as a bullock, and about as much elegance as a Bactrian camel."

" And am I to endure this insolence from a young stripling ? " cried Bodmilcar, angrily ; " am I to put up with it from a fresh-water lubber, who will cry like a baby at the first gust of wind, and implore us to put him on shore again ?   He has lived among women and scribblers till he has no more pluck in him than a garden-tortoise."

" I confess," rejoined Hanno, sarcastically, " that I have not had your experience ; I have not had the advantage of being pounced upon by the Chaldeans, or of being thrashed by my own slaves.   But let me say, I am twenty, and that I hope the first time you find me funking the sea, you

---

[1] The common cubit is about 16 inches.
[2] Nisan ; part of March and April.

HANNO CAUGHT UP A LARGE PITCHER.

To face page 11

will pitch me overboard like an old sandal. Anyhow, I
have had a voyage as far as Chittim ;[1] I have been amongst
the Ionians, and can speak their language ten times better
than any one among you."

"Talk to me about the Ionians," shouted Bodmilcar in a
fury, "and I will break every bone in your precious skin."

And, as he spoke, he laid his hand upon his knife ; but
Hanno, without flinching for a moment, caught up a large
pitcher that was standing on the table.

"Steady, steady !" interposed Himilco, "or you will be
spilling all the nectar ;"[2] and whilst I laid a firm grasp upon
Bodmilcar's arm, he rescued the pitcher, and deposited it
safely in the corner of the room.

Then addressing myself to the two excited combatants,
I said : "Now then, I cannot permit this altercation ; you are
both under my orders, and you must both submit ; conduct
yourselves amicably, or it shall be the worse for him that
disturbs the peace. But what is the meaning of this
chatter about the Ionians ? "

Hanno held out his hand to me, in token of submission,
expressed his regret for having given offence to Bodmilcar,
and assured me that he had only spoken in jest.

"You see now," I said to Bodmilcar, "Hanno is not
your subordinate, and you are bound to treat him as your
equal. However, what is it that he has said to offend you
so grievously ? "

Bodmilcar seemed abashed ; he stood twirling his beard,
and without raising his eyes, said :

" Amongst the slaves that the Chaldeans captured, there
was one Ionian girl that I thought to make my wife. I
spoke of her to Hanno, but he only jeered me ; he told me
that the girl had gone off with the Chaldeans of her own
accord, merely to get out of reach of me ; and his provoca-
tion made me angry."

[1] Chittim, the classical *Citium*, a Phœnician colony in Cyprus.
[2] Nectar ; the sweet and perfumed wine of the Phœnicians, said by the
Greeks to be the drink of the gods.

"Nay, nay," said Hanno: "I did not want to make him angry; it was a thoughtless joke; he was somewhat old, I said, for so young a bride, and Ionian girls generally like the perfume of flowers and the fragrance of sweet spices better than the smell of tar."

"It was wrong of you," I said, as sternly as I could, though I really felt inclined to laugh.

To my suggestion that they should make up their quarrel with mutual pledges over a cup of wine, Hanno eagerly responded, "With all my heart, and Ashtoreth give me my deserts if ever wilfully I offend his grey hairs again;" but Bodmilcar took the proffered hand coldly, and with evident constraint.

Seeing that all immediate peril of a smash was over, Himilco brought forward his pitcher again from its place of safety. I heard nothing more of the disagreement; but I could not help noticing that Bodmilcar was never again the same in his demeanour towards Hanno, and that he did not speak to him any more than he could avoid.

About a week later, as I was in the arsenal for the purpose of selecting the ropes for the rigging, Himilco came running to me to inform me that one of the King's servants had arrived with a message that was to be delivered to myself. I went to meet the messenger. He was a tall Syrian eunuch with frizzled hair and painted face, arrayed in a long embroidered robe, and wearing large gold earrings after the fashion of his country. He held a long cane surmounted by a golden pomegranate, and spoke with a languid lisp.

"Are you Captain Mago, the King's naval officer?" he asked, as he eyed me from head to foot.

Receiving my reply, he continued: "I am Hazael, of the royal household; here on my finger you may see the signet which empowers me to exercise my authority. The purpose of my visit is to inspect the vessels you are building; but specially my object is to give instructions that proper accommodation shall be provided for myself.

and for a slave that I have to conduct from my master to Pharaoh, King of Egypt. Two proper berths must be prepared ; and the King's orders are that you are to remit us to Egypt after you have visited Jerusalem."

" As to your directions about berths," I replied, utterly astonished at his cool effrontery, "you must permit me to remind you that on board ship the captain, with his pilot under him, invariably allots the place for every passenger."

" Be it so," rejoined the eunuch ; "yet it is imperative that separate apartments, tapestried and carpeted suitably, should be provided for myself and for the royal slave. Impossible for us to live in contact with the rough and tarry seamen."

I felt a strong inclination to let Hazael experience how he relished lying full length upon a heap of rubbish that was close at hand ; but I controlled my indignation and said :

" I will contrive something. I will either make a partition in a corner of the hold, or put up a cabin of planks upon the deck; but whatever is done must not interfere with the working of the ship. When I have made the provision in space, I leave you to fit and furnish as you please; but mark you this, your curtains and carpets will be ruined in the first tempest that we get. However, that is your concern, not mine."

"Each of the cabins," complacently continued the eunuch, "must be twelve cubits by six; there must be six benches of sandal-wood and ivory; the bedsteads must be inlaid; the windows must be framed and fitted perfectly."

"Fitted!" I rejoined: "have I not told you already that you may furnish and adorn the cabins as you will: their size, their position must rest with me: in such matters my authority is supreme. You may tell your royal master from me that adequate accommodation shall be provided, but that with my arrangements no one is at liberty to interfere."

The eunuch looked aghast at my temerity; but he seemed somehow to comprehend that I was not to be trifled with. He muttered a few words to the effect that I had better see that everything was duly done, and without a word or gesture of leave-taking, turned on his heel and sauntered leisurely away. I watched him for a moment, and turning to Himilco, who had been near enough to overhear the conversation, I said:

"Unless I reckon badly, that fellow will give us some trouble before we have done with him."

"Ah, no; I'll take care of that," said Himilco. "Sooner than the painted hound should interfere with us too much, I'd have a rope to his heels, and he should dangle, head in the water, all the way from Joppa to Tarshish. 'Tis not for us to permit ourselves to be treated like dogs."

"No," said I; "but maybe, all will go well; Moloch will be our guardian; and once at sea we shall not fail to secure the protection of our Ashtoreth. To tell you the truth, I am really far more apprehensive about Hanno's pranks with Bodmilcar."

"We must hope for the best," replied Himilco. "Bodmilcar will be on board the gaoul, and we will contrive for Hanno to come with us in one of the galleys."

"True," I assented; "it is indispensable that they should be separated. But with regard to this eunuch's requirements; I hardly see whether it will be better to provide the cabins in the gaoul, as being the more roomy, or to have them under my own supervision. Plague upon the slave and eunuch both!"

At that moment Hanno come up, with his roll of papyrus in his hand, and caught the tenor of our conversation.

"A slave and an eunuch to go!" he exclaimed. "Surely the charge of them ought to fall to *my* lot. Such duties ever belong to a scribe. Besides, I have made some progress in the studies of a magician; and better even than a magician I could humour their fancies, and understand their likes and dislikes."

I expressed my opinion that they would have enough of magicians in Egypt whither they were going, and resolved that I would keep them under my own eye.

"There's an end then to all my pretty scheme of teaching them caligraphy, rhetoric, and what not," said Hanno, smiling. "I must fall back, I see, upon my own accounts."

He unfolded his roll, and submitted to me his reckoning of the amount that would be requisite to pay our sailors and our oarsmen, at the same time handing me his statement of the sums that had already been expended in the purchase of the goods for barter.

The outlay far exceeded the golden talent, the thousand shekels, which the King had advanced. He had, however, commissioned me to spare no expense, and had promised to meet all reasonable demands, so that I felt no uneasiness, but sent Hanno straight to the palace to exhibit the accounts and to ask for a further grant. The request was most generously met.

Meanwhile, Himilco and I continued to employ ourselves

in having planks of fir from Senir [1] fitted to the flanks of our vessels, and in rigging our heavy masts of oak with yard-arms of cedar.

Our work progressed to our entire satisfaction. The *Gadita* was repaired and entirely refitted ; the figure-head, an immense horse, was illuminated with dazzling enamel eyes ; the sides of the vessel were painted red upon a black ground ; and twelve shields of bronze, each glowing in the centre with a polished copper boss, were hung outside.

After everything had been completed, I obtained permission for the *Gadita* to be conducted with great ceremony, to the music of trumpets and cymbals, into the basin of the harbour. For the occasion the naval suffect lent me a large purple sail, reserved expressly for state festivities ; twelve armed sailors, lance in hand, stood behind the shields of bronze; and twenty-two oarsmen, plying their oars in regular cadence, made the ship glide swiftly through the water. Gisgo, the helmsman, from his station in the stern, deftly wielded the tiller, according to the directions of Himilco, whose place was at the prow. Bodmilcar, Hanno, and myself were upon the poop. We were all of us in state attire, and were conscious of a keen enjoyment of the admiring gaze of the crowds of sailors who thronged, not only the adjacent quays, but the terraces of the arsenal and of the admiralty palace, and watched our manœuvres. The naval suffect was himself one of the spectators; he was seated at the grand entrance of the palace, just above the flight of steps that led down to his official wharf. So pleased he was with the appearance of the *Gadita*, that he invited all the officers to sup with him in the evening, and sent a sheep, a large jar of wine, two baskets of bread, a supply of figs and raisins, and twelve cheeses, for the entertainment of our sailors.

Arrived at the palace, we passed up the narrow staircases and dim corridors of the eastern tower, and found ourselves in a large round room with a lofty dome, from the centre

[1] Senir, in Libanus, now Djebel Sannin.

of which there hung a polished copper lamp. The suffect paid us many compliments ; and, on learning that we should be ready for our outfit within ten days, he gave me permission to go next morning and to choose whatever arms would be requisite for the expedition.

After our entertainment we embarked from the suffect's private wharf, intending to return, all of us, to our own quarters on shore ; but all at once Bodmilcar declared himself so enamoured of the *Gadita*, that he resolved to sleep alone on board. As our boat was silently threading its way along the canal that intersected the mainland, cutting off an island by its course, Hanno commenced singing in a foreign language. My attention was arrested, and I asked him what language it was. He replied that it was Ionian, and expressed his surprise that I did not understand it.

" No," I answered ; " it is strange to me. I have sailed but rarely along those coasts. But haven't you done with the Ionians yet ? "

" Oh, Bodmilcar is not here to get in a rage, and we have not got the slave amongst us to be affected by any songs of mine."

" The slave ! " I exclaimed with wonder. " I did not imagine that the slave would care for your songs. Is she an Ionian ? "

Hanno laughed, and made me no answer ; but after a while he yielded to my persuasion, and made me acquainted with all he knew.

" Hazael the eunuch," he said, " is a chattering fool. When I went to the palace I saw him, and wormed out of him that the slave in question had been brought from some Chaldean merchants, and that she had been originally carried away from her own country by a Tyrian pirate, so that the whole truth was not hard to guess."

" Not a word of this," I said ; " not a word to Bodmilcar. More than ever it makes me resolve to have both eunuch and slave on board my own galley ; otherwise I foresee there

C

will be no end of mischief.   Neither you nor Himilco must breathe a syllable until we have seen our unwelcome passengers securely landed at their destination."

Each promised faithfully to preserve the strictest reticence : Hanno, for his part, vehemently asseverating that if a word upon the matter should escape him, he would forthwith cut off his tongue, and devote himself to Horus, the Egyptian god of silence.

As we now reached our lodging, the conversation dropped, and for the next few days we were far too much engaged in active duties to think any further of what had transpired.

I gave my own personal superintendence to the weaving of all the sails, which were made strictly after the directions prescribed by the goddess Tannat.[1]   I saw that my ropes were well twisted and thoroughly tarred ; and I arranged the benches for my oarsmen with such compactness that there was only an interval of a hand's breadth between the seat of the rower on the upper tier and the head of the man in the tier below.

To give extra strength to the masts and yards, I had them bound at regular distances with bands of ox-hide, and finally I had the entire hulls plated with sheets of copper, fastened together with bolts of bronze.

Never had prouder ships been launched upon the Great Sea.[2]

[1] The Grecian *Tamith ;* according to the Phœnician legend, she was the inventor of sails.
[2] The Mediterranean.

CHAPTER II.

THE SACRIFICE TO ASHTORETH.

Two days before the great spring festival which celebrated the re-opening of navigation, and which was observed as a national holiday, our ships were ready in the stocks, and in the course of three hours were launched without difficulty.

The two galleys were each seventy-two ordinary cubits (or sixty-two sacred cubits) long by seventeen wide. The gaoul, with its keel of one solid piece of cedar, was sixty-seven cubits in length by twenty in width; it had three decks and, as I have said, two tiers of rowers; the decks were four cubits apart, and were raised fore and aft, so as to make the elevation sixteen cubits above the water, whilst in the centre it did not exceed twelve cubits. The galleys, when carrying their full burden, and the double line of oarsmen, stood each eight cubits above the water-line. Each contained space enough to take 150 sailors and 50 rowers; but hitherto I had only engaged 200 seamen, expecting that I should be able to enlist the services of 100 soldiers and archers who would be willing to take a share of the working of the vessel. The number of the crew of the gaoul was complete; the *Gadita* had likewise her full complement of thirty-seven men, and the barques their crews of eight. These two small craft were to be kept constantly in tow, and would consequently be in no need of a pilot; but each of the larger vessels was provided with two pilots one at the prow, one at the stern, Himilco being pilot-in-chief. At the top of every mast, there was a look-out place, constructed of fir-wood from Senir, for the purpose of sheltering the man on watch. The apertures for the oars were arranged at equal distances along the sides ; and all the vessels, after they had been caulked and tarred, were made to correspond with the *Gadita* by being painted black with red lines. Hanno had drawn up a document for each of the captains, containing the names of the respective crews, and a complete list of every piece of spare rigging on board, with a register of the place where every article was stored. All the arms, the bedding, the cooking-utensils, the water-barrels, had their positions carefully recorded, and in the crew's quarters between decks, each seaman and rower had his berth distinctly marked with his own name. The cabin under the raised deck at the stern was reserved for the use of the captain and pilots, whilst that under the prow was set apart for the officers of the crew, and the captains of the men-at-arms. On all the vessels the arrangements were identical, with the exception that at the stern of the galley which I had chosen for myself I had ordered a boarded cabin to be erected, divided into two compartments by a partition, and lighted by two small windows, for the especial use of the eunuch and the King's slave under his charge.

Hanno was extremely interested in the selection of good and appropriate names for the ships. At his wish, the gaoul, which was under the command of Bodmilcar, and numbered a large proportion of Tyrians amongst its crew, was named after Melkarth, the god of Tyre. One of the galleys was named the *Dagon*, being placed under the protection of the Philistine god of fish ; whilst the one on which we ourselves were about to embark was dedicated to the Sidonian goddess Ashtoreth, to whom we were per- sonally bound by an especial reverence. Associated with these divinities, of course it was out of all character that the *Gadita* should retain her previous name ; accordingly, at Himilco's request, and in consideration that she was to sail at the head of the squadron, we gave her the designation of the *Cabiros*. Bodachmon, the high priest of Ashtoreth, undertook to present us with images of the various deities to be kept on board the ships which were severally dedicated to them.

Bodmilcar was assigned the command of the *Melkarth*, and her attendant barques ; Hasdrubal, a Sidonian, was appointed to the charge of the *Dagon* ; and the *Cabiros* was confided to the care of Hamilcar, another Sidonian, a bold and experienced seaman.

On board the *Ashtoreth*, my flag-ship, I took for my personal staff Hanno as scribe, Himilco as head pilot, and Hannibal of Arvad (whom I knew to be a strong, brave man) as commander of my men-at-arms.

Fore and aft of each of the ships Hannibal placed two machines of his own invention for hurling stones and darts, and called " scorpions ; " thus, with the exception of the *Cabiros*, which being small could only carry two, every vessel was provided with four of these powerful engines.

We worked hard throughout the greater part of the night and all the following morning in packing and stowing the freight of our little fleet as it lay in the inner basin of the trade harbour, and the *Cabiros* joined us to receive her portion of the cargo and provisions. Towards the middle of the day we found time for rest and refreshment. Anticipating our departure on the morrow, several of us met for a frugal meal in a tent that had been erected for our accommodation on one of the quays. The three captains, the commander of my men-at-arms, the chief pilot, and myself, had just seated ourselves at the table, when the curtain that covered the entrance was drawn aside by one of the sailors, and Hazael the eunuch was announced.

Hazael entered with his usual lazy saunter ; behind him was a train of six slaves carrying baskets, boxes, and bundles, and accompanied by a workman with a hammer and a variety of tools. Outside, mounted on white asses, were two women, one of them closely veiled ; the face of the other was uncovered, and by her red skull-cap with

its gold band and dependent white veil, as well as by
her frizzled hair and prominent features, I recognised her
at once as a daughter of Israel.

"We have come," said the eunuch, without pretence of
courteous salutation, "to take possession of our berths, and
to stow away our baggage."

Hanno started to his feet. I laid my hand upon his
arm, and asked him what he was about to do.

"To stow away the baggage for them," he replied;
adding, "unless, captain, you forbid me."

"Better for you," I continued, "to remain where you are;
I have other business for you to do. This falls best to
Himilco's duty. Go, Himilco," I said, turning to the pilot,
"go and assist Hazael to arrange his property and see to
the accommodation of the women."

Himilco emptied his glass, and, not without a longing
glance towards the jar of wine round which we were sitting,
left the tent. Hanno, who had fallen back to his seat with
an assumed air of indifference, now asked:

"And what is the business for which you want me?"

"You must go," I answered, "to the temple of Ashtoreth

to prepare for our sacrifice to-morrow : you must procure us some birds to take with us on board our ships ; in stormy weather they will show us which way lies the land : you must find the naval suffect, and deliver him a list of all the crews, and a catalogue of all the cargoes ; most of all, you must wait upon the royal treasurer and furnish him with an abstract of all accounts. Is not all this enough for you to do ?"

"No time, I see, then, for me to lose," said Hanno, with impetuous eagerness ; and snatching up his papyrus roll, he ran hastily away. It was my impression, as I caught sight of him through the half-opened curtain of the tent, that he turned, not in the direction of the temple, but towards the harbour-basin ; however, when he came back in the evening all his commissions had been fully and faithfully executed, and I thought no more of the matter.

On his return he was accompanied by one of the officials of the temple, carrying on his head some large bird-cages made of palm-wicker. Hanno himself held a smaller cage, containing four pigeons of a rarer sort, a beautiful shot plumage glittering gaily on their breasts.

" If these birds don't bring us good luck," he said, " I am sure no others will ; they come straight from the temple of Ashtoreth, and were handed over to me by the priestess herself, who made me promise that they should be prized according to their worth."

Each of the captains selected his proper share of the birds, with the exception of Bodmilcar, who contemptuously refused.

"Don't the birds suit you ?" said Hanno ; "what's the matter with them ?"

"I want no pigeons," retorted Bodmilcar ; "ravens are the birds for me, and I have taken enough of them on board already."

Hanno turned his back ; but Himilco, who had witnessed what was passing, remarked :

"Fortunate for the passengers that they will not be on board the *Melkarth*. Far more congenial, I should think, the cooing of doves than the croaking of ravens, to the ears of an Ionian!"

"Ionian!" ejaculated Bodmilcar, turning pale, "is the slave an Ionian?"

In an instant I gave Himilco a sharp dig below the ribs to recall him to his senses, and as quickly he clapped his finger on his forehead, pretending to recollect himself: "No, no; not an Ionian; I mean a Lydian." And turning round to me he asked me whether he was right.

I made a sort of a gesture which I hoped would satisfy Bodmilcar, but he was manifestly still agitated; he made no further remark, but shortly afterwards quitted the room, mumbling unintelligibly as he went. As soon as his back was fairly turned, Hanno, who had been seated quietly arranging his papyrus leaves, rose from his seat, and advancing towards the door, made a low and solemn bow, a proceeding on his part that caused Himilco to burst into a roar of laughter.

"Our friend Bodmilcar," remarked Hannibal, "seems to be rather a morose sort of gentleman."

"Nothing of the sort, I assure you," said Hanno, satirically; "I hardly know a man of a brighter and more genial temperament; however, I confess that we may thank our stars that we have not to sail in the same ship with him."

Hannibal smiled, in token of assent.

Time to retire for the night had now arrived. We indulged in a parting glass, in recognition of our mutual hopes for the successful issue of the enterprise before us, and with no little emotion, parted to seek the repose which should prepare us for the ceremonial of the morrow.

Early in the morning I repaired to the arsenal, but not too soon to find the crews assembled each round its own captain. Hannibal had been successful in collecting together all the archers and the men-at-arms. Every captain was attended by his own trumpeter, in a scarlet tunic, the trumpeter of the military captain being distinguished by the magnitude of his trumpet, which was double the size of the others.

With effective precision Hannibal had arranged his soldiers in their ranks. The first rank was composed of twenty archers in white tunics, their heads covered with white linen caps, which were encircled by a band of leather studded with nails, and of which the ends hung down behind. They all wore scarlet waistbands, in which were inserted ivory-handled broadswords ; their quivers were attached to a belt of ox-hide, that passed over the shoulder, and was ornamented with a profusion of copper studs. In his hand every one carried his long Chaldean bow, the upper extremity of which was carved to represent a goose's head. Next behind the archers were two ranks of armed men, twenty in each rank : they wore cuirasses composed of small plates of polished copper, and had helmets of the same material. Their tunics were scarlet, and hung below the cuirasses ; on the left of their belts was a strong Chalcidian sword, and on the right an ivory-hilted dagger ; one hand carried a large circular shield, ornamented in the centre with a deep-red copper figure of the sun ; the other hand bore a lance, furnished with a long sharp point of bronze.

Hannibal stood at the head of his troop. He wore a Lydian helmet, surmounted with a silver crest, which was further adorned with a scarlet plume. The image of the sun in the middle of his shield was likewise silver, and around that was a circle of the eleven planets. His sword-handle was carved into the figure of a lion, the lion's head forming the guard. Like all the rest of the company he commanded, his feet and legs were protected by leather greaves or gaiters, laced up the front, and turned upwards at the point in the Jewish fashion. He no sooner saw me approaching than he unsheathed his sword, and his trumpeter sounded three blasts, an example which was followed by the other trumpeters, all blowing in unison, after which the captains and pilots advanced and made me a general salute.

Our seamen were provided with neither belts, shields, nor helmets, but carried large cutlasses below their kitonets; they wore pointed caps that covered the nape of the neck, similar to those that are constantly seen at Sidon. Hannibal proposed that they should be drawn up and drilled like the soldiers, but I did not acquiesce in his suggestion; I preferred allowing them to rove about at their pleasure, knowing that they could be drilled far better on board ship, after they had been regularly assigned their proper place and duties.

Hanno and Himilco, who had gone by my directions to see that everything was in readiness for the sacrificial rites, now joined us. They were accompanied by two men, each leading a superb bullock covered with purple housings, and with their horns decorated by fillets of embroidery, to which were attached little bells, which tinkled as they moved. Close in their rear followed my slave, carrying on his head a large basket of pomegranates, covered with a napkin embroidered with silver.

After he had stationed our four trumpeters in couples behind his own, Hannibal gave me to understand that he was only waiting for me to give the signal to march. No sooner had I signified my permission, than he shouted out the word of command, and the archers and men-at-arms doubled file and faced about with an alertness that elicited universal commendation. The trumpeters led the way with a flourish that was well-nigh deafening; the archers followed two and two; then came Hannibal at the head of his warriors, all shouldering their lances. My own place was the next; and I marched on, supported by Hanno and Himilco, and immediately followed by my slave and the two men who were in charge of the oxen devoted as victims for the altar; whilst behind us were the four troops of sailors, not marching in any special order, but each headed by its own captain and pilots. This irregular company brought up the rear.

The thoroughfares along which we passed were decorated gaily. In honour of the great yearly festival of Melkarth, which attracted the mass of all the surrounding population, they were profusely hung with coloured canvas of many a hue, and floating streamers of linen, dyed with the richest shades of purple, orange, green, and vermilion were interspersed amongst waving branches of palms and massy boughs of cedar. Each separate window was a separate centre of display. The people, in holiday attire, were wending their way in crowds in the direction of the island upon which stands the temple of Melkarth, but they stood aside in every portico to allow us to proceed; they were eager in their inquiries as to the meaning and purpose of our formal progress through the streets; and when they understood that we were marching to the shrine of the goddess Ashtoreth to make our sacrifice, and to intreat her favour upon an expedition to Tarshish which we were about to make, they rent .the air with their boisterous acclamations. Men expressed their wonder at the concourse of our sailors and the quality of our oxen; women admired our attire and the carriage of our officers, being especially lavish in their praise of Hanno; the children ran after the procession, attracted equally by the glittering crest in Hannibal's helmet, by the glowing red of the trumpeters' tunics, and the swelling notes of their martial music. Every one was unanimous in declaring that never before had so magnificent a retinue left a Phœnician city on a distant enterprise.

As we passed along beneath the sycamines in front of the King's palace, the vast concourse that had assembled in readiness for the royal procession parted asunder to allow us room to pass, and the King's trumpeter and musicians, who were stationed at the gateway, broke out into strains of welcome. A messenger was observed hurrying down from the palace, and it was soon known that he came

with orders for us to halt. Hannibal immediately made
his men face about ; the sailors, as it were involuntarily,
turned towards the palace, and I myself, with Hanno and
Himilco, advanced in the direction of the window at which
the King is accustomed to show himself to his people, and
which is easily distinguishable from the others by the
gilding and tapestried hangings with which it is decorated.
Meanwhile our trumpeters had taken up the strains of the
royal march in concert with the King's musicians, and
the melody was re-echoed by various bands in other
quarters of the palace-yard.

Only a short time elapsed before the King presented
himself at the window. An attendant, gorgeously attired,
held over the King's head a purple canopy embroidered
with gold and richly jewelled ; behind him could be seen
the glittering helmets and cuirasses of his body-guard.
Without a word of preface, he called me forth by name ;
and having prostrated myself to the earth in deep obeisance, in another moment I was standing with folded arms
before him awaiting his commands.

He spoke to this effect :

"Mago! content I am with the preparation you have
made. Well pleased I am with the way in which you
have collected your seamen and equipped your warriors
in behalf of my friend, my royal ally, King David. You
quit these realms for the distant shores of Tarshish. May
our guardian gods protect you ! Hazael will deliver you
the letters signed by my own hand, which you are to
present to the various sovereigns who are my allies ; to him
I have further intrusted the papyrus roll on which my
instructions are inscribed. Onwards now, fulfil your ob-
lations to your goddess Ashtoreth. I go to render my
sacrifice to our great Melkarth ; but when I have discharged my vows, my purpose is to be myself a witness
of your departure, and you shall not fail to have still
further tokens of my favour."

Again I prostrated myself before the King, who then

retired, leaving me to proceed upon my way, still heralded by the trumpets and greeted by the continuous acclamations of the people. We had hardly turned away, when the great gate of the palace was thrown open, and, headed by a band composed of trumpets, sistra, tambourines, and flutes, there issued the grand procession on its way to the island upon which rose the columns of the temple of Melkarth, the supreme deity of Tyre.

We had hardly reached the limit of the royal court-yard, when Bodmilcar, who had quickened his pace to overtake me, came to my side and said mysteriously,

" Melkarth is a great god ! "

" Assuredly ! " I said, but did not in the least comprehend his meaning.

" A great god is Melkarth of the Tyrians," he repeated. " Melkarth requires greater sacrifices than Ashtoreth : his sacrifices are large as Moloch's ; and they are going to offer him some children to-day."

I assented, yet still failed to see his purpose ; but after a little hesitation, he said :

" Might it be permitted me to take my Tyrians and to join the worship of our own Melkarth ? "

The discovery of his intention vexed me exceedingly ; it was mortifying to myself to see the number of my own retinue diminished, or to allow the dignity of our own observances to Ashtoreth to be curtailed ; but I felt that I had no alternative than to comply with his request to make his sacrifice to the god of his peculiar veneration Reluctantly I gave him my assent, and when we reached the steep street that led up to the elevated groves of " Baaltis-Ashtoreth,"[1] I saw that, instead of continuing with us, he dropped out of our line and joined himself with about thirty of our sailors to a procession that was conducting a chariot, resplendent with gold, and surmounted by a canopy ornamented with plumes of ostrich-feathers. This chariot was conveying the children that

---

[1] Baaltis, feminine of Baal, lord.

were to be offered as the victims of the sacrifice. To welcome the addition to the throng, the shouts of the populace and the clang of the cymbals burst forth with redoubled vehemence.

"How I hate that sacrificing of children!" said Hanno to me.

"Yes;" I concurred, "but if Moloch and Melkarth demand it, what can be said?"

"With all due reverence for Moloch and Melkarth," he continued, "I cannot but rejoice that Ashtoreth of Sidon makes no such request."

We had now turned into the pathway through the grove that winds up to the temple of Baaltis. By far the greater proportion of the temple-officials were absent, having gone to join the general celebration of the city in honour of Melkarth; only six priests and four priestesses remained. Seen through the hazy glow of the rising sun, the grove and temple looked surprisingly lovely, and one could hardly help being conscious of some feeling of regret at having to leave such charming scenes. But amidst all the fascination of the prospect, I realised how a perpetual residence in such an abode would make a man effeminate, and unfit him for peril and adventure; and proudly I recalled the recollection that apart from the enterprise of her sons, Phœnicia could have known no luxury: it was her commerce that had brought her wealth; and had it not been for their bold and undaunted navigation, the people might have seen their shores the prey of invading kings.

Hanno had manifestly been under a like influence, and had been following a kindred train of thought.

"Yes," he said, as if uttering aloud the conclusion of his own reflections; "yes, even if Pharaoh, Melek-David,[1] the Chaldeans and Assyrians all were to concentrate their hosts and fall on us Phœnicians, we could betake ourselves to our ships and brave them on the seas. Aye, though

[1] Melek was the title of the Kings of Judah, as Pharaoh was that of the Kings of Egypt.

they should drive us out from our own domain, build ships, and encounter us upon the ocean where the supremacy has hitherto all of late been ours, yet we have Chittim, Utica, Carthage, Tarshish to fall back upon; the whole world is ours!"

"True," I replied; "in a sense, the world is ours: but it is nothing except our own undaunted perseverance that has made it so. We have had no kings to lead us on to vanquish neighbouring states; we have had no generals to gain us victories and acquire us power; but depending only on our native resources, trusting simply to our own courage, and relying on the good protection of our gods, we have traversed regions that were unexplored, and discovered wealth that was unknown. And now, none dares to assail us; we command the respect of all. None too proud to ask our aid, none too independent to own our service. Who procures Melek-David his choicest timber, his silver and gold? Who provides Pharaoh with balm, his jewels, his copper and his tin? From whom does the Assyrian seek his purple and glass, his ivory and embroidery? Who is the great purveyor of every luxury for every prince and magnate of the world? A Tyrian may well be proud when he claims all this for the mariners of Sidon and the merchant-princes of Phœnicia."

Stirred to emotion by my enthusiasm, Himilco took up the strain: "Yes; great and deservedly great is Tyre's renown. May her spirit of adventure never flag! For my part, give me but the favour of Cabiros for my guiding star, and I would not exchange my peaked sea-cap and ragged kitonet for the tiara sparkling with its fleur-de-lys,[1] and the mantle gorgeous with embroidered work that grace the King of Nineveh!"

Whilst we were thus indulging the spirit of our national pride, the priests within had been lighting the altar-fires and preparing the sacrificial basins, some of which they filled with water, leaving the rest empty. Hannibal had

---

[1] See note on Chap. II. at end of Volume.

drawn up his men in order upon the temple-steps, making an imposing array : he had just put them in the form of a crescent, of which the archers in double file at the top were the extremities, the centre being made by the men-at-arms, four deep, and below, an avenue was left for the progress of myself and my companions, the oxen being conducted into the temple by an entrance at the back.

On our approach, our trumpeters gave a loud flourish, which was answered by the flutes and instruments within. The high priest advanced towards us and, in sonorous tones, exclaimed :

"Let Mago, the Sidonian, the son of Maherbaal, now draw near. Commander of the expedition, he comes to present himself before the goddess. Let him now approach, and all his followers attend him !"

Obedient to the summons, I ascended the steps, followed immediately by my slaves ; Hanno and Hannibal were on my right hand ; Hasdrubal, Hamilcar and Himilco on my left ; behind us was the general throng of sailors and of oarsmen. At a sign from Hannibal, the soldiers shouldered their bows and lances, and having faced about, entered the temple by the two side doors, and completely lined the edifice.

An official proclaimed silence. "Order!" he shouted ; "Mago, son of Maherbaal, makes an offering for his people."

It was the work of but a short time to bring in the oxen, and have them slain and quartered, and while this was being done my slave distributed amongst us the pomegranates he had brought. The high priest with much formality presented me with the shoulder of one of the victims, upon which, according to rule, I laid a purse containing six shekels of coined money. The officiating priest accepted the offering, and while he was proclaiming my liberality aloud, the sacerdotal scribe was inscribing the names of myself and my captains, together with the amount of my donation, in the temple register. The chief priest then took the breasts of the victims and placed them upon the altar, whence the smoke ascended high towards the round window in the dome. The black stone at Sidon is the true goddess, but here at Tyre, Ashtoreth is merely represented by a statue. Standing with his face towards this, the priest made his invocation and chanted some prayers to music, which gradually died away into perfect silence.

During the time that these ceremonies were proceeding, the remaining portions of the oxen were being steeped in the lavers, after which they were thrown into great caldrons, part to be boiled over the chafing-dishes in the temple-kitchen, and part to be cooked in the open air of the sacred groves. The sailors lent their ready assistance in kindling the fires and superintending the boilers.

The chief priest next handed me one of the bullock's breasts. I raised it on high with both hands before the goddess, and delivered it back to the priest, who turned it round three times, as if solemnly dedicating it to the deity on my behalf. Hanno went through a corresponding ceremony with the other breast, which was turned round seven times in behalf of us all.

I had given the scribe five shekels to provide us with bread for the entertainment, and in the name of the captains, pilots, and sailors, Hamilcar gave him eight shekels, a part to provide us with wine, a part as a free tribute to the goddess. He entered the several sums upon the registers, and the officiating priest again made a public announcement of our liberality. One after another we prostrated ourselves before the image of the goddess, the high priest made a short final invocation, and full of joy we withdrew from the temple to the adjacent grove. At a sign from Hannibal, the soldiers, who had stood mute and motionless throughout the ceremony, fell out of their ranks, and rushing in wild confusion, mingled with the sailors to assist them in preparing the banquet.

I took my seat at the foot of a noble cypress, and Hanno, Hannibal, and Gisgo, placed themselves as my supporters on either hand, Himilco charging himself with the duty of

D

superintending the filling of a large earthenware vase with wine. My slave arranged the drinking-cups by placing mine (which had a lion's head at its mouth) in the centre, and disposing those of the captains in order round it. Hannibal's cup was of plated copper, with a stem and two handles, and embossed with flowers and bunches of grapes. Having done this, the slave went away, and returned ushering in two soldiers, who carried a huge caldron; they let the caldron down heavily on the ground, their cuirasses rattling again with their exertion. The lid of the caldron was at once removed; a large basket of bread had been handed round preparatory to the repast, and each man having brought out the wooden knife and spoon that he carried at his waist, the whole of us set ourselves to enjoy an abundant meal.

When the wine-cups had been distributed and charged, I rose from my seat, and raising my cup on high, drank to the health and welfare of the whole assembly.

"A goodly draught is this!" said Hannibal, when he had drained his cup to the very dregs; "it is the wine of my own city Arvad; it gives life and strength to those that drink it; hence Arvad's wide renown for wits and warriors."

"And Arvad's warriors," I said, turning to the captain, "deserve their fame. By-the-by, have your wide wanderings by sea and land ever taken you into Judæa before? Thither it is, you know, that we first direct our course."

"Truly, yes;" replied Hannibal, with his mouth full; "this very sword that I am wearing, and this purple shoulder-belt, were presents from Joab, the general and cousin of the King. I commanded twenty archers under him at the battle of Gebah, when the Philistines were defeated at the mulberry groves. Nor was that the only time. I was garrisoned for a year or more at Hamath, with the troops of Nahari, Joab's armour-bearer, one of David's thirty-seven mighty men. It was on returning thence that I had the command of the soldiers on board the ship of our friend Hasdrubal here, at the time when the galleys of Sidon were sent to engage the Cilician fleet."

"Aye, I have heard of that expedition," said Himilco; "at that time we were far away at Gades."

"And we," broke in Hamilcar, "were in the service of Pharaoh, sailing along the coast of Ethiopia, beyond the Sea of Reeds.[1] What splendid shells were there, containing precious pearls! and one great fish there was that could swallow a man entire!"

At this moment one of the young priestesses approached our party, and handed Hanno a small packet, carefully wrapped in linen.

"This," she said to him, "is the image of Baaltis. Over it I have burnt the costliest perfumes; I have anointed it with the rarest ointments; I have laid it before the goddess, who has graciously accepted it. To you, Sidonian, I now entrust it, and may it bring good fortune to yourself and all who share your enterprise."

The high priest came in person to deliver us the other images of the gods, that of Melkarth alone excepted, which Bodmilcar himself was to convey from the temple to which he had separately gone.

The priestess offered to accompany us to our ships, that she might sprinkle the images on board before we took our departure.

Himilco craved permission to carry the image of the Cabiros down to the quay before resigning it to the keeping of the captain.

"How about your vow of twenty shekels and a bullock that you made to the Cabiri?" I asked him, as we rose to go.

"That will have to wait," he answered, "till I have come across that Tarshish rascal who deprived me of my eye. The patient gods, I have no doubt, will give me credit, and not require me to pay at once, or in advance."

Meantime Hanno had been uncovering his image of Ashtoreth, and was standing holding it in both hands and

---

[1] Jam Souph, the Red Sea.

gazing at it with the profoundest admiration. It was an alabaster figure, with a necklace of three rows of gold beads and a pointed cap, beneath which flowed ample masses of wavy hair.

" I, too," said Hanno, " have made a vow to my goddess, but she has promised to abide my time, and to tarry till my expectations and my longings are fulfilled ; " and as he spoke, he stooped and kissed the face of the image. I know not whether it was imagination on my part, but I certainly thought the cypresses around gave a soft yet perceptible rustle in response to his words. Perhaps the priestess observed it also, for she smiled on me, and laid her hand on Hanno's shoulder.

" But now, Captain Mago," she cried, " let us start. The time for embarkation is at hand, and the goddess pronounces that it is a favourable hour. Come, let us proceed ! "

" To your ships, men ; to your ships ! " I shouted ; and turning for a moment towards the temple, said, " Farewell, Baaltis, Queen of Heaven : to-night thou shalt behold us on the waters of the Great Sea ! "

Hannibal, who had resumed his helmet, made a signal to the trumpeters to summon the soldiers and sailors. Hanno and the priestess came on one side of me ; Himilco, carrying the image of his god, took his place on the other, and in the same order in which it had come, our *cortège* wended its way along the decorated streets down towards the port. The roads adjacent to the harbour and all the quays were so densely thronged, that it was only with considerable difficulty that we could force our way along. Every nation seemed to make its contribution to the crowd : besides the native Phœnicians, there were Syrians in their fringed and bordered robes ; Chaldeans with their frizzled beards ; and Jews in their short tunics and long gaiters, with panther-skins thrown across their shoulders. Again, there were Lydians with bands around their foreheads ; Egyptians, some with shorn heads, and some with enormous wigs ; Chalybeans, wild in aspect, and half naked ; and

men of Caucasus, gigantic in size and strength. Many a
far distant land had sent its sons to our Phœnician cities
as the headquarters and the home of industry and commerce; Arabs and Midianites were here looking with
astonishment at the height of the houses, and bewildered at
the multitude of the population; whilst the Scythians of
Thogarma, their legs strap-bound, moved with heavy
strides, and looked around amazed, perplexed at the absence
alike of horses and of chariots from the narrow streets.

The air was filled with songs and shouts of many a
different tongue; the people jostled one another in their
eagerness to catch a sight of whatever company came last
in view. Every band of musicians enlisted its own
admirers; every troop of priests attracted the closest
scrutiny. Every regiment with its painted shield excited
a perpetual interest; and as our own procession, with
its trumpeters and soldiers and promiscuous groups of
sailors, could not fail to draw a large and curious concourse,
it was in the midst of a veritable whirl that we passed the
arsenal and made our way to the reserved quay, where
our ships, poops inward to the shore, had been left under
the care of a few sailors.

Bodmilcar and the eunuch had arrived before us, and
were standing in eager conversation on the gangway that
led to the poop of the *Melkarth*. As soon as they
observed us, they stopped abruptly, and Bodmilcar whistled
for his sailors, whilst the eunuch advanced to meet me.

"Is all your baggage duly stowed on board?" I asked
Hazael.

"It is," he answered; "but it disappoints me much
that our berths have not been made upon this larger
ship; here we might have far more space and comfort:
however, it matters little; at the first point we touch we
can make a change. Bodmilcar thinks it will be best
we should."

"It cannot be," I said; "the King's slave has been
entrusted to myself, and under my supervision she must

be. The *Melkarth* is a transport, and the captain of a transport has no concern with passengers. I must hear no more of this. Do I understand aright that you have letters for me from the King?"

Without one word in reply, the eunuch handed me a box of sandal-wood, which I opened, and found it to contain several sheets of papyrus, on which were written various instructions to myself.

I was about to give orders to my trumpeter to proclaim silence, but before the words were out of my mouth, Bodmilcar rushed forward and threw himself into my arms.

"I have been sacrificing to Melkarth," he exclaimed; "I have paid my vows to my god, and I must unburden my conscience. I wish to ask pardon of any and of all to whom I have shown insolence or ill-temper."

Without hesitation, Hanno offered him his hand, assuring him that he fully forgave everything that had happened in the past, and that, forgetting all previous quarrels, for the future he would show him all proper deference, and yield to his authority. Pleased with this open reconciliation, I expressed my satisfaction that we were able thus to set out with so universal a spirit of harmony and of concord.

In the meanwhile the captains had severally collected their crews, and Hannibal had told off his men-at-arms, reserving ten archers and ten soldiers for our own ship. The priestess then, with the accustomed solemnities, presented each vessel with the image of its own peculiar divinity.

Before we started, our host, with whom we had been sojourning, accompanied by his wife and son, forced his way through the guards that had been keeping the inclosure, and came in haste to me.

"Mago, dear friend," he said, "I could not suffer you to go without seeing you once more. Here are cakes, and here is a basket of dried grapes; but, most of all, here are two goat-skins of genuine nectar. Accept them from me in token of my good-will. Farewell, and the gods grant you a prosperous voyage!"

"Farewell, honest pilot," said my host's wife to Himilco; "for you I have brought this goat-skin of Byblos, because I know there is no wine you like so well."

"Thanks, good hostess, many thanks," replied Himilco; "to me there is no wine that can compare with the rich and luxurious produce of Phœnicia. I shall not forget your bounty, and if only our star shall favour us, and the *Cabiros* shall safely bring us home again, I promise to bring you such a gift as shall make the Tyrian women die with envy."

The son, a youth of about sixteen, was devotedly attached to Hanno, and only with the greatest difficulty could be dissuaded from accompanying him upon his voyage. As a farewell gift, he had brought his friend a large packet of the choicest reeds for writing; and the two parted with mutual expressions of affection.

Amongst those present there was yet another whom I regarded with the profoundest reverence, and whose knowledge was accounted as little short of divine. This was an aged priest, named Sanchoniathon,[1] the historian and chronicler of past events; although no traveller himself, he had acquired the fullest information concerning well-nigh every country of the world.

Addressing himself to me, he said: "Mago, my son, Hanno your scribe has undertaken to transmit to me, in writing, an account of whatever he may see rare or wonderful in the far-off lands to which you go; his genius seems bright and quick, but his youth renders him wild and unstable as a kid. Is it too much to ask of you that you will urge him on to keep his word?"

"To gratify you, my father," said Hanno, "I will do all I can to control the caprices and irregularities of my youth. My own indebtedness to you is great. I trust that I may

---

[1] I am guilty of an anachronism here for the mere satisfaction of introducing the name of the great historian.

not forget the lessons you have taught me; and if I can render any aid in enabling you to keep the Phœnicians informed of the wonders of the world, I shall be ready to show myself a pupil worthy of my master."

The aged Sanchoniathon then gave us his blessing. He had scarcely concluded his benediction when the priestess of Ashtoreth came by, returning from the ships. As she passed Hanno I distinctly heard her say in an undertone:

"She is as good as she is beautiful!"

"Hush!" he murmured; "I must forget her! Happy Pharaoh!"

Everything being reported ready, I ordered the trumpeters to sound the signal for departure, and we proceeded to embark. The first man to step on board was old Gisgo, the pilot of the *Cabiros*, commonly known as Gisgo the Celt, and perhaps still more frequently spoken of as Gisgo the Earless. He had been eight times on a voyage to the Rhone, and the story went that on one of his visits there he had married a Celtic wife, with yellow hair, who was still awaiting him in her native forests; on another occasion he had been taken prisoner by the Siculians, who had cut off both his ears. Having mounted the poop, the old man waved his cap and shouted cheerily:

"Mariners, mariners all! quick and ready! quick on board! rulers of the ocean! sons of Ashtoreth! listen to your captain's call. Tyrians and Sidonians! To sea! to sea! and long live Captain Mago!"

The men all hastened to their several ships, and as soon as I had taken my station on the raised bench of the poop of the *Ashtoreth*, my standard was hoisted as the signal of departure, the gangways were removed, the boathooks were driven vigorously towards the facing of the quay, and we were on our way.

The *Cabiros*, with its twenty-two oarsmen, took the lead; next came the *Ashtoreth*; the *Dagon* towed the *Melkarth*, which was too large to hoist a sail in port. Our little squadron floated on past the numerous ships that lined the quays, making its way through crowds of boats that darted to and fro, conveying the countless visitors to the island where the feast of Melkarth was still in course of celebration. Our trumpeters continued to blow, our oars rose and fell in regular cadence, and the voices of thousands of spectators kept up a perpetual acclamation.

From my own position I could overlook the decks of all the other vessels. Hanno was at my side, and Himilco stood at the bow giving his orders to the helmsman. Hannibal had made his warriors hang their shields over the

ship's sides ; every one had betaken himself to his proper post, Hazael the eunuch being no exception, as he had retired to the privacy of his own cabin.

Passing the mouth of the trade-harbour, with its two watch-towers, we entered the canal that led to the island ; it was covered with boats decorated with holiday-trappings ; above it rose the palace of the naval suffect, its terraces all decked with coloured hangings, and thronged with a motley crowd. Beyond again, in the centre of the island, I could see the dome of the temple of Melkarth, the blue smoke of the sacrifices rising high above its ochred roof. I could even hear the uproarious clanging of the cymbals and the other instruments within.

The royal galley, escorted by the galley of the naval suffect, came forth to meet us. On the poop of the royal vessel was a raised platform, which shone as if it were a mass of solid metal, being covered entirely with cloth of gold and silver. The oars were faced with ivory ; the sails were embroidered with silver thread, with representations of Melkarth, Moloch, and Ashtoreth, the large hyacinth-coloured sail in the middle being worked with green to imitate waves, from which rose the figure of Ashtoreth protecting the fish from the fury of Dagon. A full band of musicians was playing at the bows, and, on deck, a number of graceful women, wearing state tiaras and triple necklaces, performed upon gaily painted tambourines, and waved light rods adorned with little bells and tassels of pale green and purple. At the stern sat King Hiram. He wore a Phœnician cap, his beard was frizzled in the Syrian fashion, and he had two gold bracelets on each arm. His throne was of gold and enamel ; the back of it was carved into the image of a ship, and the arms were representations of dolphins. In attendance, standing with folded arms, were his scribe and the keeper of the seals ; behind him stood two officers, one of them holding the purple canopy of state, fringed with gold, the other carrying the royal standard, which bore, worked in silver on a hyacinth-coloured ground, representations of the sun and the planets, with the crescent moon above. The suffects were on board the Admiralty galley, surrounded by guards in Lydian helmets, whose silver shields and cuirasses glittered brightly in the sun.

At sight of the royal *cortége* I ordered my men to ship their oars and to bring our vessels to a standstill. A corresponding order was given to the royal ships, and it was but the work of a few minutes for the slaves to throw the ebony gangway across, and to cover it with a brilliant carpet. King Hiram rose from his seat and stepped oυ

board, and I had the honour of conducting him all over my
vessel, and of showing him the double deck, the stowage of
the cargo, and the great earthen reservoirs of water. He
went, unaccompanied, to visit the berth that had been
provided for the slave, and before leaving, presented me,
through his treasurer, with two talents of silver. When he
had returned to his throne, the temporary passage was
withdrawn, and at a signal from me, our hundred and
twenty-two oars cleft the water without a splash. The
trumpets sounded ; soldiers, sailors, rowers, raised a tremendous cheer, and from my place I shouted aloud :

"Farewell, my King ! Tyre and Phœnicia, farewell ! And
now, children of Ashtoreth, my crew, forwards, forwards !"

Quickly the squadron made its way past the two towers
that guarded the military harbour, and on which perpetual
watch was kept. I cast one look back at the canal with
its swarm of gala-boats ; at the quays still thronged with
the motley crowd ; at the city, rising like a vast white
amphitheatre intersected by the threading of its narrow,
crooked streets ; at the mass of the yellow temple of Melkarth ; at the great Admiralty Palace, above which were
the glittering walls of the temple of Baaltis ; and, last of
all, at the heights of Libanus beyond, standing out green
and black against the background of the sky. I turned
away to give my attention to the ships that were dashing
the snowy foam from their prows. The *Cabiros* was riding
the waves like a dolphin ; the *Melkarth*, now no longer in
tow, and the *Dagon* were crowded with sail.

A favourable wind bore us onwards to the south-west,
so that I gave orders that the galleys should hoist their
sails, and that half the rowers should ship their oars and
take an interval of rest. I sat down and gazed upon the
broad and glittering ocean.

We were now fairly on our way to Tarshish.

CHAPTER III.

CHAMAI RECOGNISED BY THE ATTENDANT OF THE SLAVE.

IN order to clear the White Cape in the south-west, I took an oblique course across the bay, on the north of which stands the city of Tyre. From White Cape [1] I should sight the distant promontory of Mount Carmel, and avoiding the deep waters of the bay to the north of this point, I should double it and coast along direct to Joppa.

The *Cabiros* was quite capable of making 1300 stadia [2] in twenty-four hours ; but the gaoul, which was always in ordinary weather worked by sails and was now heavily laden, could not attain that speed ; neither could the galleys. I succeeded in accomplishing a rate of 1000 stadia in the twenty-four hours, so that in about three hours after our departure we had rounded White Cape, and holding on by a south-west course, by nightfall had lost sight of land. Towards midnight Himilco roused me with the announcement that we were off Mount Carmel. I could just discern its bluff peak standing out in the moonlight, and gave instructions that our course should be changed to the south ; at the same time I took the precaution to signal to the *Melkarth* to clew up her sail and use her oars, because we were again approaching the shore. A brisk breeze in the morning brought us in sight of the low, level coast of Palestine, and before noon we recognised Joppa by its elevated towers and surrounding groves of palms and wild fig-trees.

[1] Now Ras-el-Abiad.
[2] That is, 32½ geographical miles, the rate given by Herodotus.

MY SALUTE.

To face page 45

After passing the mouth of a river which empties itself about forty stadia north of the port, the *Cabiros* neared the shore, while the *Melkarth* and the two galleys, owing to the shallowness of the water, were brought to anchor at about a stadium and a half away.

The harbour of Joppa is insignificant, and has neither basins nor piers; scattered about the beach are a few cabins and dilapidated hovels, in the midst of which rises the small fortress of rubble built by King David when he opened traffic with the Phœnicians, and made Joppa the port whither the firs and cedars hewn down in Lebanon were brought on floats. A large Phœnician barque, and a miserable Egyptian craft, with a goose as its figure-head, were ·stranded in the mud below the beach, and on the beach itself were a few wretched boats belonging to the Jewish fishermen.

Taking Hanno and Hannibal with me, I went on shore in one of my small boats, for the purpose of paying a visit to the governor in command of the little garrison that occupied the fortress. Before, however, we had gone far, we saw the governor himself coming to meet us, followed by about fifteen men armed with swords, lances, and square shields. They wore linen girdles, fastened at the side by a strap, which was finished off at the end with a cut and polished flint. Their heads were bare, but their hair was arranged in a lot of little tresses; upon their feet and legs were long laced gaiters, and a panther's skin, according to Jewish habit, was thrown across their shoulders. The captain alone was distinguished by a cuirass, which was of copper, and badly made. As soon as I was within a few paces of him I stopped and made him my salute, a courtesy which he acknowledged, giving me to understand that he was already aware I came as an envoy from King Hiram.

" Peace be with you!" he said. " Having been informed of your arrival, I have come to offer you the escort to Jerusalem which you require. But now, I beg you, come to the fortress and partake of what hospitality we have it in our power to give."

We were pleased at our reception, and followed our host to the vaulted gate of the tower that overhung the fortress. He conducted us to a lofty chamber overlooking the sea, and made his servants spread a carpet over the floor, that was but roughly paved. The walls of the room were of the coarsest rubble and perfectly bare, the entire building being of the most meagre construction. Water, bread, dried figs, and cheese was the simple fare that was set before us, to which, however, there was added some very palatable wine, which the Jews, since their conquest of Syria, had been able to procure from Helbon.

While the repast was being prepared we interchanged mutual inquiries about ourselves and our respective kings, but the meal was no sooner ready than the Jewish commandant set us the example of eating by cramming his mouth chockfull of cheese.

Presently, as he observed me throwing glances round the room, he said :

"Ah, yes, you are thinking that we have not your Phœnician skill in building ! We lack your taste and finish. But, remember, we have not your wealth nor your materials. However, you must recollect that this is only a poor straggling village ; patience ! and you shall see our populous cities, as well as our fertile country, before you reach Jerusalem."

" The land of Judah," said Hannibal, " is not unknown to me. I have traversed it already, and can bear witness to its richness and fertility ; truly it is a land of olives, dates, and corn and wine. And not only are you husband-men, you are proud of being warriors. Every nation has its own pursuit. We men of Tyre and Sidon for the most part are sailors full of ardour, and merchants full of enterprise : but yet I think we may boast of our warriors, too : Arvad, for instance, need not be ashamed of the generals she can show."

"True enough," rejoined the other, as his eye rested with involuntary admiration on Hannibal's arms and cuirass, "and no doubt Phœnician soldiers are well equipped."

"I can tell you," said Hannibal, "something that may perhaps surprise you. In spite of your keeping no standing army, and of your never admitting strangers into your service, I have myself served under your king. It happened in this way: when I was very young I was taken to the town of Cana, in the heritage of the sons of Asher; I grew up as a child of the tribe, and eventually, at the regular age, I was enlisted into your army."

The Jewish captain was delighted; he rose and embraced Hannibal, and in token of their friendship they partook of a cup of wine, which was afterwards passed on to Hanno and myself. "I belong," he said, "to the tribe of Judah, through whose inheritance we shall have to pass as we go to Jerusalem. The King is maintaining some troops at his own expense, and I am one of the captains of twenty. My mission here is to await your arrival; the requisite horses and asses are provided for your journey, and you may start whenever it suits your wishes; this very evening, if you choose."

"Impossible to-night," I answered; "I cannot be absent from the ships until I have returned and made all things ready. To-morrow, however, I shall be prepared."

As there seemed time at our disposal, he inquired whether he might not be permitted to visit our ships, suggesting that as we were Phœnicians, we might probably have commodities to offer that they might be glad to purchase.

I explained that being in the royal service we were not carrying any goods for commercial transactions, but had only such articles on board as we hoped to barter for the provisions that we might require on our way.

"In that case," he said, "I may perchance further your designs; we have flocks of goats, and we have balm and olives in abundance. I will serve you in any way I can. I am Chamai, the son of Rehaiah; my father is well known throughout the country."

I acquiesced in his wish of visiting our ships, and he followed me down after a very short interval.

During my absence the sailors had been displaying on the beach the few articles that they had brought for their own private benefit, and were driving a briskish trade with the fishermen and shepherds that had gathered round them. On board the *Melkarth* some of the barter-goods were already unpacked, and Hanno was not long in drawing up a list of such things as I was ready to part with, and such as I was anxious to procure in exchange. The additions to my store of which I was in especial need were ten measures of grain, two measures of oil, a barrel of olives, half a measure of balm, six baskets of dried figs, six baskets of dates, and fifty cheeses ; and I further instructed Bodmilcar, who superintended the exchanges, to purchase some sheep and kids, in order that our men should be adequately supplied with fresh meat until our arrival in Egypt. Other supplies would be requisite ; but for these I reckoned upon the generosity of King David, and upon what I should be able to buy at Jerusalem.

Chamai expressed his great delight at the order and arrangement of our ships ; and as almost everything presented some feature of novelty to him, he could hardly find words to describe his admiration. The discipline of the crews and the completeness of the rigging seemed equally to fill him with surprise. He accepted my invitation to remain to supper ; and as we were all seated on the poop of the *Ashtoreth*, he gave a deep sigh, and exclaimed :

" How glorious your long voyages are ! How glorious to be able to obtain the wealth that the Great Sea can give ! Here, in our mountains, we are as ignorant as goats. From time to time we may plunder a few villages, but our chiefs always get the lion's share of the prey, which, after all, is meagre enough compared with what you gain by commerce."

I reminded him how that there was something more to charm an adventurer on the seas than merely getting wealth; there was the advantage of seeing the wonders of the world.

"Ah, yes," he assented. "I have heard your Phœnician merchants tell of enormous serpents, and of fishes fifty cubits long. I have listened to their tales of valleys full of precious stones, and mines with inexhaustible stores of silver and of gold. I know, too, that they relate wonderful stories about giants, and about mountains that belch forth fire and smoke."

"No doubt," I said, "you must allow a little for exaggeration in travellers' tales; but beyond a question there are strange sights for travellers to see."

"And do you not," he asked, "occasionally have to fight? I have had some experience in fighting; I have slain Moabites and Philistines with my own hand. I could fight again; and if you are likely to have any more fighting I should like to go with you. Could you not take me?"

Hannibal laid his hand upon Chamai's shoulder, and said: "Look here, captain. If you are in earnest, perhaps that might be done. I want forty recruits as archers. Would it be in your power to get them for us?"

"Yes, yes!" he cried eagerly, adding his accustomed oath, "in the name of El, the Lord of hosts."

"Get them then," I said; "and if they are forty sturdy fellows, fit for soldiers, you shall have the command of them, under Hannibal." I further delighted him by promising him a new cuirass, and a Chalybean dagger with an ivory handle.

"Long live the King!" he cried, in an ecstasy of joy; and Hannibal rubbed his hands with glee at the prospect of so successfully recruiting the number of his troops, saying that now they might face the world and conquer kingdoms.

"Whatever kingdoms I conquer," broke in Hanno, "I shall sell forthwith, subjects and all; I shall put them up to auction to the highest bidder, and shall purchase my palace with the proceeds. You, Himilco, shall be appointed

E

cup-bearer. 'When the goat is gardener, the goat-skins are taken care of;' you know the proverb."

"But instead of talking about *your* feast," said Himilco, drily, "we may as well proceed to enjoy our own;" and he moved towards the table on which the supper had now been laid.

We had hardly commenced our repast, when a sailor came from Bodmilcar to announce that he had completed all his purchases. I inquired why the captain himself did not come to join our party. The man said that he could give no other reason than that he believed Bodmilcar had invited the eunuch to supper with him on board the *Melkarth.*

Hanno turned pale.

"That rascally eunuch, I fear, is manœuvring some mischief," I said, when the sailor had left us; "however, let us hope that the women are not in the plot."

Hanno was on the point of hurrying off immediately to the cabin, when the door opened, and the waiting-maid made her appearance, followed by her mistress, closely veiled.

"Never fear, captain," said the maid, smiling; "the hawk may fly, but the doves do not follow."

"Did he tell you to follow him?" I asked angrily.

"He did not insist upon it," replied the girl; "and we preferred remaining here; we had no taste for taking up our quarters on that big black ship."

I told her that she had only done right, and that I should reprimand Hazael most severely if he made the slightest attempt at removing them from my immediate supervision. She then made a request, to which I willingly acceded, that they might enjoy a stroll in the fresh air upon the deck; but before she turned away, Chamai, who had hitherto been engrossed in some military discussion with Hannibal, caught sight of her face, and suddenly starting to his feet, exclaimed:

"Abigail, you here!"

"Chamai, is it you?" she answered; and in an instant they were grasping each other's hands; and gazing in each other's eyes, they wept aloud.

As soon as Chamai had recovered his composure, he asked her by what strange chance it happened that she was on board a Phœnician vessel.

"Did you not know," she asked in return, "that the Philistines came down on Guedor, our native village, and carried me off to Askelon, and afterwards sold me to the Tyrians?"

"No," he said; "all this is new to me. I was away in the north, fighting against the King of Zobah, and since that time, have not been home."

It did not take Abigail long to regain all her wonted cheerfulness and vivacity; and she went on to tell how she had been purchased by the King of Tyre, and was now on her way to Egypt in attendance upon the Ionian lady, whom King Hiram had bought at the same time as herself, and whom he was now sending as a present to Pharaoh.

Chamai, in his turn, informed her that he was to be allowed to accompany us in our expedition, but was loud in expressing his regret that the voyage to Egypt would be so quickly over; he could have wished, he said, that it would take as long as his forefathers' wandering in the wilderness.

Touched by the incident of this mutual recognition, I invited the girl to sit down for a little while amongst us; and requested Hanno, who was acquainted with the Ionian dialect, to ask the lady to do the same. With a graceful obeisance, she took her seat on a cushion that was placed for her.

The evening meal proceeded pleasantly enough. Abigail and Chamai entertained us with the story of their attachment, relating how in the days of their early childhood they had tended goats together in their native pastures. I could not refrain from expressing my sorrow that they had met to be parted again so soon.

"But perhaps," said Abigail, "Pharaoh will not want to

keep me; of such as I am, King Pharaoh must have thousands. My mistress here is sent for him; but me, surely, he will send back again."

Chamai clenched his strong fists, and gave an appealing look at me; but I could give him no further consolation than by remarking that it was very probable the company of the waiting-woman was only required for the lady during the voyage.

"Apart from that," said Hannibal, "she would be lonely and desolate enough. Little is the trouble that the eunuch Hazael puts himself to for the sake of entertaining her."

Meanwhile, Hanno and the Ionian lady had entered into a conversation so close, and apparently so confidential, that it gave me a feeling of uneasiness; and in order to interrupt it, I took the opportunity, while the wine-cups were being replenished, of asking Hanno whether, as he had a reputation for playing the psaltery, he could not persuade the lady to allow him to accompany her while she sung one of the songs of her country. She had some slight acquaintance with Phœnician, and answered for herself that she should have much pleasure in singing as I wished.

Hanno fetched his psaltery, and as soon as it was tuned, the captive damsel turned back her veil and revealed a countenance of peculiar beauty. She was dressed as a Phœnician, in a purple robe embroidered with silver, and wore a necklace composed of three rows of gold beads and gold ornaments of elaborate design. Her head was bare, and her hair was arranged in the fashion of her own country, turned back from the forehead and secured in the middle. We sat in silence, as though riveted by a spectacle of surpassing beauty.

As soon as my slave had attached the earthenware lamps to the supports that were ready for them in the ship's side, the Ionian, in a rich harmonious voice, commenced one of the songs of her native land. I cannot profess to be familiar with the Ionic tongue, but in the course of my

THE IONIAN COMMENCED ONE OF THE SONGS OF HER NATIVE LAND

wanderings I had gained sufficient acquaintance with it to be aware that the verses which she sung were in celebration of the wars made long, long ago by her countrymen, the Achæans, against Priam and the city of Troy. Ever and again, as her voice rose in thrilling sweetness, Chamai's eyes could be noticed flashing with emotion, and Hannibal's fingers seemed to be feeling for the hilt of his sword ; and even those who could not comprehend the meaning of the words were all enraptured by the melody of the song and the bewitching loveliness of the singer. When she had finished, she rose and retired with a step stately as that with which Ashtoreth might move along the floods.

Immediately after she had gone, Hanno moved to the ship's side, where he stood for a considerable time gazing moodily into the water. I missed his merry voice from our party, and going up to him asked him what was the matter.

"Nothing but what will soon pass away," he replied.

"Take my advice," I said, "and let nothing be told Bodmilcar about what has transpired this evening. I neither trust him nor the eunuch."

"Let Bodmilcar do as he pleases," replied Hanno, quickly. "For my part, I shall abide by the promise I have made. What I want now is to get to Tarshish, and to find adventures to divert me. I think I shall be a good sailor yet, captain ;" and his tone brightened as he spoke. I shook him heartily by the hand. Somehow or other I felt myself every day to be drawn closer to the youth.

When I rejoined the others I found Chamai on the point of returning to shore.

"Good-night, Chamai," said I ; "we meet again in the morning."

"Good-night, captain ; good-night all :" and as soon as he was in the boat he shouted, "Good-night, Abigail, my charming dove !"

"Good-night, my pretty lamb !" responded Abigail, saucily, as she looked forth from the interior of her cabin.

At this very moment the eunuch arrived. "The fellow has good lungs," he sneered, as he passed ; "but I question whether King Pharaoh would be best pleased to know that his slaves had been displayed to all the world."

"No, nor if he should learn that they have been entertained by a ship's captain and his scribe," put in Bodmilcar, contemptuously kicking aside Hanno's psaltery, which had been accidentally left upon the cushion that had been occupied by the Ionian.

"Your proceedings displease *me ;*" I began, in a tone of reproof ; but Bodmilcar interrupted me by saying sharply : "Hazael has the King's authority for placing the slaves wherever he thinks best."

This was too exasperating. It was intolerable that a Syrian eunuch, himself a mere slave, should presume to set up his authority over me, a free man and a captain of a Sidonian fleet, and I stared steadily at Bodmilcar, as if he could hardly be aware of what he said ; but he only returned my gaze with a look of defiance.

He proceeded in a haughty tone : " This Ionian damsel

was once mine, but she was stolen from me by men who sold her to the King. The King sends her to King Pharaoh as a present, and I shall do my duty to the King by preventing his present from falling into the hands of your scribe."

I answered firmly: "In all these matters I alone am judge. On these vessels my authority in all things is supreme, and woe to any one who questions it."

"Well spoken!" cried Hannibal. "Discipline and obedience for ever!"

"I shall do *this*, then," he began, with a voice half-choked with rage; but I took him up coolly and decisively: "You will do what I order; you will go back to your ship and look after your sailors. I shall be away five days."

He retreated slowly towards the boat, muttering threats and oaths as he went, but to these I did not pay the slightest heed.

When he was gone, Hazael said: "And now I shall go and chastise that girl."

I laid my hand upon his shoulder to deter him; but he shook himself free, and was about to open the cabin-door, when the powerful grasp of Hannibal was upon him, so that he was twisted completely round.

"How?—how now?" he stammered out, looking first at me and then at Hannibal, who still retained a firm hold upon him. I folded my arms and looked steadily at him.

"Listen!" I said; "listen to me. The rule of a Phœnician ship is this: whoever defies the captain's orders is tied to a rope from the yard-arm and dipped three times in the water. Do you understand me?"

Quivering with fear, the eunuch only bowed his head in assent.

"Remember it then," I added; "and remember, too, another rule: when any one curses another he is fastened tight to that mast and flogged; five-and-twenty lashes. Do you understand?"

He bent his head again.

"And don't forget," I said, "that Abigail has a busy tongue, and that I have sharp ears. Now, Hannibal, let him go."

Hazael made his way to his cabin without a word. Hannibal could not suppress his glee. He exclaimed: "Bravo! captain! all right! no good doing things by halves; mutiny in a ship is as bad as rebellion in a camp."

Early next morning I sent for Bodmilcar.

"Bodmilcar," said I, "you are an old Phœnician mariner and ought to be trusted, but I am afraid the influence of that eunuch has turned your head. He will not be long with us; and when he takes his women ashore, I hope you will be yourself again: but meanwhile you must give me your word that you will not be promoting further discord."

He attempted to deny that he had in any way fostered discord, but I was not to be put off; I insisted upon the promise being distinctly given, and when he had yielded and made me the promise I required, I said to him:

"Now, attend to my instructions. You will remain here in command of the vessels, while I am gone to Jerusalem. Hanno and Hannibal will accompany me, but Hasdrubal, Hamilcar and Himilco will remain with you, and you will be under the protection of the soldiers. We will make it our business to get provisions in the interior of the country, so that you will have nothing to concern yourself about in the way of purchases."

"And what becomes of the two women?" he inquired.

"That is my affair," I answered; "I shall see that they are provided for on shore. But we are off at once; so look to your duty. Farewell!"

I directed Hanno and Hannibal to get into the boat, and ordered my slave, with two sailors carrying the baggage, to accompany them. As Hanno passed Bodmilcar, I noticed that the latter scowled and spat upon the ground. Hanno merely shrugged his shoulders.

Before I took my own place in the boat, I saw the women and the eunuch safely on board the other boat, and told two sailors to go with them, and take on shore all that they might require. Hazael tried to invent some pretext for remaining behind; he would look after the baggage, he said, but on hearing me cry out, "No, no," he embarked without further remonstrance.

Everything being ready, I gave the word for starting, and the two boats moved off. Bodmilcar stood upon the poop watching us gloomily, whilst Himilco, who was by his side, bade us good-bye with a friendly cheer.

A very few strokes of the oar brought us to land; Chamai had been impatiently awaiting our arrival, and hastened to assist Abigail from the boat. We made our way straight to the village, which lies in a grove of wild fig-trees, about two bowshots from the fortress, and is provided with a good cistern. In front of the house that seemed by far the most important in the place, there were tied two horses and about a dozen asses. The horses were well caparisoned with embroidered bridles, and had their heads decked out with scarlet network, trimmed with little bells and parti-coloured rosettes, their tails being tied up with scarlet bands. The asses' manes and tails, according to a general custom, were dyed with henna, and these animals, like the horses, were all well harnessed.

"This," said Chamai, "is the house of Bichri; he is one of the men that I propose getting to join you on your voyage. He is young and strong, and skilful in the use alike of his bow, his sword, and his shield. He has been a vine-dresser on the mountains, and has learnt the art of making wine."

Bichri himself at this moment came forward to give us his greeting; he was accompanied by another man with a young woman.

"This is Barzillai, one of my captains of ten," said Chamai, introducing him to me; "and this is his wife, Milcah; she is the sister of our friend Bichri here, and is famous for the honey-cakes she makes."

Hannibal suggested that Barzillai and his wife should join us on our expedition, but Chamai explained that nothing would induce them to go to sea.

I next proceeded to make arrangements for lodging the two women during my absence. I found that they could either be accommodated in the tower, or that they could be received into Bichri's house, where they would be near enough to Barzillai to have the companionship of his wife, and the protection of his men-at-arms. At first Chamai was disposed to murmur when he learnt that Abigail was not to accompany us to Jerusalem; but when he understood that it was my wish that she and her mistress should remain together where they were, he acquiesced without another word of disapprobation. To Barzillai I give the strictest injunctions to allow no one, except the eunuch, to see the Ionian lady on any pretence whatever, and he struck his hand upon the hilt of his sword as a guarantee that he would be faithful to his trust.

"And where am I to lodge?" asked the eunuch.

"Wherever you may choose," I answered; "in Bichri's house, if you like."

"In my house!" cried Bichri; "a Syrian of Zobah in my house! No, no, captain, by your leave, I'd rather not. It cannot be."

"Why not?" yelped out the eunuch; "are we Syrians not as good as you?"

"No; Syrians are slaves: our King conquered you at Zobah and Damascus both; you are fleas, dead dogs!"

"True," chimed in Chamai; "the Philistines of Gaza and Askelon are foes worth conquering, but as to Syrians, I could spit a dozen of them on my lance and carry them across my shoulder."

"Ha, ha!" laughed Hannibal; "Chamai dearly loves a joke; he will make good sport for us along our way."

To Barzillai's inquiries whether the women were ever to be allowed to go out, I replied that Abigail, since she belonged to the country, might occasionally take a walk in company with Milcah, but that the Ionian must not be allowed to leave the house until my return. They engaged to make the lady's time pass agreeably, and Milcah undertook to initiate her into the art of making cakes and other delicacies.

Having thus satisfactorily made our preliminary arrangements, we entered the house to partake of some refreshment before our departure.

In order to ensure that the guard should be sufficiently strong, Barzillai had offered to find quarters in the village for fifteen of our men in addition to his own. Hannibal accordingly sent to the ships for fifteen archers to come on shore, and I took the opportunity of sending by the same messenger to Hamilcar and those who were with him, to inform them what I had done by way of putting an effectual check upon any scheme that Bodmilcar and the eunuch might concert between them.

The eunuch had declined joining our meal, and had returned sulkily to the ships. Milcah conducted the Ionian to her apartment, but soon reappeared, bringing a supply of her renowned honey-cakes, three for every guest. So engrossed, however, were Abigail and Chamai with each other's society, that they forgot all about taking their own shares, which Hannibal was nothing loath to eat for them.

Bichri went out first to see that the horses and asses were in readiness, and we followed him as soon as we had taken our leave of Barzillai and Milcah. The parting between the young lovers, it need scarcely be said, was somewhat protracted. Thoroughbred Sidonian as I was, more accustomed to the rolling of a ship than the curvetings of a steed, I declined mounting the high-spirited horse which the Jew offered me, feeling that I should be more at my ease upon a pacific steady-going ass. By my directions Hanno had made a present to our host of a piece of scarlet cloth ; to his wife I had given a pair of silver earrings, with which she was extremely delighted ; and we had distributed a number of earthenware dolls and toys to the children who crawled about or clambered on our knees. Chamai (who had donned his new cuirass and bestowed his old one upon Barzillai), detained us by running back a dozen times upon some frivolous pretext, which ill disguised his real design of saying good-bye once more to his sweetheart, but at last made up his mind to mount the horse which Hanno, as well as myself, had refused to ride. Hannibal had already mounted the other horse, and was exhibiting his skill as an equestrian, by cantering about us. Of the asses, four were laden with our baggage ; Hanno, the two sailors, and my own slave, got upon the others ; and Bichri, with his strong mountaineer's stride, marched on ahead of the caravan to pioneer the way.

CHAPTER IV.

KING DAVID.

AFTER crossing the fertile corn-fields of the low-lying plains, thickly studded with groves of figs and dates, and with clumps of the stunted trees which abound in Judæa, expanding their parasol-like foliage, we began to ascend the mountain by narrow pathways, bordered by forests of terebinths, alternating with vineyards and plantations of olives. This route, delightful in its shade, brought us to the little town of Timnah, on the ridge of the hill, where Chamai introduced us to a man who found us lodging, and provided shelter for our beasts. Timnah is not only small, but it is most irregularly built; it is encircled by an embattled wall, with two gateways and twelve circular towers; the houses are only of one storey, being detached, and generally surrounded by gardens.

We were tormented by myriads of fleas, which appeared to be especially remarkable for avidity. There were also countless swarms of flies; and Hannibal, who had taken off his cuirass in order that he might more effectually scratch himself, remarked, with some show of reason, that he thought the inhabitants of Judæa ought to implore Beelzebub, as the god of flies, to relieve them of this plague of vermin.

On the following morning, after traversing several ravines, and crossing several ridges of the hilly but well-cultivated country, we came in sight of a deep valley, sterile and deserted. The rocks that formed alike its bottom and its sides were scattered over with human bones, that were bleaching in the air Towards the east some eminences could be discerned, surmounted by a fort, whilst the valley again sloped upwards towards the ridges that bounded it on the south.

"This is the Valley of Giants," said Bichri, as he turned over a skull with the end of a staff he carried.

"Well enough I know it," broke in Chamai. "When I was young I was Benaiah's armour-bearer. Benaiah was one of King David's mighty men, a captain of a hundred; one snowy day he killed a lion in a pit; and once in single fight he slew an Egyptian giant; and here in this very vale of Rephaim, when I was serving under him, we routed the Philistines so utterly, that the men of Ashdod have been tributary to us ever since."

"And I, too, can recall it well," said Hannibal. "The Philistines were up there to the right, designing to storm the fortress in our front; half-way down the valley the King encountered them and drove them to their heights again. The heat of the battle was in the valley, but the greatest carnage was on the flight up yonder ridge."

As we proceeded, Hannibal pointed out to us on the further side of the valley the thirty stakes to which the King had had the chiefs of the Philistines bound after the battle; fragments of the skeletons were still attached to them.

"Ours is a good King," exclaimed Chamai; "Absalom, his son, rebelled against him, but I stood fast by David."

"And I, too," said Bichri; "and a battle followed in which I killed Othniel, the son of Ziba: I sent a javelin clean through his temples; this girdle of purple linen, which I am wearing now, was his."

All along, as we proceeded, Chamai, Hannibal and Bichri continued in this way to point out the sites, and to recall the history of places and events to which any interest attached. Whenever we passed a village or a town, the inhabitants, recognising us as Phœnicians, came flocking towards us with offerings of milk, dried grapes, figs, wine, or other refreshment, but were always eager in their inquiries

SHORTLY BEFORE SUNSET WE REACHED JERUSALEM.

whether we had any commodities of our own to sell. Bichri invariably told them that if they wished to inspect our merchandise, they must either come to Jerusalem, whither we were going, or go down to Joppa, where we had left our ships. Occasionally the goat-herds, who were in charge of fine flocks upon the hill-sides, accosted us, but we bought nothing of them except a couple of the excellent cheeses of the country, for which we paid only a few zeraas. As we were eating the cheeses under the shade of a terebinth, some girls brought us cool water from a neighbouring spring, and in acknowledgment of their attention, Hanno gave them a number of glass beads, with which they seemed highly delighted.

Shortly before sunset, on the evening of the second day we reached Jerusalem, a city very strongly built upon a steep and elevated plateau. The distant view of the city is extremely striking ; the soil on which it is built is undulating and irregular, so as to produce an effect of the whole place being literally studded with domes and terraces ; the whiteness of the walls, and the numerous roofs that are imbedded in the foliage of the olive-yards that skirt the walls, all combine to make up a picture that cannot fail most favourably to impress the traveller with its beauty.

After crossing a road that was bounded on one side by the torrent of Kedron, and which was lost to view as it deflected towards the deserts, we had surmounted the last of the olive-covered hills, and passed the last of the ravines, and soon began ascending a paved street, wide enough to admit three horsemen abreast, of which the houses were of brick, their gardens being enclosed by low clay walls. Night was coming on, and Chamai, who had galloped on ahead (leaving us to the guidance of Bichri), was now awaiting us at the gate of a large garden attached to a handsome brick house of two storeys. This house was the residence of Ira, one of the King's officers, to whom the duty was specially entrusted of providing for the entertainments of foreign ambassadors. Immediately on

our arrival, some slaves came to take charge of our beasts,
and to carry our baggage into the dwelling, where we were
first conducted into a long low room, and water was
brought us for our feet.   It was not long before Ira himself
appeared to bid us welcome, and to offer us refreshment.
I informed him of my name and errand, and showed him
the letter I bore from King Hiram to King David.   He
raised it to his head in token of his respect, and promised
to give his sovereign an immediate notice of my arrival.

When we had completed our repast, I began to prepare
my presents for King David.   First of all I chose a hyacinth-
coloured under tunic, made of the finest Egyptian linen,
and a purple upper tunic embroidered round the neck and
sleeves with flowers, and bordered with silver fringe ; to
these I added a girdle wrought in gold and silver, with a
lion's head in gold for a clasp, the eyes being of bright
enamel.   This girdle was a most elaborate specimen of
Egyptian workmanship, being one of four that I had purchased of a native artist, intending them for presents to
any monarchs to whose presence I might be admitted in
the course of my progress.   Another gift that I selected
was a drinking-cup of silver with two handles ; it was raised
upon a stem, and embossed with ornaments, worked in gold,
representing fruit and flowers.   The whole of these I
deposited in a box of the sandal-wood of Ophir, curiously
inlaid with gold and mother-of-pearl.   Remembering that
the King was not only fond of music, but was himself a skilful
performer, I further looked out for him a three-stringed
harp of sandal-wood, ornamented with coloured tufts, and
surmounted by the figure in solid gold of a bird with open
beak and outstretched wings.   This instrument could not
be matched out of Phœnicia, and the wood of which it was
made, like that of the box, had been brought from Ophir.
I had procured the harp from Khelesh-baal, a Sidonian,
to whom it had been given by the Queen of Ophir as an
acknowledgment of his having designed some ships for her
which could brave the open sea.

Early next morning when Ira came to inform me that he had announced my arrival to the King, he expressed his astonishment at the presents which I showed him I was about to make ; he told me that they would be most acceptable to the King, who was very desirous of seeing me.

About two hours afterwards some of the royal slaves arrived, bringing a calf, some bread, several cheeses, a basket of cakes and figs, a large jar of olives, and a still larger jar of the good wine of Helbon ; one of them, saluting me as an ambassador from King Hiram, said:

" I am instructed by King David to conduct you and your companions to the palace : come at once."

I gave the box containing the presents to my two sailors to carry, and collected my people together. Hannibal donned his helmet and cuirass, Hanno put his official inkhorn in his girdle, and we lost no time in setting off. Chamai and Bichri both accompanied us: they were in high glee, the latter especially, as, although he was one of David's subjects, he had never hitherto seen his King. On our way he remarked :

" David wronged our tribe of Benjamin ; but he made amends by his kindness to Saul's kindred. He is truly the glory of the tribes : I shall be rejoiced to see him ; I have never seen him yet."

" And after all," said Chamai, " he did not want to be hard upon the tribe of Benjamin ; it went against his heart. Think, too, of his love for Jonathan, and of his marrying Michal ; and Jonathan and Michal were both Saul's children. And how he avenged the death of Saul himself ! He has no ill-will against you children of Benjamin."

" He is a valiant King," said Hannibal ; " and valiant, too, is his general, his sister Zeruiah's son. He and Joab, both are warriors worthy of their renown "

While this conversation had been going on, we had been making our way through a succession of steep, narrow streets, with houses, one or two storeys high, and gardens on either hand. Seeing that we were ushered along by the royal

F

servants, easily recognised as these were by the purple
borders of their white garments, all the people saluted us
respectfully as we passed, an evidence of the high esteem in
which the King is held by his subjects.

We crossed a quarter of the city known by the name of
Millo, and came to a canal which runs out in the direction
of the open country, and which is overhung by an eminence
called Sion, the entire space between Sion and Millo being
occupied by houses recently erected at the King's own cost.
In the surrounding wall there still remained the breach
which had been opened by David, when he took the city
from the Jebusites. On the summit of Sion stands a
fortress, in the interior court of which the royal palace has
been built. Designed by Tyrian architects, this is three
storeys high, with a central dome, and is surrounded by
magnificent gardens, the edifice for the most part being
constructed of hewn stone and sandal-wood. On either
side of the gateway are two stately pillars of bronze, and
against the wall, to the right of one of these pillars, is
placed the seat where the King sits to administer justice ;
the gallows for the execution of capital sentences being
close at hand. In the rear are other gardens, and the
buildings set apart for the women of the household.

Ira was at the palace-gate to meet us, and conducted us by
a winding staircase into a square apartment, well lighted, and
hung with tapestries figured with birds and flowers. At one
end was a raised sandal-wood dais, three steps above the
level of the floor ; upon this stood the throne, which was
likewise of sandal-wood, but perfectly plain and unadorned
either with carving or gilding, a lion's skin stretched out at
its foot. On the right hand stood Joab, the King's general,
in helmet and cuirass ; at a little distance behind was the
royal armour-bearer holding the King's sword, while his
lance rested against the wall ; several officers were stationed
upon the steps ; and in front four of the King's body-guard
of mighty men, with their swords drawn.

Seated upon the throne was the monarch himself, a man

WAITING FOR THE KING TO SPEAK.

To face page 90.

of moderate stature and slight build, advanced in years, but nevertheless retaining unimpaired every symptom of agility and vigour. His straight, uncurled beard was perfectly white, but his hair was dressed in the ordinary fashion of his countrymen. His costume was very simple; neither frontlet nor coronet adorned his brow; no bracelets encircled his wrists; no rings were upon his toes; he wore a plain white tunic with a purple border, and instead of the high-heeled shoes usually worn by kings, he had on his feet a pair of mountaineer's sandals. There was nothing in his attire to distinguish him from ordinary men; only by the penetrating glance of his clear blue eye could he be marked out as one that was born to reign.

My people having ranged themselves in a line behind me, I stepped forward and prostrated myself at the foot of the dais; then rising, I stood with folded hands, waiting for the King to speak. He began by bidding me welcome, and proceeded to ask whether our voyage hither had been prosperous, and made numerous inquiries after the welfare of the kings of Tyre and Sidon and their subjects. Expressing his satisfaction at the tenor of my answers, he called for King Hiram's letters to himself. I handed the sealed papyrus to one of the officers, who presented it open to the King. The King perused it deliberately, and turning to me with a kindly smile, said:

"Mago, son of Maherbaal, I rejoice to see you. Who are these that you bring with you?"

One by one, I introduced my companions.

The King expressed his approval at seeing Chamai and Bichri amongst my followers, and said:

"I like my younger people to travel; it gives them courage, as well as wisdom and experience. I am glad, too, that your soldiers are under the command of Hannibal; he is an able leader; I remember him well. And now," he continued, "Jehoshaphat the recorder shall prepare you a catalogue of the materials which I require you to procure and I leave it to your own discretion to purchase, in addition, whatever else you may meet with that is curious or rare. It remains for me to inquire what are the supplies you need before you start."

I explained that I was anxious that forty experienced men should be added as recruits to Chamai's force, and that a sufficient store of corn and wine and oil, and other things that would not be the worse for keeping, might be provided to maintain us on our voyage.

"Just and fair are your demands," replied the King. "Joab shall choose you out forty men, whom Chamai and Hannibal may command, and my treasurer shall hand you over the money needed for their pay. Ira shall take you to the storehouses, and you shall be at liberty to select what stores you please ; he will provide you also with asses to convey them to the ships. You have only to say what you require, and it is yours."

Again I prostrated myself before the King in token of my gratitude, and requested him graciously to accept the presents that I had been commissioned to deliver. He seemed highly gratified, and inquired with the liveliest interest about the history of each gift, as it was shown him ; he then rose, and bade us follow him into an adjoining room, where wine was prepared for us. He insisted upon drinking from the cup which I had just given him, and when he had taken his seat again upon his throne, which had been brought in after him, he honoured me still further by asking me about the various countries I had visited. His curiosity seemed wakened by my replies, and amongst other things, he asked me whether peacocks and asses were not found in the West. I informed him that they came from Ophir, whither, subject to his permission, I contemplated making a voyage upon my return.

"You are a dauntless man," he said, "to talk about a second voyage before you have accomplished a first. I admire your courage, and confess that Hiram has done well in choosing you for this undertaking. I want now to show you the site of the temple that it is in my heart to rear."

With a tread elastic as a young man's, the King conducted us from the palace to an adjacent hill upon which
was a threshing-floor. The name of the hill was Moriah.

" I have just bought this threshing-floor and some oxen,
for fifty shekels of silver, of Araunah the Jebusite," he said ;
adding, "to my mind, the spot is adapted equally for a
temple or for a fortress."

Hanno remarked, " I have heard it said that the King
has taken more fortresses than he has built, and that his
sword is the best stronghold of his people."

" You are a flatterer, scribe," said the King, smiling ;
" nevertheless, I believe that bold hearts do more to defend
their country than any masses of piled-up stone."

" Then I am no flatterer," rejoined the scribe ; " I do
but echo the King's own sentiments. Happy the people
whose pride and confidence are in their King ! "

" If you use such silvery speech to women," replied the
King, " you must ultimately marry a princess."

Hanno coloured : the King laughed, and turning to me
said that I had an excellent scribe.

" Ah, my lord and King," said Hanno, " we are going
where eloquence can avail us nothing. The winds and
waves of the Great Sea will not listen to the smooth speech
of Canaan. The barbarians of the West will demand a
language of a rougher, sterner sort. Compliments will not
move the men of Tarshish."

The King was evidently much pleased with Hanno, and
told him that he should be gratified if he would bring him
back a written description of whatever he might see in
the course of his voyage ; he further inquired whether he
had any of his own compositions with him Upon this,
Hanno handed him a little scroll inscribed with some verses
he had written in praise of a lady. After the King, himself
a poet of the highest order, had admired the flow of the
lines, and commended the beauty of the handwriting, he
presented Hanno with a copy of some of his own poetry.

" There is another poetry," said Hanno, " of a severer

style, which the King has written in the valley of Rephaim, and on many another battle-field: I fear he cannot give us that."

In an instant David took the sword from his armour-bearer's hand. "Here," he said, "is the pen that wrote it. Take it; it may give you the power to write verses of the character that, in the valley of the giants, I have made to the honour of my God."

"The King's word is a prophecy," said Hanno, kissing the blade; "be it my care that it comes to pass!"

We had now to take our leave of the kind and courteous King, and I went with Ira direct to the storehouses, whilst Hannibal, Chamai, and Bichri followed Joab.

The chief storehouse is a long brick building approached by a paved pathway lined with sycamines; it is built in the Phœnician style over a water-tank, and is flanked by the stables for the royal chariots and the meadows for the horses and other cattle. Hanno had prepared a list, of which a duplicate copy was written for the King: the items were a hundred measures of grain, fifty measures of oil, fifty measures of wine, equal quantities of cheese, figs, and dried grapes, and two thousand shekels of dry salt meat: to these were added salt, beans, lentils, and dates, Ira undertaking that asses, with drivers, should be ready to convey them all to the ships on the following morning.

King David is renowned for generosity; and on our return to Ira's house we found that several of the royal servants had arrived before us, bringing various presents for us all. For myself there was a shield, a lance, a dagger, and an Egyptian battle-axe; for Hannibal, a sword and a mace of Chaldean manufacture; for Bichri, a bow and quiver and an archer's belt; while for Hanno there was another sword, in addition to the one he had already received.

Towards evening Hannibal returned, bringing word that he had completed his number of men; Jehoshaphat also came to bring me the King's final letters of instruction.

On rising the next morning I found the street outside

the house crowded with asses and their drivers, the beasts being laden with the heavy packs containing our supplies ; we had therefore nothing further to do than to take leave of our host. I gave him two phials of royal perfume for his wives, and without further delay we took our departure for Joppa.

Our return journey was unmarked by any special incident. From time to time Bichri gave us proof of his dexterity by using his new bow to shoot partridges and other birds while they were on the wing, and Hanno (with his sword passed through his girdle in Jewish fashion) was as gay as ever, beguiling the time with cheerful songs.

" Every one owns King David as a prophet," he repeated more than once ; " and as I have David's sword, I should think I might conquer the world."

" I hope you do not intend to kill King Pharaoh," said I, rather startled at his martial enthusiasm.

" Pshaw ! " he replied ; " my mistress is Ashtoreth, queen of sea and sky ! She can laugh to scorn Pharaoh and Bodmilcar, both alike ! "

Bichri interrupted us by bringing a partridge he had just brought down. " Can you tell me, captain," he asked, " whether there are any vines in Tarshish ? "

" To the great regret of our Phœnician colonists," I answered, " there are no vines at all."

" It may be a good thing then," he rejoined, " that I have brought some cuttings with me. The climate is warm, even as our own, and who can tell whether ere long they shall not be producing wine as good as ours ? "

" An excellent venture of yours, archer," I replied ; " I wish your foresight all success."

The tower of Joppa and the masts of our vessels were hardly visible in the distance before we espied Abigail advancing towards us. Chamai alighted from his horse, and received her with a warm embrace.

" What news ? " said I, hurrying forward.

Learning that all was well, I left the young people

together, and made my own way down immediately to the beach. The first person that I saw was Barzillai, who informed me that the eunuch had not been into the village since my departure, and that no one had attempted to hold any communication with the Ionian lady. Very shortly afterwards, Hamilcar and all the rest, including Bodmilcar, came to greet me on my return, and we proceeded at once to embark the supplies that we had brought. I put all the fresh recruits on board my own galley, thus making up my full complement of 210 men ; namely, 50 rowers, 70 sailors, 80 soldiers, and 10 officers.

While the drivers were assisting my own people to unlade the asses, one of them, a man of gigantic size and stature, stalked up to me, swinging his arms, and stood looking at me with a fixed and steady gaze. His appearance was remarkable ; his short bull-neck was imbedded, as it were, between his immense broad shoulders, and he had long shaggy hair that hung close over his brow and was met by a thick beard that grew almost up to his eyes.

"Do you want me ?" I asked.

In a stentorian voice he answered, "I am Jonah, of the village of Eltekeh, in the tribe of Dan."

"Well, what of that ?" I said.

"I want to go with you : I want to go where the wild beasts are."

"But what for ; what can you do if you get there ? "

"I want to go," again he growled.

"But you can do nothing ; what is the use of taking you ? "

"I want to go," he still persisted.

Puzzled in my mind, I asked him whether he could in any way make himself of use on board a ship.

"I am strong," he said ; "I am a descendant of Samson ; I can carry an ox upon my shoulders, and I can blow a trumpet ;" and as he spoke he struck himself heavily in the chest.

Hannibal, who all this while had been scanning the man with the eye of a connoisseur, observed : " I don't think we shall find a cuirass big enough to fit the fellow ; but he looks as if he mightn't be a bad trumpeter;" and turning towards him, he said : " Now look here, man ; I have a good trumpeter already ; but if Captain Mago will allow it, I should like to have a trumpet-match, and see which of you can blow the best."

Of course I had no objection to allege, and Hannibal's trumpeter was summoned to the spot. A huge clarion was

fetched from the stores and handed to Jonah, and thus the rivals were brought face to face in the middle of a circle of curious listeners.

" Blow away, my men," said Hannibal, " as hard as you like !"

Both raised their instruments to their lips, and simultaneously gave forth a series of strong, clear notes, which waxed louder and louder, as the performers, with necks outstretched and inflated cheeks, seemed to grow warm to the work. After a considerable time, during which neither appeared to have much superior power, the eyes of Hannibal's trumpeter began to start painfully from their sockets, and he showed symptoms of evident fatigue ; whilst Jonah, although the veins of his neck were swollen as large as one's finger, continued to give forth notes that almost split our ears, and which seemed still louder in contrast to the enfeebled strain of his competitor. At last, when full fifteen minutes had elapsed, Hannibal's herald gave one prolonged and plaintive note, and sunk down upon a stone, breathless and exhausted. Jonah, without exhibiting any sign of distress, stood with his hand upon his hip, and raising his trumpet high into the air, gave vent to a loud triumphal flourish.

" Enough, enough ! " we shouted one and all.

" Bring out the very largest scarlet tunic that we have on board," said Hannibal; " the fellow has gained his day."

" Then may I go ? " asked Jonah.

Hannibal made him understand that I had given my consent, and told him to put on the tunic. While he was endeavouring to fasten the garment, which seemed ready to burst out at every seam, Himilco walked round him, and surveyed him with a puzzled air.

" I should like to see inside the rascal," he said ; " I have never heard such lungs."

" I am thirsty," roared the giant.

A great cup of wine was handed to him ; he drained it at a gulp.

" Do you call that a draught ? " he asked. " I should give as much to my little children ; can't you let me drink from a pitcher or a cask ? "

Himilco refilled the cup, and handed it back to Jonah. With an air of wonder, that almost amounted to terror, he muttered to himself, " An extraordinary fellow, but it will cost us something to keep him ! "

When we had embarked all our goods, we took leave of Barzillai and his wife. The Ionian bade a most affectionate farewell to Milcah, who had treated her with the greatest kindness and hospitality. Abigail was the last to leave the shore, and when she did so, it was with a look, long and lingering, towards her native mountains.

By the following evening we had rounded the point of Pelusium, easily distinguished from the surrounding lowland by its rising grove of palms. The sea was rough, and to many on board the consequent sickness was very trying. Towards noon next day we came in sight of the troubled waters caused by the outflow of the Nile.

CHAPTER V.

PHARAOH ARRIVES TOO LATE.

WE shortly hove in sight of what is known as the Tanitic
mouth of the Nile, beyond which, in the distance, could be
discerned the tall obelisks of the City of Tanis.   The de-
posit brought down by the river itself, combined with the
action of the wind and surf upon the two headlands of
the bay, has a perpetual tendency to block up this outlet
of the Nile ; and when the *Cabiros*, which had been sent
on ahead to explore the bar, returned with the intelligence
that the water was too shallow to permit a safe passage
to the *Melkarth*, I determined to push on a little further to
the Mendezian mouth, which is considerably wider, and
which leads, moreover, direct to Memphis.   Night was
coming on, so that I would not venture to stem the somewhat rapid current of the river in the dark, but brought my
ships to anchor within a bowshot of the shore.

Hazael came to me and asked permission to pass the
night with his friend Bodmilcar.   I was equally surprised
at his request, and at the submissive manner in which he
made it ; but after ascertaining that the Ionian was in her
cabin, and that Abigail was with Chamai on deck, I allowed
him to go.

Remembering that we had arrived at a land of strangers,
with whom hitherto we had held no communication, I
doubled the watch, and gave Hannibal special directions
to keep a sharp look-out.   The order in which our ships
were arranged was this : on the right, furthest to the south,

was the *Cabiros;* the *Ashtoreth* was moored to some piles about half a bowshot behind; the *Melkarth* and the *Dagon* were stationed on the opposite bank, where the water was deeper. One of the small barques was with me, the other with the *Melkarth*.

Anchored higher up the river were several Egyptian vessels, and a considerable number was drawn up upon the shore. I wondered why there should be so many at a spot where there was no regular anchorage, but I subsequently learnt that Pharaoh was about to send forth a squadron for the purpose of putting down a revolt that had broken out at Pelusium. Two officers, accompanied by a troop of soldiers, some armed with battle-axes, and some with bows, had already boarded my ship to inquire who we were and what we wanted, and had retired satisfied with my explanation. As the shades of night deepened, we could observe the lights of two galleys cruising about in the open channel, and shortly afterwards another Egyptian came on board and ordered my own lights to be extinguished, a direction which was instantly obeyed.

The night was intensely warm, and the scorching east wind, laden with the sand of the desert, blew from time to time in dry and unrefreshing gusts. The sky was overcast, and although the night was not black it was so dark that little could be distinguished except the gleam from the fires of a large camp pitched on the right bank, and the inconstant lights of the distant villages on either shore. Close in front of us were still burning the torches of the two galleys I have mentioned; but besides these, there was only the occasional flicker from some little boat that moved upon the stream.

Towards midnight, five or six hours after our anchoring, I resigned my watch to Himilco, intending to take some rest. On my way to my berth I cast my eye towards the right bank, and through the gloom I could see indistinctly that there was a crowd of vessels there; but everything was silent, and I went below.

I had not been asleep for more than a half-an-hour when I was roughly aroused by Himilco.

"We are adrift !" he exclaimed.

In an instant I was upon my feet, and rushed to examine our moorings.   They were cut asunder.

"All hands on deck! lights! light the lamps!" I cried with all my might ; and at the same time I noticed lights appearing on the left, and heard a distant voice hailing the *Ashtoreth* with the cry, "Our moorings have been cut, and we are all adrift." I shouted in reply that they should come over to us ; it was only too evident that another of our ships was in the same dilemma as ourselves.

Meantime my crew had come on deck, and had lighted several signals.   I ordered the rowers to their benches, and made them backwater gently so as to keep us steady until the other ship should join us.   At the distance of about four bowshots behind, I made out the *Cabiros* hoisting her lights, and could hear the voices of the crew in great excitement.   Almost immediately there was a splash of oars, and the *Dagon* came alongside of us.   I shouted to Hasdrubal, who was standing on board :

"Where's the *Melkarth ?* "

Getting no satisfactory reply, I immediately ordered the three ships on to the left bank.   The *Dagon* went straight across the river ; I followed, taking an oblique course, and the *Cabiros*, hastening ahead, went a little way south, and then turned back due north, keeping as close as possible to the shore.

During the time we were getting across, Hannibal had just put all his men under arms, as it occasioned us much surprise that while there was this commotion amongst ourselves the Egyptians had made no sign nor sound ; their lights were out, and their cruisers no longer to be seen. The *Cabiros* rejoined us, and reported that she had seen nothing ; nor even after we had descended the river a couple of stadia was a single Egyptian vessel visible, and it was not until we were within hearing of the roar of the waves at the river's mouth that we almost ran against some black mass that loomed through the darkness.

"Back to your moorings, Phœnicians! no leaving the river at night!" shouted a voice, in Egyptian.

"We don't want, I can tell you," I replied, "to be running away like a set of thieves. We have been cut adrift, and one of our ships has disappeared."

"Then get fresh moorings," was the answer: "you must wait till morning. By Pharaoh's orders, you cannot leave to-night."

There was no help for it but to obey; and sending some men on shore in the small boat with torches, we succeeded in finding an anchorage. But scarcely had we settled in our places, when our attention was arrested by a voice from the middle of the river gasping out in Phœnician, "Help! help!"

We put off a boat in the direction of the sound; the cry was repeated still closer to us, and in a few minutes the boat returned alongside, and one of my sailors, dripping with water, was hoisted on to the deck of the *Ashtoreth*. He was in a pitiable condition, his face all bleeding, and his head gashed open in several places.

"Treason, treason! we are betrayed by Bodmilcar!" was all he could utter, as he staggered and fell senseless on the deck. I ordered him to be laid upon a piece of carpet, whilst Abigail chafed his face with ointment, and Himilco put some wine to his lips. I had ascertained quite enough to put me on my guard, and consequently had our lights extinguished, permitting only one lamp and one torch to each ship: and I gave directions to the watch to keep a keen look-out.

Meanwhile the poor fellow had recovered his consciousness, and Hanno, Hannibal, Himilco, Chamai, and myself, pressed round him to gather what he had to say. One of our sailors supported his head to facilitate his power of speech, and Abigail and the Ionian knelt beside him, with the wine and ointment.

"I went this evening," began the man, "to visit a friend of mine on board the *Melkarth*. You know the crew are nearly all Tyrians. Bodmilcar has tampered with them all. He has had an interview with Pharaoh's general, and told him that you are spies in league with the insurgents at Pelusium ; he said, too, that you had a slave on board your ship, whom he was bringing to Pharaoh, but who had escaped. His people urged me to join the conspiracy, and when I refused they all threatened to kill me. I

jumped overboard. An Egyptian boat pursued me. I was twice struck on the head by an oar. I dived beneath the water. I suppose they thought I had sunk ; as they gave up the pursuit. Orders have been given to seize us all to-morrow. We are to be attacked in the morning, and carried off to Pharaoh. I can tell no more."

The exertion of telling all this had been too much for the brave fellow, and he fainted away again. My first impulse was to rush to my cabin for the King's letters, but to my amazement they had all disappeared ; they had evidently been stolen during my absence at Jerusalem

We were overwhelmed with consternation. Hanno was the first to speak :

"All is plain enough," he said ; "Bodmilcar is the thief. Hazael, you know, has the King's signet ring ; and the rascals have opened the papers, altered their purport, and closed them again with the royal seal. Bodmilcar has carried them and presented them ; he represents himself as leader of the expedition, and denounces you as a traitor. He gets believed : and what is the result ? why, sure as fate, we shall be made prisoners, and only too likely we shall be put to death. Abigail, of course, will be sent to Pharaoh."

"Not while I have a sword to defend her," said Chamai, stamping with rage.

"Yes," continued Hanno, coolly ; "no doubt Abigail will be handed over to Pharaoh, and the fair Chryseis will be awarded to Bodmilcar as a recompense for his service."

Hanno groaned aloud, and Hannibal furiously twirled his moustache.

"I have no doubt, Hanno," I said, "that all your conjectures are right. But it's rather soon to despair. Perhaps you haven't been with us old mariners long enough to learn our seamen's song about the Egyptians ? "

I began to whistle an air, and Himilco, with a merry laugh, broke out with the gay refrain :

> "The bull-head tribe, with all their skill,
> Must catch the man they fain would kill."

The effect was instantaneous. My whole party almost smothered me in their delight. Hanno threw himself at my knees and grasped one of my hands ; Abigail seized the other, and covered it with kisses ; Hannibal caught hold of my cuirass on one side ; Chamai lugged at me on the other. Altogether, I was in a fair way of being strangled. The Ionian, who partially comprehended my meaning, could

G

only express her gratitude by the bright glance of her soft eyes.

As soon as I had extricated myself from the embraces of the enthusiastic group, I pointed out to them a confused mass of Egyptian boats, now just visible in the dawn.

"If there were only half-a-dozen of those fresh-water tortoise-shells," said I, "our three ships could soon show them the way to the bottom of the Nile; but there is such a lot of them! Besides, they have forces on land, and the river isn't wide enough for us to get out of their reach. Bodmilcar, too, will lend them a helping hand, and he is an old stager; his ship, it is true, is not much in fighting trim, but it is manned with Tyrians. However, we mustn't give up! Patience! Trust yourselves to me!"

"Yours we are to the death!" cried Hanno; while Hannibal, with his teeth set, growled out, that if any one disobeyed my orders it should be the worse for him. Chamai, almost beside himself with excitement, clasped Abigail in his arms, and vowed he would bring her the head and spoils of the first foe he should meet, even if it were Pharaoh himself.

Hamilcar and Hasdrubal, with his pilot Gisgo, now came on board for my orders.

"I never trusted that Tyrian," said Hamilcar; "and I am glad to have the chance of fighting it out with him; and my men are as delighted as myself."

"Ha, ha! Himilco," laughed Gisgo the carless, "we shall have some sport now."

"Yes, old Celt," replied Himilco, "we will teach the rascals to swim."

I shook hands heartily with all three men, and they returned to their ships. It was now broad daylight, and casting my eye towards the river, I reconnoitred the enemy's position. Below-stream the Egyptian galleys were under way; opposite to us, on the left bank, were about forty small boats, each manned with four rowers

and five soldiers, and a troop of nearly a hundred bowmen
were assembling hastily on the right-hand shore. Looking
up-stream, I could count as many as six galleys about two
stadia away ; two large heavy ships, with hanging decks,
were sailing down the left bank ; and mid-channel I
recognised the towering sides and rounded prow of the
Melkarth, her oars shipped, and her sails furled, being
towed by a low, open rowing-boat. The camp, of which
we had noticed the fires in the darkness, was much too
far off to be visible by daylight. The shore on either
side was perfectly flat and treeless, but covered with fields
of clover and of corn that was nearly ripe, as the harvest-
time was drawing nigh. On the left bank, about two
bowshots from the water, a steep dyke, surmounted by a
causeway, had been thrown up as a protection during the
annual inundation. Far away to the south, the white
buildings of a city could be distinguished ; and in the north
could be seen the yellowish-whitey waters of the river bar,
with the broad green surface of the sea beyond.

We were hardly six stadia from the mouth of the river ;
the strong east wind and the current were both in our
favour, and once out at sea we should have little to fear. I
determined, therefore, to make an attack upon the Egyptians
before the *Melkarth* could get ahead of us, for I knew that
once in front of us, her very bulk would be a formidable
obstacle to our retreat, and that she could overwhelm
us with a storm of missiles ; while the superior height of
her deck would not only prevent our men from boarding
her, but, on the contrary, would give her men every facility
for boarding us.

My first manœuvre was to slip my moorings, and to
take up my position in the middle of the channel, so as to
be out of reach of the archers on the shore. The *Dagon*
had shifted her prow to the north, and lay half a bowshot
below me ; the *Cabiros* was to my left, her prow southward. The sails were all furled, the rowers were ordered
to backwater very gently so as to just keep the vessels in

their places, and each pilot took his stand by the side of the helmsman. Hannibal posted his archers fore and aft, and grouped his soldiers round the mast. Hanno and I mounted the prow, and my trumpeter followed. The gigantic Jonah remained with Hannibal ; he could not be persuaded either to put on a cuirass or to take a lance, but stood, clarion in hand, watching all our preparations with a curious eye.

The scorpions had already been supplied with missiles, and each vessel was provided with a number of earthenware pots filled with sulphur and pitch. We improvised, also, a quantity of fire-ships, formed of small planks, into which spikes were driven, to which were fastened well-greased goat-skins charged with combustibles.

We had not long to wait. Very soon were heard the shrill notes of the small Egyptian trumpets, and the decks of the ships were seen manned with troops. I could discern the smooth brown faces of the soldiers, and make out that they were armed with battle-axes and large triangular shields ; and I could see that the archers, with their legs bare, and poignards in their girdles, were ranged along the sides of the ships. The rowers, more than half-naked (clothed merely by a strip around their loins), plied their paddles, according to their custom, standing. On board the *Melkarth*, Bodmilcar was easily distinguished ; he was in a state of great excitement and activity, and apparently giving some explanation to an Egyptian officer, a man dressed in green and wearing a large wig, with his face and arms painted with cinnabar, in accordance with the common fashion of their men of rank.

The soldiers that manned the small boats were nearly as slightly clad as the rowers ; they carried poignards in their girdles, and were armed with axes and staves pointed at both ends, in the use of which the Egyptians are notoriously skilful. Although all appeared in considerable commotion, not one of the vessels made any attempt to advance, and there seemed a general state of expectation.

"DOWN, YOU PHOENICIAN THIEVES!"

The solution of all this was soon apparent. A large boat was seen to detach itself from the general mass, and make its way down-stream towards us. Eight rowers stood paddling on the raised bow and stern; twelve soldiers, with square plates of bronze strapped on their breasts, and armed with lances, daggers, and short scimitars, were in the middle; and amongst them was an Egyptian officer of high rank. He was arrayed in two tunics of striped gauze, crossed one over the other upon his breast; a girdle ornamented with enamel plates was round his waist, and a large gold and enamelled bird with out-stretched wings was suspended by a gold chain from his neck. His head was covered with a tall cap, bearing an enamel plate inscribed with the name of Pharaoh in hieroglyphics; his beard was enclosed in a casing of red cloth; and in his hand was a gilt battle-axe, elaborately inlaid with figures of animals and other symbols. On one side of this sumptuous personage was a closely-shorn priest or scribe, habited entirely in white, and holding an inkhorn and some papyrus in his hand; on the other, in full Syrian armour, was our old friend Hazael. I could not resist a smile as I caught sight of a pile of chains and manacles lying in the boat.

On the Egyptian officer shouting that he wanted to come on board and speak to me, I gave permission for his boat to come alongside the *Ashtoreth*, and, followed by his scribe and five of the soldiers, with the greatest arrogance he stepped on deck. Hazael had the discretion to remain behind, where he was. I received the magnate with all courtesy, and saluted him after the fashion of his own country, but instead of acknowledging it in any way, he began with the most overbearing insolence to exclaim:

"Down, down, you Phœnician thieves, and sue for Pharaoh's mercy!"

Finding that such was the tone he took, I answered sternly:

"No thieves are we, nor have we injured Pharaoh; so

far from imploring Pharaoh's mercy, we have a right to demand Pharaoh's protection."

"Out upon your falsehoods!" retorted the enraged Egyptian; "have you not this very night been attempting your escape?"

"No," I said emphatically; "we were cut adrift. The real thieves are amongst you. That rascal Bodmilcar and that vile eunuch stole the royal letters that they brought to you."

"Silence!" shouted the Egyptian in impetuous fury; "too well we understand your frauds. Out with your hands! the handcuffs are ready here, and you and the slave that you have stolen must come along to Pharaoh. Never fear but ample justice shall be done!"

The scribe was opening his inkhorn for the purpose of taking down our names, when I burst out into a roar of laug'ter.

"Do you take us for fools?" I said; "why on earth should we leave our ships to go and hear a slanderous catalogue of lies alleged against us? No, no, sire, we remain where we are."

The Egyptian literally stamped with rage. "Villains! pirates! thieves!" he cried; "every one of you shall die a death of torment."

Throughout this interview I had taken care never for a moment to lose sight of the fleet above-stream; and seeing that the ships were now in motion, without paying the least regard to the continued ravings of the grand official, I ordered my trumpeter to sound an alarm. The Egyptian, followed closely by his scribe, hurried towards his boat; his soldiers, to cover his retreat, rapidly crossed their lances. Chamai, Hannibal, and Hanno, mistaking the movement, and supposing they were making an attack on me, fell upon them with drawn swords; and the huge Jonah, throwing down his trumpet, rushed into the fray, and wresting a lance from one of the soldiers' hands, took him by the shoulders and dashed his head twice or thrice

THE SOLDIERS RAPIDLY CROSSED THEIR LANCES.

against the side of the ship. It is a popular belief that the Egyptians are a hard-headed race, but I avow that this fellow's skull cracked like a ripe water-melon.

Meanwhile, Hannibal had cut the throat of another of the soldiers, and Chamai had plunged his sword into the body of a third. I was struggling to wrench the lance from the grasp of a fourth, when taking alarm at the number of my men, he turned about, and following the example of his sole remaining comrade, sprang overboard and swam like a frog. But they were not to escape so easily; Bichri, who was standing near the wale of the vessel, hit one of them with an arrow, and the rowers stunned the other by blows with their oars. Thus the whole five were entirely disposed of ; but the real conflict was yet to come.

As soon as the Egyptians were aware of the fray, one of their galleys from the right bank drew rapidly towards us, and the whole bevy of small boats that had gathered round kept up a continuous flight of arrows, every one of which, however, either stuck in the ship's side or went whistling over our heads.

A single glance was sufficient to reveal to me the enemy's tactics. Just as I had anticipated, the *Melkarth* was being towed down the stream towards the right, obviously with the design to pass us and get below, so as to cut off our retreat. Their immediate design was to divert our attention from this manœuvre, and for this purpose two large ships were ordered to bear down upon us, and a flotilla of small boats was sent to keep up a storm of arrows. Hannibal immediately, by my directions, set his catapults to work, and a volley of stones and pots full of pitch and sulphur was discharged, right over the *Cabiros*, on to the approaching vessels. I then ordered the *Cabiros* and the *Dagon* to move simultaneously, right and left of me, but in opposite directions : the *Cabiros* northwards towards the galleys that were obstructing our way, the *Dagon* straight down upon the boat that was towing the *Melkarth.* I could see Bodmilcar upon the prow of the great gaoul,

wildly endeavouring to make the Egyptians understand
their danger, and urging the rowers to get their oars into
the water ; but he was too late. Our movements had
taken them completely by surprise. The *Dagon*, cutting
her way full speed through the crowd of small boats,
crushed or capsized all that came in her course ; the *Ashtoreth*, liberated by the departure of the *Cabiros*, effectually kept in check the ships that were trying to pass down
the stream ; and the *Cabiros*, that had gone northward, by
sending out a number of fire-floats that drifted on in
advance, completely discomfited the two galleys that were
guarding the mouth of the river.

Our tactics were a perfect success. One of the Egyptian
ships was run into by the *Ashtoreth* with such violence
that it was cut asunder, and sank immediately ; and the
other, harassed by the pots of combustibles, and alarmed at
the eddy caused by the foundering of its consort, purposely
ran aground. The *Dagon*, after staving in the towing-boat
like a piece of rotten wood, had returned to me ; and as we
had the satisfaction of seeing Bodmilcar's crew cut their
tow-rope, we both turned our attention to the galley which
was retiring from the attack and falling back upon the
Melkarth. Simultaneously passing it quite close, one on
each side, we swept off both its tiers of oars, and hurling
down upon it a final shower of arrows, we filed off to join
the *Cabiros*, which was still engaged in discharging its
missiles and fire-floats at the other two galleys.

The contest had been sharp but short. In less than
an hour we had rendered the *Melkarth* incapable of
action ; had sunk two Egyptian vessels ; had sent a third
aground : and had crushed or capsized at least fifteen
small boats.

The surface of the water was covered with the *débris*,
and not a few men could be seen drifting along in the
current. Thrown into utter confusion by our unlooked-for
attack, the rest of the Egyptian vessels floundered about in
each others' way, and totally prevented the *Melkarth* from

obtaining another tug-boat. Finding, therefore, that those
need give me no concern, I gave my attention to the galleys
in front, and sent adrift a dozen or more fire-floats, which
the crew of the *Cabiros* sent down-stream with their boathooks.   The galleys gave way; and, feeling that there
was no immediate impediment, I proceeded towards them
calmly to the north, leaving our assailants confounded by
their disaster, and Bodmilcar raving furiously on the poop
of his helpless ship.   Bichri lamented that he could not let
fly an arrow at him, but it was utterly useless, as we were
already too far away.

"A drawn battle!" said the brave archer, coming forward
from the stern.

"Yes," said I; "the rascal has had bad luck this morning;
but he will watch his opportunity. We haven't done with
each other yet."

"I hope not," said Hanno, vindictively.

Presently there was a movement among the Egyptian
ships, and three of them, having extricated themselves from
the maze of confusion, had commenced a pursuit of us,
accompanied by a number of little boats.   At the same

moment I espied a troop of horsemen galloping along the shore; and raising my eyes to the causeway on the top of the dyke, I observed a cloud of dust, from the midst of which broke ever and again the gleam of a row of bronze and gilded chariots.   There was no room for doubt; evidently the King himself was approaching with the intention of being a witness of our capture.

But the mighty Pharaoh had come too late!

Out of forty or fifty fireships which we had set afloat, two at last had run foul of one of the galleys, which was now in flames, and the terrified crew were fain to resort to the usual naval manœuvre of the Egyptians, and run their ship aground.   The vessels that had started in pursuit of us were still at least two stadia in our rear, so that we had ample time to tackle with the single galley that remained ahead to bar our progress.

"Board her! board her! Let us board her!" shouted Hannibal, Hanno, and Chamai, with unanimous accord.

"We have no time, and she's not worth the trouble," I replied; "we will sink her."

"Down she goes, then, like a stone," cried Himilco.

The *Cabiros*, without meeting with any resistance beyond a few chance stones and straggling arrows, now slipped quietly under the very prow of the galley, and with unfurled sail was making off to sea.   The *Dagon* was about to follow her, but at a signal from me, Hasdrubal bore down upon the galley's stern, whilst I simultaneously drove straight against her flank, and between us we literally cut her in two.   Down sank the galley in a whirlpool of foam; and our last obstacle being thus removed, we hoisted our sails and rode out to sea, our trumpets sounding out a flourish of victory.

Behind us rose a discordant howl of maledictions.   We were out of reach.   It was utterly impossible for our enemies in their little nut-shells of vessels to follow where our victorious prows were now cleaving the foamy billows; and when we were fairly out at sea, steering due west, I

could see, as I looked along the low flat coast, that the
Egyptian masts were quite motionless. It was evident,
therefore, that Bodmilcar had advised them to abandon
their pursuit.

Fifteen of our men were wounded, nearly all of them
slightly, and two had been killed; whilst the loss of the
enemy, including those slain by the archers, burnt by the
fire-ships, or drowned by the waters of their own sacred
Nile, must have been nearly three hundred.

It did not take long to repair whatever damage we had
sustained. Some broken oars on board the *Ashtoreth*, and
a few more on board the *Dagon*, were replaced from the
reserves; the decks were washed down, the stays strength-
ened, some broken ropes spliced, and the arrows that had
lodged in the rigging and ship's sides removed. All our
wounded had been carried below; and the bodies of the
three Egyptians, having been stripped of any spoil of value,
were thrown overboard. The bodies of our own two men
were also committed to the waves with an invocation on
their behalf to Menath, Hokk, and Rhadamath, the judges
of the infernal regions.[1] In less than three hours everything
was as much in order as though nothing had happened.
Chryseis and Abigail, who had all along rendered what
assistance they could, were rejoicing in their freedom;
Hanno, whose nerve had never failed him, and Chamai
fully sharing in their delight.

I sent for Hasdrubal to come on board, that he might
join Himilco and myself in a council of war. When we
were alone together, I said:

"Listen to me. There is no shadow of doubt that we
shall be pursued. Ascending the eastern outlet of the
river, the Egyptians will come down by the western; they
may come either by the Canopic or Phanitic branch; and
at both Pharos and Canope there is no question but that
the King has ships in readiness. They can anticipate us
there; couriers by land can arrive by early morning; we,

[1] The Minos, Eacus, and Rhadamanthus of the Greeks.

with our utmost speed, could not arrive till long beyond
mid-day. Somewhere or other we must of necessity put in
to shore again ; our supply of water is all but gone."

To Himilco's suggestion that we had wine enough to
meet our need, I vouchsafed no other reply than a shrug of
the shoulders, and continued :

" My intention was to take in a fresh supply this very
evening, but this skirmish has frustrated everything. Go
ashore we must ; and this is the scheme that I propose ;
we will re-enter the river by the Sebennitic mouth, which

is nearest to us now ; they will never suspect us of ven
turing on land so soon ; probably they will not be there at
all ; if they are, we must use main force ; but water we
must have."

My companions approved my plan, but expressed their
anxiety as to what was to happen afterwards.

" I do not think," I said, "that because we have lost the
gaoul that we need at all contemplate abandoning our
expedition. Failing to find us at either Canope or Pharos,
the Egyptians will watch for us all along the coast ; and at

last Bodmilcar, who knows our destination, will get re-inforcements from Pharaoh and will chase us right on to Tarshish. Sooner or later we shall be pretty sure of falling in with him; but for the present, at least, we can elude him thoroughly. Here is my project. The wind is north-east and favourable; by steering by the sun in the day-time, and by keeping the Cabiros a little to our left at night, I do not fear but that in five days at most we might reach the shores of the great island, Crete."

Himilco and Hasdrubal stared at me in mingled admira-tion and surprise.

"From Egypt to Crete! Across the open sea! An unheard-of thing! Can it be possible?"

Such were the exclamations with which they heard my proposition.

"Aye, harder things than that may be done," I con-tinued; "the wind isn't likely to change till next new moon; but even should it change and we happen to miss Crete, we shall only run upon the mainland, or on one of the islands of the Archipelago. Thence we can get round Cape Malea to Sicily, from Sicily to Carthage, from Carthage direct to Tarshish. That's our course, now."

"By our goddess Ashtoreth, your scheme is beautiful!" cried Hannibal; "and meanwhile the Egyptian rascals will be floundering about the Syrtes."

"And rough enough they'll find them," said Himilco. " I was well-nigh drowned there two years back; and let us hope that Bodmilcar and his Tyrian sneaks, bad luck to them! may come to grief. How I should like to hang them all like a string of fishes, fastened by their gills!"

We were not long in reaching the little town of Sebennys. The *Cabiros* was first sent ashore, and returned with the tidings that all was quiet. I paid the customary dues to the Egyptian governor of the place, and despatched a number of our sailors to procure the requisite supply of water; they took the opportunity of purchasing several baskets of onions and some good fresh meat. Before the end of the day we had turned our backs upon the land, and were making our venturous way north-west.

"And now, for our dishes and platters," I cried; "I am frightfully hungry."

We seated ourselves in the stern, and joined by Chryseis and Abigail, we formed a large and merry group. The sailors and soldiers all were served with a ration of wine in honour of the morning's victory.

"I see we have changed our course," said Hanno; "are we making for Crete?"

"Yes," I replied; and added that I supposed it was a place already known to the fair Chryseis.

Chamai inquired whether it was not the same as Chittim.

"No, not the same," I answered; "*this* island is full of mountains, upon which are goats with spreading horns like those of Arabia; the people are famous for their skill as archers."

"Bichri, then, may find his match," said Chamai. "But to what nation do they belong?"

"They are Phrygians and Dorians," I told him; "fair, tall men, with handsome faces and well-formed limbs; they have built towns in which some of our Sidonian merchants have recently settled, getting there by way of Chittim and Rhodes. Chryseis speaks the same language as the Dorians."

Chamai, ever full of interest in Chryseis, expressed his pleasure at hearing that she was about to go amongst a people kindred to herself, and was inquiring whether they were a martial race, when Chryseis interposed, and with Hanno's assistance explained that the Dorians, like the Ionians of the Isles, and the Achaians on the mainland, were renowned warriors, and that the fame of their conquests had spread far and wide.

"How large, how vast the world must be!" exclaimed Hannibal; "here is a people, famed in war, whose very name I scarcely know. But is it not from Crete that we get our Chalcidian swords?"

Smiling at his mistake, I made him understand that Chalcidian swords were made of copper from the island of Chalcis, and that the Phœnicians could not elsewhere procure copper that would take so fine a temper.

Hannibal went on to ask Hanno to inquire of Chryseis what were the military tactics of the Ionians, and how they paid their soldiers.

" Do you expect us women to know such things as these ?" asked Abigail, with a merry laugh ; " a woman knows well enough that her countrymen can fight, and she knows how to prize the spoils they bring her from the battle-field ; but what can she know of the art of war ?"

Chryseis seemed amused at her maid's vivacity, and proceeded to enumerate the most illustrious military leaders of her land. I heard her name Achilles, and Ajax, and a certain king called Agamemnon ; and I understood her to relate that two kings in her country, named Jason and Ulysses, were renowned for the voyages they had made.

" Voyages !" cried Himilco, scornfully ; " I can guess what their voyages were : creeping along and hugging the shore ; making perhaps a stadium a day ; never looking at a star. And then, what ships they had ! I am glad I haven't to trust myself in one of them from Sidon to Chittim."

Chryseis owned that, as to ships, she had never seen anything in her own country that could be compared to the ships of the Phœnicians, adding that she thought that the mariners of Phœnicia must be true sea-gods.

" And you must be their goddess," said Hanno, with enthusiasm.

" Ah, young man," yawned out Hannibal, "you should put your fine speeches in Ionian ; the lady does not understand you."

The lady, however, bent her head gracefully, and raised a laugh by saying in good Phœnician that she perfectly understood what had passed.

"Trust a woman for understanding a compliment," was Hannibal's remark.

"I should like to see the effect," said Himilco, "of one of Hanno's pretty speeches upon Gisgo's wife; her Celtic dialect is something like the croaking of Bodmilcar's ravens."

It was now getting dark, and as he spoke, Himilco moved off to his post upon the prow, and I took up my watch upon the stern. All that night, and all the following day, the wind freshened till it blew a gale; being all in our favour, its violence caused me no alarm, but well-nigh all on board, conscious of being far away from land, and beholding nothing but sea and sky, were filled with terror; and as the ship at one moment was carried high upon the crests of the enormous waves, and at another was sunk low in what seemed an unfathomable abyss, they became almost paralysed with alarm; they lost their appetites entirely, and were incessant in their invocations to their gods. The gale next night increased to a hurricane, and on the morning shifted to the south, driving us to the north at the rate of 1800 stadia in a day.

Happily, although our ships were thus flying over the sea, they kept well together. Towards evening the wind dropped a little, and on the morning of the fourth day it was comparatively calm; the sky was very clear, and, to our vast delight, the man on watch at the top of the mast announced that land was in sight. I joined Himilco on the prow, and both of us could plainly distinguish in the sunlight the peaks of some snow-capped mountains. By the afternoon the view of land was plain to every one on board, and before the stars had risen, we were skirting a coast that seemed so rocky as to be inaccessible.

It was long past midnight before we could discover any anchorage at all; at last we found a small exposed bay where a river coursing along a bottom of white sand entered the sea. Towards the east, masses of thick woods could be made out, with snowy peaks of higher ridges rising up behind them. The *Cabiros* was hauled up on shore close to the river's mouth, and, the water in the bay being found sufficiently deep, the two galleys were moored to some of the great boulder-stones upon the beach. The coast was quite desolate, and there was no sign of human habitation.

CHAPTER VI.

CRETE AND THE CRETANS.

NO sooner were the ships safely settled in their moorings, than Himilco and I, who had both been up on watch throughout the last four nights, retired to take the rest that we so much needed, and, worn out by fatigue, I did not wake until the sun was high above the horizon.

The shore was still quite deserted; the steep rocky mountains appeared for the most part to rise perpendicularly from the sea; and the little valley of the river soon lost itself in a deep gorge, densely wooded with myrtles and holm-oaks.

My first care was to send a squad of sailors on shore to fill our barrels and goat-skins with a supply of fresh water; I next ordered a guard of soldiers and archers to be landed ready for any emergency; and then despatched Bichri, accompanied by half a score of bowmen, up the gorge to explore the mountains. There was abundance of wood about, and I determined to light some fires and cook our morning meal upon the strand. I likewise pitched a couple of tents, in which I laid out some of our merchandise, in case Bichri should fall in with any of the natives of the island. Jonah made himself especially prominent by his services on the occasion; he carried wood enough on his back to load three ordinary men, and lifted a barrel of water without any assistance, remarking that, if any one would give him wine in it to drink, he would lift a barrel twice the size.

PLEASED WITH HIS MORNING'S WORK.

To fa. 128.

About midday Bichri returned, tired with his wanderings, but well pleased with his morning's work. He had come across several of the natives on the mountains ; they fled at his approach, but being an experienced mountaineer he had followed them from rock to rock, and had at length succeeded in capturing one of them. The others had pelted him with stones from a distance, but he had sustained no injury, and, in accordance with the orders I had given him, he had acted strictly on the defensive, and had not in any way returned their violence. The prisoner that he brought with him was a great strapping fellow, with a quantity of glossy black hair and a skin as brown as a Midianite's ; his eyes were black and obliquely set ; his face wide, with projecting cheek-bones, and a pointed chin. He had no other covering except the skin of a wild-goat, which was thrown over his shoulders and fastened round his waist by a cord, and on his bare neck and arms were a necklace and bracelets made of shells. A hatchet with which he had defended himself had been wrested from him by Bichri ; it was made of a highly polished stone of a greenish hue, and had a strong wooden handle.

As soon as the barbarian was brought to me he began with many gesticulations to speak in a language of which I did not understand a word. I restored him his hatchet, made him a present of a piece of red cloth,. and after showing him the goods in the tent, gave him his liberty. He bounded off towards the mountains and disappeared among the trees.

Two hours afterwards he came back with several other men, half-naked as himself, and armed with lances and rudely-made bows. When within about a hundred paces of us, they stopped and waved some boughs of myrtle. I ordered my men to do the same, and then I advanced to meet them, making Hanno accompany me, and display some pieces of red cloth and strings of glass beads. Gradually the savages gained courage and were induced to approach, and at last to enter our tent. There was one of them who seemed to be a sort of chief, and acted as spokesman; he first pointed to the sky and ejaculated, "Britomartis;" and then to the mountains, saying "Phalasarna, Phalasarna." It was evidently not the first time he had come in contact with Phœnicians, for as soon as he caught sight of our ships he cried "Sidon! Sidon!" and touching our tunics, he called them "kitons."

We gave him an old kitonet, and distributed a quantity of glass beads amongst his followers, who brought us in return a couple of wild goats, and some partridges, which they called "hamalla."

Towards evening another of their number, an old man, came to us; he wore a kitonet under his goat's skin and had on an old pair of sandals. He could speak a little Phœnician, and succeeded in making us understand that he was of the race of the Cydonians, who had been the original possessors of the island, until the Phrygians and the Leleges had made war upon them and forced them to take refuge, east and west, where the mountains were most inaccessible. The whole of the coast, and the central highland, as well as the fertile valleys of the north and south, were now occupied by the conquerors, who had subsequently been joined by a colony of Dorians, so that, altogether, the Cydonians were being gradually exterminated. I now comprehended how it was that I, who had always approached Crete from the north by way of Caria and Rhodes, had never seen any inhabitants except Dorians; whilst other Phœnician captains who had landed on the eastern extremity of the island—where they had discovered some insignificant mines, and opened a small traffic in the ore—had always transacted business with the Cydonians.

The old man likewise informed us that his people had a town, up in the mountains, called Phalasarna; also that their goddess was Britomartis, which in their language signifies "the gentle virgin." He was delighted with the wine which I gave him; and on receiving, as a present, a couple of lance-heads and a necklace of enamelled earthen beads, he promised to get us next day as much fresh meat as we wanted.

Upon its growing dark, the barbarians retired to their mountains. Hannibal took the precaution of doubling the number of his sentinels, but we were quite undisturbed throughout the night.

In the morning the Cydonians returned and brought some goats. They are not in any way an agricultural people, and consequently could not provide us with either corn or vegetables, but they brought us a quantity both of wild fruit and wild honey. I showed them a picture of an ox, and tried to make them know that that was the animal I wanted them to get me, but they explained that they had none of their own upon the mountains, and that such an animal had been quite unknown upon the island until it was introduced by the Phrygians.

Pointing in the evening to the crescent moon, the barbarians told me that it was Britomartis, their goddess of the chase. Chryseis said she knew this goddess by the name of Artemis, from which I drew the inference that the Cydonians might have taught her worship to the Dorians, who would have made her known to the Ionians. The offerings that are accustomed to be made in her honour are hinds and deer; and I have heard it said that young men have been sacrificed as victims on her altar; but this is mere tradition, and I do not pretend to state it as a fact. I feel quite certain, for my own part, that although this goddess is the moon, she is not identical with our goddess Ashtoreth, otherwise she would not have been content only to encourage them to hunt, but would have taught them the science of navigation.

The Cydonians are also acquainted with the god of the Phrygian tribes of the Curetes and the Corybantes, who have a city called Cnossus in the island, where they have built a temple. This god is a white bull, although sometimes he is known to take the form of a man. The Dorians affirm of him that he is the primitive god of the country, but the Cydonians protest against this statement, and maintain that he was imported hither by the Curetes. I myself had never heard of the god. I cannot believe that he is either the Apis of the Egyptians or our own great Moloch. Chryseis asserts that she knows him by the name of Zeus, and believes that once upon a time he crossed the strait between the Black Sea and the Sea of Ionia, carrying a fair maiden on his back. He is said to be a fine and majestic creature, and the Phrygians of Crete honour him with dances, howlings, and the music of tambourines: his priests are of the tribe of the Corybantes, the progeny of Corybis. It was mentioned by Chryseis that a bull had once married a queen of the island, named Pasiphae, by whom he had a strange offspring, half-man, half-bull; but the monster was destroyed, she thought, by some Dorian or Ionian King. I can hardly persuade myself that this bull was Zeus; and I am rather inclined to suspect that the whole story is a fable, depicting some victory gained by the Ionians over the mixed Phrygian tribes that had made good their settlement upon the island.

I openly avowed my own conviction that this god was not our own god Moloch. Moloch was far more powerful than any god of the Ionians; he was much too mighty to permit foreigners to triumph over his own people. It was quite possible that the Phrygians had not honoured their bull-god Zeus as they were bound, and he, in anger, had abandoned them to their conquerors; but this was not like Moloch; no, he was not Moloch.

"Gods! gods!" cried Chamai, who had overheard the tenor of our talk; "who are all these gods? There is one only God; and El is His thrice-holy name. Another name He has, but *that* we are forbidden to pronounce. In His sight Moloch, Zeus, Artemis, Melkarth, all are nothing. Chemosh could not defend the Moabites against our hosts; Dagon could not protect the Philistines of Gaza and of Askelon; Nisroch could not lead the Syrians at

Zobah on to victory; Adrammelech was impotent to gain a triumph at Damascus; and Baalim could not prevail in behalf of the Amalekites. They all are nothing. It is the Almighty El, the Lord of hosts, the Maker of the heaven and the earth, that is the only God. He has brought us out of Egypt; He has established us in our goodly lands. He is the God invisible and true, the God of vengeance and of power."

"However much I may confess," said Hannibal, interrupting Chamai's earnest protest, "that your mighty El may be the god of the mountains and the plains, it cannot be denied that our Ashtoreth is the goddess of the ocean. See what glorious victories she has gained for us Sidonians; she has made us monarchs of the sea! For Moloch and Melkarth I have no reverence whatever; but still I think that Baal and the gods of Arvad should be honoured in the countries they have favoured with their care."

"And don't forget our great Cabiri," put in Himilco; "what would all our Tyrian pilots do without their guidance and protection?"

"I know nothing about pilots," Chamai said; adding, "for my part I shall be content to worship El, our Lord Almighty, by land, by sea, and everywhere."

So ended the discussion; and every one having made his invocation to his own special divinity, all retired to rest.

There was little more to be gained from the Cydonians; accordingly, on the following morning, having made a few trifling purchases, I prepared to start. My own intention was first to round the western limit of the island and to steer full north; next, having sighted the two Cytheras, to coast along the mainland till we reached the mouth of the Achelous, where I hoped to replenish our supply of water, and to transact some profitable business with the natives; thence, passing between Zacynthus and Cephallenia, I reckoned I could take our course between the mainland and the island of the Siculi; once there, I would coast along the north of it to Lilybæum, from which headland the distance was only 380 stadia across to Carthage. Such was my project ; but whether any of the gods had been incensed at our discussion the preceding night, or whether they were disposed to put the capabilities of our vessels to the test, certain it is that they had decreed that our course should be very different.

The sky was dull and lowering, and Himilco drew my attention to some lurid clouds that were gathering in the south-west.

" No time to lose," I said ; "unless we can get ahead of the hurricane that is brewing down there, we shall run the risk of being dashed on this rugged and unsheltered coast. There is safe anchorage on the northern shore, and thither with all speed we must betake ourselves before the storm shall break."

The weather was unnaturally calm ; but I knew the necessity of urging the rowers to full speed, and the ships made rapid progress to the west. In the course of twelve hours I calculated we had made about 450 stadia, and had got quite clear of the island ; but by this time the sky had become obscured with low heavy clouds, and there was no room to doubt that the tempest was approaching. I continued to keep well out to sea, and fortunate for us I did so ; for at nightfall, when we were, as I conjectured, about 150 stadia from the land, the storm overtook us in its fullest fury. The hurricane blew from the south-west and feeling satisfied that by abandoning ourselves to its violence we should be carried nearly north between Crete and the lesser Cythera, I ordered a sail to be hoisted, and permitted the wind to drive us on before it.

Throughout that night we knew not where we were The rain poured down in torrents ; wave followed wave in quick succession, dashing masses of water on to our decks, and our helmsmen had the utmost difficulty in controlling the vessels so that they should not present their broadsides to the squalls. The crash of the thunder was incessant, and by the vivid glare of the lightning we could see where the seething foam was rent asunder into black and yawning chasms.

In spite of the heavy seas that they continually shipped, our vessels, all three, bore up admirably. I made the rowers and the soldiers set to work with scoops to bale out the water, and under the supervision of Hannibal and the oarsman in command, who spared neither fair words nor hard blows to keep them to their task, they worked away with a will.

In a voice loud enough to be heard above the roar of the tempest, I shouted to Chamai that now was the time to invoke his God. To Bichri's inquiries whether the danger was really great, I answered that I had experienced worse weather in the Syrtes, and had known worse peril on the sea beyond the Straits of Gades, the swell out there being very long; but here, though rough and strong, the sea was short, and the ships seemed as though they might hold their own.

Chryseis and Abigail were in their cabin locked in each other's arms. Chamai and Bichri, although quite un-accustomed to the sea, and scarcely able to maintain their footing, kept up their spirits bravely, and to their very utmost assisted the sailors in securing the rigging and making fast the stowage; but nothing could exceed the terror of the great hulking Jonah, who, in the most abject state of alarm, threw himself down upon the floor of the hold, where, like a big bundle, he was rolled about at every pitch and lurching of the vessel.

"Oh, oh! why did I come?" he groaned, in the agonies of despair; "why did I come? why did I leave the village where I had plenty, and more than plenty? I shall be drowned, drowned in the sea, and the fishes will eat me! Oh, oh!"

"Out of the way, you great camel!" said Hannibal, giving the poor wretch a tremendous kick in the ribs; "you will be smashing something if you keep floundering

about in this way ; you all but threw me down just now.
Here, some of you," he called to the sailors, "come and
lash this fool to the foot of the mast."

The unwieldy giant was rolled helplessly along, and
bound securely as Hannibal directed.

Going to the stern, I found Himilco doing his best to
instruct the helmsman. He informed me that he had
quite lost sight of the *Dagon*. Just as he spoke, an
enormous wave almost dashed the *Cabiros* against our
side, and a vivid flash of lightning revealed Hamilcar and
Gisgo gesticulating vehemently to their men.

" A fine beginning to our voyage ! " shouted Gisgo, as he
passed us.

" Hold on, man ; face it out ! and we shall conquer in
the end," I screamed in reply.

To Hanno, who stood clinging to a rope, gazing out
upon the sea, I said :

" Keep up your courage, Hanno."

" I have courage enough for Chryseis and for myself as
well," he answered, cheerily ; " but I confess," he added, " I
have never seen weather so bad as this."

At this moment we were startled by the voice of Himilco,
shouting vehemently :

" The sail ! the sail ! look to the sail ! "

The sailors flew to the yard.   We were all but capsized ;
an immense wave had turned the ship's side to the wind,
and the sail was driven tight to the mast. A flash of
lightning, more dazzling than any that had gone before,
threw its vivid glare upon a great round vessel right in
front of us.

" The *Melkarth !* Bodmilcar ! " cried Himilco and Hanno
the same instant.

A second flash. There was no mistake ; beyond all
doubt there was the *Melkarth*, and Bodmilcar, standing
erect upon the poop, seemed to be controlling the very
winds and waves.

A third flash gleamed out amidst the continuous crash·

"THE MELKARTH"

ing of the thunder, but it revealed nothing except the raging waste of waters ; the *Melkarth* had vanished in the darkness.

"Khousor Phtah[1] is working away up there with his hammer," said Himilco ; "but let him hammer ; he will not harm us ; we have the Cabiri on our side."

The next hour was a period of intense anxiety. As far as I could judge the tempest was bearing us northwards, but I had no means of knowing for certain whether it was so. Every wave threatened to break upon the ship's side, and the *Cabiros*, which was quite close to us, appeared sometimes towering high above our heads, and at others gulfed down far below our feet. I was standing with Himilco and the two helmsmen over the stern cabin, when a sea, heavier than any we had yet encountered, swept clean across the deck. I clung to the ship's side, and when I raised myself, half stunned and half blinded by the shock, I found that Himilco and one of the helmsmen had disappeared. Fortunately the helm had not been carried away, and by exerting all my strength, I succeeded in pushing the tiller round, and bringing the ship back into the current of the waves ; then confiding the helm to a seaman who had just come up, I leaned over the side, and kept shouting " Himilco ! Himilco ! "

Day was beginning to dawn, and in the glimmering light I could just distinguish Chamai ; he had cast himself down before the cabin-door, and was imploring the God of Israel to spare the lives of the two women, even though it should please Him to destroy the lives of all beside.

Noticing the agitation of my voice, Hanno rushed towards me, expressing his alarm that something must have happened to our good pilot. I was telling him how much I feared that he had been washed overboard, when a voice reached me from behind :

[1] The god of subterranean fire and of the hammer. Compare Phtah with the Hephaistos of the Greeks.

"All right; I came down on my head;" and Himilco emerged from the hold with a goat-skin in his hands.

His appearance was a great relief, the more so when he explained that he was quite unhurt.

"The water carried me clean over the hatchway," he said; "and by good luck my head struck against this goat-skin in the hold. Strange to say the goat-skin hasn't burst. Praise to the good Cabiri! they have been good guardians. But what has become of Cadmus, who was at the helm?"

I could only point mournfully to the sea. Himilco seemed to comprehend, but he made no reply, and having seated himself upon the poop, began to refresh himself with the contents of the goat-skin he had found.

All of a sudden Bichri came towards me, and said he should like to speak to me. He began:

"As I am no sailor, perhaps I ought to apologise for giving an opinion, but my eyesight is very keen; and I am certain that I can see mountains over there to the right of the poop."

Himilco started to his feet; without relinquishing his hold upon the skin of wine, with his single eye he steadily scanned the horizon in the direction in which Bichri was pointing. After a few moments, he said:

"The archer is right; my eye seldom deceives me; we are to leeward of land."

Notwithstanding the incessant downpour of rain, I could just see enough through the mist to discern that there were mountains behind us to the right. Feeling sure that we had been driving to the north, I had no doubt in my own mind that the land we saw was some promontory on the north coast of Crete; and so ultimately it proved.

Our first business now was to get clear of the whirlwind, and to make for the shore. I signalled to this effect to the *Cabiros*, and doubled the number of the rowers by making a soldier as well as a sailor work at every oar. In the next place I inspected the stowage, and was rejoiced to find how little it had been displaced.

In a few hours the wind had almost dropped, and shortly afterwards a ray of sunlight darting through the clouds, cast an enlivening gleam upon our course.

" The Lord has saved us," said Chamai; "but I confess I was horribly alarmed."

Himilco wrung out his drenched kitonet, and proposed that, with my permission, he should give Bichri, who had been the first to spy out the land, a draught of wine from the skin which he still retained. I acknowledged that he well deserved it.

The two women were now induced to come from their cabin; although they were still somewhat tremulous with their recent fright, they had a bright smile upon their faces.

"Here they are." said Hanno, as he escorted them on to the deck; "they are like the weather, half smiles, half tears."

Chamai declared that he would rather contend with ten armed men than with one angry sea; I told him, however, that he had behaved admirably, considering it was his first squall, but recommended him to be cautious for the future how he spoke irreverently of the gods.

Emerging from the hold, helmet in one hand, cuirass in the other, Hannibal came up to us, saying:

" I have had such sharp work all night in keeping those beggarly rowers up to the mark, that I had no time to look to my armour; I expected to find it battered to bits; but thanks to your gods, Ashtoreth or any one you like, it is all safe and sound. Happy to see you, ladies; I hope you have recovered your fright, and regained your appetites. I am hungry enough."

And as he caught sight of Himilco and Bichri, enjoying themselves over the goat-skin, he hurried off to join them.

By the afternoon the sun had dispersed the clouds entirely, and the deep blue waters shone brightly in

contrast with the verdant land from which we were distant
not more than thirty stadia. I sent the *Cabiros* on ahead
to find a suitable place for anchorage, where we might
rest and repair our damages. Whilst we were sitting on
the deck of the *Ashtoreth*, basking in the sunshine, and
taking a simple repast of dried figs, unleavened bread, and
raw onions, to our great delight we saw the *Dagon* coming
on behind us. She had lost her yard-arm with its sail
attached, but drifted along by the tempest, she had sur-

mounted all further perils. Happily we had a good store
of spare sails to replace what were lost. We came up
with the *Cabiros* as she was lying off the head of a high
promontory, waiting to announce that on the southern
slope of the headland there was a fine bay, into which a
river debouched from an open and fertile valley. All
three vessels accordingly rounded the point, and steering
to the south, along the coast, by nightfall had reached the
middle of the bay, whence the shore recedes considerably
to the east. Here the *Dagon* and the *Ashtoreth* were

brought to anchor, and the *Cabiros* was drawn up on shore. The anchorage was very good, and the weather continued beautiful ; inland we could see lights gleaming from several villages, and thus feeling secure, with light hearts, though with weary bodies, we laid ourselves down to rest, and slept soundly throughout the night.

CHAPTER VII.

CHRYSEIS PREFERS HANNO TO A KING.

I LOST no time in setting our men to work to restore all damages. The cargo had been too well packed to sustain any material injury, and I had a selection from various bales of merchandise carried out into a field and displayed under the shade of a clump of trees. I took Jonah likewise on shore, bidding him bring his trumpet. No sooner did he feel the dry ground beneath his feet, than he began to yell and to jump for joy.

"Out of reach here, of the jaws of Leviathan!" he roared triumphantly. "Now I am safe. Here on dry land I care not what monster I face; and the sooner the better!"

I put a check, in some degree, upon his excitement, by ordering him to take his trumpet and to sound it as loud as he could; and the noise he made had the effect not only of summoning the residents of the neighbouring village, but of collecting a considerable number of the shepherds who were pasturing their flocks upon the adjacent hills. Assured of our peaceful intentions, they all flocked to us with perfect confidence, raising as they came the cry of "Pheaces! Pheaces!" as an intimation to their companions that some Phœnician merchants had arrived.

The people were all Dorians; tall, well-built men, with fair complexions, straight noses, and dark curly hair clustering over lofty foreheads. Nearly all of them came quite unarmed. Some of them were attired in old kitonets, evidently of Phœnician production; others wore a tasteless imitation of the same, made of coarse cloth of their own manufacture. For the most part they were bare-headed, the exceptions being the few who wore a kind of flat hat of plaited straw. There were some women of the party, and these well-nigh all were much to be admired in face and form ; they were attired in long plain dresses, almost as simple as sacks, with openings at the seams to allow the head and arms to pass through ; but these were covered by short open bodices, coming just below the

waist, and becomingly slashed on either side. No jewellery nor any ornament whatever was to be seen about their persons.

Before my visitors arrived, I took the precaution of making an enclosure for my merchandise by driving some strong upright stakes into the ground and running a rope along from one to another, and told Hanno to make the natives understand that they could not be allowed to pass the rope. They readily understood him, and appeared to be altogether very intelligent, although somewhat reserved in their manner.

One of their number, who carried a long copper-headed staff and wore a cloth band round his head, acted as spokesman. He was evidently a sort of chief, and his companions waited in silence while we listened to what he said. The Dorians appear to be addicted to long speeches, and the chief stepped forward, and scarcely raising his eyes, made us a formal harangue. Hanno interpreted sufficiently well to enable me thoroughly to comprehend the purport of his speech. He began by bidding us welcome, and proceeded to pay us a variety of compliments, addressing us as demi-gods, calling us kinsmen of the tutelary deities of our ships, and concluded by asking that he and his people might be allowed to inspect the wonderful commodities that we had brought from the divine city of Sidon.

I was already aware that all the tribes that bear in common the name of Hellenes are accustomed to regard the Phœnicians as being of divine origin. The magnitude of our ships, the length of our voyages, the mysterious remoteness of our cities, all combine to confirm them in their belief, and it was not for our advantage at present to undeceive them ; the time would come when they would be brought into closer relationship with our colonies, and they would find out by experience that we were ordinary mortals like themselves. Meanwhile they regarded us as superior beings, and listened with eager attention to whatever tales we pleased to pour into their ears.

By my instructions, Hanno informed the chief that we had brought with us many strange things from Caucasus, the land of giants ; from Cilicia, where the mountains are the open mouths of the infernal world and spit out flames of fire ; from Sidon, the metropolis of the gods ; from Arabia, the land of the devout, where men live for three centuries and more ; and from Egypt, where there are bull-gods, crocodiles, and serpents two stadia long. I made him understand that if his people could bring us ox-hides, Chalcidian copper, woven wool, or goats' horns, we, in exchange, could give them coats, glass beads, perfumes, nectar, or nearly anything they liked to ask for ; and without delay, he despatched a number of the men back to the village, to procure such goods as we required.

"What awful lies!" said Chamai to me, aside, "didn't you tell them that the Midianites are a devout race ? And didn't you say that the children of Ishmael live three hundred years ? And did I hear aright that you should say there are gods in Egypt ?"

I only smiled at this outburst of indignation ; but Himilco laughed aloud and said :

"Never mind, Chamai ; there may be worse lies than these ; they will answer their purpose if they make these folks good buyers."

The chief had offered to sell me some *pilegech*, or young female slaves that he had captured in a recent raid upon the mainland ; but I declined to make any purchase of the kind, knowing that there was no market for women-slaves either in our Libyan colonies or in Tarshish. Our word "pilegech" he pronounced *pellex*. The Dorians manifestly have considerable difficulty in articulating our language ; for example, they say "kiton," for *kitonet ;* "kephos," for *koph*, and "kassiteros," for *kastira*. Sometimes, like other savage nations, they fail to understand the true meaning of a word, and pervert it altogether ; for instance, when speaking of the great sea beyond Gades, instead of calling it the Sea of Og, they describe it as a river named "Oceanos," and believe it to be a god.

The men that had been sent back by the chief soon returned with a very fair supply of good copper, ox-hides, and goats' horns, some of which were large enough to make good bows. They likewise brought some very excellent woollen cloth which they had themselves imported from the mainland. For all their goods the prices they demanded were singularly moderate.

It was now necessary, in order to find space and leisure for repairing our ships, that the throng of buyers, which seemed continually increasing, should be drawn away from the neighbourhood of the beach.   To effect this, I placed a quantity of the merchandise under the charge of Hadlai, one of the most trustworthy of the sailors, and sent him into the interior of the island to dispose of what he could, instructing him to be sure and return to us in eight-and-forty hours, by which time I expected to complete the repairs.   Bichri volunteered to act as an escort; and Jonah, with whose trumpet the Dorians seemed immensely amused, was sent to summon the natives to the sale.

In the course of the day I sent eight of my men to cut down an oak from the forest on the valley side, to make a new yard for the *Dagon*.   The Dorians permitted us to take whatever wood we wanted without any charge, deeming it a sufficient compensation to themselves to watch our carpentering, and to listen to the wonderful tales of such of our sailors as could speak anything of their language.   They were most attentive in bringing us firewood, water, and what else we wanted; and whatever they may be in their bearing to other nations, I can testify that to us Phœnicians they were most courteous and considerate.

The Dorians plied Chryscis with countless questions about the *Pheakes*, and made all kinds of inquiries about their country, their cities and their king; and she, pleased with the sound of a dialect kindred to her own, conversed with them willingly, and made them stare with surprise, as she recounted the glories of our temples, and the magnificence of our palaces.   They had no clear idea of what Phœnicia really was, but imagined it to be an island, evidently confounding it with our colony of Chittim, or with our settlement at Chalcis, which was considerably nearer to them.   They almost seem to think Phœnicians ubiquitous, for they give the name of Phœnicia to the coast of Caria, where our merchants have established some marts. This is really the country of the Carian Leleges, who, together with the Phrygians, were the Dorians' predecessors in the isle of Crete, and the first to drive the Cydonians to

the highlands. The Dorians assert that the Leleges and
Pelasgians preceded them on the mainland, and that many
of them still remain. I can readily understand that the
Carians, Æolians, and others, whom we drove from their
own coasts, succeeded in reaching Crete ; for the Carians
were not ignorant of navigation, and at that part of the
Archipelago, where the sea is thickly studded with islands,
the voyage from the coast of Asia hither, even in small
boats, would be by no means difficult. It is a fact, too,
that the principal mountain in Crete is known by the
Pelasgo-Ionian name of Ida, the same as that borne by
the mountain in Æolia, opposite the island of Mitylene ;
the evidence, therefore, is very strong that the Pelasgians
and Leleges, who were of the same race as the Carians,
Æolians, Lycians, and Dardanians, must have occupied
not only the entire coast from the Straits of Thrace down
to the regions opposite Rhodes, but likewise all the mainland
and islands between Thrace and Cape Malea. The Cydonians must be a remnant of some still earlier inhabitants of
quite another race, driven back, first by the Pelasgians and
Leleges, and afterwards by the Dorians, Ionians, and those
others who are now advancing to establish themselves
alike upon the coast and in the islands. The accuracy of
this conclusion is borne out by the fact that our ancestors
were acquainted with the Pelasgians long before they knew
anything of Dorians and Ionians, and it is well known that
there are still in existence cities large and populous, though
badly built and weakly fortified, such as Plakir and Sculake
in the Propontis, some distance north of Dardania and the
isle of Tenedos.

I enter into all these details because I consider it part
of the duty of a Phœnician mariner to make himself
acquainted not only with the configuration of both land
and sea, the movements of the heavenly bodies, and the
laws of navigation and of commerce, but also with the
origin, language, religion, and habits of every nation with
whom he may be brought in contact ; and my experience in

my naval life has taught me that although the knowledge thus acquired is to be very cautiously revealed to strangers and foreigners, yet it cannot be too freely disseminated amongst one's own countrymen.

The Dorians acknowledge themselves to be a people akin to the Ionians, and are, like them, a branch of the great family known by the name of Hellenes, Ræci, or Græci. These Hellenes, like the children of Israel, are comprised of twelve peoples or tribes; the Thessalians, the Bœotians, the Dorians, the Ionians, the Perrhebians, the Magnetes, the Locrians, the Eteans, the Achæans, the Phocians, the Dolopes, and the Malians. Their own account of themselves is, that on reaching the south of Thracia they settled in the district known as Hellopia, of which they were still in possession, and whence they spread themselves over the peninsula and the islands. Hellopia is the country traversed by the River Achelous, which empties itself into the channel that divides the island of Cephallenia from the mainland. The two oldest cities in Hellopia are Dodona and Delphi, which are both the abodes of the chief gods. It is from the name of their city that the Hellenes are sometimes called Dodonians, although they are far more frequently referred to by us as the Ionians, or sons of Ion or Javan. Amongst themselves, however, they are invariably designated Hellenes, Graii, or Græci.

All the Hellenic tribes recognise four special bonds of fraternity : first, they are of one common origin ; secondly, they speak a common tongue ; thirdly, they worship the same gods, and in the same modes and places; and fourthly, they cultivate a general uniformity in manners and disposition. They all send representative chiefs or elders to Dodona, and I presume to Delphi also, for the purpose of settling any common difference ; and there they take a threefold oath, never to destroy any city that has ever been admitted into covenant with them ; never to intercept the supply of water to any city of their fraternity, and always to unite to punish those who should violate their pledge.

Their principal god dwells at Dodona, and is named Zeus. They believe him to be the same as the Zeus of the Leleges and Pelasgians, whom the Curetes of Crete honour with songs and dances. Like Baal Chamaim, he is the god of the air and sky, and son of the heaven and the earth. He it was who, in the form of a bull, carried off the Phrygian goddess Europa to Crete ; and on the south of the island, in the valley of a little river, Lethe, the Dorians have a city which I have never seen, but which they call Hellotis, where there is a plane-tree, under which Zeus and Europa are said to have reposed. Another town there is in the island, named Cnossus, founded, I believe, by the Phrygians, where Zeus has one of his places of abode.

Another deity, almost equally powerful, is Apollo, the archer and soothsayer. He is known as the Pythian prophet, and dwells at Delphi, where he is consulted about future events. He is held in especial veneration by the Dorians, whom he is said, under the form of a dolphin, to have conducted across the seas. Probably he may be the same as our Phœnician archer-god, Baal Chillekh, whom we have ourselves taught the Hellenes to worship, and it may be that because he taught them navigation, they represent him as a dolphin.

The mysterious Hermes, the god of the hidden forces of nature, is likewise an object of their high regard. It is not unlikely that they learnt his worship from the Egyptians ; but whether it be so or not, it is quite certain that he has been known amongst them from a very remote antiquity.

The Cydonians have made them acquainted with Artemis, and we are ourselves leading them to the knowledge of Ashtoreth or Astarte, whom they are gradually learning to venerate above all their other divinities.

Of Beelzebub, Baalpeor, El Adonai, Chemosh, or the Cabiri, the Hellenes know nothing. They are absolutely ignorant of the position of the Cabiri, and have no conception of guiding their course in sailing by the seventh Cabiros or Pole-star: to say the truth, they are very cowardly sailors, rarely venturing to lose sight of the shore. Their boats are large but very badly built, having no decks, ill-contrived rigging, and very defective arrangements for ballast; consequently they are equally unsteady whether they are impelled by oars or worked by sails. The people have little idea of distance; they are profoundly ignorant of the shape of the country, and are at once deterred from a voyage by the least stress of weather, or by the most insignificant current.

The towns are built in places that are difficult of access, and are rudely fortified with piles of uncemented stones. The houses are made either of rough stone, or of bricks that have been baked in the sun, and are very little better than cabins. The people are not at all skilful in any handicraft; and they can scarcely do more than manufacture their copper lance-heads, hatchets, breast-plates, and helmets, which, although very ill-formed, are covered with ornaments. They have no cavalry and very few archers, and rarely use swords in fighting; lances are their favourite weapons, and these are used by their chiefs either on foot or from the top of their chariots. In close combat they employ a kind of poignard, which very frequently is seen curved at the point into a kind of hook. By way of pastime, Hannibal and Chamai occasionally made Hanno practise with the sword, and on these occasions they would be surrounded by a group of Dorians, who were struck with wonder and admiration at the variety of the thrusts, passes, and parries of the fencing, as exhibited in the different practices of the Chaldeans, the Philistines, and the Israelites, and the dexterity they all alike required.

The shields which they use are round, and made of ox-hide, those of the chiefs being faced with copper and ornamented with paintings. Before we left the island, the Dorian king of Hellotis came to visit us, and for one of our bucklers of wrought bronze offered me five-and-twenty

R. P. Philippoteaux

BORNE TO ITS RESTING-PLACE.

To face page 123

oxen; but I allowed him to have it for some agates, to
be used in making jewellery, and for an enormous pair of
boar's tusks which he had brought from the mainland, and
which now adorn the temple of Ashtoreth at Sidon.

On the third day after our arrival in the island, one of
the sailors, who had been struck by an arrow in the
Egyptian engagement, died, the wound having gangrened.
According to our national custom, I had all the ships hung
with black, and made inquiry of the natives for some
cavern in the neighbourhood where we could inter the
body. They showed me a cave in the mountain side about
thirty stadia distant, and were quite ready in any way to
assist me, as they are themselves very careful about the
burial of their dead; in fact, there is nothing of which they ·
entertain a greater dread than of being deprived of funeral
rites, and this is one great reason that deters them from
venturing out far to sea.

After the corpse had been washed, it was borne to its
resting-place, a considerable crowd of Dorians following in
the rear, amongst them a large proportion of women, who
kept up loud cries of lamentation. The cave in which we
laid the body was very deep, but by no means lofty; in it
we left not only the body, but the planks and the two oars
which had formed the bier. When the opening had been
closed by piling up a heap of large and heavy stones,
Hanno, in a solemn voice, made an invocation to Menath,
Hokh, and Rhadamath, the judges of the souls in Cheol.

All these three gods of our nation are known to the
Dorians, who call them by the names of Minos, Eacus, and
Rhadamanthus. They believe that Minos, previous to his
appointment as a judge in the infernal regions, was a king
of Crete, and that, being a skilful navigator, he had sailed
as far as the mainland to the Ionians, who, by way of
tribute, gave him a number of boys and girls. With regard
to Rhadamanthus, they suppose that he was brought to the
island of Chalcis by the Phœnician demigods; but the truth
is, that they have made some strange confusion between

the god himself and the Sidonian sailors through whom
they had become acquainted with his existence.   In the
same way, I believe, that Europa (the goddess who was
carried off by Zeus) and Ariadne (known first to one of the
demigods, and then to Dionysus, the god of rivers) are
nothing more than other names for Ashtoreth, surviving
from the period when the Phœnicians first imported wine
to their shores.   From us, too, they have derived their
knowledge of Khousor Phtah, the god of the forge, whom
they call Phtos or Phaistos ; and in short, whatever fami-
liarity they have either with literature, wine, or with the
use of metals, all seems to have been derived from the Sidonians.   As for our own knowledge, that (according to our
ancestors long, long ago) was obtained from the Egyptians,
and the Egyptians derived theirs from the still more ancient
Atlantes, who, when the Great Sea was still to the south
of Libya, came from lands in the West that have since
passed away, traversing Ethiopia in their course.   How
true it is, that though nation may follow upon nation, the
gods are immortal !

The Dorian people gave us their word of honour that
the cavern in which we had buried our companion should
never be desecrated, and we returned to our ships, which
remained hung with black for the remainder of the day.

Towards evening Hadlai and his party made their appearance, bringing a goodly supply of purchases.   Jonah,
marching along with a consequential air, and encircled by
a crowd who had followed him down from the mountains
was carrying a calf upon his back.

" What are you going to do with that calf ? " I asked.

" Eat it," he said ; " I have earned it."

" How ? by blowing your trumpet ? "

" No ; not by blowing my trumpet, but by wrestling :
they matched their strongest against me, and I levelled
them all ; and so I won my calf.   A capital country is
this !   I will knock them over, every one, if only they
will give me a calf every time."

And, catching sight of the King of the Dorians, who had come with a herd of oxen, he shouted to him :

" Yes, you too ; give me a bullock, and I will knock you down. Give me two, and I will break every bone in your skin."

" Silence, fool ! " I cried, hoping to bring him to his senses. The King did not understand Phœnician, and asked what the man was saying ; but I did not think it necessary to enlighten him.

Jonah continued muttering and grumbling to himself : " Why should I not fight them, if they like it ? If I were to challenge a man of the tribe of Dan or Judah, I should soon find a knife in my ribs ! But here they like it, and give me a calf. Fine country this ! "

That evening the wind blew briskly from the north-north-west, but not with violence enough to make us hesitate about taking our departure next morning. The Dorians were full of surprise at our determination to put to sea, and owned that nothing would induce them to face the peril of such a wind.

" Can it really be," asked one of the chiefs, " that you intend to start upon your voyage with this gale in your very teeth ? "

Upon my assuring him that I had fully made up my mind, he continued :

" And that, too, with the recollection so fresh of the terrific storm in which you came ? Truly, you are demigods indeed ! "

" Aye, yes," I said ; " children of Ashtoreth we are ; and we rode the seas that night in a way that was worthy of our fame ! "

" And were not the Cabiri considerate for me ? " interposed Himilco ; " the salt sea made me thirsty, and they sent me a goat-skin full of luscious wine."

Without noticing him, the chief continued :

" Assuredly the Phœnician deities maintain a careful watch to guard their children. I shall not soon forget how

I saw their mighty chariot roll above the waves to your assistance."

It was now Himilco's turn to look astonished.

"Chariot upon the waters!" he exclaimed; "what was it like?"

"It was high, and round, and parti-coloured, and had great sea-monsters drawing it over the raging sea."

He spoke with a kind of awe; but it struck me that he might perchance have seen Bodmilcar's gaoul, and that the lightning's glare had given it the variegated effect which he had noticed. I suggested this, in an undertone, to Himilco, who only said:

"If Bodmilcar were the sea-god, I should like to have the chance of getting into the sea-god's chariot and ringing the sea-god's neck."

While we had been talking, I had observed Hamilcar and several others closely scrutinising something that the waves had cast upon the beach. Curious to see what was interesting them, I joined them, and found some fragments of a ship.

"This is no Phœnician work," said Hamilcar, pointing to a bolt still hanging to one of the planks.

"No," I agreed; "and from the thickness of the wood, and from the bolts being driven in without wedges, I have no doubt that it is an Egyptian craft that has been wrecked."

"Look here!" cried Himilco; "here is proof positive; the goose's neck from the prow!"

"It may be," I said, "that some Egyptians accompanied Bodmilcar, and have come to grief in the tempest."

"I hope Bodmilcar has not shared their fate," said Gisgo; "drowning is too good for him; I want him to have a stout rope round his neck. And besides, the rascal has three-quarters of our merchandise that I should like to get back."

"Rather too much to expect, I am afraid," I said; "however, we must now embark. We are bound for Sicily where perhaps you may recover your lost ears."

A grim smile passed over the old pilot's face.

"Until the wind changes," I observed, "we shall have to keep on tacking;" and I moved towards the ships.

At this moment the Dorian King approached me with the air of having something important to communicate; he broke out abruptly:

"You are a Phœnician, a ruler of the sea: I am a Dorian prince, a ruler of my people: so far we are equal. These oxen, these horses, these chariots are all mine; from my thirty villages I can summon twelve thousand men. I am favoured of the gods. I am mighty."

I thought he surely was about to make some demand, but a single glance satisfied me that he was not in a position to exact anything by force; not only were Hanno, Chamai, Bichri and Jonah still on shore, but Hannibal, too, was close at hand, supported by forty of his men, while the King was attended only by about a score and a half of lancers. I made no reply, but waited for him to proceed.

"Ruler of the Phœnicians," he said, "I want you to sell me your pilegech Chryseis: you have only to name your own price for the Ionian, and that price is yours."

Hanno made a start forward, but I held him back.

"King of the Dorians!" I said, "Chryseis is not designed for sale. However, she is free to answer for herself. To us your kindness and courtesy have been great; and I am ready to consent, in return, to give the maiden up to you. But this one condition must be fixed; she must become yours by her own free choice."

Hanno glanced eagerly at Chryseis, and imploringly at me.

The King advanced to where the girl was standing, and proffering his hand, said:

"Daughter of the Helli! kinswoman of our tribe! come and be the Queen of the Dorians of Hellotis!"

She stood with her eyes fastened on the ground, but made no reply.

"Zeus and Apollo guide your choice!" continued the King, "and inspire your answer! Listen and consent. No

Dorian maid has ever yet made good her hold upon my heart, although there is not one who would not be proud to be the object of my choice.   Honours and luxury await my bride.   She shall have slaves to surround her, and do her weaving, and obey her slightest wish ; her table shall be spread with the choicest diet, the produce of three hundred goats and fifty cows ; and her home shall be full of all the comforts that wealth can buy."

He waited for her to speak, but still she made no sign.

"My house," he went on to plead, "is a house of stone, like the Egyptians', and stored up within it, Chryscis, there are chests, in which are necklaces, and pearls, and golden bodkins for your hair.   All shall be yours, and you shall be first and noblest of all the women in Crete."

Chryscis slowly raised her eyes from the ground, and laying her hand upon Hanno's shoulder, in a firm, deliberate, and yet gentle voice, said :

"Our holy Zeus has given me to Hanno, and with Hanno I shall remain."

The Dorian, mortified and excited, literally stamped with rage.

"What !" he cried, "prefer a Phœnician subject to a king of the Hellenes ?"

"A Sidonian scribe," said Hanno, "is the equal of any king on earth.   I own no superior except my captain and the gods above."

"Though he were the lowliest sailor in the service,' declared Chryscis, "my heart is his.   His goddess Ashtoreth has delivered me in the hour of peril, and Zeus, my god, pronounces that I am his."

The Dorian could do no more : in vain he pointed to the smiling meadows and the shady forests of the island, and contrasted them with the abode upon the raging water of an angry sea ; Chryscis maintained that the water had charms as many as the land.   Unable to prevail with her, he made a final appeal to me ; but finding me firm in my resolve to leave the girl unfettered in her choice, he gave a growl of anger, and without turning his head, remounted his chariot and drove rapidly away.

"Mine, henceforth," said Hanno to Chryseis, as he led her to the ship. "You are as a priestess of Ashtoreth, the guardian of us all!" and he drew her closer to his side.

The sail was soon hoisted, and the rowers settled to their seats. Leaving the shore, we made long tacks to get to windward, and in five hours had passed the northernmost extremity of Crete. In the course of the night we were coasting the rocky land upon the north of the lesser Cythera.

Two days' safe, though tedious, navigation brought us to the mouth of the Achelous, a stream which from the colour of its water is known to our sailors as the White River. We passed between the fertile and indented shore of the mainland, and the islands of Cythera, Zacynthus, and Cephallenia. In these navigable waters, where land is never out of sight, we perpetually came across Hellenic vessels of every size, engaged in a brisk trade not only in their own native productions, but also in the manufactures of the Phœnicians.

The sea was calm when we reached the mouth of the Achelous, but a fresh breeze sprung up from the north-east, which was just what we wanted to carry us to the Sicilian straits. It is usual, in order to break the length of the sea-passage, to follow the Hellenic coast as far as the island of Corcyra, but under the present favourable circumstances this would have been merely to waste time. We had an ample supply both of provisions and of fresh water; I therefore quite abandoned all thought of visiting the metropolis of the Hellenes, and determined to make with the wind across the open sea direct for the southern point of Italy. As we were passing along the channel that divides Cephallenia from the little island of Ithaca we fell in with a Sidonian galley and a couple of gaouls, and hailing them, we found that they were on their way home from the mouth of the Eridanus on the Iapygian Sea. Bodachmon, the captain of the galley, proposed that we should lay-to off Ithaca, so that we might send any commissions by him to Sidon. I availed myself of his offer, and went at once on board one of his gaouls. His cargo consisted of a small supply of gold, both in dust and nuggets, but principally of rock-crystal, which the people on the banks of the Eridanus obtain from those who reside on the mountains near its source. Bodachmon agreed to take some of my heavier merchandise for a part of his light freight, and to do any-thing he could to assist me after the loss we had sustained of our own gaoul through Bodmilcar's treachery. His indignation at Bodmilcar's conduct knew no bounds. Such an act of faithlessness, he said, had never happened within his experience ; and he would take good care that not only should it come to King Hiram's ears, but that Bodmilcar should be denounced throughout Phœnicia, so that if the traitor should attempt to land anywhere either in Phœnicia, or in Chittim, or any other of her colonies, he should be visited with the punishment he so justly merited.

"But now," said Bodachmon, "let us proceed to business. What commodities have you to offer ?"

I answered that I had just obtained goods in Crete, for which he would be sure to find a ready market either in Egypt or at home—copper, ox-hides, woollen cloth, and enormous goats' horns ; I told him, moreover, that if he would visit Crete for himself, he would be able to purchase any number of young female slaves at the most reasonable rate.

He said that he thought he should act upon my advice, and that he was sure we should be able to make exchanges between ourselves which would satisfy us both. He pro-ceeded to inquire whether I could let him have any wine, as his own supply had been exhausted six months ago, and that in his intercourse with the Iapyges and Umbrians he had had no opportunity of replenishing it.

Our own ships were well provisioned, and I was pleased to have the opportunity of inviting him with his two mates and pilots to come on board the *Ashtoreth*, and to partake

HOMER

To face page 127.

of our fresh meat, onions, dried figs, cheese and wine. They all admired the completeness of our arrangements ; and Bodachmon made an inspection of the goods that I proposed to barter, telling me that he should be able to pay a good price, if I would accept his rock-crystal.

All of a sudden Bodachmon exclaimed : "By Ashtoreth ! I think I can give you a treat in return for your hospitality. In Corcyra I took up one of the Hellenes, whom I promised if I could that I would land in Crete. He is an old man and nearly blind, but he seems to know the history of all the world ; neither Sanchoniathon, nor Elhanan the Israelite, could know it better. He sings the exploits of his country's gods and heroes, accompanying his singing on his lute ; he has no other means of paying his passage. You shall hear him."

The venerable bard was sent for, and was soon conducted on board. He had a dignified bearing, and commanded an involuntary reverence. His long beard was very white, and he carried in his hand a lute made of tortoise-shell. His name was Homer.

Addressing us, he said :

"O Pheacians ! ye sea-kings, who explore the marvels of the earth ! may the divine gods protect your ships ! My eyes are dim ; no longer do I discern the meadows with their pasturing herds, nor the warriors with their dazzling armour ; nay, scarce can I perceive the glorious beams of day. But the Muses from their blest abode, beside the Peneus, have endowed me with the gift of harmony and song, so that wherever I may go, I celebrate the achievements both of gods and men."

I handed the old man a cup of the choicest nectar, and, with invigorated spirit, he began to sing his songs. To me their meaning was barely intelligible ; but Hanno, familiar with the Hellenic tongue, was perfectly enraptured, and made the venerable minstrel a present of his mantle. which was woven of the finest wool of Helbon, and exquisitely embroidered with flowers.

K

"Never have I heard anything to be compared with this," exclaimed the scribe; "in spite of their ignorance of trade and navigation, these people cannot be quite the barbarians we supposed."

Hannibal, who had hitherto looked on in silence, now observed:

"Once, when I was in the city of Our in Naharan, I came across an extraordinary man, of whom this wandering poet reminds me. He was an Egyptian, travelling about, and singing songs to his own lute, just like Homer here,

but he was not so old, and the remarkable thing was that he had an ape with him that used to mimic all the events about which he sung. Now when Chryseis sings her war-songs, it is pleasant to listen, although one does not understand a word; her voice is itself a charm. But this old minstrel's songs are dull; he ought, I think, to have an ape with him, to act as an interpreter of what he sings."

Hanno sneered contemptuously, and said:

"Hannibal is wonderfully clever. I should fancy ne could play the ape's part to perfection."

Not discerning the satire, Hannibal replied with the greatest gravity :

"I don't know about my being more clever than any of my people from Arvad ; but I think that if I could understand the old man's tongue, I could perform for him better than an ape."

CHAPTER VIII.

AN AFFAIR WITH THE PHOCIANS.

HAVING entrusted Bodachmon with various commissions, and especially with the duty of delivering a letter from myself to King Hiram, I took my leave of him and his companions. In the afternoon, the breeze being favourable, we resumed our voyage to Italy. In order to pass between the islands of Cephallenia and Leucas, it was necessary to deviate somewhat to the north, after which we should have to steer nearly due east for the south of the great Iapygian gulf.

The *Cabiros* was about ten stadia ahead, and consequently so far in advance that she was lost to sight as she rounded the southern cape of Cephallenia; but she had hardly disappeared beyond the headland, when it struck me that I could hear her trumpet sounding signals of distress. Having sounded an alarm, I put my men in readiness for any emergency, and it was well I did so; for when we had rounded the promontory far enough to get her within view, we saw her not only surrounded by nearly twenty large boats of the Hellenes, but the object towards which some fifty other boats were making their way with the greatest speed.

The fact was, that while we had been coasting along the east of the island the enemy had made their way by the west, and thus the *Cabiros*, rounding the headland, had found herself unawares in an ambush, which, with her superior sailing power, it would have been quite easy to

UNAWARES IN AN AMBUSH.

escape if there had been any previous warning. As it was,
she was completely taken by surprise ; and her tonnage
being too light to allow her to carry a copper beak for
attack, she could only avoid being boarded by the expedient of rapidly making her way round and round in a
circle.

There was not a moment to be lost. The *Dagon* put on
all speed and made her way direct towards the promiscuous cluster of boats that was coming up beyond, whilst I
hastened to secure the rescue of the imperilled *Cabiros.*

The antagonists with which the *Dagon* had to contend
did not appear to be be of a very formidable character. A
very cursory glance at the unmartial appearance of most
of the crews, and at the cargoes, which consisted mainly
of agricultural produce and implements, made it evident
that we had come into collision with some convoy of
emigrants. Hannibal had manifestly come to the same
conclusion that there was nothing to cause him any alarm
for I noticed that after having given his men a sign that
there was no occasion to draw their bows, he made a con-

siderable sweep to leeward, and then dashed furiously in upon the crowded craft.

But my more serious attention was demanded in another quarter. The adversaries that I had to face were less numerous, but far more formidable, being all armed men. It was in vain that I hurried forward with all the speed at my command ; before I could get within two stadia of the *Cabiros* she was already boarded, and the deck of the gallant little ship was becoming the scene of a desperate struggle. From the midst of a whirl of lances I could distinguish Hamilcar, protecting himself with his shield in one hand, and dealing tremendous blows with his sword in the other ; whilst Gisgo stood with his back supported by the top of the poop, and had just raised the battle-axe with which he had cloven the skull of one of his assailants. To prevent us from rendering any assistance, five or six large boats advanced towards us to obstruct our progress, and I could hear the shrill voices of the warriors on board chanting their exciting war-cry, "Io Pœan! Io Pœan!" A fine-built man, who seemed to be chief in command, was standing at the prow of the highest boat ; he had a crested helmet ; his shield and greaves were faced with copper, and he was brandishing his long lance like a maniac. I was about to point him out to Bichri, but he, ever on the alert, was already upon one knee with his arrow to his bow, watching his opportunity, and no sooner were we within range than the bowstring was up to his ear, the arrow whizzed through the air, and the chief, throwing both hands aloft, fell head foremost into the water.

"Now, men, now's your time !" I shouted ; "down upon the savages ! Down upon them ! Quick !"

With a tremendous spurt, the *Ashtoreth* dashed violently into the boat, which sank instantly in an eddy of foam, our magnificent success setting us at liberty to concentrate our attention upon another boat which was harassing us on the right.

In their eagerness to be ready to climb up into our ship

the crew of this boat had inconsiderately crowded altogether to one side. Knowing the unscientific build of the Hellenic boats, and how easily they are overturned when heavily laden, I tacked round suddenly to the opposite side, and putting on full speed, capsized it without the slightest difficulty.

But the need, meanwhile, was becoming more and more urgent that we should reach the *Cabiros*, although she was holding out with a vigorous defence. I had to manœuvre by taking a long semicircular sweep to get beyond the reach of the boats around me, but the delay had its advantage in giving Hannibal opportunity to arrange his men. He very judiciously placed the archers in the stern, and divided his remaining force into two companies; one of them under his own leadership to be prepared to follow him on to the deck of the *Cabiros*, the other to remain and protect their own ship from being boarded.

About the *Dagon* I had little or no anxiety. I could see that she was not only holding her own, but that by dashing backwards and forwards amongst the medley of boats around her, she was crushing or sinking all that she came athwart, and by discharging volleys of arrows and pots of combustibles, she succeeded in distressing the men on board to such a degree that we could hear their howlings of mingled rage and dismay.

Hannibal's instructions to his soldiers were very brief; telling those whom he left behind that they were to obey Chamai's orders, and that he trusted them to do their duty, he turned to those under his own command, and said:

"Soldiers! the fight before you is a fight hand-to-hand; no room for lances! Draw your swords, stand ready at the prow!"

I gave orders to the rowers to pull steadily ahead; but they had scarcely laid themselves out to their work, when we fouled two of the boats which had detached themselves from the others, and were endeavouring to get alongside of us.

"Quick! to the engines!" I cried; "and, archers, draw your bows!"

In an instant Bichri's men were at the scorpions, and a perfect torrent of stones, arrows, and combustibles, fell on either hand. Hannibal's men did not stir from their attitude of readiness, and Chamai kept his detachment grouped close around the mast, abiding the time for a charge to be ordered. Bichri's party laid aside their bows, and drew their knives and swords; and Jonah, laying his trumpet on the deck, armed himself with the ponderous handspike usually employed for heaving the anchor, and which two ordinary men could scarcely carry.

"Come on, Dodanim!" he shouted; "if you can afford a calf for a little shaking, perhaps you will pay better still if I lay this rod across your shoulders. I should like a few bullocks and a good skin of wine. I am quite ready to begin pounding away, like Samson at the mill."

The time for action had come, and I gave the word of command to push ahead, straight at the foe. A dash and a crash! and cries of mingled wrath and consternation rose from beneath our prow as it made its way in a vortex of foam. We rushed past the first boat, leaving it hopelessly far astern; we disabled a second that was designing an attack upon our starboard, and we capsized a third that was coming on our left; and when our men drew breath after their paroxysm of exertion we were within half a bowshot of the *Cabiros*. So close we were, that I could see Hamilcar with his head all bleeding, and Gisgo, with dishevelled hair, laying about him desperately with his hatchet, whilst a dozen sailors who had retreated to the stern, were making a vain effort to repel the invaders, who continued to make their way on board.

"Help! Mago, help!" shouted Hamilcar, imploringly, as he saw us drawing near.

"Cheer up, mate!" I replied; "we shall soon be with you."

I made a rapid survey of our position, and having

instructed the helmsman to bear up hard to starboard, I called to the oarsmen :

"Now, men, once again, a good strong pull with might and main ; then ship your oars, and we shall be right alongside!"

So vehemently did they put forth their strength that our prow was lifted high above the flood, and the impetus given to our speed was so great that another of the opposing boats was cut clean in two. In another minute we had gained the side of the *Cabiros*. Hannibal seized a rope and sprang upon the deck ; and followed by his men was quickly in the midst of the mortal struggle.

I had no time to watch the issue of their intrepid venture. They had hardly left our deck when I was startled by the urgent voice of Hanno :

"Look, captain ! they have us now !"

And turning round I was face to face with a throng of the Hellenes, who had not only brought their boats into close quarters with the *Ashtoreth*, but had forced their way on to her stern. Into the breast of the foremost man, who was rushing towards me with uplifted lance, I thrust my sword well-nigh to its hilt ; and Hanno showed how well he had profited by the fencing lessons he had had on board ; he parried a blow with his left hand, and almost in the same instant felled an opponent by driving his weapon into his shoulder with his right. Sometimes bending himself down, sometimes rearing himself to his fullest height, Chamai wielded his sword with the most extraordinary dexterity : three men set upon him at once ; one of them soon reeled and fell heavily at his feet ; a second, grasping his sides in agony, was seen to stagger back amongst his comrades ; whilst the other, putting his head between his hands, cowered down to the ground, the blood trickling through his fingers.

Bichri also, single-handed, had to engage quite a little group of antagonists. It seemed a desperate fray ; but, strange to tell, he got the better of them all, and retired triumphant, his blood-stained sword in one hand, his dagger in the other.   Nor did good fortune fail Himilco; closely pressed as he was by his adversary, he succeeded in catching him by the throat, and, holding him back firmly against the mast, he thrust his sword into his heart.

But for rendering effective service no one surpassed the redoubtable Jonah.   Such wholesale slaughter was never seen.   Skulls were fractured; limbs smashed; ribs broken in; back-bones, breast-bones, collar-bones, shoulder-blades contused, crushed, splintered, as the ponderous handspike, swinging backwards, forwards, upwards, downwards, made the very air reverberate.

" Room, I want! give me room!" roared the giant, as he brandished his enormous weapon; "bring me bullocks, sheep, calves, cakes, wine, anything, and I'll earn my dinner honestly."   And striking out more furiously than ever he roared again, " Room, room! elbow-room, I say!"

Three or four of the Hellenes now made a simultaneous attack upon myself.   I succeeded in slashing the face of one of them who had knocked my shield out of my hand with his lance, but in a moment I felt myself grasped round the throat by another, who forced me backward, and was about to cut off my head with his scimitar, when Hanno caught him by the wrist and plunged his sword beneath his armpit.   The two of them came down heavily upon me, and we were all three rolling on the deck together; a third man darted forward, and I could see the gleam of a lance as it pointed to Hanno's breast, when Chamai rushed to the rescue, and dealing a powerful blow, sent the fellow staggering back.   Hanno rose, and placing his foot upon the dead man's neck found it taxed all his strength to withdraw the sword with which he had slain him.   As I regained my footing, I caught sight of Chryseis standing near her cabin-door; her hands were tightly clasped, and her face was deadly pale, but she had not lost her self-command.   Abigail was close beside her; like a true daughter of Judah, she had seized a sword which she was pointing defiantly against a soldier who had lost his lance, and who, as though scared at being challenged by a woman, was cowering behind his shield.

Chamai's keen eye soon discerned what was passing, and followed by Hanno, he rushed like a wild bull through the crush, knocking down friends and foes alike, as he made his way to the protection of the women.

Meanwhile Himilco and fifteen of the sailors, cutlass and hatchet in hand, forced their way along and grouped themselves close to me. Telling them that now was their chance, I led them forwards and succeeded in effectually clearing the whole fore-ship, the Hellenes stumbling over ropes and rigging in their precipitous retreat. On reaching the prow I turned, to make the reassuring discovery that Hanno and Chamai had been equally successful in clearing the stern, and that they were closing in towards Bichri and his men at the mast, where they were engaged in repelling a fresh contingent of the enemy. Above the mass of heads and shields I could see Jonah's handspike swinging to and fro, and above the confusion of cries and yells I could hear his sonorous shout of defiance :

"Come on, Dodanim! I am your man. Let me earn my dinner. Come on! Come on!"

With such determination did Bichri and his supporters beat back the assailants, that ere long the middle deck was as clear as prow and stern, and there rose a frantic cheer of triumph. The *Ashtoreth* was free from her enemies.

The cry of success was followed by a shout of welcome to the *Dagon*, which at that moment came dashing up at a prodigious speed, sinking a boat as it approached, and discharging a volley of arrows amongst the boats that still persevered in hanging around us.

I now signalled to my helmsman to hold himself ready, and sent my rowers down the hatchways to their oars ; they found some Hellenes skulking in the hold, but they soon despatched them ; and it was the work of only a few minutes to get clear of the remnant of the attacking boats, and to bring the *Ashtoreth* sharply round until she was in a position on one side of the *Cabiros* corresponding with that of the *Dagon* on the other. Hannibal had returned to us, and gave us whatever assistance was in his power. Yet another boat was sunk ; and the crews of two more, over-whelmed in terror, leaped overboard and swam after the fugitives, who, under a shower of arrows, were making their way off.

No longer called upon to act upon the defensive, we next turned our attention to the main company of the convoys, of which three already had been abandoned by their crews and were drifting helplessly on the waves. As we were steering towards them, I chanced to look astern, and to my surprise I found that the boat we had in tow was crowded with armed men, who had evidently got into it with the design of boarding us, and had not been able to make their escape with their comrades. I made Bichri come on to the poop with a party of his bowmen, and he succeeded in hitting one of the Hellenes in the shoulder just as he was about to sever the tow-rope with his scimitar.

"Lay down your arms!" I shouted in Ionian.

But the man was not daunted. He renewed his effort to cut the rope asunder, an attempt in which he was foiled by receiving a second arrow in his throat.

"Shall we shoot them all ?" asked Bichri.

"No ; wait a bit !" I said ; "they look sturdy fellows, and ought to fetch a good price at Carthage ; we may as well do an extra stroke of business."

Again I called to them to lay down their arms and to surrender, but they made no sign of submission. One of them hurled his lance at me, just grazing my shoulder ; but another, apparently convinced that the case was desperate, jumped overboard, and as we were a long distance out at sea, was probably drowned.

Fifteen men still remained, and I made Hanno and Chryseis bespeak their attention in their own language

HANNO AND CHRYSIS BESPEAK THEIR ATTENTION

and thus succeeded in bringing them to terms.   Hanno, by
my instruction, promised them that their lives should be
spared, and that they should be conveyed to a land where
they might earn good pay as soldiers of a king, and have
good treatment besides.   After a while they yielded, and
laid down their arms, which were immediately hauled up
on deck ; and then a rope was thrown down, and one by
one the men, crestfallen and agitated, climbed on board.

The remainder of our assailants were now flying in complete disorder.   Night was coming on, and to them a voyage
in the darkness was scarcely less terrible than a second
battle.   Although some of the boats were quite uninjured,
we could see that several of them had sustained so much
damage that they could hardly make any progress, and
that more than one had been set on fire by the combustibles
discharged by the *Dagon.*   From the distant shore we
could hear the lamentations of the women bewailing the
fate of the drowned and slain.

Hamilcar and Hasdrubal obtained my leave to go in
pursuit of the fugitives, and I told off thirty men under
Bichri and Chamai to go with them.   While they were
absent I sent some men to take in tow the two boats that
had been abandoned by their crews, and found that they
contained a number of dead bodies, the whole of which I
had stripped and thrown into the sea.   The two ships
returned very shortly, bringing three prizes and twenty-two
prisoners.

I deferred making any detailed examination of the spoils
until the morrow, and tired as we were, I should have
been glad of repose for myself and my men ; but it was
absolutely necessary that we should at once wash the
decks, collect the scattered armour, and do something to
repair the disorder inevitable after so hard a conflict.
The corpses of the Hellenes who had been killed and
about twelve of the wounded were thrown overboard.   Of
our own men, twenty-three had been wounded and eleven
killed ; the bodies of these were wrapped in cloth and laid

side by side on the fore-deck, that they might be com•
mitted to the sea in the morning, with the rites and
invocations of their religion.

As the *Dagon* had sustained less injury than any of our
ships, I had all the captives, including my own fifteen, sent
on board her and fastened securely in the hold.

Our losses were very serious. The *Cabiros* had eight
killed and ten wounded ; the *Dagon*, three killed and
seven wounded ; making, with the casualties on my own
ship, a total of twenty-three dead, and forty wounded.
Here was a melancholy proof that we had been matched
with no mean opponents ; and to confess the truth, their
courage and energy were such, that if they had had any
practical notion of naval tactics, and if their boats had been
more manageable, and their weapons not so ill-adapted for
this character of warfare, our chances of success would have
been very small.

Both Hamilcar and Gisgo had sustained serious though
by no means dangerous wounds. Hanno had a gash
across his shoulder, Chamai a lance-cut in the arm, and
Himilco a large bruise on the head, but neither of the three
was incapacitated from going on with his accustomed
duty. Our senior seaman, Hadlai, was among the killed.
Jonah had five lance-wounds, which he regarded as mere
scratches ; and after he had smeared himself all over with
ointment, he declared that the day's proceedings had not
only given him a tremendous appetite, but had made him
desperately thirsty.

It was impossible accurately to estimate the losses of
the Hellenes ; but they must have amounted to several
hundred ; thirty-six dead bodies had been found lying on
the deck of the *Ashtoreth* alone, and the *Cabiros* had
thrown overboard thirty-eight more.

We contrived to get some brief repose before morning,
but it was still quite early when under a fair east wind we
started again on our way to Italy. The eight prizes were
all taken in tow, and in order to make our progress more

easy I sent a few men into each of them, either to put up a sail or to work them with oars.

Our ships were hung with black in honour of the dead, and the usual invocations were made to the gods of the departed. There were several bullocks amongst the booty we had captured, and I ordered one of them to be hoisted upon each vessel and slain for a sacrifice. On board the *Ashtoreth*, Hanno recited the prescribed petitions to the goddess, and after the slaughter of our beast, the fat and a portion of the flesh were set apart to be smoked and dried, the rest being allotted to the funeral feast. The children of Israel, meanwhile, after their own fashion, were sacrificing a sheep to their God, El-Adonai. As soon as the sacrifices were finished, I made a distribution of wine ; but before this was allowed to be tasted, the trumpets were sounded, and the bodies of the dead solemnly committed to the deep. The black hangings were then removed ; and we gathered together for the general repast. Every one's spirits revived under the influence of food and drink. Weariness and wounds were soon forgotten, and the men, one to the other, were cheerfully recounting their own experiences of the fight.

"Hannibal," I said, "you, as captain of the guard, and your men under you, have acquitted yourselves admirably and, according to the covenants of the charter-party, you are entitled to a share of the spoil."

"For my part," said Hannibal, "I am quite ready to give up all further claim if I can only have a new set of armour ; my cuirass is terribly battered about, and my helmet has lost both crest and plume. I have no doubt there is a good suit of Lydian armour on board ; let me have that and I shall ask no more."

"With all my heart!" I answered : "and in addition I shall give you a flask of fine Sareptan wine."

"Aye, a good thought!" said Himilco ; "I, also, shall be only too happy to dispose of my claim for three skins of Berytos."

Chamai maintained that he must be entitled at least to a bracelet and a pair of Syrian earrings. "Give them to Abigail," he said, "and I will cry quits for my share."

"And now, sir scribe," I asked, turning to Hanno, "what shall I do for you? There are sheep, oxen, armour, wines at your command."

"By Ashtoreth!" he answered; "there is nothing I want. Take my portion and distribute it amongst the wounded; they need it more than I."

Struck by this generosity, Hannibal and Chamai shook him heartily by the hand, and Chryseis showed her approval by the most beaming of smiles.

One of the pilots came to me, as a deputation from the crew, and requested that I would sell the whole booty in a lump at the first opportunity, and let them have their shares in money: meanwhile they hoped that I should not object to make them an advance of what they might expect. The fact was that the men knew that Phœnician coin was current at Utica, Carthage and Gades, and reckoned upon going ashore and enjoying themselves at all these ports. I saw no reason for refusing the men what they wanted, and accordingly instructed Hanno to draw up a list of all the plunder, to every article of which I appended the price in shekels which I was willing to pay for it. The priced catalogue was affixed to the mast of each ship for the sailors' inspection, and as it gave universal satisfaction, I paid them the amount to which they were severally entitled that very evening.

Chryseis and Abigail spent the night in administering to the wants of the wounded.

Next morning, I sent for the prisoners. They had some rations served out to them, and were brought from the *Dagon* to the *Ashtoreth*, looking downhearted and full of mistrust. I enlisted the services of Hanno as interpreter, and having selected the most intelligent-looking of the group, had him questioned as to his nationality and his home.

"We are Hellenes," he said, "of the tribe of the Phocians. We have no regular home, but we have been in the country round Mount Parnassus. We left our haunts there at the bidding of Apollo, who told us to depart, and to seek for other settlements. With our wives and children we were on our way to join our kinsmen, the Ionians, either in Epirus or in Corcyra. We were hoping there to find a happy and a settled residence."

Great tears stood in his eyes, and his companions in

adversity could not suppress their sobs. I assured him that it was far from my wish to aggravate their misery, and that I really pitied them in their misfortune, so that they need not fear any harsh treatment at my hands.

"If we had been meeting you in regular warfare," he continued, "we should have fought on to the very death, and would have borne disaster and defeat without a murmur; but now who shall blame us, if we weep for our wives and dear ones perished in the waves?"

"But why, then, did you attack us?" I inquired

L

"Listen, and you shall hear," he answered : "three days ago, we fell in with a great Phœnician ship; it was not alone, but was accompanied by several others. The captain hailed us and asked us to sell him some provisions : regarding the Phœnicians as all divine, we were all most ready to oblige them ; we sent them oxen, fruit and corn ; my own poor son and many others went besides ; but no sooner had they got the supplies on board, than the pirates hoisted sail and made away. We had no remedy ; there was no hope of recovering our people or our property ; our boats cannot compete with yours in speed. In our fury we swore that we would be avenged, and vowed we would attack the first Phœnicians we should see. You were the first. Now you know all."

"Bodmilcar! by all the gods !" ejaculated Himilco. "It is Bodmilcar that has involved us in this trouble. To him we owe the death of our brave Hadlai, and the loss of all our men ! Ten thousand curses on him ! Moloch's bitterest curse be on his head !"

Anxious to learn whether this suspicion was well founded, I made inquiry as to what the Phœnician ship was like, and not only ascertained that it was large and round and high, but that the men on board were quite different to the men upon the smaller boats, who had brown faces, and wore dresses of another shape. These boats, too, carried the figure of a goose's head at every prow.

"The *Melkarth* and the Egyptians beyond a doubt !" I cried.

The Phocian looked astonished at my agitation.

I soon recovered my composure, and asked whether there were any men amongst the captives upon whose courage and discretion he could rely. He informed me that his own brother was one, and that five of the others were his cousins ; he added, moreover, that the wife of one of the cousins had been carried off on board the Phœnician ship.

"Call them forward !" I said ; and in a few minutes

six young men, all apparently strong and active, stood before me.

"You would like to see your son again?"

"My son!" echoed the man. "Restore my son, and you shall be counted divine indeed."

I informed him that the Phœnician who had borne him off was my avowed and mortal enemy. "But serve me with fidelity," I added, "and you may recover your son even yet."

Turning to Hannibal, I ordered him to provide the seven men with kitonets and arms, and to take them into his own force; the remainder I sent to assist the rowers. It would be easy, I knew, to dispose of them all at Utica or Carthage, where there is a constant demand both for oarsmen and for mercenaries.

The seven Phocians kissed my hands, and wept for joy; the remainder went below with lighter hearts than they had brought on board.

CHAPTER IX.

THE LAND OF OXEN.

ON the third morning after the battle we sighted the mountains of Italy,[1] and having entered the gulf,[2] along the north of which extends the Iapygian Peninsula, we soon came to the mouth of a river that meandered along a fine plain, in which the broad pastures were diversified by groves of pines and oleanders. Inland, about a hundred stadia from the shore, rose a range of grey mountains, partially wooded, and crowned by a ridge of ragged peaks. The anchorage was tolerably good, and as we required fresh water and provender for the cattle, I determined to lay to at once. I had all the animals sent on shore. This was a work of some difficulty ; Bichri with a few armed men was put in charge of them, and he was to employ the prisoners to drive them where they could find proper pasturage ; my intention in doing this was that the animals should follow the ships along the coast as far as the Sicilian Straits, where, unless I succeeded meanwhile in disposing of them, they should be re-embarked.

"Not much chance of selling them here," said Himilco ; "we are in Vitalia, the land of oxen. If we could have brought them some goats now, like those we let the Ionians have, we might have found a market. Of cattle such as these they have more than enough already."

"Probably so," I answered ; "but first of all we must find some inhabited spot amidst all this desolation ; we

---

[1] Italia, from ἰταλός, *vitulus*.   [2] South of the Adriatic.

must try and meet with some of these Italians or Vitalians,
whichever they are called.   There must be some Iapygians
here too in the south, as well as in the north.   Do you
know the Iapygian dialect?"

Himilco said that, although he was not acquainted with
that dialect, he had some knowledge of the language of the
Vitalians, as well as of that which was spoken by the Opsci,
the Marsians, the Volscians, the Samnites, the Umbrians,
the Sabellians of the eastern coast, and the Latins of the

western.   He mentioned also that Gisgo was tolerably
familiar with the tongue of the Rasennæ, away to the
north-west.

The spokesman of my seven Phocian prisoners now
approached me somewhat timidly, as if he had something
to ask.   His name was Aminocles.   He began by addressing me :

"King of the Phœnicians!"

I stopped him and told him that my proper appellation
was not king but captain.

"Captain of the Phœnicians," he said; "will you please to tell me what country we are in?"

"Italy," I answered; "Italy, the land of herds."

"But in what part of it?" he asked.

"In that part," I replied, "which is inhabited by various tribes of Vitalians; south and north-east dwell the Iapygians; far away to the north are the Rasennæ, who build great cities, and have a king in the fertile vales beyond the mountains."

"We know nothing of them," said Aminocles.

"Patience!" interposed Himilco; "perhaps we can refresh his memory. Phocian, listen to me. Have you ever heard of Opsci?"

"Of Opici? yes," he answered; "our ancestors have left it upon record that long ages back, before we built Dodona, nay, before we settled by the Achelous, while we still were dwelling in the cold regions beyond Thrace, we were in association with a people called the Opici. At that time mainland and islands both were inhabited by Leleges, Pelasgians, giants, dwarfs, and monsters; but the gods slew them all and made way for us. If your Opsci are the same as those Opici, I suppose I ought to have heard of them before."

"It is of no use perplexing the man," I said; "you see he does not understand you."

"Wait a bit," Himilco remonstrated; "perhaps I shall succeed even yet. Tell me, Aminocles, did you ever hear of Tyrsenians?"

"No," said the Phocian.

"Strange!" muttered Himilco to himself. "Again and again I have heard the Hellenes speak of Vitalia, and call the natives Tyrsenians or Tyrrhenians; I must try again. Do you know the Siculians, the Cyclopes, the Læstrigonians?" he asked aloud.

The man's countenance changed in an instant.

"What! do you mean"—he exclaimed, in a voice

agitated with alarm—"that we have come to the land of such people as those?"

"Aye, that we have," said Himilco, with a chuckle of satisfaction; "this is the country of the Lœstrigonians; and down there is the island of the Cyclopes, the Siculians, and all the rest of them. We are going to pay them a visit, when we have steered safely between Scylla and Charybdis."

And he laughed outright when he heard Aminocles, wringing his hands, groan out:

"Oh! better, better far to have perished in the fight than to have come to this land of monsters. Oh!"

We all laughed. The ridiculousness of the fellow's terror was irresistible.

"Silence, simpleton!" I said; "the Lœstrigonians will not hurt you; we shall see plenty of them, but they will not eat you up."

While I was speaking, my attention was directed by the man on watch to a party of about fifty men, who were advancing across the plain. Their attitude was far from confident, and they halted on the edge of a wood, apparently in indecision whether they would come on or retreat. At length I took upon myself to encourage them to come forward, and, according to my custom, went alone towards them, making them every sign of good-will. Presently two of them advanced to meet me. They were stout, thick-set men, square-shouldered, and of middle height; they had light complexions, thick beards, and frizzly hair, that overhung low brows and wide faces. Their legs and arms were quite bare, and their heads uncovered, but they wore a kind of coarse woollen kitonet, with another loose garment thrown crosswise over one shoulder. They were all well armed, having two short copper-headed lances and a poignard; most of them carried knives or swords in their girdles, and about a dozen had slings or bows.

One of the two who had come on in advance shouted in Italian :

" Who are you ? and what have you come for ? "

Himilco, who had followed me, shouted back in the same language that we were merchants who had come from distant lands, and that we wanted to open a trade with them.

" But are you not Rasennæ ? and is it not your design to rob us our cattle ? "

" Nothing of the sort," we answered ; " we are Phœnicians from the east.   Come down to the shore, and you shall see our merchandise."

Both the men retired to their comrades, and appeared to deliberate ; but very shortly they returned, and one of them called out :

" You see these two trees on each side of me ; these must be our boundary."

And, driving his lance firmly into the ground midway between them, he continued :

" If you advance one step beyond this lance, I take it up, and we declare ourselves your foes."

Himilco repeated his assurance that we had no wish to do them the slightest injury, and they came up close to where we were.   The leader told us that they were Sabelline Samnites, and that they wanted to know what payment we were going to make them for the pasturage of our cattle.   I made Himilco satisfy them that they should have a proper remuneration.

It was now my turn to erect a barrier.   This I did by driving stakes into the earth, and stretching a cord across, beyond which I made the Samnites understand that I should not permit them to pass.   They raised no objection to my measure of precaution, but crowded up to inspect our goods, their curiosity meanwhile extending to our ships, ourselves, and our costume.   They were rougher in manners than the Hellenes, and more suspicious, and I had some trouble in inducing them to negotiate with us

"IF YOU ADVANCE ONE STEP BEYOND THIS LANCE."

at all ; but after a time I succeeded in securing their confidence to a certain degree, and they informed me that they were not an agricultural people, and had no cereals nor vegetables to bring us, but could supply us with any number of sheep and oxen. They subsequently brought several half-wild pigs, which particularly attracted the attention of Chamai and Bichri, neither of whom had seen animals of the kind before. Not understanding the art of making bread, the Samnites ordinarily eat a kind of pulp called "masa ;" but, as they had on previous visits of other Phœnicians tasted some loaves, they were now very anxious to be shown how to make them ; they made a number of inquiries likewise about our wine, but for this they did not seem to care to the same extent as the Hellenes.

Next morning they came to us again in considerable numbers. I had observed that during the night they had lighted a good many beacon-fires over the land, and naturally conjectured that they were signalling for a gathering of their countrymen, and I accordingly doubled my ordinary guard. I soon found, however, that there was no cause for alarm, and that they had no hostile intentions ; on the contrary, they were quite content to follow my injunctions that they should not approach our boundary line in groups of more than fifty ; they awaited their turn with the utmost patience, and altogether were far less noisy and demonstrative than we had found the Dorians.

Amongst other things they brought a great quantity of coral, which after rough weather is washed up on their coasts, but which they also procure by diving from frail rafts of their own construction ; for although they are very indifferent navigators, they are for the most part excellent swimmers. The most expert coral-divers are the Iapygians, those who dwell amongst the Samnites and the Bretians, as well as the natives of Iapygia proper. Some few of them were to be noticed amongst our Samnite visitors ; they were generally tall and wore no beards ; they had round heads and brown skins, being in many respects very like the Cydonians : in their manners they were more polished and in their conversation more communicative than the other Italians. They seemed to me to bear a marked resemblance to the Siculians ; and I cannot help thinking that the Iapygians, the Siculians, the Cydonians, and the natives discovered by our forefathers in Malta, are the aborigines of their respective countries. Afterwards, from the coast of Asia came the Leleges and the Pelasgians (tribes that bear a strong likeness to the Lydians, Lycians, and Carians), and these settled in Dodanim and the isles, being succeeded by the Hellenes and Italians, who came southward from the confines of Thrace. Of the origin of the Rasennæ I am perfectly ignorant : all I know is that Phœnicians who have visited the mountains whence the rock-crystal is obtained, and which lie north of the Eridanus, at the head of the Iapygian Gulf, have reported that they have fallen in with a people who call themselves Rhœtians, and who speak a language in many respects identical with that spoken by the Rasennæ.

Two days were spent in bartering my cumbersome booty for coral, which could be compactly stored away. As the captured boats were emptied, I had all but two of them broken up. I reserved only the planking, which was sure to be useful, and the masts, which might be of service if we should require extra spars. After the spoil had been all exchanged away, I commenced paying for what I purchased with glass-beads, lance-heads, and sword-blades ; the last of these articles were so eagerly coveted, that for four blades, worth about a shekel a-piece, I obtained at least four hundred shekels' worth of the finest coral. When I expressed my surprise at the quantity of coral in their possession, they explained that it was the accumulation of a very long time, adding that they had intended disposing of it at one of the emporiums which the Phœnicians had established on the western coast, but that our arrival had saved them the trouble of the journey

They told me that they should have been glad if I could supply them with goats, and stated that those which had been brought over by our countrymen, and purchased by the Marsians and Volscians, were rapidly spreading in the mountains of the north.

The Samnites have no regular towns, but live in small scattered hamlets, consisting generally of a few thatched huts built of boughs of trees cemented with mud. They have very little notion of agriculture, and the Latins of the west coast (especially those of the valley of the Tiber) are far superior husbandmen ; the Latins, however, have a city named Alba, occupying a secure position between a mountain and a lake. Along the coast I know only of a single sea-port, and that belongs to the Rasennæ, and is named Populonia. These Rasennæ are no contemptible sailors ; that they were bold and unscrupulous pirates, I had long known by hearsay, but here on the Samnite coast I was destined to have a confirmation of the fact from my own experience.

Having completed all the business that was practicable, I was preparing to renew our voyage, when one of the Samnites came running up to his associates, and shouted something which appeared to throw them into a state of great excitement.

"What ails the fellows ?" said Himilco ; "they seem going mad. Is the cock-head Nergal at their heels ? "

The commotion was soon explained.

" Pirates ! Pirates !" shouted a number of the Samnites in a breath. " Quick, Phœnicians, on your guard ! The Tyrrhenians are coming ! They are rounding the point ! they will be on us directly ! Away ! Away to the mountains !"

Without losing a minute, I made Jonah sound an alarm and summon our men to their ships. Hannibal donned his helmet and marshalled his men, including the seven Phocians ; the overlooker of the rowers, scourge in hand, hurried the oarsmen to their benches, and in a short time we were three stadia from the shore and ready for **action**. Chamai congratulated himself that although his right arm was disabled he was still capable of doing good execution with his left.

"What new friends are we to have the pleasure of seeing to-day ?" asked Bichri, with a smile, as he fastened on his quiver and strung his bow.

I told him that they were Tyrrhenians, or Rasennæ, from the north-west of Italy, who traded a little, but did a good deal more in the way of privateering along the coast ; and that, although I was not aware of their having ever hitherto come into collision with Phœnicians, I had very little doubt they carried freight enough to make it worth our while to risk an engagement with them.

"Yes, they are new to me," said Hannibal ; "and perhaps we can give them some new lessons in the art of fighting ; they may like a taste of the Chaldean mace that King David gave me."

Anxious to understand the true position of things, I sent the *Cabiros* ahead to reconnoitre, ordering her to keep as close as possible to the shore until she reached the extremity of the headland, whence she could command a view of the whole line of coast ; she returned with the intelligence that there were five ships, which seemed of a long build, advancing leisurely towards us by making short tacks to catch the wind, and that in about half an hour they would be in sight.

Whilst I was pondering in my mind what line of action I should follow, my eye fell upon the two boats of the Hellenes which had been spared in the general demolition, and it occurred to me that I could make them of service.

"How about our soundings, Himilco ?" I said.

"Ten cubits, and a rocky bottom," was the pilot's prompt reply.

Gisgo was on board the *Ashtoreth*. He had come to bring the report of the *Cabiros*.

"Tell me, Gisgo," I said, "how much water do those Tyrrhenian privateers draw? Is it six cubits?"

"Aye, six at the very least; they look low upon the water, but they sink very deep; it is their excessive weight that keeps them from lurching."

"Very well; now go to those two boats, scuttle them, and sink them there, right in front of my ship. *There!*" I said, pointing with my hand.

Himilco and Gisgo chuckled again with delight as they went to do as they were ordered, and in the course of twenty minutes the boats were both sunk, and formed a regular stockade about three cubits below the surface of the water.

My next proceeding was to direct the *Cabiros* to lower her sail, and to pretend to be dragging herself with difficulty towards the headland, as though she had sustained some serious injury. I then made the *Dagon* sheer off about two stadia out to sea, ordering her to make her way back to the *Ashtoreth* by short tacks, as if she were coming to her assistance. Meanwhile I gave my ship the appearance of being a disabled merchantman; I lowered my sail, made my rowers struggle with their oars without propelling the vessel, and told all my soldiers to slip their shields, and to lie down flat upon the deck so as not to be seen.

"What's up now, Captain?" said Chamai raising his head, with a merry grin.

I told him that I was giving a sprat to catch a mackerel; and that if he would have patience I hoped he would be satisfied with the haul.

It was a very short time now before the Rasennæ caught sight of us. Immediately one of the five ships bore down directly upon the *Cabiros;* two of them started off in pursuit of the *Dagon*, which was still out to sea, and the remaining two steered for the *Ashtoreth*, which, as though perfectly helpless, exhibited no sign of resistance.

When they had come within a stadium of me I had ample opportunity of examining the details of their boats

and equipments. Although the boats were long, they were
very ill-constructed ; they had only a single deck, and
were each manned by thirty rowers ; the stern was somewhat raised, but the deck was almost level with the sea ;
on the prow was painted a pair of huge red and white eyes
which seemed to stare fixedly at the waves. The men on
board were very tall ; they had large heads, wide flat faces,
reddish complexions and thin beards ; although their
limbs were muscular and well-developed, their gait was
very awkward. They were armed with ponderous lances,
hatchets, bucklers, and round helmets which had no crests ;
whilst their legs were protected either by sandals or by
pointed gaiters. Most of them wore tunics of some dark
colour, which, though longer than our kitonets, were
shorter than those worn by the Syrians. On their arms
and throats was a profusion of bracelets and necklaces, and
their girdles, which were very wide, were ornamented with
plates of polished bronze. After looking at them steadily
for a time, Abigail declared that she would rather die than
fall into the hands of such revolting creatures.

Coming within hail, the Rasennæ began shouting furiously
at us, but we took no heed. Finding that their challenge
was unanswered, they sent one of their boats in front of me,
whilst the other passed round the stern intending to cut
me off from the shore ; but they reckoned without their
host. The former boat dashed itself violently against the
stockade of concealed boats, and after two or three ineffec-
tual efforts to disengage herself, heeled over on her side,
and remained with her stern considerably sunk below
the sea.

My trumpet sounded, my oars dipped, my warriors
started to their feet, and a shout of triumph rang through
the air.

Thoroughly taken aback by our sudden revival, the other
boat endeavoured to tack about to get out of our way ; but
so clumsily did she set about the manœuvre, that she only
succeeded in running her stern aground, and being thus

entirely at my mercy, I poured into her such a shower of missiles as probably her commander and crew had never before conceived possible.

"Here, Tyrrhenians, Rasennæ, or whatever you call yourselves," shouted Hannibal, as he worked away at his scorpions; "here is a heavenly shower of manna for you! If these arrows and Cretan pebbles are not to your taste, we can find you a nice little lot of spiked stakes."

Bichri, too, was quite in his element. With such an immovable mark within bowshot, he selected his victims just as he pleased, and was careful to choose those who wore any article of apparel or any ornament that particularly struck his fancy.

"Look at that fellow," I heard him say, "with the necklace of gold beads inlaid with blue and enamelled with white: I must have him; but I must hit him on the head, or I shall be spoiling that charming bit of embroidery he is wearing."

As our deck was several cubits higher than that of our antagonists, their archers were comparatively powerless; and in order to protect themselves under the incessant discharge of our missiles, they took refuge in their hold. Observing their retreat, Hannibal, Chamai and Bichri, with a few followers, leaped down upon their deck; Jonah, in his impetuous haste to go after them, came sprawling down headlong with a tremendous thud, but rising rapidly to his feet, caught hold of the heels of an unhappy Tyrrhenian who had not had time to make his escape, twirled him round and round in the air like a sling, and dashed out his brains against the side of the vessel. Short work was made with the few who still remained above board, and in a few minutes more, our people, who had forced their way down the hatchway, reappeared, bringing with them twenty men, of whom, to my surprise I found that no less than eleven were Phœnicians. Their costume and physiognomy revealed this at a glance.

Free now to turn my attention from the shore to the

sea, I found that the *Dagon* had already sunk one of the privateers, and in concert with the *Cabiros* was driving the remaining two fast inland. I joined in the pursuit, and after a short chase, one of the boats, overwhelmed by the volleys of stones which we threw from our engines, found all further resistance useless, and made signs of surrender. The capture of this vessel cost us the lives of two of our men, and while we were engaged in securing our prize, the remaining boat took advantage of our occupation to effect an escape.

We lost as little time as possible in making our way back to the coast towards the prizes we had left there. We were only just in time. The Samnites had been watching the issue of the contest, and were hastening down from the heights to pillage the abandoned vessels; but as I sent some detachments of men to keep guard, they had for the present to keep their distance, and to be content to bide their time before they could enjoy the crumbs of the expected feast.

Our first business now was to empty the boat that had struck upon the sunken stockade; it had already nearly two cubits of water in its hold, and was consequently liable to sink at any moment. There were no prisoners to be made here; during our engagement with the other vessels some of the men had escaped in a small boat, and the rest had swum to shore, but only to be captured by the Samnites. The *Cabiros* and *Dagon*, however, had thirty-three prisoners, making, with the nine I had myself taken, a total of forty-two, who were first stripped of everything of any value that was found belonging to them, and then distributed amongst our three crews, who would be entitled to dispose of them to our colonists on the coast of Libya, where no doubt they would be in demand either for soldiers or artisans.

The eleven Phœnicians were highly delighted at what had befallen them; their capture was really a deliverance They told me that they had formed part of the crew of a

Sidonian gaoul which had been wrecked off the coast of Sardinia, and that they had escaped in one of the small boats. They had attempted to reach one of our settlements in the island, but tempestuous weather had frustrated their plan, and they had been carried out to sea, and finally drifted to the mainland. They had next tried to make their way northward to one of the Phœnician marts, established on the coast; and it was more than a week ago since they had fallen into the hands of the Rasennæ, who had sent them to serve on board their privateers. All of them were ragged, and more than half-starved; and their rejoicing seemed unbounded, when I not only provided them with clothes and food, but allowed them to enter my service on an equal footing with the rest of my crews. Amongst them was an experienced helmsman and a master mariner; so that all our losses were to a great extent replaced, especially as the whole of the wounded were in a fair way of recovery.

Stripping the dead, collecting the booty, conveying it on board, and making lists of it all, occupied us till the close of the day, and it was past sunset before we were at liberty to avail ourselves of the wind, which was quite favourable for our coasting along towards the Straits of Sicily. We left the captured boats, and whatever plunder was too heavy or too valueless to be worth carrying away, to the Samnites, who, with shouts of joy, rushed forward to take possession of their unexpected prize.

The evening meal was merry. Our successful negotiations, our victorious skirmish, our release of our countrymen, our valuable booty, were all topics of mutual congratulation. Hannibal was loud in his praises of my stratagem of the stockade.

'Ah! that's an old trick," said Himilco; "we once played it off upon the Carians of Rhodes, and took eleven of their ships and no end of plunder. Old Tarshish mariners are adepts at schemes of that sort."

Chamai held up a pair of twisted bracelets, and a necklace of a similar pattern, ornamented with a large flat crescent.

"Are these solid gold, captain?" he asked me.

"Aye, and of the finest sort," I answered; "it is the gold they get from the Eridanus and the Rhone; you are to be congratulated on your lucky prize."

"Not one man did I either kill or catch," said Hanno; "and I suppose I shall have to be content with my share-and-share-alike portion of the plunder; but I confess I should be very pleased if I might have a vase which I discovered amongst the captured goods; it is exquisitely painted, and I have no doubt that these Rasennæ, ugly as they are themselves, are highly-skilled as artists."

I told him that I saw no difficulty in yielding to his wish, and requested him to submit to me his inventory of the spoil. Casting my eye at it, I was not surprised to find that the articles made of gold were considerably larger in number than those made of silver. I knew that the Tyrrhenians had little or no communication with Tarshish and the other silver-producing countries, whilst they have free access to the sands of the Eridanus, and that by the road made by the Ligurian convicts they could cross the mountains to the Rhone. There were a good many articles of copper which came from Lower Vitalia, and amongst them some figures, which were evidently images of gods.

I sent for Gisgo to come on board and interrogate the prisoners in their own language. In their peculiar muffled accent they informed us that they had come from Populonia, and were subjects of King Tarchnas, who ruled over twenty Tyrrhenian cities. Populonia, they said, was their only sea-port, and thence they always set sail upon their cruises, their ships being manned with Ligurians as oarsmen and sailors, whilst their fighting men were nearly all Rasennæ. Two of their chiefs they mentioned as having been killed in the fight, whose names were Vivenna and Spurinna; Himilco gave it as his opinion that these names were identical with the Vitalian Vibius and Spurius.

Upon being shown the copper images of the gods which

CLOSE TO ETNA.

had been found amongst the plunder, the prisoners recognised them at once, and told us the names. There were Turms, the Hermes of the Hellenes ; Turan, whom I believed to be our Ashtoreth ; Sethlans, the same as our Khousor Phtah ; Fouflouns the Dionysus of the Hellenes ; and another called Menvra, of whom I had never heard, but whom Himilco declared to the Vitalian goddess Minerva.

The Tyrrhenians went on to say that they were allies of the Latins and of the Opsci, or Occi, a name which in our language signifies "workmen ;" and that the semi-barbarous Samnites, although of the same race and speaking the same tongue as the Opsci, had committed depredations against them on the river Volturnus, or "the rolling stream ;" and had likewise attacked the Latin settlement of Novla, or "the new city." In defence of their allies, the Rasennæ had declared war against the Samnites, and were on their way to attack them when they encountered us, and fell into our power. This was all the information they had to give me, and I sent the men back to the care of the crew, and we all retired to rest.

The day had hardly dawned when I rose, and looking a little to the left, I could see behind us the light, the flames, and the lurid smoke that issued from the crater of Mount Etna. The two women and all the men, who had never before seen such a spectacle, looked on, some in astonishment, some in downright terror. Hannibal was as surprised as anyone, and declared that except he knew to the contrary, he should have taken it for the mouth of hell ; adding, that he thought it a great pity that all that mighty force of fire could not be utilised : it would make a splendid apparatus for reducing an obstinate city in a siege. To my inquiry whether he had never seen the burning mountain in Cilicia, he replied that, although he had passed several times, it had never been his good fortune to be there at the time of an eruption.

We passed sufficiently close to Etna to be able most distinctly to hear its roar. The women, really alarmed,

betook themselves to their cabin.   Hanno asked what was
the distance of the volcano from us.

"Sixty stadia at least," I answered; "you seem surprised at our seeing it so plainly, but in the broad daylight
it will not be nearly so conspicuous, although it is very
lofty. My own reason for coming so close to it now is
that we may the more directly steer into the Straits of
Sicily."

Jonah, who at first had been terribly alarmed, did not
disguise his satisfaction that we were not going any closer
to the mountain. "All very well in the distance," he said;
"it is the kitchen of Nergal, the old cock, whose head is up
in the sky and his feet here on earth. Yes, it is his kitchen;
where he roasts his behemoths and leviathans; his smallest
platter is a good deal bigger than this deck. But the time
is coming when El-Adonai shall demolish him, and the
children of Israel shall feast upon him and his dainties!"

"Hold your tongue, you fool!" said Chamai. "None of
your idiot stories of Dan, and your fables of the drunken
Ephraimites!"

"Neither stories nor fables!" retorted Jonah; "have you
not a proof before your eyes that it is all true? What will
the people of Eltekeh say when I tell them I have seen
Nergal's kitchen?"

"Hush! I say! Shut up!" And as Chamai spoke, he
gave the giant a violent blow across his mouth with his
open hand.

"Humph!" he growled; "I must hold my tongue,
must I?"

We now made rapid headway towards the north, and as
we approached the strait, Himilco and his sailors amused
themselves by working up Aminocles and the other
Phocians to the highest pitch of terror.

"That is the mountain of the Cyclopes that you have
been looking at," he said to them; "now's your time to
look out sharp to the right and left, and you shall see
Scylla and Charybdis. You know who they are. They

are the ravenous monsters that swallow up whole ships and all their crews. Listen! you can hear them roaring now; they seem desperately hungry."

"I remember," said one of the sailors, "seeing Charybdis suck in three gaouls and two galleys at one draught, just as easily as I could drain a cup of wine."

"And would you believe," interposed the man who was at the helm, "that I have seen the heads of Scylla shatter a whole fleet with such violence that the admiral was pitched clean over there into the jaws of the volcano?"

Himilco, of course, could not allow himself to be outdone by the men, and proceeded to say:

"I have been nearer to Scylla than any of you. One cloudy night I was at the prow, vainly endeavouring to make out the Cabiri, when all at once I felt her foamy mouth open gently, close behind me, and snap off my cap —lucky it wasn't my head too—and before I could turn round, Charybdis had swallowed a whole bottle of my best Berytos and three whole cheeses!"

Jonah, who was looking on intensely interested, said:

"And what did you do, pilot? I know what I should have done. I should have given her a good crack across her muzzle."

"O, it was no good my saying anything to her; she wouldn't have understood me; the only language she can comprehend is that of the Loestrigonians."

He could hardly speak for laughing; but Aminocles cowered down upon the deck, and covered his head with his loose tunic, the other six Phocians scampering off in dismay to secrete themselves in the hold.

CHAPTER X.

GISGO THE EARLESS RECOVERS HIS EARS.

NOTWITHSTANDING the strong and rapid current which bears down upon the promontory to the right, and which has given rise to the marvellous stories with which sailors delight to awaken the fears of the inexperienced, we passed through the strait without the slightest difficulty ; and so well did I know the channel, and so manageable were our ships, that we had no necessity to diminish our ordinary speed.   The coast on either hand was covered with fine wooded hills, surmounted by jagged grey rocks, rising up almost perpendicularly, like the battlements of a fortress ; there was good anchorage everywhere, and more especially in the bay on the side of the island in the strait itself.   I did not, however, lay to, but hastened on with as much speed as possible, in order that before nightfall I might reach the roadstead in front of the promontory of Lilyboeum, to which our countrymen are accustomed to pay periodical visits for the purpose of purchasing sulphur and lava-stones.   The Siculians have a few cabins on the margin of the roadstead, and are on the whole less savage than their countrymen in the south and west of the island, more frequent intercourse with strangers having tended to soften their manners ; but the ever-increasing immigration of the Latins is so continuously overwhelming their numbers, that in my opinion they will before long have entirely disappeared.

Rounding the cape, I steered due west along the shore

of the island, leaving the Æolian peaks to our right, and by evening had reached the anchorage upon which I had settled, and where I found good moorings about two bow-shots from the beach. I did not feel altogether sure of my quarters, so that I would not land any of my merchandise that night, and I resolved, moreover, to hold no communication of any kind with the natives till the morning. Some men came with torches to the water's edge and made signs of friendly intentions, but I merely told them that they might bring what sulphur, coral, or mother-of-pearl they could on the next day ; and finding that I was resolute in my refusal to negotiate with them then, they went away.

They had not been gone very long, when Himilco pointed out to me some shoals of tunny-fish within reach, and asked permission to try and catch some. As it was some time since our men had tasted fresh fish, I could not refuse, but allowed him to make up a party of the most experienced fishermen he could select. A lot of harpoons and tridents were lowered into a boat, into which got Bichri and two archers, carrying some lines to be attached to the harpoons to haul up the fish that were hit. Jonah, ever on the alert when food was in question, asked permission to join the party, and was allowed to go under condition that he brought his trumpet and some torches to attract the fish. It had been ascertained that Aminocles was a skilful hand at this pursuit ; and as soon as he was satisfied that there was no fear of his encountering any of the monsters of which he had heard so much, he was induced to accompany them.

" How was it," he said to Himilco, " that we escaped Scylla and Charybdis so completely ? I looked out once or twice, but I saw nothing alarming."

" Neither did I," said Himilco, gravely. " The truth is, the old monster does not show herself every day, or, maybe, something scared her ; perhaps Hannibal's red crest, or perhaps Jonah's big trumpet. Anyhow, there's no accounting for the freaks of these monsters."

" She was quite right in keeping out of my way," said
Jonah ; "now I have seen Nergal's kitchen, I have courage
enough for anything."

Aminocles was still not quite easy in his mind, and with
reference to the volcanoes, asked whether we were quite
out of the reach of the flames.

" Out of reach!" repeated Himilco ; "why, the flames
are six hundred stadia away from where you saw them ;
you only saw the reflection in the clouds."

" Nergal's kitchens, all of them!" said Jonah ; " plenty
of them! nice and hot! He can fry and he can bake!
He's a capital cook!"

The sailors were immensely amused at all this talk ; and
when Himilco, with imperturbable seriousness, proceeded
to interpret Jonah's remarks to the credulous and timid
Aminocles, their laughter became perfectly uproarious.

The fishing was a great success. Several good hauls
were made ; and before daylight the boat returned, and
the men retired to their well-earned rest.

In good time next morning the natives whom we had

seen the previous evening, came with a considerable increase in their number, and one of them swam boldly out from the shore, and was received on board the *Ashtoreth*. He was a man that might be regarded as a fair type of the Siculians; tall, with a low forehead, thin nose and lips, beardless chin, and copper-coloured complexion. He addressed us in the Latin tongue, and was eager to tell us that the Latins were now in possession of the eastern portion of the island, and were the bitterest enemies of the Siculians. I replied that I was a Phœnician, and that Italian Latins, or Italian Samnites, Umbrians, or Sabellians were all the same to me; what I wanted was coral, sulphur, and lava; and if the Siculians could bring me these, they should have a liberal price in return. He replied:

"We are subjects of King Morgesh, who will only permit us to transact business inland. Come with us to yonder mountains; we have plenty of the commodities you want. There we may make our exchanges."

The persistency with which he urged our going on shore with our goods aroused my suspicions; but without exhibiting any sign of mistrust I pretended to acquiesce in his proposal, and at once proceeded to land my bales of merchandise and sixty armed men, taking the precaution, moreover, of placing all my archers on board the *Cabiros*, which, with her machines ready for action, was moored within a few cubits of the shore.

"What need to bring so many men?" asked the Siculian, when we had landed; "we can carry your packages to the mountains."

When I replied that I did not intend to go inland at all, and that if they wanted to effect any bartering with us they must bring their own merchandise down to the beach, the man was evidently very much disconcerted, and went away to consult his companions. While he was absent, I availed myself of the opportunity of replenishing all our water-casks from the copious brook that flowed into the bay.

On the man's return, he was accompanied by two of his colleagues.

"Do not be afraid of the fatigue of ascending the mountain," they urged; "we will not only convey your property, but we will carry all of you too, if you like. Only come."

And with repeated solicitations, they assured me I should be pleased with the bargains I should be able to make.

I represented the impossibility of my yielding to their wishes. It was my determination to set sail again that very evening; consequently there was no leisure for us to quit the shore. While I was talking, I made my people unfold to the view of the savages some specimens of my wares—glass beads and trinkets, bottles and bright caldrons, and some parti-coloured stuffs. These proved too much for their cupidity, and unable to stand out any longer, and convinced of my inflexible purpose of remaining where I was, they hurried off to fetch their own commodities.

Rough and brutal in their manners, they haggled over every item; and whenever they saw anything that especially attracted their fancy, they tried to snatch it from our hands; or, if small enough, they would endeavour slyly to pilfer it; but we kept a sharp look-out, and as fast as I completed my purchases, I despatched them either to the *Dagon* or to my own ship. The throng of the Sicilians gradually grew larger and larger, and in proportion as their numbers increased, their demands became more and more encroaching; so much so, that fearing some outbreak of violence, I thought it prudent to send for Chamai, Bichri, Himilco, and a score of men to supplement my body-guard.

All at once, Gisgo, who had been sitting quietly on the beach watching the proceedings, started to his feet, and touching Himilco's shoulder, drew his attention to a sudden stir that had begun amongst the Sicilians in the rear. Following with my eye the direction of his finger, I per-

ceived in a moment that some king or chief was passing
through the throng, which was falling back to allow him a
passage. Before him was carried a number of rods, all
painted red, and ornamented with coral, mother-of-pearl,
and other glittering substances. From the end of the longest
of these rods dangled some ill-defined objects, which to
my unpractised eye looked like nothing so much as strings
of faded leaves. But Gisgo was better informed.

Pointing to the rods, and with a voice almost choked
with excitement, he said :

" Captain, there are my ears !"

" Your ears ! What do you mean ?"

" There, there! on that stick ! strung together ! I know
what they are well enough."

And he muttered to himself : "A man knows his own
ears."

It was all in vain that I strained my eyes to see which of
the shapeless and withered cartilages Gisgo maintained
were his : I could make out nothing to distinguish one pair
of ears from another.

" Never mind," said Gisgo ; " I recognise them ; and I
recognise something else ; that chief is the blackguard who
cut them off."

The impropriator of my pilot's ears had now advanced to
me, and commenced negotiating in person. He sold me a
quantity of sulphur, and appeared to be conducting his
transaction in a friendly and equitable manner ; but just as
I was about, as usual, to embark my purchase, he declared
that in addition to the stipulated price, he must have a
cuirass like Hannibal's. I told him peremptorily that he
could not have anything beyond the contract, whereupon
he caught hold of the cuirass that Hannibal was wearing,
and tried to drag it from him by main force. Hannibal,
however, was too strong for him, and repelled him with a
blow so violent that he stumbled and fell to the ground.
In a moment, doubtless at a preconcerted signal, we were
assailed by a shower of stones and lances. I was quite pre-

pared ; my measures of defence had all been arranged, and at a sign from me, the *Cabiros* set her catapults at work, and discharged a volley of missiles over our head into the throng of the enemy, whilst Hannibal and Chamai, each with his own troop, charged right and left.

But Gisgo was beforehand with any of us. Before the chief could regain his feet, the pilot rushed at him, and with the help of Himilco (who drew his sword, and hurried to his assistance) he had split open the chief's skull, and laid two of his staff-bearers dead, or as good as dead, by his side.

My fighting-men meanwhile succeeded in driving back the foremost Siculians half a stadium from the water's edge, and as soon as our boats were loaded and ready to start, I sounded the signal for retreat. Finding themselves no longer pursued, the Siculians faced about and followed us back at a safe distance, trying to harass us by stones and javelins; but I made my people embark a few at a time, and when there were only about fifteen of us remaining, just enough for one boat's load, I was congratulating myself that we had been so little molested ; but at that very instant a large party of the Siculians made a dash towards us, and if it had not been that the *Cabiros* skilfully protected us by her engines, we must inevitably have fallen into their hands. As it was, we all managed to embark ; and although they pursued us with hideous yells as far as they could into the water, we got right away, the *Cabiros* slipping her moorings and following us without sustaining any injury.

One of our Phocians had been killed, and another seriously wounded, and eight of our own people had received slight cuts and contusions ; but we had obtained fifteen hundred shekels of coral, mother-of-pearl, and sulphur, so that on the whole I considered we had come out of the affair without much to regret. I rejoiced that my prudence and resolution had spared us from falling into any ambush of the treacherous foe.

Gisgo was in high spirits ; he considered himself amply avenged, and came on board the *Ashtoreth* t) show me his trophies ; he brought two rods that he had captured, to each of which he had affixed a pair of bleeding ears, freshly cut from the skulls of his fallen adversaries. With regard to his own ears, nothing could convince him but that he had found them amongst the string of others, and the pair he selected was ever afterwards preserved most carefully in his leather purse.

During the night we passed through the group of the Ægades, which lie off Lilybœum, and where the Phœnicians have established a naval station. After hailing one of the guard-ships, we directed our course south-west, hoping that we might, with a calm sea and a light wind from the east, succeed by the following afternoon in reaching the fine bay which encloses, on the one hand, the roadstead of Utica, the metropolis and arsenal of our Libyan settlements, and on the other the harbour of Bozrah, its newly-built rival.

Eager to catch sight of the first important place at which they were to rest awhile, my people next morning were up betimes. Hannibal was especially interested ; he had long wished to visit both Utica and Carthage, and asked me if it were true that Carthage had formerly been called Bozrah, and had not been known as Carthage for more than twenty years.

I replied that his impression about Carthage was quite correct ; it had originally been Bozrah, which means " the citadel ;" but Utica had been in existence for more than a century. He would find it a noble city ; its Cothôn, or war-port, contained sixty dry-docks, above each of which was erected a magazine, and the whole place landwards was rendered impregnable by a triple wall.

Before disembarking, I satisfied myself that my prisoners were all in good condition, and after they had been well washed I ordered them to be supplied with double rations. The Rasennæ generally are very superstitious, and my captives were no exceptions. My proceedings with regard to them caused them much misgiving ; they imagined that the extra food and cleansing implied that their last hour was come, and that they were about to be offered in sacrifice to the gods. Every moment in the dim light of the hold they fancied they could hear the winged Turms coming to conduct their souls to the shades, and they even went so far as to persuade themselves and each other that they could make out the shrieks of the tortured who were being scourged below. I was glad to relieve them of their fears. When I made them aware that the object of my preparations was to make them ready for sale in a fine city, where they would be employed according to their abilities ; would be well fed and well clothed ; and where, if they conducted themselves meritoriously, they would have a claim to the spoils of war, they were full of glee, and fell to their double portions of meat with a double relish. One only regret they acknowledged ; they mourned their removal from their Hestia, or hearth-goddess, but they soon consoled themselves with the reflection that as the gods are everywhere, they might fairly hope to find a Hestia in their new country.

The Phocians had carried off the body of their comrade who had been killed by the Siculians and had conveyed it on board. I promised to try and procure them a piece of ground where they might bury him according to their own rites ; and so gratified were they by my endeavour to meet their wishes in this respect, that they declared they would encounter any perils by sea now that they found it did not deprive them of their rites of sepulture. Another circumstance which had some little effect of reconciling them to their position was that Himilco, although he had great difficulty in bringing them to believe what he said, explained to them that the Siculians, with whom they had just had an engagement, were really the Lœstrigonians that they had so much dreaded.

CHAPTER XI.

OUR HEADS ARE IN PERIL.

WHEN I returned to the deck, the promontory of Utica (or, as the point on the Libyan coast facing Sicily is sometimes called, the Cape of Hermes) was clearly visible.

In honour of our arrival at so important a city we all took extra pains in dressing ourselves. I put on my best kitonet and my embroidered cap; and Hannibal donned his plumed helmet, and wore a handsome tunic under his cuirass.

We could ere long see not only the cape but the city of Utica itself; and further south, at the other extremity of the bay, a confused white mass, which unquestionably was Carthage. Leaving this on our left, we steered due west right into the bay, and having rounded the headland, coasted for some miles along the low-lying shore that continued all the way to the city, which seemed to rise in gentle gradations from the deep blue waters to where the "bozrah" formed its lofty crown. The red and brown domes of the buildings and the battlements of the citadel stood out in sharp relief against the azure sky; and the masses of verdure all around the city formed a fitting background for the dazzling whiteness of its lime-washed walls.

Having passed a number of imposing edifices on the island, which is separated from the mainland by a canal that forms the trade-harbour, we entered the war-port, in the centre of which, high above the crowds of shipping, rose the massive walls and towers of the Admiralty palace.

I found that there was room for my ships on the left-hand quay, where I had them laid to, and then in company with Hanno I got into a small boat and rowed across the harbour to a jetty, wide and paved, that led from the Admiralty to the mainland, and which, being in connection with all the surrounding quays, is always thronged with passengers going to and fro upon business at the Admiralty offices.

From the jetty we passed through a high vaulted gateway, flanked on either side by a tower, into an outer courtyard. Here the sentinels asked our names, and sent us on through another lofty gateway, across a hall hung with red and yellow tapestry into a long dark lobby, at the end of which was a half-open gate leading into the large inner court. We crossed this court, and entered another lobby exactly like the one we had just quitted ; and leaving this, we found ourselves in a low square room with a vaulted roof, whence we passed, by a side door, into a gloomy room with a circular dome. We had, however, still farther to go : after ascending three long and very narrow staircases we entered an apartment with a lofty dome on the second floor of one of the towers ; but even yet we had not reached our destination. We had now to descend a few steps and pass along a corridor, from which we ascended another staircase, and finally reached a spacious apartment, circular in shape, well lighted by loop-holes in the wall, and having a handsome vaulted ceiling.

I could observe that we had thus made our way to the left-hand tower of the four which are ranged along the north front of the palace, one at each end of the building, and one at each side of the gateway, this one commanding a view of the Admiral's private basin, beyond which I could see my own vessels lying in the Cothón.

The apartment was hung with strips of tapestry alternately red and yellow, and the paved floor was covered with mats. The guards who had ushered us all the way from the outer courtyard remained standing at the door, and having given us permission to enter, Hanno and I advanced alone towards a window, where, seated in a chair of painted wood, I recognised old Adonibal, the naval *suffes*, or suffect.

Nearly every one is aware that our Libyan cities are subject to a government in many respects similar to that which existed among the children of Israel before the time of King Saul ; that is, they are ruled by suffects, whose office corresponds very nearly to that of the "judges." A council, all eligible as suffects, are nominated by the people, and these from their own number elect two (whom, however, the people reserve to themselves the power of displacing), one to be " naval suffect," entrusted with the control of all maritime matters ; the other, popularly called the "sacred suffect," to have the superintendence of all inland affairs. But it is not so generally known that for the last ten years the Libyan suffects have been appointed without any sanction either of the Kings of Tyre or Sidon. The representatives are chosen independently, subject only to the condition that no Tyrians are admitted to the office at Utica, which is essentially a Sidonian colony, and no Sidonian can be elected for Carthage, where it is the Tyrians who have been rearing the new city around the ancient Bozrah.

At the time of our visit, Adonibal, the son of Adoniram, had been for eight years the naval suffect, and it was universally acknowledged that he wielded his magistracy with a resolute and steady hand. After many years of adventure both by sea and land, he had settled at Utica, where he had carried on his affairs, both in trade and warfare, with great success. He had led the forces of the city against the Libyans, had made incursions upon the coast of Tarshish, and in a great measure had contributed to the establishment of Massalia, the city of the Salians, at the mouth of the Rhone, in the land of the Celts. In return for his services, and as a proof of the confidence they had in his judgment and experience, the people of Utica elected him their naval suffect, and the way in which the city and its dependencies prospered under his rule convinced

N

them that their choice could not have fallen on a better
man.

In the course of my many voyages I had at various
times been brought into contact with Adonibal, and although
I was quite aware that he had been a daring freebooter, I
knew him to be a brave sailor and a clever merchant.   It
was therefore with much pleasure that I advanced towards
the chair in which the hale old man was seated.   Although
he had a flowing white beard, his upper lip was shorn perfectly smooth in the old Chittim fashion; he wore his
mariner's cap pressed closely over his ears; and his nose,
slightly redder than of yore, betokened that he had more
than a slight acquaintance with the luscious produce of
Helbon and Berytos.

I bowed, and congratulated him that I found him looking
so well.

"Ah!" he said, speaking in a sort of facetious way that
had become habitual to him, "here's Mago, the Sidonian,
the 'cutest captain that ever took cedar ship to Tarshish!
And who is this young man with you?"

I introduced Hanno as my scribe and fellow-townsman.

"And the brave fellows that were with you when you
came here before; how are they all?" continued Adonibal,
stroking his beard; "Himilco with his one eye, and Gisgo
who had lost his ears, how are they?   And what has become
of the notable *Gadita*?"

Flattered by the accuracy with which he retained me and
my people in his memory, I replied that they were all well
and with me, and that he had only to turn his head to the
window and he would see all my ships in the harbour,
amongst them the *Gadita,* whose name had been altered to
the *Cabiros.*

The old man laughed significantly.

"I shall see your ships quite soon enough for your liking,"
he said; "I shall not lose much time in making my official
inspection of them.   The *Melkarth* left here only three
days since."

"The *Melkarth !*" I exclaimed in astonishment.

Seeing my amazement he began to jeer me. "An old stager like you! you surprise me very much by trusting yourself here so soon after Bodmilcar."

"Bodmilcar!" I repeated; "surely you must be unaware of how Bodmilcar has acted!"

"I am only aware of this," he said, his eye twinkling as he spoke; "you and your scribe must lay down your swords and be trotted off to the dungeons, and the rest of your people will very soon be trotted after you."

I stood dumb with bewilderment; but Hanno, with whom neither patience nor reticence were prevailing virtues, laid his hand upon the hilt of his sword, and said:—

"This sword was given me by Melek David, and whoever demands its surrender shall first know the feel of its point in his bosom."

White with passion, the old man started to his feet. In an instant a couple of guards had laid their hands upon the shoulders of my impetuous scribe.

"Let him alone!" he bawled; "I can defend myself."

Then suddenly controlling his fury, he said very slowly, addressing us both :

"Lay down your swords at once, or by Baal-Peor! within a quarter of an hour your heads shall be swinging from the highest battlement of this very tower!"

I knew that Adonibal was not a man to swear lightly by his god, and I knew, moreover, that a few heads more or less were a matter of no moment to him. Seeing, therefore, that he was somewhat calmer, I summoned all my courage, and said as firmly as I could :

"My lord suffect, you are bound to show justice to all mariners alike ; you would not, I am sure, commit a Sidonian captain to the dungeons without giving him a fair hearing."

He had recovered his equanimity sufficiently to resume his bantering tone :

"They have gone for the handcuffs : they will soon be back ; but perhaps you will have time to tell me what you want, while they are fetching them. And, really, I am curious to know what defence you can possibly make for your treachery to Bodmilcar, under whose command, as I see by his letters, you were placed by King Hiram."

"I have but one question to ask," I said ; "and if the answer convicts me, why then you may behead me, hang me, or crucify me, as you like. Have you any documents bearing Bodmilcar's seal and signature?"

From a bag that was hanging beside him he drew out a papyrus-roll, which he opened and laid before me.

"There," he said, "is Bodmilcar's deposition, written, signed, and sealed by himself. That convicts you plainly enough, I should think."

"Just the contrary," I replied calmly ; "Bodmilcar is caught in his own trap. Here is our charter-party." And taking the deed from the hands of Hanno, I showed it to the suffect.

"Yes," I continued, "that is the indenture which sets forth the contract, and you need only glance at it to see

that Bodmilcar covenanted to sail under my command.
Why, the very seal with which he ratified his deposition
was bought with the few coins I gave him to rescue him
from starvation at Tyre! Let me ask you now, who is the
traitor?"

Adonibal perused the document carefully, and seemed
much distressed. In a few moments he rose and said:

"Mago, my friend, I have manifestly misjudged you.
Nothing could be more completely demonstrated than
Bodmilcar's faithlessness. Forgive me my too hasty conclusion. I ought to have known that neither you nor your
brave companions could ever have been guilty of such
treachery."

He went on to say that he should be interested in hearing our whole story, and that he should be only too ready
to do us justice. As I detailed the particulars of Bodmilcar's conduct, he could hardly restrain his indignation.

"By Baal-Peor of Berytos!" he said, "if ever Bodmilcar
and his crew come within reach of my clutches, they shall
all be crucified within an hour."

He then addressed himself to Hanno:

"You, sir scribe, seem to have a spirit of your own, notwithstanding your tender years."

"My lord," replied Hanno, "I should not have been so
presumptuous if Mago had not already told me how renowned you were for discrimination and for justice. I felt
that there could be nothing to fear from one who knows so
well how to unmask the truth."

"You have a sharp fellow here, Mago," said Adonibal to
me, smiling as he spoke; "but, come now, we must all
drink wine together. I have much to tell about Bodmilcar,
and presently I shall hope to see as many of your people
as you please, seated at my own table."

Thanking him for his hospitable offer, I made Hanno
write down a list of my officers, which was delivered to one
of the guards. Wine, meanwhile, had been brought in, and
Adonibal himself handed us each an ivory goblet with a

rim of Tarshish silver. While we were drinking, he observed that he took it for granted we had not come to Utica empty-handed.

"I am quite aware," he said, "that the bulk of your cargo is for King David; but I reckon that you are rather too old a sailor not to be doing a little business on your own account. What have you got to dispose of?"

I told him that I had brought some sulphur and lava-stones, articles which always used to command a ready sale in Libya.

"And so they do now," he said; "you will be sure to get a good price for them. But what else have you?"

"Well, my lord suffect, you know I have been in three little skirmishes off Ionia and Sicily. You must naturally suppose I have managed to pick up a trifle or two."

"Ha! ha!" he laughed; "you are a genuine Sidonian. Out with it, man!—how many have you got?"

"Sixty-one," I answered; "and fine sturdy fellows they are—as fine a lot as one could wish to see. Perhaps the council might like to purchase them. I would take any reasonable sum, and should prefer selling them in bulk rather than in separate parcels. I hope the republic may be induced to take them off my hands."

"Good—good, my friend," said Adonibal; "it is worth consideration. We have had some rough encounters lately with the Libyans, and must replace our soldiers. Your Hellenes may be a good investment. Under Phœnician generals they often do very well in the forts, and if they get killed, the loss is not very serious. I think I can arrange to take the lot. I can put them with a batch of Egyptians that I bought of Bodmilcar, and send them off in divisions; some into garrison, some to the works, and some to fell trees. The Egyptians are good hands at building."

"Do I understand you aright?" I asked, "have you purchased Egyptians from Bodmilcar? There seems no limit to the scoundrel's treachery. Those Egyptians were lent him by Pharaoh to go in pursuit of us. Some of their ships were wrecked off Crete."

" He sold them to me, ships and all," said the Admiralty-lord. "They made a pretty good howling at first ; but a day or two in the dungeons, and a little low diet, corrected all that, and to-day they are as quiet as lambs."

I could not help smiling as I realised the adroitness with which Bodmilcar had taken advantage of his allies.

" You may laugh ;" said Adonibal, half-amused and half-vexed ; "the rascal has bamboozled the Egyptians, and outwitted you, crafty old salt as you are. Perhaps it may entertain you to learn that he has gone off with two of my galleys and three hundred Phœnicians."

" Good Ashtoreth ! " I exclaimed ; "how has he managed that ? "

He emptied his wine-cup and went on :

" Three hundred criminals sentenced to transportation in the mother-country had been landed here. My prisons were already full, and I resolved at the first opportunity to forward them to the mines at Tarshish. Bodmilcar arrived ; I gave him the commission. I lent him two galleys, and furnished him with written credentials from myself But what did the knave do ? the curse of Khousor Phtah be on him ! he saw that they were a sturdy set, gave them their freedom, put arms in their hands, and enlisted them into his service. And now they are ready to attack you with my galleys as soon as you will give them a chance."

" No doubt," I said ; "but never mind ; I daresay we shall be a match for them."

We were interrupted by the arrival of Hannibal and the rest of my officers, who had received the suffect's invitation.

" Welcome, friends ! welcome to you all ! " he said ; " I ought to recognise some old faces. Aye, there's Hamilcar ! I remember him when he was a cabin-boy on board my ship. And here, too, here's Himilco, learned in the stars ! and if my memory fails me not, no bad judge of a good cup of Helbon. It is so still, Himilco ? "

My pilot professed that he retained his taste both for the astronomy and the wine.

"And you, Gisgo, did you ever find your ears again?"

"Aye, that I did," was the prompt reply; "and here they are, safe in my purse. And not only my own, but those of the brute who cut them off." And to the amusement of the suffect, Gisgo gave a graphic description of his splitting the skull of the Siculian chief.

Adonibal had a kind word for all my men, and promised that he would visit them on board their ships, at which he said that he had been looking from his window, and had already formed a favourable opinion of them.

Bread and meat were now laid before us; and while we were sitting at table I asked Adonibal whether amongst the Egyptians that Bodmilcar had sold him there were not some Hellenes.

"Certainly," he said; "a dozen Phocians."

"A woman and a boy?"

"Yes; both a woman and a boy; but as I had no use for them, Bodmilcar kept them; he had an eunuch to take care of them."

"You saw the eunuch, then?"

"Yes; and a great lubberly Syrian he was."

"What did he talk about?"

"Why, he seemed to say nothing except to ask how he could get from here to Tyre."

"Is he going back?"

"No; Bodmilcar has him, and I do not think he will let him go in a hurry."

When we had finished our repast, some slaves appeared with torches to attend us to our ships. We did not quit the palace the same way as we had entered, but after descending the staircase to the next lower floor of the tower, we passed through a door into the sloping gallery of what is called a "curtain;" into this the quarters of the soldiers opened, the chambers themselves being built in the thickness of the outer wall; we then passed into a vaulted hall, whence a corridor brought us to the gate of the palace adjacent to the Admiralty-basin. A private barque was waiting to convey us to our ships, where we found the sailors, who by my orders had not been allowed to leave their posts, making all manner of plans for the next day.

The trumpets on the various vessels were soon heard summoning the crews for the night, and the countless lights in every direction testified to the crowded condition of the harbour ; over these, high and bright, were the lights in the city, while in the east the flickerings from the loopholes of the Admiralty made the building look more sombre and massive than ever.

In the morning I had everything put in readiness for the admiral's promised visit, and before noon I saw his twelve-oar issuing from his private quay. As soon as he had mounted the deck of the *Ashtoreth*, he turned and glanced impatiently towards the top of the palace.

" Idiots ! " he muttered ; " how long they are ! when I was young an order was executed in half the time."

He had not finished speaking before several men appeared at the summit of one of the towers and fastened a score of heads along the battlemented parapet.

" Right at last ! " he said ; " it ought to have been done a quarter of an hour ago ! "

Finding his equanimity restored, I proceeded to show him my cargo, and had the captives brought forward for him to see. Without any haggling (for Adonibal was really a generous and large-hearted man) he agreed to pay a liberal price, alike for the sulphur, the lava, and the slaves.

He next made a complete inspection of my ships, and expressed himself much pleased with their construction and arrangements. Eager to make amends for his rough reception of us on our arrival, he promised me that I should be allowed to put my ships into a dry dock, free of dues, saying that this would give me an opportunity of examining the copper sheathing. He then gave orders for his purchases to be embarked, and for the slaves to be

properly guarded, adding that he himself was going across
the bay to settle some disputes that had arisen amongst
the Tyrians. He summoned his officers to accompany him
with their ropes and scourges, and said to me :

"Farewell, for the present, Mago; I see that your men
are all longing to get ashore. I was young myself once,
and I have not forgotten what it is to have some shekels
burning holes in your pocket."

He made a sign to his attendants, and preceded by his
scribe and officers, re-entered his boat and departed.

Having thus disposed so satisfactorily of my property,
I no longer delayed giving the men the permission that
they were anticipating, to go on shore ; and with the exception of the few who were of necessity told off to take
charge of the ships, they lost no time in availing themselves
of their liberty.

The Phocians had wrapped their dead comrade in a
winding-sheet, and proposed to carry him to a cemetery
of which one of my sailors had told them. Before they
started, I presented Aminocles, as a token of my appreciation of his services, with a couple of silver shekels. He
stared at them, quite bewildered.

"Ah !" said I, "I forgot that you barbarians do not
know anything about coined money ; but never mind—the
sailors who are going with you will show you what to do
with them. Trust them for that."

Accompanied by Hanno, Hannibal, Chamai, and Bichri,
and taking the two women. I landed on the principal
quay, Himilco and his friend Gisgo, with Hasdrubal and
Hamilcar, preferring to go in another direction. We all
had well-filled purses, and those who had never before seen
the famous city, were impatient to inspect its wonders.

Our first resort was to the temple of Ashtoreth. This
was at the basement of one of the forts that protect the
entrance to the harbour, and was at a very little distance
from the place where our ships were lying ; and as neither
Bichri, Chamai, nor Abigail wished to make any offering

ITHACA.

To face page 187.

to the goddess, they waited for us upon the quay, entertained, they said, in watching the numerous vessels going
in and out both of the Cothôn and of the trade-harbour,
of which the outer basin was visible from this point.

Being built in a fort, the construction of the temple is
necessarily very simple. Eight unornamented pillars support the roof, and, like the walls, are stuccoed with yellow
ochre ; at the further end was a recumbent figure of the
goddess, with a golden crescent on her head. From the
tariff of sacrifices which was posted up at the entrance I
made my own selection, paying the sum of five shekels ;
and having made my offering, I obtained permission from
the governor of the fort, who was an old acquaintance, to
take my party on to the terrace upon the roof, whence there
was a fine view of the city. Chamai, Bichri, and Abigail
joined us there. Looking towards the sea, we had on our
left the Cothôn and the Admiralty palace, and on our right
the island which had been the original nucleus of the
colony, and the trade-harbour which separated it from the
mainland. Landwards rose the white buildings and terraces
of the city, threaded by dark winding streets, and studded
with domes painted red and brown, and culminating towards the south in the massive citadel, the residence of the
sacred suffect. A double line of fortifications encircled the
whole city both by land and sea, and outside this a moat
and palisade, that followed the undulations of the soil,
formed a third advanced line of defence ; beyond this
again stretched the country with its rich foliage and
yellow crops, amongst which lay imbedded the snow-
white terraces and brown domes of the country-houses,
farms, and cisterns.[*]

The Cothôn at Utica, although not to be compared
with the harbours at Tyre and Sidon, is still the finest
of any that have yet been constructed in our western
settlements, and is well adapted to the climate. It is 480

---

[*] The description of Utica is from M. Daux's admirable book, ' Fouilles
executées dans le Zeugis et Byzacium.'

cubits, or nearly three-quarters of a stadium square, and is capable of holding as many as four hundred ships of war; a small dry basin is annexed to it, having a passage flanked by two lofty columns, and leading into the great harbour of the arsenal.   On three sides it is bounded by paved quays, twelve cubits wide, which are very little above the level of the water; the fourth side being formed by a strong mole.   Behind the quays rises a wall of rubble-work faced with Maltese stone, in which at regular intervals are pierced the arched openings that form the entrances to the dry docks.   The dry docks, as I had told Hannibal, are sixty in number; they are sixteen cubits high, but as they are only forty cubits long by twelve broad, they will only hold small vessels like the *Cabiros*, larger ships being sent for repairs into the basin in front of the arsenal.   The docks are covered in by a flat pavement which forms a second quay as wide as the lower one; upon this, over the docks, and partitioned symmetrically with them, stands the range of magazines and storehouses, fourteen cubits high, of which the flat roofs form a third terrace, which is on a level with the city.   The whole of these fine edifices are built upon cisterns.

On the innermost side of the harbour the lowest quay is broken in the middle by the jetty which maintains the same level, and connects the quay with that of the Admiralty; the shore end of it breaks the line of magazines, and is a wide open space, generally thronged with busy crowds; it terminates in a flight of paved steps that leads up to the second and third terraces, from the uppermost of which, through openings in the embattled wall that encloses the whole, there is direct access into the city.

The entrance to the Cothôn is defended on one side by the fortress containing the temple, and on the other by two more forts connected by a curtain, and these form the boundary of the mole.   The channel, at the mouth, is considerably encroached upon by the towing-quays, which are so broad as only to allow a passage thirty cubits in width. The outer basin of the arsenal is defended in a similar manner by two forts, one of them being at the other extremity of the mole; and other forts have been erected, one at each end of the interior side of the Cothôn, the lower storey of one of them being appropriated as another temple. A solid embattled wall starts from the mole, and after running round the arsenal and its outer basin, joins the city wall at the left-hand fort, while a corresponding wall, pierced by a lofty square opening, flanked by loop-holes, separates the basin from the arsenal. As a connoisseur in such matters, Hannibal pronounced the whole to be wonderfully well devised, and expressed his conviction that, protected as they were by their forts and by the wall that was connected with the city wall, the Cothôn and arsenal were capable of resisting the most determined assault.

The mole itself is a remarkably fine structure. It is built upon piles, and extends the whole length from the arsenal-basin to the entrance; it is no less than twenty-four cubits thick, and its massive substance of rubble is pierced by slanting apertures or air-holes, the effect of which is to rebut the waves and very materially to diminish their shock. The noble work does great credit to Adonibal, under whose supervision it was constructed.

The Admiralty palace in the centre is a handsome edifice, consisting of a main building flanked by six circular towers and four bastions. It is a large irregular parallelogram, with one of the round towers at each exterior angle, and having an open court in the middle, upon which open all the apartments of the palace, and around which runs a gallery on pillars, supporting two tiers of arches. The two other round towers are on the sides of the gateway on the north front of the palace, which opens on the naval suffect's private landing-place; there is likewise a gateway on the south front, which is protected by walls pierced with loop-holes and built into the sides of the palace. It was through this gateway that I had myself passed into the outer court-yard, and from which I had been conducted up one of the two interior towers, of which only the tops were visible from the spot where we were now standing.

After leaving the temple, I conducted my party along the quay to the open space at the end of the jetty, and then mounting the steps, we passed through the arches in the enceinte of the Cothôn, thus making our way towards the city. We passed the baths, and taking a turning to the left, wound our path upwards in the direction of the Bozrah; there, at the base of the plateau on which the citadel is built, is a large square, the common resort of the sailors; under the shadow of the trees was a number of stalls for the sale of food and drink; there was likewise music as well as amusements of various kinds; and at the farther end was a market for the disposal of wild animals, ivory, slaves, and whatever else was the produce of the interior of Libya. For many hours of the day the place is thronged by people of every rank; and musicians, acrobats, men with monkeys, dancers of both sexes, hawkers of caps and sandals, singers, vendors of cakes, fruit, and cooling drinks, all press upon the sailor fresh from his voyage, and endeavour to attract for themselves a share of the shekels which he is sure to have brought on shore. It had not been my intention to come to this spot, but early association made me almost involuntarily turn my steps in this direction.

Everybody seemed bent on pleasure, and it was not long before I saw several groups of my own men laughing, shouting, singing and pushing along in true sailor fashion, jostling their neighbours, and buying wine and other drinks from every hawker that they met.

Hannibal was breaking out into loud admiration of the life and gaiety of the place, when Hanno drew his attention to a row of heads that, by order of the sacred suffect, had been ranged along the battlements above the gate of the Bozrah. Hannibal paid but little heed to the ghastly sight, scarcely turning his eyes to look, but proceeded to rhapsodise

To face Page 238

A HUGE ELEPHANT WAS BEING LED PAST.

over the difficulty of scaling such fortifications, and to expatiate upon the impregnability of the position, until he was recalled by an exclamation of surprise made simultaneously by Bichri, Chamai, and the two women. A huge elephant was being led past by some Libyans.

"What monster have we here?" cried Hannibal, equally astonished.

"Heavens!" exclaimed Bichri; "how many arrows would it take to slay such a brute as that?"

"It must be the Behemoth, of which we have heard so much," said Chamai, gazing in amazement.

I explained to them that the animal which had so much excited their wonder was an elephant; that the great teeth projecting from its jaws were ivory; and that the rope-like appendage to its head, which it wielded so adroitly, was its trunk.

"What a line a herd of those creatures would make on a field of battle!" said Hannibal, his thoughts turning as usual to military tactics; "I cannot imagine how any infantry could hold their ground against them; the only thing would be to open their ranks, let the brutes pass through, and then attack them from behind."

"You are not the first soldier, Hannibal," I answered, "who has had the same idea. Some of these animals have already been tamed, and trained to carry on their backs a tower full of archers. They are brought from the banks of the Upper Bagradas, and from the forests in the borders of Tritonis, a lake in the interior of Libya."

Besides the elephant, we saw a hippopotamus, or river horse, and a couple of rhinoceroses, with their big horns. The whole of these were a portion of the tribute (consisting of ivory, tame elephants, and other animals), which had been imposed by the sacred suffect upon the subjugated Libyans on the Bagradas, and which happened now to be on its transit to the Bozrah.

A well-known voice, harsh and sonorous, at this instant caught my ear, and turning round, I saw Jonah towering head and shoulders above the crowd, and encircled by a group of my sailors, all in roars of laughter.

"Now, at last," the trumpeter was saying, "I am where I wanted to be! Now I am in the land of strange beasts! This is the first animal I ever saw in my life with two tails, one behind and one at the end of his nose! I wonder how many onions it would take to season the carcase of such a brute as that! I wonder, too, how long it would take a fellow to eat it!"

Leaving the sailors to their diversions, we bent our steps towards the market, where red-skinned Libyans, with aquiline noses and long plaited hair, were being offered for sale. Entering a tent where provisions of all kinds were sold, I ordered some refreshments for myself and my party, and a Syrian slave, who was serving instead of the owner, brought us two guinea-fowls, some stewed beans and onions, some olives, bread, and very fair Helbon wine. Hannibal seated himself near the stove to feast his eyes upon the wheat-and-honey cakes that were being fried upon the top.

We had not long been in the refreshment-booth before Himilco and Gisgo made their appearance; they were followed by a dancing-girl and three other girls, one playing the flute, and two the tambourine. The dancing-girl was one of the western Moors; she had a copper-coloured complexion, and her hair twisted in coils like so many serpents; her nails and eyebrows were dyed red; her face was tattooed with three parallel stripes in regular Mahouârin fashion; and on her wrists and ankles she wore rattles that clanked again as she moved. The flute-player was a native of Barbary, with a fair skin and light hair, parted over a high, narrow forehead. Both girls were dressed alike in gay skirts, open as high as the knees; in their hair they had bodkins, of which the heads were grotesque figures; their necklaces and girdles were of glass and enamel; and their earrings were great crosses. The tambourine-players were inconceivably ugly; one of them appeared to belong to the Rasennæ, and the other had her face so daubed with red and blue paint, and made such hideous grimaces, that it was idle to speculate upon her nationality.

Himilco was in high spirits ; he came up to me and said that he and Gisgo had been spending the morning in going from tavern to tavern, and that they had engaged the orchestra, which we now saw, to accompany them for the day wherever they went, and to entertain them while they regaled themselves.

" Poor girls ! " said Abigail ; " are they obliged to perform for all the sailors alike ? "

" No, indeed," I replied ; " they take good care never to perform unless they are well paid, and I suppose there is not much hardship in that."

The Libyan had now commenced her performance. We stayed for a few minutes watching her contortions, and then left the tent.

The first person we met in the square was Hamilcar, carrying a monkey.

" Hamilcar with a monkey ! " cried Hannibal. " Where did you get it ? The very thing I want myself. I want to teach it to fight."

" I should like to have a monkey," said Hanno ; " I would teach it to dance."

Bichri said he was sure he could make it learn the use of the bow ; and Chamai declared it would be capital fun to teach it to make grimaces, and to mimic the mighty Jonah.

On all hands it was agreed that we must have a monkey on board the *Ashtoreth.*

Hamilcar told them that they would have to go down towards the trade-harbour, through the square where the rich merchant Hamoun resides ; and at the corner of the street which leads to the temple of Moloch they would find a dealer who had a whole cargo to dispose of.

" You will have a choice there," he said ; " there are apes of all sorts, all sizes, and all colours. You may have them

O

brown, or red, or grey, or black, or green; with tails or with-out tails; with long hair, short hair, or no hair; wild or tame; only ask for what you want, and you will be sure to get it."

On our way down towards the trade-harbour we met Aminocles, quite drunk. He was being dragged along by a couple of sailors, singing at the top of their voices. He had learnt only too soon what was the use, or abuse, of the silver shekels.

We had no trouble in finding the monkey-dealer's, and Hanno, who had taken it upon himself to select the most intelligent monkey he could see, chose one which appeared to meet with general approval.

"And now what are we to call it?" said Hannibal, who liked everything to have a name.

"Don't you think," said Hanno, "that it has a very striking resemblance to old Gebal, the judge at Sidon? Look at it now. Isn't it like him when he rolls his eyes and scratches his poll, just before giving sentence?"

"Exactly!" said Hannibal, "the very facsimile! and Judge Gebal he shall be called!"

We now made our way with our new purchase down to the quay, whence a small boat carried us across the trade-harbour to the opposite island, on which are built the hand-some residences of the more wealthy inhabitants of the city; for during the last ten years many of the merchants have amassed considerable fortunes, and abandoning sea-life, have settled down in homes replete with luxury. We walked to the extremity of the island, and after leaving the two women at the noble bath-room at the top of the wall above the small basin in which the pleasure-boats of the rich inhabitants are kept, we betook ourselves to the men's baths, and enjoyed the refreshment of a wash and a shave. Rejoined by the women, we rowed across to the nearest point of the Cothôn, and paid a visit to the signal-tower; thence we went on foot to the magnificent gardens that lie between the citadel and the lower town. Here I

showed my party the temple of Achmon, and took them to
see the public fountains, the constant resort of both sexes
for lounging and gossip.

Night coming on, we returned to the *Ashtoreth*, on which
the lamps were already lighted.   Going on board, I found
the slave of the man who had entertained me during my
former visit to Utica waiting for me with an invitation
from his master to dine with him next day, and I sent
a message that we should be pleased to avail ourselves
of his hospitality.   During our day's absence my cook had
prepared a sumptuous repast, which we all thoroughly
enjoyed.

The trumpets now sounded the signal for calling in the
sailors.   They came dropping in two or three at a time,
all more or less tipsy, and some of them inclined to be
noisy ; but so strong was their habit of submission to discipline, that no sooner had they stepped on board than they
relapsed into their wonted silence, and retired quietly to
their berths.   Himilco was among the last to return, and
to his credit I feel bound to record that he was quite able
to walk across the deck without any assistance from his
friend Gisgo.

CHAPTER XII.

I CONSULT THE ORACLE.

I MADE it my first business on the following morning to go to the great market-place, near the trade-harbour and the temple of Achmon. It is surrounded by lofty houses upon an arcade, under which are the retail shops of the tradespeople, their warehouses being in courts at the back. In these shops every variety of Libyan merchandise was exhibited for sale. There were hides, dressed and undressed; stones prepared for engraving; Numidian copper; lion-skins from Mount Atlas; thongs of hippopotamus-hide from Lake Tritonis; elephants' tusks from the Macar; corn from Zeugis and Byzatium, and wool from the land of the Garamantines. I spent a considerable time in making purchases of ivory, and procured a good supply at a very fair price; and later in the day went with Hannibal and Hamilcar to fulfil the engagement I had made on the previous night. Hanno and Chamai preferred escorting Chryseis and Abigail about the city; and Bichri went for an evening's diversion with Gisgo, Hasdrubal, and Himilco.

Barca, our host, one of the richest shipowners in the colony, had prepared us an elegant entertainment in a handsome tent pitched upon the terrace of his house. As soon as the meal was ended, wine was brought in, and musicians and dancing-girls performed for our amusement; and one of Barca's slaves, an old Libyan, who was well versed in the songs and traditions of his people, repeated his tales about the mystery and wonders of their origin.

According to his account, there had formerly, south of Libya, been an extensive sea, which received the water of several rivers, and to the south of which again lay the land of the negroes, who had faces like monkeys. This sea was the original Lake Tritonis, or Pallas, and the chain of lakes, at the foot of the Atlas Mountains, extending from the vicinity of Gades to Karth,[1] in Byzatium (now known to us as the Tritons), are either marshes formed by the overflow of two great rivers from the south, whose waters have been diverted by Mount Atlas, or, when salt, are probably the remains of the same great sea. There are then, he represented, two mountainous ridges, the more southernly of which outpours its streams as far as the Tritonis and Mount Atlas, and the other sends its rivers, the Macar and the Bagradas, into our own Great Sea. Further west, issuing also from Mount Atlas, are other important rivers, which lose themselves in the sands. These, however, long centuries back, had an outlet into the inland branch of the great Atlantic Ocean, which, at that remote period, was the southern boundary of Libya, and extending eastwards towards the confines of Egypt, ultimately joined the Syrtes. Libya was thus a great peninsula, connected with the mainland only by a narrow isthmus, now the Straits of Gades, and enclosed on every other coast by water; on the north and east by the Syrtes, by which it was separated from Egypt; on the south by the inland sea that covered the present sandy desert; and on the west by the ocean itself.

But as time went on great changes were evolved. His face beaming with intelligence as he spoke, the old man told of mighty convulsions of the earth, and how they changed the isthmus of Gades into a strait, and how the waters were swept back by the shock, so that the whole flood of the ocean rushed through to the Great Sea, and the Great Sea receded and yielded to the upheaving of the land.

[1] Karth, the town; later Cirtha, the actual Constantine.

I listened with increasing interest. I knew already how the sea could overwhelm the land. I was also aware how the Siculians maintain that long ages back a neck of solid land had joined their country to the continent of the Vitalians. Many times, too, I had heard amongst Phœnicians how a deluge had detached the isle of Chittim from the mainland. And now I was hearing the wondrous tale of how the sea had retreated from the south of Libya.

He went on to say that when the waters rolled away they submerged an immense number of islands, leaving the Fortunate Islands[1] (of which I shall have to speak hereafter) as the sole representatives of what had previously been a vast archipelago, that had made communication easy, even in small boats, not only with the land of the Atlantides, but with that other great country that lies still further to the west. Now, however, that Atlantis has disappeared, all intercourse has been dropped with that remote land, from which both the red and white Libyans assert that they originally came, and whence migrating eastwards they founded cities as they advanced, became the first settlers in Egypt, and spread far and wide the knowledge of their gods, which were really the Dionysus and Minerva of the Hellenes and Vitalians, and Zeus, known among us Phœnicians as Baal-Hamon. According to their own account (which is confirmed by the Hellenes), the Pelasgians, under the leadership of Melkarth-Ouso, came into Libya, but afterwards retreated to the east. Then came the great convulsion when the land was upheaved and the waters receded, and the earth subsided into its present configuration ; then, too, the Sidonians, protected by their gods, began to assert their sovereignty on the sea, and sending forth ships to every region of the world, opened emporiums of commerce, discovered mines, founded cities, taught the art of writing, and disseminated knowledge of every kind.

[1] The Canaries.

More and more as the aged Libyan recited his ancient legends had we become rapt in attention. Hannibal sat with his eyes wide open, and from time to time gave vent to ejaculations of astonishment; and I, though less surprised, for I had already speculated very much on these matters, was nevertheless deeply impressed with the clearness with which they had been laid before us. I retired that night with my brain agitated by excitement, and dreamed that I was commanding a magnificent fleet, and that we discovered the land beyond Atlantis; and when I woke in the morning, I made a vow in my mind that no sooner should my present expedition to Tarshish be completed, than I would set out on a voyage of discovery to the west.

We had been in Utica three days when Adonibal sent me a message that he wished to speak to me. Without loss of time I presented myself at the palace, and was conducted to the apartment from which the admiral can at once overlook the city, the harbour, and the sea. To his enquiry how long it would be before I took my departure, I replied that having taken in my cargo I hoped to sail in two days.

" Here, then," he said, " are letters for the suffects of Rusadir and Gades; and I intend to give you ten seamen to supply the places of those you have lost. I am sure there ought not to be any deficiency in your numbers in the event of your coming into collision with Bodmilcar."

I was proceeding to thank him for his liberality, but he stopped me, and said that he should have to trouble me for fifty shekels that I owed him.

I professed myself quite ready to pay anything that was due, but said that I was very much amazed to learn that I was in his debt.

" It is a mere trifle," said Adonibal, in his usual facetious way; " it will not ruin you. I should not mention it at all, only you know it is a matter of principle with a true

Phœnician to keep his accounts straight. The truth is, it is a little fine. Some of your men have been half-killing a couple of my Ligurians. The knaves are down in the dungeon sleeping off the effects of their drinking-bout ; but just pay their fines, and I will give you an order for their release, and, if you like, you may go yourself and fetch them out."

"Ah," said I, laughing, "you wanted to show off the efficiency of your police."

I could not help asking him whether the circumstance did not remind him of the time when I was his helmsman, and he had himself come to liberate me from the prison in Chittim, where I had been locked up for smashing the skull of the grand merchant from Seir.

"You mean when I was captain of the *Achmon*—and a noble ship she was," said Adonibal. "Yes, to be sure—I remember it perfectly : we were both of us younger then than we are now. When I was a youngster I was always getting into scrapes as often as I went on shore with a purse-full of money ; now I am only a poor hulk, dismasted and stranded here on the shore. Such is life ! while we are young we entertain ourselves with breaking each other's heads, and when we are old we busy ourselves with cutting them off."

"But, seriously, how have my men been committing themselves ?" I asked.

"As far as I understand the matter," replied the suffect, "they took it into their heads to play pranks with one of the priests of Dionysos ; they treated him to some wine, made him perfectly tipsy, smeared his face all over with red and blue paint, and then insisted upon making him dance. Some of my Ligurian soldiers, seeing what was going on, tried to protect the priest—an interference that your men were not in the mood to allow. They had tripped up two of the soldiers, when the Admiralty-guard came to the rescue, and quietly walked off four of your drunken fellows to me. I sent them to the dungeon, but I have not had them flogged ; I am generally as indulgent as possible in the case of a sailor's spree. I am an admiral now, and old in the service, but I do not forget that I was once a young pilot."

The subterranean vaults to which I now descended were very dark : most of them were used as armouries or store-houses, but a few were set apart for prisons. The turnkey opened the door of one of these, and by the light of his torch I could distinguish Bichri and three of my sailors, all looking very sheepish, and I had some difficulty in repressing my inclination to laugh. However, I assumed a serious air, gave them a severe reprimand, and sent them out with a notice that they were not to quit their ships. They did not wait for any second bidding to be off ; the Admiralty dungeons are no enviable quarters, and those who find their way into them rarely leave except for the cross or the gallows.

Returning to the quay, I passed along the subterranean passage to the arsenal, and spent the remainder of the day in directing the repairs of my ships. By the evening everything was finished ; and I was so gratified by the rapidity with which the work had been done, that in my good humour I not only forgave my four men who were in disgrace, but allowed them, on promise of good behaviour, to have another holiday on the following day.

For myself, I resolved to spend that day in an expedition to a small temple of Baal-Hamon, a short distance from the city, and to take with me no companion whatever except my friend Barca's old Libyan slave.

This temple is situated in the gloomy recesses of a forest ; it is oblong in shape, and has neither door nor window ; its only external aperture is a hole in the roof to allow an escape for the smoke of the sacrifices ; and it is entered by an underground passage, the mouth of which is closed by a large stone concealed by the brushwood. Three old and half-naked Libyans were waiting outside, and after a brief consultation, in whispers, with the slave I had brought with me, quietly raised the stone and pointed to the orifice. I entered the passage, followed by the men, and in a short time found myself in a small dim chamber, in the further wall of which was a flat stone, which turned on a hinge and formed a door, just affording room to pass, and opening into a second chamber, that was at once misty and red with the glare of two smoking lamps. Let into the wall of this compartment was another flat stone with a hole in its centre, which one of the men turned slightly round upon its pivot, allowing me to peep into a third chamber, which was a mere cell, containing a niche, where a shapeless notched stone was deposited, which my guide informed me was the god himself. In obedience to the directions that were given me, I prostrated myself three times before the deity, and remained waiting where I was. After a time, a black sheep that I had brought with me was conducted into the cell, and slaughtered before the niche in such a way that its blood flowed into a hollowed stone let into the ground to receive it. When the sacrifice was finished, the stone was turned back, shutting the god with his newly-slain victim into the inner cell. I was told to apply my ear to the hole in the stone, and to listen for the voice of the deity. The lamps were then extinguished, and I was left in silence and in total darkness.

Presently a deep muffled voice, that seemed to issue from the abysses of the earth, came to my ear :

"Phœnician mariner, what wouldst thou ask of me ?"

Awestruck, I could scarcely speak, but making an effort to reply, I said :

"Oracle of Hamon! I would know whether it be possible to sail westward beyond the Straits of Gades, and whether there is land."

"There is land," the voice repeated.

"Is it to be found north, west, or south ?" I inquired.

"There is land to the north, there is land to the west there is land to the south," the oracle replied.

I PROSTRATED MYSELF THREE TIMES.

Emboldened by the answers I obtained, I asked again :

"And the proper route—is it by the sacred promontory, or must I sight the head of Gades ?"

"Mortal !" the voice declared, "you ask more than it is permitted mortal to know. Go ; I tell no more."

The stone doorway turned on its hinge, and we groped our way back through the gloom out into the open air. I recompensed the attendants liberally, and returned to the city—perplexed, it is true, but confirmed in my resolution to explore the ocean and seek for land, far or near, beyond the Straits of Gades.

In the course of our walk back, I inquired of my companion whether there were many of these subterranean temples in Zeugis and Byzatium. He told me that in the interior there were several very much more elaborate, with arches and domes, but they were not nearly so ancient ; the true temples of the Atlantides were all like the one which we had just left. Some there were, indeed, that were still more simple, consisting only of three stones, flat and unhewn, of which two were placed upright on their ends, and the third laid horizontally across them ; others were formed of stones arranged in a long covered avenue. Of these, some were in the open air and some concealed under mounds of earth, at the top of which several stones were reared, while round the base circles of still larger stones were grouped symmetrically. No doubt some of these erections were not temples, but tombs, and were occasionally found in such numbers as to cover a large extent of ground, and were laid out in set figures, representing men, serpents, eggs, and scorpions.

Such was the Libyan's account of his religious edifices. When, however, I began to question him about their signification, and why some were underground and some above, and what was the design of their peculiar construction, I could elicit nothing from him but that it was the result of magic, of which his people had inherited the great secret from their forefathers.

Early the following morning, with the suffect's permission, I set to work to take in a supply of fresh water
from the fine cisterns on the quays.   Each cistern is
divided into two compartments ; one to collect the rain-
water in its turbid condition from the paved streets, the
other to receive the same water when it has undergone
the process of filtration; the two tanks being connected
by square-headed cocks turned by a wooden key.   All
the private houses, as well as the public buildings, in the
towns, are provided with cisterns of a similar construction,
the country villages being supplied with water from open
tanks formed by two circular compartments, of which one
acts as a receptacle and the other as a reservoir.

Hannibal, who had been paying a visit to the ramparts,
returned highly gratified with what he had seen.   He informed me that all the forts were built upon cisterns, and
that the rubble-work of the walls was twenty-four cubits
thick at their base, and eighteen at their top ; that the
soldiers' quarters were on the second and third storeys,
out of the reach of the battering rams, and built in the
thickness of the walls ; also that about three-quarters of a
bowshot in advance of the inner line there was a wall half
the height, and outside this again a strong palisade, with a
moat and intrenchment.   He thought, however, that his
eye had been keen enough to discover one weak point to
the right of the city, where the arsenal was overlooked
by an adjacent hill, and I concurred in his opinion that
another fort ought to be built upon the wall to cover any
attack from the eminence.

The sundial on the Admiralty palace marked the hour of
noon when, having made my roll-call, and satisfied myself
that my men were all on board, I went to take leave of
Adonibal.   The aged suffect bade me a kind farewell, and
wished me a prosperous voyage.   I lost no time in giving
the signal for departure, and as we left the harbour we
raised a hearty cheer for the admiral, who was watching us
from his balcony.   Four other vessels, heavily freighted

and bound for Massalia, at the mouth of the Rhone, left
Utica immediately after us.

The distance from Utica to the Straits of Gades is 8800
stadia, and by fast vessels can be accomplished in about a
week.   A strong west wind, however, had made the sea so
turbulent that all navigation was very difficult, and it was
not until after four days that we sighted the **Cabiri** (or the
Seven Capes), a point which is usually reached in two ;
and even then, in order to clear the promontory, we were
obliged to make such long tacks that we quite lost sight

of land, and were carried far towards the north.   But at
length, on the seventh day, I recognised the first great
cape[1] on the mainland, south of the Pityusai Islands.

" Tarshish !" shouted Himilco, who had been so fully
occupied that he had scarcely spoken before.   " Tarshish at
last ! "

There was a rush to the deck ; but so blinding were the
rain and the spray, that it was impossible to distinguish
anything on shore.

[1] Now Cape Palos.

I had taken in enough water to last us for a fortnight, and it was well that I had done so, for we found ourselves experiencing the difficulty, not at all infrequent, of approaching this dangerous coast, and had to continue to make very long tacks.

After three days' perpetual struggle with the elements we were still off the Libyan coast, but the wind then moderated, and the rain gave place to sunshine. In the course of the next night Himilco and I, whilst well-nigh every one was asleep, recognised the tall perpendicular peaks of Calpe and Abyla, and soon afterwards we passed under the wall of rock that forms the southern limit of Tarshish; by the morning we were within sight of the level tongue of land south of the magnificent bay of Gades All along the headland rose the white domes and terraces of the town, imbedded in luxuriant foliage; high above all was the semaphore beside the temple of Ashtoreth. As we entered the basin of what serves equally for trade-harbour and war-port, our trumpets were sounded, and we saluted the town with three ringing cheers.

We had reached our goal, and were in Tarshish at last.

CHAPTER XIII.

THE SILVER MINES OF TARSHISH.

THE town of Gades, though not large, is neat and trimly
built, and in the well-kept gardens in the environs, pomegranates, oranges, and lemons, which have all been introduced by the Phœnicians, flourish in great abundance.
About the centre of the town, and in direct communication
with the harbour, is the market, the emporium not only for
the wedges of silver brought from the mines in the interior,
but for barrels of the salted murenæ that are caught on the
neighbouring shore ; for Tarshish cats,[1] to be used in rabbit-
hunting ; for iron, which is obtained in small quantities
from the north ; and for the promiscuous curiosities in which
the strange and remote region abounds. The market-place
is surrounded by the offices of the rich merchants and
money-changers, who, as proprietors of the mines, were
ready to exchange their silver for copper, manufactured
articles, and fancy goods. I was not long in making my
way thither.

Having seen my ships properly moored in the places
assigned them at the quay, handed their pay to my seamen
and soldiers, and notified my arrival to the naval suffect, I
turned into the thoroughfare that leads to the town, and had
no difficulty in finding the office of Balshazzar, the rich
merchant with whom I had had many business transactions
during my previous visit. Balshazzar was dead, but Ziba,
his widow, was carrying on the business in partnership with

[1] The ancient name of ferrets.

several other merchants. She received me very cordially, and insisted that I should send for the two women, and for my sub-captains and pilots, to come and take refreshment at her house. She provided a handsome entertainment, during which I had the opportunity of explaining to her the object of my voyage, and of asking her advice as to the best means of obtaining silver, either in lumps or ingots. I found that, according to her statement, the current price of silver was just then very low, so that I might hope to purchase on favourable terms, either in the town, or by going inland and bartering with the savages. Some large mines, she informed me, had quite recently been discovered on the River Bœtis,[1] about four days' march up the country, and the only reason why they had not been opened and worked was the scarcity of labour ; the great bulk of the population of the town being either merchants or mariners.

"We ought," she concluded, "to have plenty of soldiers stationed here."

"Beyond a question," exclaimed Hannibal, warmly, "the prosperity of a country is to be measured by the number of soldiers it maintains."

Ziba's long residence in the colonies had rendered her quite unaccustomed to the ideas and manners of military men, and she looked at him in some amazement.

"Yes," she said, "we do require a large number of slaves, soldiers, and transported felons here."

It was now Hannibal's turn to look amazed.

"Soldiers and felons ! What do you mean ? Do you suppose that soldiers are to be associated with slaves and malefactors ?"

In explanation of her remark, she said that in order to establish a firm footing in the silver-producing districts, she thought that the merchants ought to club together, and either buy or hire soldiers to drive back the native barbarians. The prisoners they took ought to be sent to the mines, and to these there should be added as many slaves as could

---

[1] The Guadalquivir.

be bought, and any number of transported criminals who would cost nothing but their keep.

Seeing that Hannibal was about to make some indignant rejoinder, I interposed by asking her whether it was possible to obtain slaves here, and whether the natives were hostile or well-disposed.

"Not a slave will you find in the market," she said; "they have been purchased as fast as they have been brought to us. As to the savages, they have hitherto been tolerably peaceable; but, aware of the value we set upon their silver, they demand most exorbitant wages for their labour."

"Peaceable you call them, do you?" broke in Himilco; and pointing to the empty socket of his eye, said, "Yes; perhaps if using their lances to scoop out people's eyes is a proof of peaceableness, the Iberians of Tarshish are supremely peaceable; but I confess I don't quite see it."

Ziba smiled. Although she was a thorough woman of business, she had a keen appreciation of a joke.

"Yes, pilot," she replied; "I very well recollect your misfortune when you were here before; indeed, it was I myself who dressed your wounds with oil and rosemary. But you may take my word for it that the tribes on the Bœtis are far more anxious to take your goods than to do you any bodily injury. In time, I have no doubt, they will become perfectly submissive to our rule."

"And then," I exclaimed, "Tarshish, like Zeugis, will be one of the brightest jewels in the crown of our glorious Sidon."

And every one, as I spoke, filled and drained his wine-cup to the honour of our noble city.

"But to return to business," said Ziba; "I think that the best plan for you will be to come with me to the naval suffect, who may probably suggest some plan by which you can get labour to open some fresh mines. The Bœtis is quite wide enough to allow your ships to ascend within a day's march of the best districts, and your soldiers and

P

sailors ought to be quite enough to protect you from any
hostilities on the part of the Iberians."

I readily acquiesced in her proposal; and the widow,
having put on a veil, mounted a richly-caparisoned mule
led by two well-dressed slaves, and preceded by a running
footman carrying a long staff.   She went in front, and we
all sallied forth after her to the Admiralty palace.   The
suffect received us in the large hall, where he was seated in
his painted chair; and when I had explained the object of
my visit, he said:

"Had you come four days sooner, you might have
arranged to accompany a Tyrian merchant who passed
through this port on his way to the mines."

The suspicion flashed instantly on my mind, and I said .
"You mean Bodmilcar?"

"Yes," replied the suffect, "Bodmilcar; and a rare
rough-looking set he had with him.   We are not generally
very particular in looking into the character of men who
go to the diggings, but I confess I never set eyes upon a
worse-looking lot.   They looked like thieves and assassins."

"Just what they were," I said; "and their leader is no better than themselves. You have only to read this, and you will learn what he really is;" and I handed him Adonibal's letter.

"By Ashtoreth!" he swore, "what a scoundrel the fellow is!"

After pondering a few minutes, he continued:

"I will tell you what I can do. I will lend you fifty armed men to help you to improve the villain off the face of the earth. I would, if I could, lend you more, as I know how advisable it is for expeditions into the interior to be well guarded; all kinds of people are at work in the mines, and nothing is easier for them than to conspire to overpower a new comer. But I really cannot spare any more. The time will come, I hope, when we shall have reinforcements enough here to make our authority properly felt in the mining districts."

Ziba now mentioned that she had made a contract with one of the Iberian chiefs, named Aitz, by which he had engaged to find porters and labourers to assist the twelve hundred slaves which she had provided to excavate the soil of a new mine; and having explained that she had erected a fortress in which were stationed a hundred soldiers, and put up a residence for an overseer of the works, she said that she was perfectly willing to hand over the contract to me under certain conditions. She was ready to surrender her sole interest, to give me an introduction to her overseer, and to allow me the protection of her little garrison, if I would stipulate to pay her a fifth part of the gross profits.

The suffect seemed to think that the proposal was reasonable; but I demurred to the proportion of the profits which she demanded, and insisted upon her accepting a sixth instead of a fifth.

After a short debate, which ended in Ziba's yielding to my terms, I made Hanno draw out two copies of the agreement which we mutually signed, and then all adjourned to the temple of Ashtoreth, where we offered a sacrifice to the goddess, and made a vow to remain faithful to the various covenants of the contract.

The time of the year was very favourable, and I was anxious to lose no time in starting. Accordingly, four days did not elapse after our arrival at Gades before our ships were again on the sea, making way towards the mouth of the Bœtis, which we reached after two days' easy sailing.

Beyond the Straits of Gades the sea is subject to tides which are even more considerable than those in the Jam Souph, and it was necessary to wait until high-water before we could pass the bar of the river. As soon, however, as the bar was passable, the river presented a very animated scene, and vessels of every description got into motion, both ascending and descending the stream; Phœnician craft, from the ponderous gaoul to the slim fishing-smack; Iberian piroques, carrying their great brown or black sails of woven bark; and the long Celtic coracles, composed of hide. Of all these, none were empty; whatever provisions are consumed in the mining regions have all to be brought from Gades, and the same ships that convey the supplies into the interior always return laden with the ore.

Having crossed the bar, as there was no wind and the current was strong, I lowered my sails and rowed up the river. The yellow waters of the river flow rapidly between banks that are sometimes wooded and sometimes barren flats. The country on both sides is mountainous and wild, and only at long intervals are to be seen any of the Iberian villages, which, consisting of hovels made of mud and branches of trees, are most frequently nothing more than roofs to holes which have been dug in the ground. The miners' villages are very similar, the chief difference being that the huts are higher and more commodious, and in the centre of each community there is a palisade enclosing a redoubt, or embattled fortress built of brick.

"Not particularly lively here," said Hanno; "the getting of silver seems rather a more dreary business than the spending of it."

Hannibal remarked that all the villages seemed to occupy positions that were naturally very strong, observing that the Bœtis itself formed a good line of defence, and that there might be a great deal of hard fighting in such a country.

"I can answer for that," said Himilco; "I know that these Tarshish barbarians would sooner pluck out a man's eye than give him a cup of wine. Here come some of the rascals. Look at them."

Every one looked where Himilco was pointing, and there, walking, or rather shambling, along the bank were rather more than a score of savage-looking creatures evidently watching our ships. They were almost naked, their only covering being a strip of woven bark around their loins, and a sort of turban of the same material on their heads; they had sunburnt skins, black hair, and small black eyes, obliquely set; they were of moderate height, and appeared to be extremely agile. But we observed that some of them seemed to be quite of a distinct race, being very tall and thin, with thick shaggy beards and very revolting countenances. All were armed with long shields, and carried either bludgeons, slings, or strong lances pointed with flint or bone.

I shouted to them, but they made no sign, and continued skulking along the bank.

"Bichri!" cried Himilco, to the archer, who was sitting on the poop with Jonah, both of them playing with the monkey, "Bichri, just put an arrow into one of those scaramouches, will you? they pretend they cannot hear the captain."

He started to his feet, and was in the act of raising his bow, when I interposed:

"Leave them alone; time enough to attack them when they attack us."

Bichri lowered his hand at once.

"Well then," he said, "I may as well go on amusing myself with the monkey; what an entertaining brute it is! he pulls my hair and scratches my face a bit; but I bear it all because he's so clever."

"Aye, aye, go back to your plaything; he's about as good-looking as the Iberians," said Hanno, laughing.

My brave young archer was not much more than eighteen years of age, and in light-heartedness and love of frolic was like a boy of twelve. The monkey, the only creature on board more restless than himself, had taken his fancy immensely, and they were continually vying with one another in feats of agility, trying which could climb the mast the faster, or which could swing the higher at the end of a rope. Another of Judge Gebal's warm admirers was Jonah. The giant seemed to have lost his concern about the land of strange beasts, and to be engrossed with the monkey, which he had admitted into his close friendship, and whose antics he was always rewarding with the choicest tit-bits on which he could lay hands. One of the creature's great delights was to mount the trumpeter's shoulder and clamber by his shaggy hair to the top of his head, where from its elevated perch it would make grimaces, scratch its pate, and grin and gnash its teeth at every one. Bichri, Jonah, and the monkey, thus formed an amicable trio, of which a little rough treatment all round, and a few cuffs and scratches, did not mar the general concord.

Towards evening by my orders we came to a standstill, opposite a miners' village. The overseer came out from his hut to speak to us. He was a coarse, ill-spoken man, rarely opening his mouth without an oath. He was a native of Arvad, and consequently an old acquaintance of Hannibal's.

"By all the infernal gods!" he began, "this is a week of visitors!"

"How so?" I asked.

"Confound me, if we hadn't another Tyrian here five days ago! Bodmilcar was his name; and a rascally set of scamps he brought. Drunken beasts they were; they sacked some houses in the village here, and, by Khousor Phtah! I vow they would have murdered us every one if we had not pounced upon them pretty hard. I have seen blackguards in my time, but never the like of those. And if any one can succeed in swinging up Bodmilcar himself at a rope's end, he will do the world a service."

"Where is he now?" I asked; "can you tell me that? I have a score of my own to settle with him."

"By the gods! you will have some distance to go. He has taken a swarm of Iberians with him into the interior. You had better be careful how you meddle with them: they are dangerous folks to touch; and they are a pretty strong force altogether."

"Never mind their force," said Chamai; "numbers don't matter; only let us get them within reach of our swords."

"All very fine for you, young fellow, to be so cocksure of your game," replied the overseer; and turning to me, he added, civilly enough: "But I see you are determined to risk the consequences. Give me a drink of wine, and by the gods! I will give you some hints that may be useful to you. Silver is silver, you know."

"Yes, and wine is wine," muttered Himilco, always keenly interested upon that topic.

I ordered a skin of good wine to be produced, that he might drink while we talked over our scheme; but the overseer had no wish to be outdone on the score of hospitality; and accordingly he clapped his hands sharply, and when the manager of his slaves appeared in answer to the summons, he gave instructions for one of his finest calves to be killed, and a feast to be laid out for us under an adjacent clump of trees.

After we had given each other the latest news of Phœnicia and Tarshish, the overseer said in his own abrupt way:

"You seem brave enough; but I have a great respect for numbers. Your wine is good stuff, and I like it. I am glad to meet a fellow-townsman. Now, in return for the wine, curse me if I don't do the best I can to help you."

After all, he had not much to tell. He informed us that in the territory adjacent to that of Aitz, who had made his compact with Ziba, there were some exceedingly rich veins of silver; and that, although the Iberians in possession were decidedly disposed to be hostile, they might readily be bought over by some trumpery merchandise, or without difficulty might be subdued by our arms.

"And how near to them can we take our ships?" I asked.

"Within three days' march," he answered. "It is not so much that the distance is great as that there are no roads; and after the ships are left there is no further communication with the river. You have to go through forests, and you have to go on foot. No horses can go; no mules."

"Nice marching that!" said Hannibal, sententiously; "and you say we have to take our own provisions?"

"As to that, I daresay you can get Ziba's overseer to lend you some Iberians; they make capital beasts of burden."

"Very good," said Himilco; "and I think I can undertake to make them trot along at a good pace. Give me a stick, and I will write a few words of their Iberian tongue upon their backs in a way they will perhaps remember."

The overseer seemed to enjoy Himilco's spiteful jest, for he laughed aloud. We emptied our wine-cups, and broke up our meeting.

Betimes next morning we were again on our voyage up the river, and in less than a day had reached Ziba's territory. Her overseer, a native of Utica, lent me two hundred slaves as porters and miners, and I divided them into gangs, which I put under the supervision of my officers. The ships, with just a sufficient portion of their crews, were left under the charge of Hasdrubal; the *Dagon* and the *Ashtoreth* descending the river for a short distance to get a better anchorage ; the *Cabiros*, as drawing less water, being left under orders to cruise about, and to keep on collecting a supply of provisions. We had been provided with a guide ; and everything being arranged, I set out upon my exploration of the new territory.

We started across an extensive plateau, and having traversed several woods and deep ravines, made our encampment for the night. Very monotonous were the journeys of the following days, over gloomy hills and across deep valleys, and it was not until the middle of the fourth day after leaving the banks of the Bœtis, that we caught sight of an Iberian village. The people were all under arms when we arrived, and inclined to take a defiant attitude, but a few presents had the effect of conciliating the chiefs, and inducing them to give us permission to encamp on a barren knoll, about three stadia off their cluster of huts. Under Hannibal's superintendence we surrounded the encampment with a trench and a palisade, and in two days were ready to commence our digging operations, in which we were directed by an experienced man, who had been sent with us for the purpose.

We were beginning an arduous task. For three long months did our labours proceed without intermission. The Iberians were always distrustful, but never committed any overt act of hostility. Yet, thanks to the favour of Ashtoreth, though our work was long, our success was great. Excavation after excavation turned out prolific, and as the result of our mining, I obtained no less than two thousand shekels of silver. Some of this I refined on the spot, and retained in my own keeping, the rest of the ore being periodically despatched by hired slaves to the *Ashtoreth*, whence I received back a written acknowledgment of each consignment as it was delivered on board.

At length I felt it was time to re-organise my caravan to return ; and under the direction of an Iberian guide, over whom a strict surveillance was kept, we set out upon our

way back to the ships, rejoicing to quit the desolation in
which we had been sojourning so long.

No sooner were our backs turned upon the encampment
than the Iberians rushed towards it, tore down the palisade,
and scrambled furiously for any article, however worthless,
that we happened to have left behind.

CHAPTER XIV.

AN AMBUSCADE.

FOR two days we continued our return march without any interruption, and reached the base of the steep ascent that leads to the plateau overlooking the river.

The mounting of this height was a matter of no little difficulty. We had to climb like goats, clinging to rocks and tufts of brushwood, trampling down branches and dry grass, and hardly succeeded, after all, in following the track which the head of the caravan had opened.

Suddenly, about half-way up the slope, the ground sank abruptly, forming a deep ravine that had to be crossed before continuing the ascent. We paused at its brink to recover our breath. Behind us the long line of our sailors and porters was slowly filing through the thicket; in front, yawned the precipitous ravine itself; and opposite to us rose the mountain-side, to its very summit a mass of sombre woods; several eagles were wheeling round above the chasm.

"A fine place for an ambush!" said Hannibal, wiping the perspiration from his forehead, and little dreaming what was in store for us.

Himilco took a draught from the goat-skin that he carried at his side, and heaved a long-drawn sigh:

"Ah!" he said, "it was in just such a plaguy hole as this that I lost my eye ten years ago. I hope the hand that thrust the lance has been rotten long since."

My own experience of the dangers of the land of Tarshish

made me very cautious, and with the approval of my two
military subordinates, I despatched Hanno and Jonah to
the rear to call together the stragglers, and to collect any
that might have lost their way in the woods; Bichri and
his ten Benjamite archers, and Aminocles with his five
companion Phocians, I sent on in front to make their way
rapidly across the ravine, and to explore the forest on the
opposite side.

Jonah's trumpet was soon heard sounding its call, and
very shortly afterwards Bichri and Aminocles were seen
entering the wood beyond the hollow. Without suspecting
that there was any cause for alarm, I ordered the guide
(who was still being watched narrowly by my sailors) to
advance, and we began our descent. Some of us had
already reached the bottom, and the main body were
making their way as best they could down the trouble-
some incline, when the guide came to a sudden halt. He
was about fifty paces ahead, just beginning to re-ascend the
hollow. As soon as he stopped, a whistle was distinctly
heard from the woods in front, and Himilco called out:

"Look out, captain—look out! there's mischief brewing."

I shouted with all my might to the guide to move on
more briskly, and the sailor who had been put in charge of
him was in the act of pushing him forward, when the
savage made a sudden dive, felled the sailor to the ground,
in two or three bounds cleared the intervening space, and
disappeared in the adjoining thicket.

"I told you so," said Himilco; "I knew well enough
that the Iberian scoundrels would be at their old games
again."

While he spoke, Jonah's trumpet sounding an alarm told
only too plainly that the column was being attacked in the
rear, and in front a frightful chorus of yells and war-cries
was followed instantaneously by an avalanche of stones
One of my poor sailors fell at my side with his skull
smashed, and all the native bearers who had entered the
ravine threw down their loads and fled precipitately.

AN AVALANCHE OF STONES.

"Form a line!" shouted Hannibal to his men; and in spite of the storm of stones that was falling around him, the intrepid leader mounted a projecting rock, and brandishing his sword, vigorously rallied his force. A party of sailors made a body-guard about the two women, and Chamai, pale with rage and excitement, rushed with his sword drawn to Hannibal's side.

"What do you think of this?" said Himilco to me, pathetically, as he picked up a great stone that had fallen within a hand's breadth of his side; "these Tarshish almonds seem to be falling pretty thick."

And as if in answer to his words, a second storm yet heavier than the first came pelting down amongst us, and knocked over several of our men; but this time it came from behind, from the quarter of the ravine that we had just quitted, and showed us that we were assailed as much in our rear as in front.

'O, if only we had some cavalry and some chariots," began Hannibal; "how easy to turn both flanks like the Khetas[1] did with the Assyrians.[2] We would send our cavalry to the right, and our chariots to the left, and a free passage for our own centre should soon be forced."

"But considering we have no cavalry and no chariots," I said, interrupting him, "we must defend ourselves how we can."

Without taking any notice of what I had said, he was proceeding to expatiate upon the advantages and disadvantages of our position, when a huge stone struck his helmet, knocking off the crest and battering in the headpiece, and enforced upon him more effectually than I had done the necessity of abandoning theory for practice. For an instant he staggered with the shock, but quickly recovering himself, he roared out:

"By Nergal! this won't do. Holy El-Adonai! this is

---

[1] The Hittites of the Bible. Kheta was the general name given by the Egyptians to the Semitic tribes.
[2] B.C. 1070

too much. They must pay the penalty for this. Archers
quick! up the slopes! shoot every one who attempts to
enter the ravine!"

And turning to me, he cried :

"Captain, will you take your sailors back again up the
very path by which you came down, and sweep round to
those vagabonds who are harassing our rear?"

"Men of Judah," he continued, "follow Chamai. Chamai,
lead them yonder to the left. And now, my men, to the
right with me. Forward!"

"Forward to the left! long live the King!" shouted
Chamai at the full pitch of his lungs, as he obeyed orders,
and led off his company in the direction contrary to
Hannibal.

The archers under Hamilcar formed a circle round the
women and the baggage, and were a guard for the bottom
of the ravine ; Himilco and Gisgo, with my party, regained
the ridge we had so recently quitted ; and thus on every
side we presented a front to the enemy.

No sooner had we scaled the side of the ridge, than my
men, cutlass in hand, began to lay about them vigorously.
The half-naked men of Tarshish, armed only with clumsy
bludgeons or wooden-pointed lances, could make no stand
against our sharp weapons, and fell in numbers beneath
our blows ; and although crowds of them disappeared
behind the thickets, we did not break our compact mass
to go in pursuit, but pushed on straight ahead. Concealed
and protected by the underwood, many of the foe continued to follow us, and to hurl javelins at us from piles
that had been secreted ready for the purpose. When,
however, we came to any open patch, clear of trees, a
detachment of our men would make a dash into the brushwood in the hope of capturing some of the stragglers ; but
the savages were generally much too fleet of foot to allow
themselves to be caught, and only about fifteen altogether
were secured in this way. To these no quarter was given.

Although we had advanced two stadia, we found no

traces of Hanno and Jonah. I did not consider it advisable to go further, and made my men halt and form a circle round a large oak that stood alone in a little glade; but Himilco, whose vengeance seemed insatiable, ventured on for about another stadium, with Gisgo and fifteen sailors. It was somewhat more than an hour before they returned. They had caught and killed two of the Iberians, but what created a far greater interest for us, they had found Hanno's writing-case all covered with blood, lying in a copse with the dead bodies of nine or ten of our adversaries, and the mutilated corpse of one of our own sailors. The trampled soil, the pools of blood, and the carcases of the savages strewn all

about rendered it only too probable that after a desperate struggle the scribe and poor Jonah had succumbed to numbers, and that they had not only been massacred, but their bodies had been carried away.

It was with saddened hearts that we made our way back to the spot where we had been first surprised, repelling our enemies all along as they persisted in harassing us. As soon as I reached the ridge, and had satisfied myself that the women and the troop around them were all safe, I closed in my ranks and told up my losses. Six of my men had fallen. Meanwhile I was beginning to feel very uneasy about both Hannibal and Chamai, but my anxiety was of no long duration; they soon appeared together on the opposite height of the chasm : Bichri, too, was with them, and the troops were in good order. They had nearly forty prisoners ; and in the midst of the ranks I could see Aminocles marching along with a child in his arms, whilst amongst the captives I could distinguish a woman, two men wearing kitonets, and another dressed in a long Syrian robe. Hannibal was in front, and no sooner did he catch sight of me than he waved his sword over his head with a triumphant gesture, while Chamai, still more excited, with his head bare and his forehead covered with blood, began running rapidly towards me. I made pretence of looking another way as he stopped to kiss Abigail in passing, but in a minute or two he was at my side, his countenance beaming with joy. All out of breath, he exclaimed :

"Close quarters ! but we have pretty well done for them now ! "

Seeing the deep gash in his forehead and his bloodstained sword, I observed that he bore evident traces of a smartish tussle with the Iberians.

"Iberians !" he said, contemptuously ; "who cares for Iberians ? No ; it is our Tyrians that have done the mischief. However, we have nabbed the scoundrel Hazael ; and Aminocles has recovered his boy ; he was only just in time to save the child's life."

"And Bodmilcar ? what of him ?" I asked, all excitement at the information.

"Ah ! we have just missed him," he said ; " Hannibal got near enough to slice him pretty sharply in the ribs, and if it had not been for this unlucky wound of mine, we should have had him here now ; but his people contrived to rescue him, and to carry him off to the wood."

Half-frantic with agitation, and impatient to exact vengeance on my hated adversary, I forgot all about our perilous position, my scattered ingots, and the fate of my unfortunate scribe, and declared to Chamai that without the loss of an hour we must go in pursuit and get Bod-

milcar dead or alive. Across the ravine, off I started,
bidding who would to follow.

Himilco had shown Chryseis the writing-case, stained as
it was with blood, and a very few words had sufficed to
make her realise what were the fears we entertained upon
the scribe's behalf. She said nothing, but while Abigail
grasped her waist and wept tears of sympathy, she walked
steadily along, her hands tightly clenched, and giving no
other outward sign of emotion than a slight convulsive
movement of the shoulders. Chamai, whom I had omitted

to inform of the too likely fate of Hanno and Jonah, hurriedly asked Himilco what had become of them, but the
pilot only answered by a significant shake of the head,
and by pointing to the woods behind.

As I drew near to Hannibal, he advanced rapidly to
greet me. He seemed in high spirits, and although he was
evidently affected by the intelligence we gave him about
Hanno, he endeavoured to disguise his feelings by saying
that we must all submit to the chances of war.

" But what's to be done next ? " he added, quickly.

Q

I told him that I was determined at all hazards to go in pursuit of Bodmilcar, who must not be suffered to escape.

"Easier said than done," replied Hannibal. "Bodmilcar not only had a large force of Phœnician criminals and de- serters, but when he attacked us he had a regular swarm of savages, all armed either with clubs or javelins. At any rate, he can keep his distance. I know not whether he is alive or dead ; but I know this, that the fellows have found out that it is not to their advantage to tackle us in close quarters. However, we are too few to surround them, and to pursue them is only to expose ourselves to another ambush."

"What is to be done, then ?" I asked, gnashing my teeth with vexation.

"You must get to the top of the hill before night," he answered, decidedly ; "you must reach the open plain ; you must not run the risk of another surprise. Once on the plateau you are secure ; you can rest your men and give them food ; they are knocked up. And you will have time to interrogate your prisoners."

Chagrined as I was, I could not resist the conviction that Hannibal's advice was judicious, and, however reluctantly, gave up all thought of immediate pursuit. I directed that the prisoners should be fastened together by a rope passed round their necks, and that forty men should be told off under Himilco for a guard, with orders to kill the first man that showed the least sign of resistance.

"You may trust me for that," said the pilot, with a vin- dictive grin ; "they have only left me one eye, but that is a sharp one."

When the captives had been securely bound, I had all the packages and silver collected that had been left strewn about by the runaway porters.

"There will be a double load for each of these scoundrels to carry," I remarked ; "I shall take good care not to trust Iberians with my property again till I have seen them well fettered."

The baggage was gathered without the occurrence of any renewed attack, and Gisgo returned from the wood brandishing a stout cudgel that he had cut from the bough of an oak.

" Here's something to make them stir their legs a bit !" he said, as he saw the men loaded with their burdens.

" Now then, get on, you brutes!" Himilco screamed in Iberian ; " and the first rogue that shirks his work is a dead man !"

Placing the prisoners in the middle, we proceeded cautiously to continue our ascent ; and while we were prosecuting our toilsome march, I asked Bichri to give me full particulars about the encounter with Bodmilcar.

" As accurately as I can," he said, "I will. On leaving you we advanced without obstruction some hundred paces into the wood, when in a moment we found ourselves with a host of Iberians in our front, and as many in our rear, pelting us with stones and darts. We ran full speed to a spot where the trees were not so thick, and planting our backs against a projecting rock, we stood on our defence ; but almost directly afterwards we espied a troop of soldiers dashing down towards us. They were Bodmilcar and his miscreants. There seemed no hope for us : in a few minutes we must have been overpowered ; but, happily, Hannibal and Chamai made their appearance, and a desperate fray ensued. I saw Bodmilcar fall to the ground ; Chamai had all but secured him, when he was cut down by a cutlass, and the Tyrians seized their opportunity to carry off their chief, the barbarians covering their retreat, and hurling an incessant shower of missiles. But we were rescued."

I had listened with eager attention to Bichri's story, and as he came to a pause, I asked :

" But how about Hazael, and the woman and the child ?"

" Patience, and you shall hear," he said. " We resolved to go in pursuit of our foe, who, we had no doubt, was seriously wounded, and we had got into the thick of the forest, when we came upon a pile of wood with a child lying bound on the top of it. Fourteen or fifteen soldiers were standing round, and Hazael, with a long knife in his hand, was on the very point of slaying the child, while two men were forcibly dragging off a woman, who had evidently thrown herself across its body. The very instant that Aminocles caught sight of the victim, he shrieked aloud 'My son, my son!' and dashed like a madman into the group; we all rushed after him, and Hazael, seeing that he was in danger, made a lunge at the child with his knife and took to his heels. However, I was too quick for him, and soon had him back again. Meanwhile Aminocles and my archers had made short work with the other men, and the boy, who had fainted, was set free by cutting the cords that fastened him, and was found to have sustained no very serious injury. The woman, too, who had been endeavouring to ward off the blow of the knife, was recognised by one of the Phocians as the wife whom he had lost. Altogether, considering we have captured the eunuch, saved the child, and restored a man his wife, I do not know that we have done a bad day's work."

But changing his tone, Bichri added, mournfully:

"And yet how it saddens all to think about poor Hanno and our big friend Jonah. I loved them both, poor fellows! I wonder what has become of old Gebal. Is he gone too?"

I said that I had very little doubt the monkey had been on his usual perch upon the trumpeter's shoulder, and so most probably had shared his fate. Bichri drew a long sigh, which seemed to convey the impression that he was almost as much concerned at the loss of the monkey as he was moved by the fate of his comrades.

We had now reached the plateau. It was a dreary plain, dotted at rare intervals with a few trees and tufts of thistles, and as far as I could estimate, about twelve stadia from the Bœtis. Our supply of fresh water being nearly exhausted, we were obliged to be very frugal with it at our evening

ON THE VERY POINT OF SLAYING THE CHILD.

ILE DE LA TENTATION.

meal; but as soon as this was finished, and Hannibal had posted his sentinels and had all lights extinguished, I summoned Hazael before me. I took my seat, supported on either side by my officers and pilots, making Bichri, Aminocles and his son, and the Phocian with his wife, likewise be present.

The prisoner was brought forward, pale and trembling; his hands were tied behind his back, and his embroidered robe was torn and soiled with dust and blood.

"You know me?" I roared out to him as he approached.

"Yes, my lord," he faltered out in a quivering voice, without lifting his eyes from the ground.

"And you know your conduct towards me?" I roared again.

The culprit made no answer.

"Do you suppose I took you with me that you should plot against me in Egypt, at Utica, at Gades?"

He still gave no reply.

"What made you dare to try and kill that child?" I said.

"I was under orders," he whined out; "Bodmilcar made me. He wanted to sacrifice to Moloch to secure his favour. I dared not disobey him; he has had me in his power all along. It is not I, it is Bodmilcar that has wronged you."

"O, that matters not," I answered. "Curses on Bodmilcar! Would you save your life? One way, one only way is open to you still."

The despicable Syrian prostrated himself till his face was on the earth, and groaned out:

"Spare me! spare my life! ask what you will! trample on my neck! make me your slave for ever! but spare my life!"

Chamai, who was standing beside me with a bandage on his forehead, turned his head away in disgust.

"Spare your life!" I repeated; "why, if I did my duty I should make your life a sacrifice this very minute to the souls of the brave heroes who have lost their lives through you!"   And after a pause, I said: "But, listen to me! do what I require, and I will give you more than your life; when we are back at Gades, I will give you your liberty."

"O, I will do anything; but swear, swear that you will spare my life!" implored the abject wretch, still grovelling with his forehead in the dust.

"Yes, hearken!" I ejaculated.   "By Ashtoreth! goddess of heaven, I swear it!"

Relieved of his immediate terror, the pusillanimous craven started to his feet, and in a tone quite brisk in contrast with his previous whinings began to ask what it was that I required him to do.

"You must first inform us of the strength of Bodmilcar's force."

"One hundred and sixty Phœnicians.   Six hundred or perhaps seven hundred Iberians."

"You must next tell us the place of rendezvous he had appointed, in case his attack should fail."

Hazael hesitated.   Chamai said that if he revealed this, he would deserve a score of hangings for his treachery. Without noticing the interruption, I said again:

"You must tell us his place of rendezvous."

Again no answer.

"Except you tell, you shall be hanged this very minute."

And to show him that I was in earnest I called for a rope.   Himilco produced a strong cable-end that he always wore round his waist under his kitonet.   Hazael quivered and turned pale.

"Stop, stop! don't hang me!   I *will* tell!"

"Out with it, then; quick!"

"At the Wolf's knoll."

"So far, so good.   But where is that?"

"In the wood, two stadia off."

"But which way?"

"Behind us; over there; there to the right."

" Well then, come and show us the way."

And weary as I was, almost worn out by fatigue, I could not resist the desire to go upon the simplest chance of meeting the adversary that I hated so bitterly. I called out to my men that I wanted fifty volunteers to go with me and hunt out Bodmilcar from his lurking-place. Many more than I had called answered to my appeal, eager to offer their services, and I could only request Hannibal to select those best fitted for the expedition, and bid the others take good care of the women and the baggage, and see that the captives were well secured.

Aminocles begged for permission to remain behind with his little son, and asked that his countryman Demaretes might likewise be allowed to stay with his newly-rescued wife ; he acknowledged that they were indebted to me for the recovery of their dear ones, promised that they would fight doubly hard another time, but pleaded that they might be excused now. Of course I had no hesitation in yielding to his request.

Before setting out I said, incidentally, that we might perchance be fortunate enough to recover the bodies either of Hanno or Jonah, or both. Chryseis rose instantly to her feet, and, pale with agitation, placed herself at my side. To my inquiry whither she was going, she replied in a steady voice :

" To seek the body of my betrothed. If it be the will of the gods, I will consign it to a tomb."

" Come, then, you shall," I said, deeply affected by her sorrow, her resignation, and her courage ; " and may Ashtoreth protect us all !"

Hannibal gave the order to march. Bichri, ever indefatigable, went to the head of the column, leading Hazael by the cord which bound his wrists ; Gisgo, with his hatchet on his shoulder, kept close to the eunuch on the other side ; and Himilco, with his sword drawn, followed on behind. We advanced in silence towards the woods, choosing such hollows in the ground as the moonlight left in shadow, and in a short time were within sight of the dark masses of foliage that bounded the moonlit plain. Making our way as stealthily as we could through the thickets, we came to a mound near the edge of the steep that we had scaled in the morning. It was an abrupt elevation of the soil, and was described · to us by Hazael as being the place known as the Wolf's knoll, and which Bodmilcar had fixed as the rally-point of his people. When we halted there was not a light to be seen, not a sound to be heard, nothing to break the gloom or the stillness of the forest.

"Before we give the signal for attack," said Hannibal, under his breath, "we ought to know what they are doing."

"I know my way," said the eunuch; "let me go and look, that I may bring you word."

"Thanks," said Himilco; "you are very good—we will not trouble you."

After this sarcastic rebuff to his very transparent pretext for eluding us, Hazael was relapsing into his former silence, when Bichri suggested that he should himself take the eunuch and go and ascertain the actual position of affairs, adding that if he made a movement to escape, he would plunge his knife hilt-deep into his body.

Hannibal gave his consent, and the two disappeared in the thicket, Bichri pushing on his prisoner before him. In less than half an hour there was a crushing of the brush-wood, and they were before us again.

"What news?" we asked.

"The rascal has deceived us," said Bichri; "we went all round the mound, not a man, however, was to be seen."

"No, no, no!" sobbed the eunuch; "I have not deceived you. I swear I heard Bodmilcar say, 'Wolf's knoll.' Cut out my tongue if I lie! I swear it."

"Stop your oaths, liar!" I exclaimed impatiently. "Lucky for you I pledged you your life; but be on your guard, or, by Ashtoreth, another time——"

"It may be," said Hannibal, "the villains have been

lurking about, and, having discovered your approach, have decamped. The eunuch may have told the truth. Anyhow, nothing can be done. I am dead-beat."

Himilco and Hamilcar both declared that they, too, were quite knocked up, so that I determined to make our way back, and seek the repose of which we were so much in need.

CHAPTER XV.

JUDGE GEBAL DISTINGUISHES HIMSELF.

ON arriving within a comparatively few paces of our encampment, we were challenged by the sentinels, who were
keeping a sharp look-out. As soon as we had entered the
lines, Aminocles came running towards us with excited
gestures, and, hardly allowing me time to inquire what had
occurred, told me in broken Phœnician that during our
absence "the little man" had been and gone, and was now
in a clump of trees hard by.

For the moment I was puzzled ; but Bichri, comprehend-
ing more quickly what the man meant, exclaimed, "Gebal!
Judge Gebal!" and dashing off in the direction indicated,
began to whistle his accustomed call-note. In a few
minutes he returned, his countenance beaming with glee.
The monkey was seated on his shoulder, and greeted us
with hideous yells and grimaces. Ugly as the creature
was, I confess I was glad to have it again amongst us ;
nearly every one came to look at it, and although it pulled
Hannibal's beard, scratched Himilco's face, and bit Gisgo's
nose, nothing was set down to spitefulness, but all was
taken in good part, until the beast tried to claw Chamai's
hand, upon which Chamai, never very patient either with
man or brute, struck it a violent blow which sent it howling
back to Bichri. As it sprang away it dropped something
that looked like the strap of a sandal. After picking it
up and examining it by the light of a torch, Chamai
exclaimed :

"By all that's good, there is something written here! it is written in Phœnician."

I snatched the strap away from him in my eagerness, and discerned in a moment that it was covered with characters apparently traced in blood. Without waiting to read it all, I cried out:

"Hanno is alive! old Gebal has brought us the news. Hanno has written to us himself."

After I had deciphered the writing carefully, I said:

"Now, listen, my friends—this is what he says: 'We are prisoners, alive and well: Jonah's trumpet saved us; savages would not give us up to Bodmilcar; their chief wanted a Phœnician trumpeter. Another chief wants a trumpeter before he will give his daughter in marriage to this chief. I am spared as well. We are to be sent off at once to the northern chief. Keep up your spirits. We will soon escape. Beware of Bodmilcar; he is laying an ambush. He means to cut you off from the river.' There, my men, that's what he says. We will hope to see him yet."

As I ceased to read, Chryseis threw herself into Abigail's arms, and wept for joy; Gisgo flung his cap into the air; Himilco took a liberal draught from his goat-skin; and Hannibal manifested his emotion by sneezing seven times in succession. As for Bichri, he took the monkey in his arms, and fairly hugged it, a piece of attention which Gebal acknowledged by plucking out a handful of his hair.

"O, Gebal, shame upon you! would you be pulling out my hair when you know how much I love you? Brave old Gebal! I was only congratulating you on distinguishing yourself so well."

The others were all equally anxious to pet the creature, and gave it quantities of almonds and raisins, which it took without leaving its perch upon Bichri's shoulder.

"Come, come!" I said, "no time for this trifling. Our water is gone; we must get to the river; we must be

beforehand with Bodmilcar.   But there is one piece of
business that we must settle first.   Bring Hazael here."

The eunuch was brought before me, and addressing him
very sternly, I said :

"Hazael, you have heard this letter.   It proves you a
liar and a traitor.   Your villainy has cost us much trouble ;
there is no reprieve this time ; you must be sent forthwith
to another tribunal.   Menath, Hokk, and Rhadamath must
be your judges.   You must die."

Flinging himself prostrate at my feet, the abject wretch
broke out into the most piteous supplications ; he implored
for mercy, but I was inexorable.   Two sailors raised him
to his feet, and Himilco having made a running noose in
his rope, slipped it round the Syrian's neck.

"Choose your own tree, my good man," said Himilco ;
"for my part I should recommend a sturdy holm."

Hazael made no reply, but struggled so violently that he
had to be dragged forcibly along.

"Don't be a fool !" cried Gisgo.   "What objection can
you have to be hanged ? it will save your shoe-leather."

"Now then," said Himilco, as soon as they had placed the eunuch under the tree, "haul away, tackle him up to the standing-rigging; there! his navigation has come to an end!"

And almost as he spoke, Hazael was dangling in the moonlight.

"One traitor gone to his last account," I said.

"And the other, I hope, soon to follow," Hannibal replied.

Brief and scanty was our rest that night; and when in the morning the sun rose in a cloudless sky, so unrefreshed were we after our fighting and toiling, that it was with the utmost difficulty that we could drag ourselves across the hot and dusty plain. My own throat was parched, and my stomach cramped with those terrible sensations known only too well by those who have suffered the tortures of excessive thirst. Himilco had drained his last drop of wine, and went feebly along through lack of stimulant; Hannibal removed his helmet, and carried it slung from his girdle; and all were too worn and weary to utter a syllable as we marched. Bichri was the only one of us who exhibited no symptom of fatigue, his wiry frame being capable of unlimited endurance.

About the middle of the afternoon a light mist, indicating the course of the river, revived our flagging energies by making us aware that fresh water was not far off. I took Bichri and a number of men carrying gourds and goat-skins, and hurried on to obtain, without loss of time, some drink for my thirsty host; but when I had got within half a stadium of the river-bank I was seized with such violent pain and nausea that I could hardly stand. I persevered however, till we were hardly more than twenty paces from the water's edge, when suddenly there was a rustling in the bushes, and a score or more of lances came whizzing about us, and we were startled by the shrill war-cry of the Iberians. Surprised, but not intimidated by the attack, we kept steadily on our way, and were close upon the river-bank, when some thirty or forty savages emerged from the rushes and confronted us with their lances, whilst as many again, with hideous yells, ran to assail the flank of our main body. Hannibal and Chamai soon dispersed their adversaries, but I with my party in advance did not fare so well, for notwithstanding that Bichri struck down more than one of the foremost of the barbarians, they succeeded in entirely surrounding us. One of the sailors had his arm pierced by a javelin Bichri had a cut in the calf of his leg, and my own movements were completely paralysed by a lance having got tightly fixed in my shield and shoulder-belt. I confess I thought it was all up with us, but at the critical moment the well-known sound of the Phœnician trumpet broke upon us, followed by the animating cry, "Courage, courage, we are here!" and a change passed upon the scene. Like a flock of startled birds the savages were off in scared retreat ; an advancing troop, doubtless Bodmilcar's own, wheeled rapidly about and took to flight ; they had descried Hasdrubal who, from the river-bank, was bringing up a company to our rescue. Never did a friend receive a warmer welcome. To my inquiry how it was that he had arrived so opportunely, he told me he had been watching the enemy's movements all the morning ; they had been too engrossed with their own schemes to observe him, but he was so convinced they were designing mischief that he lowered the mast of the *Cabiros* and brought her up to the side-arm of the river, whence he had led his men forward just in time to render us good service.

Thus happily relieved from the threatened peril, our force hastened onwards to slake their thirst, and I think it was for the first time in my life that I saw Himilco gulp down (and that with evident satisfaction) a draught of pure water. Another hour and we were descending the Bœtis, and joyously recounting our adventures.

That night, which was spent on board the *Cabiros*, was a night of well-earned rest. Next morning we started early for the spot where the *Dagon* and the *Ashtoreth* had been moored.

I gave my sailors five shekels apiece, and a triple ration
of wine, and conscious that they had been overworked, I
granted them twenty-four hours' release from labour before
finally recommencing our voyage. They spent their holiday according to their own taste ; they drank, they shouted,
they sang, they danced, and occasionally they diversified
their amusement by a little fighting ; yet, notwithstanding
the obstreperousness of their proceedings, when evening
came they calmed down quietly enough to their ordinary
discipline.

The next day found us once more on the open sea,
and for myself I felt an indescribable satisfaction in again
looking upon its green and restless face, and in hearing
its waves plash against the sides of my ship.

In two days we had reached Gades, and I settled all the
business I had to transact with Ziba.

And now the time had come for me to announce to my
officers and crew a purpose that I had long been contemplating. Accordingly I invited them all to an entertainment in a tent at some public gardens beyond the
town, and when the repast was over I rose and told them
why I had gathered them together.

"My friends," I began, "our mission is accomplished.
King David's demands are met ; King Hiram's orders are
fulfilled. King David's subjects are at liberty to return to
Palestine, and I have brought them here to bid them all
farewell."

Chamai started to his feet impatiently, and looking at me
with a keen and earnest scrutiny, asked what I meant.

"What I mean," I continued, "is soon told. I propose
to put all my silver on board the *Dagon*, and to place her
under the command of Hasdrubal. In the *Dagon* you, too,
can return. Hasdrubal shall have orders to land you and
Abigail and Hannibal, and whoever else may choose to
accompany you, at Joppa."

Upon hearing this, Hannibal, in a voice agitated with
emotion, called out :

"And you? What about yourself? And are not Himilco, Hamilcar, and Gisgo to go back with us?"

"Not one of them," I answered; "we have other work to do."

A blank silence fell upon them all. Hannibal gazed at me in bewilderment, big tears gathering in his eyes; Chamai broke his reverie by bringing his fist down so violently upon a chair that it broke under the blow; and after a space, Bichri began softly to whistle one of the

melodies of his tribe, his usual way of trying to exhibit a contemptuous indifference.

Chamai was the first to speak.

"By our holy God! captain, I could never have believed you capable of this," he blurted out.

"Yes, indeed, by all that's holy!" said Hannibal, finding his voice, "what have we done that merits treatment of this kind?"

"I am doing you no wrong," I answered; "friends we have been hitherto; friends let us part. You can surely ask no more than that I should remit you to your homes to pass the rest of your lives in ease and affluence."

"But why not return yourself?" they asked.

"I have invited you here, to tell you why. It is the resolve of myself and of the Sidonians that are with me to make a voyage of discovery. I have set my heart on finding out what lands there are, whether they be isles or continents, lying to the north. I am determined, if I can, to settle whether it be possible, by sailing round Tarshish to the west, to reach the Celtic shores. These are the problems that I seek to solve."

"And do you think," said Chamai, "that we shall be content to enjoy our repose while you are braving all the perils of the unknown sea? No, no; not quite so ungrateful as that!"

"Desert our colours in the middle of the fight? nay, that will never do," cried Hannibal: "return home, who will; my post is with you captain."

Chamai echoed his words, and Abigail averred her intention of not being parted from her lover.

I was quite overcome by the attachment of my people, and grasped them all in turns by the hand.

"The gods reward your courage and fidelity," I exclaimed. "But surely some of you will wish to return? Aminocles, what say you? do you not want to take your son back to his home? And you, Chryseis, you will hardly think of facing the perils of the untried sea?"

Aminocles replied that he could not desire his son to have a better home than the society of warriors offered; and Chryseis avowed that she was bound to me by a perpetual debt of gratitude: I had liberated her from slavery, and it might be, if she continued with me still, that her missing lover would be restored to her.

Turning to Bichri, who was still whistling some national air in a lackadaisical manner, I said to him:

"As yet, young man, we have not heard your decision. Have you nothing to say?"

R

"Not much," he answered; "I planted a patch of Ziba's land with a lot of vine-slips. I think I shall go north with you, and look in here at Tarshish on my way back, just to see how my plantation prospers."

"Well done, Bichri!" cried Himilco; "you have set a young vineyard going, have you? You will have a long generation of tipplers never ceasing to bless the day you came to Gades. May the gods smile on you and your vines!"

Bichri did not vouchsafe Himilco any answer, but went on, as though talking to himself:

"With old Gebal, and little Dionysos, I think I can be happy enough. I shall miss poor Jonah, though."

I had thus learnt to my great surprise that there was not one of my companions who was disposed to leave me. I took measures, therefore, for consigning the charge of my cargo, including the silver, to a Sidonian captain who was about returning home, and then, without loss of time, laid in an ample store of provisions for my voyage over the untraversed waters of the West.

On the morning of my departure I went to take my leave of the naval suffect and of Ziba. As I passed along the quay by the entrance of the harbour, I found a great concourse of people gathered together for the purpose of witnessing the erection of two great pillars, one of which bore a figure of the sun, and the other a statue of our god Melkarth. I was naturally curious to ascertain the meaning of the columns, and was informed that they indicated the limits of the habitable world, and that beyond them there was nothing but ocean. But the response of the oracle was still echoing in my memory: the world for me had wider bounds, I smiled, and went my way with a hopeful heart.

CHAPTER XVI.

PERILS OF THE OCEAN.

FOR a whole week I followed the coast steadily to the north, and having rounded a lofty promontory, bore towards the east. In all my previous navigation I had never experienced such difficult sailing, nor seen waves more angry than those which dashed against the cliffs that formed the shore. One headland there was which took us little short of four days to double, and it was not until we had been battling for more than a fortnight with continual tempest that we found ourselves in calmer waters and off a flat coast, of which, after the mountains had come to their limit, the direction was again northwards. We were all greatly fatigued.

Before we had proceeded much further we came to a river with a mouth so wide that at first I imagined it to be a gulf; the shores on either hand were wooded and undulating, and the general aspect of the country was so inviting that I determined to lay to, and had no difficulty in finding excellent anchorage about half-way up the estuary.

"By all that's good!" exclaimed Gisgo, "I recognise those cabins. That's a Celtic village;" and he pointed to a cluster of huts, with conical roofs made of thatched reeds, and without more ado made four rowers pull him ashore in a boat to pay a visit to his former acquaintances.

He was not mistaken. In half an hour our vessels were surrounded by the ill-made coracles of the inquisitive Celts some of whom were so eager to scrutinise us that they swam out all the way from the shore; and our decks were soon invaded by numbers of them, who, with loud laughter and much gesticulating, began talking all at once in a language which was anything but euphonious. They appeared perfectly friendly, and were far less barbarous in their manners than the people of Tarshish. They were dressed in very short tunics, made of coarse material woven by themselves, and their legs were covered with trousers that came to the ankles; their faces were round, and generally bore a good-humoured expression; their eyes were bright, and for the most part blue; their hair light brown, and occasionally quite flaxen. Some of them had bronze weapons and jewellery, which had found their way from Phœnicia along the Rhone by means of the Salians; the majority of them, however, still retained their wooden, stone, or bone implements, many of which were very well made.

The Celts, as I learnt on visiting one of their villages built upon piles in the water, are very expert fishermen. I bought some gold dust of them in exchange for some of my goods, which they seemed glad to obtain. They all agreed in affirming that they had come from the north-east, and had been established for nearly a century in their present localities, whence they had driven out some people resembling the Iberians and Ligurians; and they said that in the regions behind them there were some other tribes of Celts, whom they called Gauls and Cymri.

After leaving their "mas," as they termed their village, I returned to the ships, and we resumed our northward course. Eight days' moderate sailing brought us into a labyrinth of rocky shoals and islands. On the mainland we found some more Celts, who told us that the name of the country was Ar-Mor, that is to say, "the land of the sea;" and relying on their statement that north of their own country there was a large island both rich and fertile, I resolved to prosecute my voyage in that direction.

Two days later we were overtaken by a tremendous tempest, and the sea being at the same time overhung by a dense fog, which my people called "the lungs of the ocean," we were tossed about by the foaming waves, and seemed for several succeeding days to be wandering in the gloomy realms of the dead. By the evening of the fifth day we had lost all reckoning of our position, and were drifting helplessly at the mercy of the wind and waves. Towards midnight, overcome with fatigue, I was dozing at the foot of the mast, when I was aroused by Himilco's stentorian shout, "Breakers ahead!"

In an instant I was upon my feet, and at the helmsman's side.

"Backwater!" I shouted, "and signal the other ships."

All hastened to light the torches and lamps; but it was too late—a long cry of distress made us aware that the *Dagon* had already stranded, and as I tacked about to effect a retreat, I witnessed the heart-breaking spectacle of the *Cabiros* completely heeled over, and lying in the very midst of the breakers.

The *Ashtoreth*, although she was hitherto uninjured, was environed by reefs which were level with the surface of the water. The current was so strong that all my efforts to get back to the channel by which we had entered were unavailing, and after an hour's struggle I still found myself near enough to hear the surf curling over the peaks of the rocks. For nearly the twentieth time I gave the order to tack, when a sudden and ominous crash revealed the appalling fact that we had struck the shoal, and were aground; and all through that pitch-black night we had to endure the torture of believing that all our vessels were irretrievably lost.

The wind dropped with the first streak of dawn, and beyond the breakers I could distinguish that the sea was calm, and that we were not much more than half a stadium from the shore. Shipwrecked though we might be, our lives were spared, and our situation was not altogether so desperate as we had imagined. The *Cabiros* was safe, in spite of her disaster, and had been hauled up on shore; but the *Dagon*, it was only too evident, was in a very critical position. I ordered all my men to abandon the ships and make for land. Some of them hung back, unwilling to leave me; Chamai being so reluctant to go that he had to be sent ashore by main force, and Hamilcar Hasdrubal, Gisgo, and Himilco all pleading so earnestly to remain with me that I was forced to consent. My own resolution, of course, was to abide, while the planks held together, with the ship that had carried us so far in safety.

As the day advanced the swell gradually abated, and the pale-blue sky was broken by fleecy clouds; not far away we could see the green shore, where our people were standing on the water's edge waving signs of encouragement, and very soon Bichri and Dionysos managed to clamber over the rocks and to come aboard our vessel.

At low tide I made a careful examination of the keels, and found that not only was the keel of the *Ashtoreth* very little injured, but that her stern was wedged so tightly between the two rocks that her position was secure; at the same time she had not been jammed in so violently but that I hoped a high tide might float her again. With the *Dagon*, however, the case was unfortunately very different; she had been dashed so hopelessly against the jutting crags that she must inevitably go to pieces, and I lost no time in beginning to unload her.

Our people had discovered a stream of fresh water, and a neighbouring wood afforded fuel, so that the spot was very favourable for a camp, the whole arrangement of which I deputed to Hannibal, who immediately enclosed the site with an intrenchment. Having completed the task of unloading both ships, we took down the mast of the *Ashtoreth*, and rescued from the *Dagon* as much planking and as many fittings as we could, as well as the best part of her copper sheathing. Lightened by the removal of her cargo and rigging, the *Ashtoreth*, under the influence of a stiffish breeze,

I DID WHAT I COULD TO CONSOLE HASDRUBAL.

To face page 247.

was set afloat on the third day amidst general acclamation, and so admirably was she managed by Himilco, that she was soon brought to land, and laid high and dry upon the shore.

I did what I could to console Hasdrubal for the loss of his ship, but he wept tears of bitter sorrow as he saw his ill-fated *Dagon* break up before his eyes.

For some days we had seen no trace of any natives, and were in want of provisions. I was preparing to send out two boats on a fishing excursion, when we caught sight of a long coracle rounding the point that sheltered our position. It was made of hides stretched out upon a wooden frame, and was paddled by four men, half-naked. On nearing us they hesitated, but we made signs to them of our friendly intentions, and they came on and landed. Gisgo, recognising them as Celts, both by their physiognomy and general aspect, began to address them in their own language, and they answered him very volubly, making many gesticulations all the time they were speaking. So delighted did they profess themselves at meeting with people who understood their tongue, that they insisted on kissing us; and notwithstanding the smell of their long hair, which was reeking with rancid grease, we were obliged to submit to their embraces.

Gisgo told us that although they spoke a language similar to that of the southern and central Celts, they were really the Cymri, a kindred tribe from the north, where they inhabited an island which they called Prydhayn; they seemed restless and inquisitive, overwhelming us with all manner of questions; they were tall and handsome, and had pink and white complexions, eyes of azure blue, and hair of the colour of ripe corn.

"Fine soldiers these fellows would make," said Hannibal; "I should like to have a thousand of them to drill; I would soon be more than a match for Bodmilcar."

To Bichri's remark that they seemed to have no bows, Gisgo replied that he had seen them with bows occasionally, but that their ordinary weapons were lances and hatchets, of which the stone tips and blades were always sharp and often beautifully made.

I had the men questioned as to whether they had any previous knowledge of the Phœnicians. They said that their kinsmen, the Cymri of the north, had often spoken of strangers with dark skins and black hair, who came in large ships and brought beautiful merchandise, but that they themselves had never been thrown into contact with them.

I made them a number of presents, and much to Himilco's annoyance (for he knew our supply was rapidly diminishing), I gave them some wine. This exhilarated them very much for a time, although their shouting and screaming ended in some bickerings amongst themselves; to us, however, they were civil, and in spite of a little roughness, we found their manners so kind, that it was impossible to be in any way alarmed at them. When they went away they promised to return in the evening, and bring their whole population and some goods in return for our presents, but we saw nothing more of them until the next morning, when they came followed by a whole retinue of men, women, and children, but all of them quite empty-handed. Rushing into the camp with great excitement, they overwhelmed us with their embraces, and asked such countless questions that I was quite bewildered; they insisted upon helping us to arrange our camp, but introduced disorder wherever they went: loud in their praises of what they saw, they were scrupulously honest, and did not attempt to purloin the smallest article, but their inquisitiveness and their meddling rendered them a perpetual nuisance. They tried Hannibal's temper sorely, by handling his cuirass and helmet; the more he pushed them off the more they laughed and enjoyed his annoyance. Chryseis and Abigail had a hard matter to keep them from stripping them, in their curiosity to examine their clothes. Judge Gebal did not fail to provide them boundless amusement, and they roared with laughter as Bichri and Dionysos made their mischievous little quadruped

JUDGE GIDAL.

show off his antics. Some of my people regretted that we had lost the attraction of Jonah's trumpet, but there was a sufficient variety of objects without that to give them abundance of diversion.

Amidst all this, however, I did not suffer myself to forget either of the two grand objects of my voyage, the discovery of new lands and the acquisition of rare commodities ; and accordingly I took much pains to examine the people about the situation and configuration, both of their own islands and of the land we had just left. They seemed a very intelligent race, and I found that they were adventurous, frequently accomplishing long distances in their canoes of hide. According to their information we were now on the largest and most important of a group of twelve small islands,[1] but that the great island Prydhayn was so large that it took them no less than two months to circumnavigate it in their canoes, from which I drew the inference that it must be as large as Tarshish. I requested the men to bring me whatever food they had for sale, and they never failed subsequently in keeping me well supplied with fish and venison. Seeing at once that they were not an agricultural people, I made no demands for corn and vegetables ; but as some time afterwards a small quantity of barley and some other edible grain arrived from Prydhayn, I conjectured that some of the natives are beginning to have some notion of husbandry.

I was much struck by the number of trinkets that the Cymri wore about their persons ; and observing that the metal of which many of them were made was singularly white, I was curious to know what it was and where it could be procured. To my surprise, and I may add to my delight, I was informed that the island on which we were encamped yielded it in great abundance, and I lost no time in investigating the veins of ore. Accompanied by a few men, I set out upon a search which was rewarded by the discovery that the entire island was one vast mine of tin.

---

[1] The Scilly Islands, the Cassiterides, or Tin islands of the ancients.

A scheme suggested itself to my mind which I resolved to carry out. With the wood obtained either here or from the neighbouring large island, I determined to build a new ship to replace the shattered *Dagon ;* and during the time that it was being constructed I purposed gathering such a store of metal as would form a cargo far surpassing anything of the kind which Phœnicia had witnessed before. Every one around me most heartily approved of my project.

In return for a few trifling knick-knacks, and for some fragments of the old copper sheathing of the *Dagon,* the natives willingly acquiesced in our working their mines, and in letting us portions of their territory for as long as we pleased to retain it ; in fact, they seemed to wish that we would settle permanently amongst them ; they volunteered their assistance in every way, and our camp was quite over-stocked with the produce of their hunting and fishing, whilst for the presents we made them they were profuse in their expressions of pleasure and gratitude. In spite of their restlessness, inquisitiveness, and love of talking, I have no hesitation in pronouncing them the most favourable specimens of savages we had hitherto seen.

Our arrangements were soon made. Hamilcar, with Bichri and twenty archers, started on board the *Cabiros* to explore the islands and the coast of Prydhayn ; Hasdrubal and Gisgo undertook the supervision of the working of the mines ; I remained with Himilco in the camp to devote myself to the construction of our new ship ; and, first of all, in order to protect our men against the rainy and rigorous climate, I had some substantial huts erected, as being more suitable than the tents. For Hannibal and Chamai there was no definite employment, and they spent most of their time in hunting and fishing, and in joining in the sports of the islanders, whom they began to instruct in military drill ; and never had they found more apt or devoted learners.

One day Hannibal and Chamai made their appearance among us with their chins closely shorn, and no hair left on the face except a moustache on the upper lip ; they had fraternised so far with the savages as to conform to their fashion.

"You cut fine figures," I said, laughing ; "go and paint your faces, and you will make capital Cymri."

Hannibal tried by very elaborate reasoning to justify his proceeding, alleging that one ought to conform to national customs, and that as the warriors here had their faces shorn, it was right that he as a warrior amongst warriors should do the same.

"And Abigail," said Chamai, "thinks the change is very becoming to me."

This argument being unanswerable, I had not another word to say.

Days, weeks and months glided on whilst we continued our active though somewhat monotonous labours.

When Hamilcar returned from his cruise, he informed us that he had not only made his way along the west coast of the great island, but that, still farther to the west, he had discovered a somewhat smaller island which he had completely circumnavigated ; the natives, he said, called it Erin, or "the green isle," from its remarkable verdure, and I retained the name.

The winter came on, cold and drear. I have no power to describe the consternation of those of our party who had never before seen frost or snow ; nothing but the sternest necessity could induce them ever to leave their huts. The poor monkey suffered excessively.   Bichri and Dionysos alone seemed unaffected by the fall of temperature ; they were always ready to join the young Cymri in games of snowballing, and would glide along the frozen surface of the water until their faces glowed again with the exertion.

Under Bichri's tuition the little Phocian boy was be· coming an adept in the use both of the sling and of the bow ; he seemed always delighted to be bringing back from his hunting excursions fresh trophies of his skill.

The most hipped of all the party was Himilco ; not that the sturdy pilot had more dread than the rest of mists and frosts, but because he was much disconcerted at the rapid diminution in our stock of wine.

"Ah me !" he would sigh, as each goat-skin was drained ; "another gone ! we shall have nothing but water with which to greet the advent of spring.   Ah, yes ! it is time we were back again in Phœnicia ; it would do one good to see the vines on the hill-side of Berytos."

In his forebodings Himilco found a genuine sympathiser

in Hannibal, who (although I should not like to say that
there was one amongst us who would not be sorry for all
our wine to be exhausted) was the only one who openly
shared the regret of our thirsty pilot.

At length the days grew longer and brighter, and the
sea, which had been almost always angry and restless,
settled down into something of a calm.   Our new ship was
finished.   We launched it on our feast of navigation, and
not only did the Cymri come to assist, but in honour of
the occasion their priests and priestesses stripped themselves of their clothes, and stained their bodies with blue
and black paint.   In the evening we had a banquet of fish,
venison, barley, and some of the esculents of the country.
We also finished the last drop of our wine.

"Let us drink to our prosperous return," said Himilco.

"It is much too soon to speak about that," I rejoined ;
"our voyage as yet is far from its end."

Every one looked at me in bewilderment ; it had never
occurred to them that we could be bound elsewhere than
for Sidon.   Chamai asked whether we were going to have
a little further benefit of "the lungs of the sea."

"You are perfectly at liberty to go home," I answered
him.   "This new ship has been built, and I am quite
prepared to let her return with her cargo and as many of
you as are no longer disposed to encounter the cold and
mists."

Chamai started to his feet, and said impulsively :

"Surely, captain, you did not suppose I was in earnest ;
you cannot believe I was thinking of leaving you.   I
profess I do not like this chill and dreary climate ; but you
may rely on this, wherever you go, I shall go also."

I gave him my hand, assuring him that I had every
confidence in his fidelity, and then proceeded to explain
the motive that induced me to extend my voyage.   I
showed them a fragment of a transparent yellow substance,
which appeared to be comparable to some of the jewels of
our own land.   The Celt who had given it me called it

amber, and told me that thirty days' sailing to the east would bring me to the shore of a large continent where it was washed up in great abundance. Here truly was a gift from Ashtoreth !

"And who knows," I continued, "whether the vast ocean which is united to the Great Sea at the Straits of Gades may not again be united to it in the east ? Hitherto we have learnt nothing about the northern shores of the Black Sea, and who can tell whether we shall not be able to return to Sidon by way of Caria and Chittim ?"

The familiar sound of these names rekindled the courage of my people, who one and all avowed their intention of accompanying me eastwards to the amber-coast.

"Yes," said Himilco, "although the wine is all gone."

Our new vessel (which was called the *Adonibal*, after the naval suffect at Utica) was well freighted with our cargo of tin ; like the other ships, she took in a good supply of water and a quantity of dry salted meat, as well as some grain and some of the sour native fruits.

After bidding farewell to the kindly-disposed Cymri, who had contributed so much to our comfort during our long sojourn among them, we put out to sea. The islanders accompanied us for some distance in their canoes, but we soon outstripped them and left them out of sight as we doubled the western extremity of Prydhayn.

Six days' rough sailing brought us to the eastern extremity of the island ; thence steering due east I came to a low flat coast, along which I continued to advance very cautiously. This took us a week, at the end of which we found ourselves in a wide estuary, on the far side of which the coast resumed its northerly direction. In spite of the violent wind and angry sea I persisted in following the coast for yet five days more, seeking a passage towards the east, holding no communication with the natives, although the glow of the fires inland demonstrated that the country was inhabited. But at last the state of our provisions and the continuance of rough weather compelled us to abandon all hope of discovering a passage, even if one existed, which probably after all was not the case, and we turned back, meeting on our way four large Cymrian canoes coming back from the continent, where their crews had been collecting amber. They assured us we should find unlimited quantities on the eastern shore, and I was preparing to proceed thitherwards when we were enveloped in a fog so dense, that we were forced to lay to. We sent some boats out to reconnoitre ; these had some difficulty in getting to the shore, but considerably more in getting back again to the ships, although I had lighted a number of torches and lamps as beacons.

When the fog lifted a little we made our way very gradually until we came to what looked like land. This was the amber country.

"Since there is nothing to be found at sea," I said, "let us disembark."

But disembarkment was no easy matter. We had entered, without knowing it, into what seemed to be the estuary of a river ; but we were literally imbedded in mire, and it was next to impossible to define the boundary between the muddy water and the slimy shore ; in the gloomy atmosphere, earth, air, sky, seemed all to be blended into one. After four or five hours' toil the *Ashtoreth* was moored in a small creek, and the other vessels were drawn up on what was the nearest approach to dry land that the sodden sands afforded. It took the rest of the day to dig a trench round the ships, and to make a kind of encampment for ourselves ; the fog again became extremely dense, and the gloomy day yielded only to a gloomier night.

Bichri, who with twenty men had started on a foraging expedition, returned shivering with cold ; he brought some good faggots, which, though they were damp, were very resinous, and burnt well. We lighted as many fires as we could, and heedless of the volumes of smoke which they emitted, we crouched closely around them as we cooked our supper.

Chamai, who had wrapped himself tightly in his mantle, was the first to break the depressing silence.

"Frightful, odious country!" he exclaimed ; "can human creatures exist in such a desolation as this ? It is a place for monsters, not for men!"

"It would just suit old Jonah, then," said Hannibal, with a sigh ; "it would cheer us up, too, if Hanno were here to entertain us with a sprinkling of his wit."

" I do not think we need have much fear on their account," I said ; "by this time, I should hope, they are pacing the sunny streets of Sidon, or enjoying the fragrant heights of Libanus."

"Yes ; I daresay," Himilco assented ; "and no doubt they have plenty of good wine to drink ; wine, rich as nectar, from Helbon, Byblos, and Sarepta!"

"There now, enough of that," cried Hannibal ; "cease your talking, or you will be making me as much a wine-bibber as yourself."

" Call me a wine-bibber ?" groaned Hannibal, holding up a goblet of turbid water ; "do you think this is the kind of stuff to get tipsy on ?"

The dull mist grew more and more chilling, and every one appeared quite benumbed. Gebal was wrapped up in folds of woollen cloth, which Bichri had provided for him, but was almost too paralysed to make a grimace. We crouched down still closer to our fires, and obtained what unrefreshing sleep we could.

The morning dawned, grey, and almost as gloomy as ever, without one streak of sunlight. Red with anger was Chamai as he exclaimed impatiently :

"I suppose the sun does not shine in these cursed regions !"

"Oh yes !" replied Gisgo, "he does come now and then, but he finds everything so confoundedly ugly, that he is glad to get back again to the Great Sea, and to his own dear Phœnicia."

Aminocles once again became subject to his nervous

fancies ; he was sure that we must have entered Hades, and implored us to lose no time in offering a sacrifice to propitiate the gods of the lower world.   Naturally enough we ridiculed his fears, but it cannot be denied that the influence of the climate is most depressing, and conducing to hypochondria.

I urged upon my companions the importance of our seeking communication if possible with the natives, and as soon as we had taken our morning meal we arranged to set out and explore the river.   Bichri and twenty men went forward as an advanced guard ; I followed with Hannibal and the main body of the fighting force ; Hamilcar, with about thirty more, brought up the rear.   Hasdrubal and fifty men were told off to keep guard over the ships and encampment during our absence.   Just as he was setting out Bichri remarked that he wished he had Jonah with his trumpet to attract the attention of the inhabitants, but I bade him not to indulge just then in unavailing regrets.

After wading through such desperate quagmires that we could hardly determine whether we were going by land or by water, we arrived at some forests consisting of black firs, and some other trees that were remarkable for their slim- ness and scanty grey foliage.   The soil everywhere was marshy, and often broken by large pools.   Although we did not come across a human being, we observed many vestiges which showed that the place was by no means untrodden by the foot of man.   In four places we passed some ruined reed-huts, surrounded by piles of ashes, numbers of shells, and some gnawed bones that bore the marks of fire.   But if men were wanting, animals abounded.   At every turn we noticed prints, large and small, of cloven hoofs, betokening that we were traversing the haunt both of bullocks and deer, some of the impressions being obviously those of very enormous creatures.   Bichri, who followed one of the tracks for some distance into the wood, remarked that branches had been broken off the trees by the animals' horns at so great a height from the ground, that he was convinced it had been done by a beast several hands taller than the largest horse. On our way back to the camp we saw two deer of a smaller species; Gisgo recognised them as the same he had seen in the country of the Celts, who call them renns or reindeer; they took to flight immediately they caught sight of us, a circumstance that convinced me that the inhabitants were accustomed to hunt them; Bichri and Dionysos, however, not only contrived to get within bowshot of them, but brought them both down, a great boon to us all, as we were in much need of fresh meat. The renns were about the size of a donkey; they had very slender legs, large hoofs, thick grey hair, a white spot upon their breasts, and large branching horns.

Next day I sent Hamilcar with two boats to cruise along the coast, and taking nearly all the rest of my people and thirty archers with me, went myself to make a more thorough exploration of the country. We were met by a herd of wild bulls. We attacked them as vigorously as we could, but at the first touch of our arrows the brutes charged down upon us so furiously that we were obliged to take refuge behind the trees. One poor soldier who could not succeed in getting out of the way was trampled under the animals' feet, and another was tossed into the air so violently that his back was broken by the fall. Three of the bullocks were killed, and after being cut in pieces, their flesh was conveyed to the camp.

On our way back Bichri wounded a gigantic stag, which Chamai succeeded in killing by stabbing it just below the shoulder-blade. It was of a kind which Gisgo said was not often seen by the Celts, and he called it an elenn or eland. Elenns are considerably larger than horses, and as a general rule feed upon the lower branches of trees, their necks being so short and rigid that unless they can graze upon soft soil into which they can sink nearly to their knees, they cannot get their heads down sufficiently low to reach the grass; they have very formidable antlers, which do not stand high, but branch out very wide on both sides;

BICHRI AND DIONYSOS BROUGHT THEM BOTH DOWN.

their strength is enormous, and, unlike the rest of the deer tribe, they do not exhibit terror when attacked, but boldly front the hunter.   They are consequently animals which it is by no means prudent to assail in close quarters, as we subsequently learnt by our own experience.

Hamilcar returned, bringing a fair supply of amber that he had collected along the coast.

We remained in our quarters here for more than a fortnight, spending our time in gathering amber, and subsisting upon whatever renns, elenns, or wild bulls we were able to kill.

The poor fellow who had been killed was buried where he had fallen. Over his grave was placed a stone engraved with his name and an invocation to the gods.

CHAPTER XVII.

JONO, THE GOD OF THE SUOMI.

AFTER sixteen days' sojourn, finding the amber beginning to run short, and the game getting very wild, I resolved to proceed, and sailed eastwards for five days, until the lack of provisions, no less than the desire of exploring, induced me to enter the mouth of the great river we had previously seen. The aspect of the place was scarcely more inviting than where we had landed before, but we hauled up our ships, and made an encampment as near to them as we could.

On setting out next morning to explore, we had proceeded but a little way before we came upon traces proving beyond a question that human beings had been in the neighbourhood quite recently. We entered nearly a dozen of the conical huts that we came to, in one of them finding a fire still burning, and in several of the others a variety of arms and implements, consisting of weapons made of polished stone, hatchets, and some copper caldrons. Examining them with greater minuteness, we ascertained that the huts had been abandoned in great haste; not only were there fragments of partially-consumed meat and fish, but one of the litters of reeds covered with moss was still warm from being lately occupied. I felt convinced that the natives must have evacuated their tenements in alarm at our approach, and suspecting that they were still lurking about, I ordered some red cloth, some beads, some bracelets and necklaces, and other things which I thought might attract their interest, to be displayed in one of the most spacious of the huts. I next made my people retire about three hundred paces, and waited to see the result of my device.

Before long the savages returned, and seeing us stand quietly, without any apparent wish to molest them, they allowed themselves to be seen, and came nearer to us. I took Gisgo and advanced to meet them ; but when he addressed them in the Celtic tongue, I found that they did not understand a word he said, but replied in a language that neither of us had ever heard before. Pointing first to a neighbouring marsh, they cried, "Suom, Suom," and then pointing to their own breasts, they said, "Suomi, Suomi," from which I conjectured that they called a marsh "suom," and that they were themselves "people of the marshes." When they showed us their stone weapons, they pointed to the north-east and said "Gothi ;" and what struck me as remarkable, they used the same word when they spoke of their articles of Tibarenian bronze. I had never before heard of a people of that name, but could not help wondering whether these "Gothi" could by any possibility be Caucasians.

I had seen many savages in my time, but I had never seen savages so frightfully ugly as these ; their huge heads, flat faces, small eyes, enormous mouths, sallow complexions, made up a physiognomy that was simply hideous ; their short, thin legs appeared scarcely able to support their clumsy bodies. They made us understand by their gestures that their friends the "Gothi" were taller either than themselves or us.

Besides being ugly, their appearance was most sordid. None of the ornaments so frequently worn by savage tribes adorned them, but their bodies were scantily protected by fragments of skins, and their weapons, for the most part, were clumsy bludgeons, stone lances, and a kind of harpoon tipped with bone. One alone wore a necklace made of shells and pieces of uncut amber. He appeared to be a sort of chieftain, and as a token of his good-will he held out a wild bull's horn full of some yellowish fluid ; I was on the point of taking the horn into my hand, when Himilco, ever ready to guzzle, raised it to his lips ; but no sooner had he tasted the contents than he dashed it to the ground, and began spitting and spluttering with every expression of disgust.

"Ugh ! the vile stuff !" he said, as soon as he could speak ; "it's nothing in the world but beastly fish-oil ! Ugh !"

We all roared with laughter ; but the chief, highly offended at the way in which we received his proferred attention, assumed a threatening attitude, and in spite of my attempts to pacify him, withdrew with his followers to the woods.

Poor Himilco looked very penitent when he saw the mischief he had done.

"What a besotted idiot I am !" he exclaimed ; "I declare I deserve nothing less than to be swung up to the nearest oak. But who was to know that what looked so tempting was nothing but stinking oil ?"

" Well, well," I said ; "never mind, you will have better luck another time. I don't fear but that we shall soon have another opportunity of improving our acquaintance with these barbarians."

As we proceeded up the river we met occasional groups of the people, who were always full of gesticulations ; they snatched greedily at any gifts we offered them, but took themselves off directly we attempted to open any negotiations.

A clearance in the wood made us suspect we were approaching a larger settlement, and we soon came to a large sheet of water, in the middle of which was an island crowded with conical huts, that in the centre being much higher than the rest. The island had been connected with the land by a narrow causeway, which the natives made us understand we were not to cross ; but they were not altogether indisposed to transact business with us, and

HE DASHED IT TO THE GROUND.

parted with some amber at a very low rate. But although
they attached so little value to their amber, it was far
otherwise with their weapons ; we could not induce them
to part with one of their clumsy lances nor one of their
smallest bone hooks for any article that we could offer
them. They showed us various implements of polished
stone, and appeared to be desirous of getting more like
them, exhibiting some surprise that we had none to
exchange away. Bronze they had seen before, and they
were acquainted with the use of bows and arrows ; they

pointed to the birds upon the trees, as an indication that
they wanted Bichri to shoot some ; a desire on their part
which he was more than ready to gratify.

Not thinking it prudent to remain all night in our
present position, I gave orders for making our way back
to the ships, yielding, however, to the wish expressed by
several of the Suomi to accompany us ; but so dark was
the night, and so bad were the roads, that we utterly
lost our way amidst the quagmires. We wandered about
till near daybreak, when six of us—Hannibal, Chamai,
Himilco, Bichri, one of the sailors, and myself—found

ourselves up to our waists in a swamp. After extricating
ourselves with much difficulty, we discovered that the rest
of our party was out of sight, and although we shouted
with all the strength of our lungs, we failed in making ourselves heard. Terrible as our situation was, there was a
still greater dilemma in store. While we were anxiously
endeavouring to find some waymarks to guide us, we were all
at once surrounded by nearly two hundred of the savages,
all stoutly armed. Resistance would have been useless even
if it had been possible. The men had started, as if called

by an incantation, from the tufted brushwood around, and
before we could lay our hands upon our swords, they had
felled us to the ground and pinioned our arms, yelling and
dancing all the time. They did not allow us time to regain
our feet, but pounced down upon us. Two men seized
me by the arms, two by the feet, and a fifth, after taking
away my sword, my cap, and my shoulder-belt, came
dancing along behind, every now and then leaning close
over me to peer into my face. They had all evidently
tricked themselves out for their adventure; their hair was

dyed red, and their faces were tattooed blue and black with war-paints.

After about an hour we were made to cross the causeway from which we had been repelled the day before, and alternately pushed and pulled, we were thrust into one of the huts. Hideous women and still more hideous children followed us in groups until we reached our destination, where a matting was fastened closely over the doorway, and we were left upon the cold damp ground in complete darkness, pillaged, bruised, and bound. There was the sound of retreating footsteps, and soon the noisy yells lapsed into perfect silence.

If we had been pinioned with rope we might perhaps have contrived to extricate ourselves, but we had been tied with a tough twist made of bark, which lacerated our wrists every time we made an attempt to release them. Chamai groaned aloud with agony.

"Who's groaning?" asked Hannibal, his voice being at once recognised in the darkness.

"I cannot slip these cursed cords," said Chamai.

"No," said Himilco, "you might as well try to break a ship's cable;" and remembering that he had not heard either me or Bichri speak, he asked whether we were there.

Bichri replied :

"Here we are, both of us ; and I only wish old Judge Gebal was with us ; he would have got us out of this dilemma."

"What do you mean ?" I said. "I don't understand what good the monkey could do. Anyhow, we must now help ourselves ; and that doesn't seem a very easy business."

"If Hamilcar and Hasdrubal do not come to our rescue, I shall think them the vilest cowards on the face of the earth," said Hannibal.

"Ah, you must not judge too hastily," I answered ; "I do not doubt but that they will do all in their power, but it is only too likely they have been attacked, and are in the same plight as ourselves. Besides, I hardly see how they are to get across that causeway."

"No difficulty there," said the general, warming into enthusiasm; "archers, right and left; fighting men in a column, four abreast; sound your trumpets and——"

He stopped abruptly; the clang of a trumpet had caught his ears.

"They come! they come!" cried Chamai, all excitement; "The Lord of hosts be with them!"

Another blast.

Hannibal continued to expatiate very scientifically about columns of four and columns of eight, and bewailed his fate that he was not in command; Bichri, less calm, fancied himself at the head of his troop.

The notes of the trumpet seemed more and more distinct.

"I cannot make out that trumpet," said Himilco; "it does not sound like one of ours."

"Whose else should it be?" replied Hannibal, testily. "Savages do not blow trumpets."

The pilot now insisted that the sound did not come across the water at all, but from the very centre of the huts.

"And yet," he said, "if it means an attack, I wonder we do not hear the war-cry."

We were all bewildered, and no less so when we heard three loud shouts rend the air, and the trumpet notes which had been going on at intervals for a quarter of an hour come to an end with a prolonged and thrilling flourish.

"I never knew but one pair of lungs that could make a clarion ring out like that," said Himilco.

The name of Jonah rose simultaneously to the lips of us all, and Bichri said he should like to see Gebal come in and confirm our impression.

"Nonsense," I said, "why indulge these foolish fancies? we must be practical. If we are rescued by our troops, well and good; otherwise we shall either have to buy ourselves off by a ransom or invent some ruse to escape."

SEVERAL OF THE SAVAGES ENTERED THE HUT.

To face page 267.

The sailor who was with us, speaking now for the first time, reminded us that there were several canoes moored to the causeway, and Himilco recollected having noticed them. This set us speculating whether we could devise any means of getting at the canoes, and using them to facilitate our escape. Hannibal declared that we should still be in the clutches of the savages, even if we got to land ; but Bichri and Chamai maintained that once free they could take good care of themselves.

I interrupted them to inquire whether any one amongst them had a knife, but it proved, as might have been expected, that the savages had not left us anything of the sort.

" Then roll yourself over here, Bichri," I said, "and see whether you cannot gnaw this twisted stuff off my hands."

" I have pretty good teeth," replied the youth, " and I will try."

Silence fell upon us all as we listened to him shuffling along the ground and panting with his exertions. I cannot tell how long it was before I felt his warm breath upon my hands, but it seemed to me at least half an hour. He nibbled indefatigably at the cord, giving my flesh an occasional grip in the process, until the material was reduced to the substance of twine, when by a slight effort of my own I burst it asunder, and I was free. An exclamation of delight broke from my lips, and I was about to liberate the others, when Himilco, who was lying across the doorway, said :

" Hush ! some one comes !"

In an instant I twisted the broken cord around my wrists, but only just before a party of several of the savages entered the hut. One of them having fastened back the covering at the door, took a long pole and pushed up a kind of trap that had closed the aperture at the top that served the purpose of a chimney, and the gleams of light afforded by these two openings allowed us to inspect our place of confinement.

The hut was perfectly empty, without an article of furni-
ture ; the walls were grimed with soot and smoke ; upon
the clay floor three rude stones formed a kind of fire-place,
which was filled with ashes and the refuse of some victuals.
A cold drizzling rain penetrated the hole in the roof, and
pattered down upon the ground below.

The men that had entered were elaborately covered with
their war-paint. One of them had the head and skin of a
bear drawn over his face like a mask, in the way that I
have seen done by the Assyrians ; another wore upon his
shoulders the head and horns of an elk. A third, who
carried a stick in his hand, ushered the other two into the
middle of the hut, where they began dancing and making
the strangest of contortions, but all without uttering a
word. After this had gone on for some time, one of the
two, who wore a necklace made of the teeth of wild animals,
and who apparently was the chief, walked up to me, and
stood gazing in my face. I noticed that he had my own
sword in his hand. He began a long harangue of which
I could not understand a word, but observed that he repeatedly said "Jono," and as often as he did so, all the
others gave a loud shout. When his oration came to an
end, the savage sprinkled us with some stinking liquor,
which he poured from a horn ; and having in chorus muttered
some kind of refrain that ended in "Jono," they all quitted
the hut, fastening the doorway securely behind them.

" No chance of making terms with such brutes as these,"
I indignantly exclaimed, when we were again alone.

" Patience !" said Hannibal ; " only let me get my hands
at liberty, and I'll guarantee to floor half-a-dozen of them,
unarmed as I am."

Himilco avowed that he was burning for a chance to
avenge himself for the filthy fish-oil ; and Chamai protested
that though the brutes should be as countless as the palms
of Jericho or the fleas at Shechem, he would outwit them
yet, and find his way back to Abigail.

While they had been talking in this strain, I had disengaged my hands, and very soon succeeded in freeing Bichri, who assisted me in liberating all the rest. Once again upon their feet, they stretched their stiff and weary limbs, and Hannibal, Chamai, and Himilco each armed themselves with one of the stones that formed the fireplace.

"Here's something that may smash a skull or two," said Chamai, as he poised his stone aloft.

"Not altogether a military-looking weapon," was Hannibal's remark, whilst he examined the cumbersome missile; "but our forefathers have done good execution with worse."

Picking up a few fragments of stone, Bichri was beginning to lament that he had not a sling, when Himilco in a moment produced the rope which he invariably wore, and tore off a piece of the goat-skin that had carried his wine, and with these materials the young archer was not long in putting together a sling which he hoped might do him good service.

Night closed in. It was still raining; the wind blew furiously. Everything seemed to favour our escape.

"Now's your time, my men!" I said. "Make your prayer to your gods, and we will be off at once."

It was agreed that if we should find more than one sentinel, we should fight our way through and make for the canoes, and that if we failed in that attempt, we should take to the water, and swim to the far end of the causeway. Our watch-word should be three raven-croaks.

"Now, invoke your gods," I repeated.

There was silence in the hut, and I noticed that Himilco raised his single eye to the aperture in the roof, as though looking for the Cabiri, but there was nothing to be seen except the pitchy blackness of the night.

I was about to lead the way, when, on peering out, I not only heard the sound of footsteps, but saw the glimmer of a torch. My heart beat fast, and I made my companions arrange themselves on either side of the doorway, so as to guard the entrance. It seemed to me that there were not more than one or two approaching. Chamai pressed his back against the wall, ready to brain the first savage that came within reach ; but whoever they were that were coming, it was evident that they were not hurrying themselves: they paused in quiet conversation outside, and at intervals we could again catch the mysterious word " Jono."

" I wonder whether they are going to give us any more of their beastly sprinkling," said Himilco.

" I have something here," muttered Hannibal, " that may give them a sprinkling they don't expect."

Breaking the silence of the night, we now heard the ringing notes of the trumpet, followed by yells and vociferations. The clamour was obviously a signal, for at the same moment the covering at the door was raised, and a man carrying a torch entered the hut, and closed the entrance behind him. But scarcely had he advanced a step, when four strong arms arrested him. Chamai's hand was across the intruder's mouth, effectually stopping any outcry he might raise ; I took possession of his torch ; and Himilco, having lifted the stone above his head, was about to hurl it on his victim, when he let it fall to the ground, and ejaculated :

" Merciful Cabiri !"

I raised the torch to the visitor's face, and in a moment had thrown myself upon his neck. It was Hanno.

The sailor picked up the torch that I had dropped in my excitement, and enabled Hanno in his turn to recognise us.

We were speechless.

For some moments we could do nothing but grasp each other's hands and embrace our long-lost friend.

Hanno himself was the first to speak.

" Don't strangle me quite. What a joyful surprise is this !"

" Out with a joke, Hanno!" cried Hannibal, " or I shall never believe it's you !"

Hanno did not smile, but inquired anxiously about Chryseis. Hearing from me that she was safe and well, his eyes filled with tears, and he murmured :

"Ashtoreth be praised !"

A violent thumping outside brought us back to a sense of our real position, and when the thumping was renewed Hanno went to the door, and having addressed some one with a few guttural words, which were received with a half-approving grunt, he returned to us.

"And now," he said, his voice assuming its old tone of vivacity, "perhaps you would like to know what brings me here. I am come to conduct you to the grand temple of the Suomi ; and a fine structure you will see it is, built of reeds and fish-bones in tip-top style. You are there to be sacrificed to the great god Jono."

"So then Jono is a god, is he ?" I said ; "but if you are his high priest I presume we need not give ourselves much alarm."

Himilco said that if this Jono were the god of fish-oil he most heartily wished that he might be sent some hundred fathoms down below the sea.

"Gently, gently, good pilot !" said Hanno, with mock solemnity ; "you must not speak disparagingly of the great divinity. I can, however, tell you one thing. Jono has no more liking for fish-oil than you have yourself. No one loves a draught of good wine better. And I may as well tell you at once who he is. He is none other than our friend Jonah of Eltekeh ! our incomparable trumpeter, Jonah !"

"Ah ! didn't I say," cried Himilco, "that no one but Jonah could bring out such a flourish as that ?"

Hanno went on to tell us that the people were already assembled in the temple awaiting the arrival of ourselves, their destined victims, and in reply to Chamai, who suggested that we should rise up and attack them bodily, informed us that there were more than three thousand of them, so that any resistance on our part would not only be useless, but must result in our immediate destruction.

"No;" he continued; "you have no alternative but to trust yourselves implicitly to the influence of the mighty Jono and of his high priest Hono, your humble servant. My first proceeding will be to acquaint the assembly that I have released you from your bonds, and that by the agency of magic I have rendered you quite mild and submissive."

"Allow me to interrupt you for a moment," I said; "but I am intensely anxious to learn whether you know anything of our comrades?"

"They are now on their way hither," replied Hanno; "and the very object with which the Suomi propose to sacrifice you is to propitiate their god, so that he may vouchsafe them the victory."

Hannibal burst out enthusiastically:

"I knew our fellows would come to our defence; brave souls they are! we'll conquer yet!"

"Not so fast," was the reply; "you must be content to leave everything to me. I will send a message to Hamilcar and Hasdrubal. See now; I have my writing materials ready; I made myself a calamus from the marsh-reeds; my ink is some of the Suomi war-paint; and for papyrus I have a piece of deer-skin."

Hanno wrote and talked at once; and as soon as he had finished he turned to us:

"Now then, follow me to the temple. You need be under no apprehension yet. I will take care that the god shall declare that he does not require your lives at present. This will give some hours' respite. In the interval I shall be able, I trust, to send my letter to our friends. Let us go: but one more word of caution; you must be careful above all things not to laugh at any of our proceedings."

"You will have to conjure pretty cleverly," I said, "if you are going to conjure us out of this dilemma."

"Well, you know," he said with a smile, "I have had some education in this line. I have learnt a bit of the craft of a priest and a magician; though I acknowledge I did not anticipate that I should have to practise under the present circumstances."

Taking his torch, he led the way; and with downcast eyes, and much to the amazement of some savages who were waiting outside, we filed demurely after him.

The island which we proceeded to cross was considerably larger than it had at first sight appeared. The huts were arranged in irregular clusters, each group surrounded by its own palisade. The road was very dark, and we had to ford a number of pools of water, while the rain splashed heavily down upon our bare heads. After winding through the labyrinth of huts, we reached an open place in the heart of the village, lighted with torches, and thronged with a crowd of Suomi, armed and coloured with their paint. The central hut into which we were conducted was much larger than the others, and served the purpose of a temple; it was circular, and had the appearance of a gigantic beehive. The interior was lighted with torches, and with pans of oil, furnished with flaming wicks, which had been made of bark; it was crowded with the savages, and what with the fumes of the torches, the vile odour of the burning oil, and the stench of the grease with which the savages had smeared their bodies, the atmosphere of the place was positively sickening.

On first entering the assembly the mist was so thick, and the confusion from the noise of the savages, who were raving like maniacs, was so great, that I could not distinguish the venerated deity; but as I gradually got accustomed to the smoky glare and the boisterous hubbub, I made out that there was a kind of dais or altar piled up with every conceivable variety of natural products,—skins of beasts, intestines of fishes, bladders of sea-calves, feathers of birds—mounted upon which, daubed with blue and crimson, and adorned with bulls' horns and sea-calves tusks, was the god himself. Not a feature could I distinguish; one only object seemed familiar; in one of his crimson hands the god held the very trumpet which I had

T

purchased for twelve silver shekels of Khelesh-baal the merchant of Tyre.

The savages did more than make room for us to pass ; they thrust us forward till we were close in front of the altar-shrine. Hanno placed himself at the side of the god, who, at a given signal, raised his trumpet to his mouth and blew a deafening blast. A few words from Hanno made the entire assembly, except ourselves, prostrate themselves with their faces to the very ground, and thus left standing conspicuously above the rest, the god could not fail to recognise us.

No words of mine can describe Jonah's amazement. Eyes, nose, and mouth, were all distended until the very paint broke in scales upon his face. He was dumbfounded for the time, and only after a long stare of astonishment, exclaimed :

"Baal Chamaim ! lord of the heavens ! "

A sensation of terror thrilled through the prostrate worshippers. The mighty Jono had spoken !

"Hold your tongue, you fool ! " exclaimed Hannibal, with sonorous solemnity, but in plain Phœnician. The god started, and said no more.

The crowd of worshippers shivered with awe.

All at once a piercing shriek echoed through the temple. A black-haired object, ill-defined, had made a tremendous bound, and perching upon the head of the divinity himself, began tearing his hair, scratching his face, and hugging and caressing him with wild delight. The savages started to their feet in consternation, and some of them fled at once ; but when they saw their god drop his trumpet and take the apparition in his arms, and heard him say to it, "Gebal, Gebal ! dear little man ! and have you found out your poor old Jonah ?" their terror knew no bounds, and they rushed frantically out, leaving us absolutely by ourselves.

Chamai on one side gave the god a good dig in his ribs, while Hanno on the other kicked him pretty sharply on the

THE GOD JONO.

leg, but neither of these attentions seemed to disconcert him in the least ; he came forward and said :

"Delighted to see you all, my friends ; an unexpected pleasure : you know I am a god now ; what shall I order for you to eat ?"

"Back to your seat, jackanapes !" cried Hanno, severely, "and don't speak another word until I give you leave."

For a moment Jonah's dignity seemed somewhat wounded, and he hesitated about complying ; but upon my promising him a good skin of wine, he returned to his shrine without further murmuring. Hanno re-arranged the trumpery jewellery with which the god was bedecked, and Bichri whistled the monkey back to his own shoulder.

"Here's a messenger," said Hanno, "that I think will answer my purpose very well."

And turning to the creature, who was making the oddest grimaces, he said :

"Now, Gebal, take this to Hamilcar, quick ; and you shall have some cake."

The monkey appeared perfectly to comprehend what was wanted, snatched the piece of skin that was held out to it, gnashed its teeth, and on three legs hopped rapidly out of the temple. A buzz of mingled surprise and fright made us aware that the animal had passed through the crowd outside.

"So far, so good," said Hanno ; "now for the next scene. You must all prostrate yourselves to the ground before Jonah. I am going to recal the Suomi."

Jonah was taken aback, and modestly remonstrated against this humiliation on our part ; but Chamai, by way of enforcing obedience to Hanno's injunction of silence, gave him a sharp blow across his mouth, and then came and took up with the rest of us his posture of outward reverence and awe.

Standing at the doorway in the character of Hono the priest, Hanno encouraged the people to re-enter their temple. Gradually the more courageous were induced to return, and ultimately about fifty, still tremulous with their recent alarm, were assembled in front of the shrine. Jono once again made the building ring with a tremendous blast, and Hanno delivered a brief oration, which seemed to have a soothing effect. The Suomi quietly retired, and we could hear them placing sentinels outside to prevent any one from entering.

Finding that we were not likely to be disturbed again, Hanno extinguished all the lights except two torches, and led us into the darkest corner of the temple, whither Jonah, after flinging off all his gew-gaws, was only too delighted to follow us.

CHAPTER XVIII.

JONAH WAXES AMBITIOUS.

" WHERE'S my wine ?" was Jonah's first inquiry.

"Coming in good time," I answered ; "but you must have patience to wait, it may be a few months."

The giant looked aghast and stup'fied, until he was recalled to himself by a friendly poke from Chamai.

"Glad to see you amongst us again, old tippler!"

"And I am glad too," he said ; "but what am I to do next ?"

"Whatever else you do, you must obey Hanno," I said ; "he is trying to accomplish our escape to our ships."

What I informed him seemed to have the effect of plunging him into a deep reverie ; he knitted his forehead till a layer of red paint peeled off, and at last roused himself to ask if he should have to accompany us.

"Certainly," I replied ; "unless you prefer remaining with these barbarians."

"And with their revolting fish-oil," put in Himilco.

"But here I am a god," said the trumpeter, slowly, as if pondering the matter. "On board ship, Chamai knocks me about, and Hannibal kicks me, and every one calls me a lubber : but here it is all different ; instead of being thumped, I may thump whom I please ; I gave the god of the savages in the north such a thrashing that he died an hour afterwards. At home too, in Eltekeh, the little children used to call me a blockhead, and the men used to make me carry olive-baskets on my head and sacks of corn on my back, and scant measure of wine did I ever get ; but here, I blow my trumpet, and in there comes no end of good things, meat and venison and fish, more than I can eat. It's no bad thing to be a god."

We all stared in amazement.   He had never been known to make such a long speech before, far less to arrive so logically at any conclusion ; at any rate, his deification had expanded his ideas, and inspired him with a new ambition.

"So then," I said, "you do not mean to go back with us."

He hesitated ; but soon said that where Hanno went he should go too.

Himilco began to jeer him :

"O ! you mean that you like Suomi fish-oil better than Helbon wine ? and you prefer the chilly fogs of the marshes to the olive-yards of Dan ? and you like slices of rein-deer more than wheat and honey cakes ?"

A tear stood trembling in the giant's eye.

" I think," he said, " I would rather go with you."

"And surely," added Hanno, "you would wish to go back to Eltekeh ; you must want to tell them all about the leviathans, and the behemoths, and Nergal's kitchen, and how you have been a god yourself."

" They would'nt believe me !"

" And think," said Bichri, " we shall have old Gebal with us to show the men of Dan !"

This last appeal was too much for Jonah, and fairly bursting out into tears, he sobbed out :

" Yes, I must go ; I must go with you and Gebal."

Hannibal laughed outright at what he called Jonah's calf's tears, but declared that he was really very pleased to have his trumpeter back again, and pulling out two silver shekels from his purse, which he had contrived to retain, he said :

" There, man, take these ; they will pay somebody to give you a good wash when you get on board."

Hanno now proceeded to explain his scheme.   The

written message he had sent to Hamilcar was to the
effect that he should parley with the Suomi until he heard
the sound of Jonah's trumpet, and should then answer the
signal by his own trumpet.

"I shall pretend to the savages," he continued, "that
their god has ordered them to lead out their victims for
sacrifice, and if by this stratagem we can once get over the
causeway and within reach of our own people, everything
is easy."

Approving of his plan, I merely observed that there
might be some difficulty in knowing when our comrades
were holding their parley ; but Hanno at once assured me
that the savages would not do anything without consulting
him as their priest, so that he should be fully informed of
everything that transpired.

We had now been twenty-four hours without food, and
were suffering from fatigue and hunger. Hannibal ventured
to ask whether some provisions were not to be had, and in
an instant Hanno went to the door and uttered a few
syllables that sounded something like the croaking of an
old crow.

"I have told them," he said, "that Jono wants something to eat. They know what his appetite is ; I daresay they will bring enough for you all."

Very shortly there was a knocking at the entrance of the
temple ; some savages had brought platters of boiled fish
and roast venison, and several large horns full of drink, the
whole of which Hanno took from their hands at the door
and passed on to us. Half-famished as we were, we made
short work with the dishes, the god appropriating as his
own modest share a fish half as large as a tunny, and a
reindeer-steak. Hanno joined us, and asked innumerable
questions all the time we were eating Both he and Jonah
drank freely from the horns, which had been placed with
their small ends on the ground ; but Himilco and Hannibal
could not conceal their disgust at seeing them swallow
what they supposed to be rancid oil. Hanno, however,

soon explained that the contents of the horns was a liquid made of fermented barley and some vegetable juice, and that it was the common beverage, not only of the Suomi and Cymri, but of the Celts of the west, the Gothi of the east, and the Germani of the south.

"I should not think of saying that it is in any way equal to the juice of the grape," he said ; "but it is really not unpalatable ; you may safely taste it."

Hannibal looked doubtful. Himilco said that he had heard Gisgo speak of some preparation of the kind before, and that he was not sure he had not himself tasted it at the mouth of the Rhone ; he raised one of the horns cautiously to his lips, sipped, and said nothing.

We all in turn followed his example. Bichri pronounced it very acid ; Chamai declared it was detestably bitter ; the sailor and I both recognised it as very like what we had tasted elsewhere.

"Not good for much!" said Hannibal, after he had taken a good draught ; "is it intoxicating ?"

"Most assuredly it is," replied Hanno.

"The most villainous stuff I ever tasted," said Himilco, the last to pass an opinion. "However, I think I will have a little more."

And he drained another horn.

"Disgusting!" he sputtered out ; but he seemed so thoroughly to have reconciled himself to the flavour of what he abused, that I was only fearful that he would take more than was good for him.

By the time we had finished our refreshment, day was beginning to dawn. and Hanno was summoned outside ; he returned almost immediately, ordered Jonah to sound his trumpet, and bade us all be prepared to start.

Jonah went to the doorway and delivered a ringing blast.

Himilco hastily emptied every one of the horns, protesting all the while that it was odious stuff, sickening to the palate, and almost as vile a drink as plain water.

In answer to Jonah's signal we soon heard the reverberation of our Phœnician trumpets, and without loss of time, Jonah and Hanno at our head, we marched out of the temple. The crowd outside, regarding us with a superstitious reverence, allowed us to pass freely through them, and to proceed onwards without hindrance, so that in the course of half-an-hour we were in the midst of our friends, Hanno clasping Chryseis in his arms, Jonah hugging Judge Gebal, and Chamai so engaged with Abigail, that he did not notice how Hannibal, Himilco,

and Bichri had been mercilessly thrashing a group of the nearest savages.

Our reception by our party had the immediate effect of opening the eyes of the barbarians to the terrestrial nature of their supposed god ; and they no sooner became aware how we had escaped their clutches than they began to assail us with showers of stones and lances, so that our retreat to the ships was a matter of considerable peril. No one, however, was seriously injured ; there were many slight contusions, and Jonah's nose was ignominiously bruised by a stone hurled at him by one of his late worshippers.

Once safely on board, we made no delay in turning our

backs upon this inhospitable shore, and steering west-
wards, made towards the island of Prydhayn.

With a calm sea and a favourable wind, our progress
was easy; and anxious to learn all that had befallen
Hanno and Jonah since we had lost them, we assembled
on the stern of the *Ashtoreth* expressly to hear their
story. Jonah, who had been well washed, insisted upon
being dressed in Phœnician costume, and took his seat,
with the monkey upon his shoulder, by the side of the
scribe, who proceeded to recount their adventures.

"It is now, you know, more than a year since the day
when we were caught in the ambush of the men of Tarshish. When we were first captured our lives were in the
greatest jeopardy, for according to what we were told by
a Phœnician I met, we were at once to be handed over to
Bodmilcar, who was close at hand. Negotiations to this
effect were going on, when it transpired that one of the
Iberian chiefs had been so fascinated by Jonah's trumpet
that we were to be retained, and not given over to the
Tyrian, who was reported to be wounded. During this
respite I contrived, by means of a stick and some blood
from a wound of my own, to write a message for you on
my sandal-strap; I had no doubt that the instinct of
Gebal would take him back to Bichri, and accordingly I
resolved to make him my messenger."

"Yes; and your message came that night," I said.

"I conjectured so," he continued, "by the monkey not
returning. We were soon sent off towards the north,
under the guardianship of a troop of Iberians, who did not
by any means treat us badly, and after a toilsome journey
came to a region where the mountains were so high that
they were all covered with snow; they separated the land
of Tarshish from the land of the Celts, and were called the
Pyrenees. Here we were handed over to the chief of the
Guipuzcoa, for whom we were destined. These Guipuzcoa
are sometimes known as Bascons; they are a warlike
people, perpetually engaged in hostilities with the Aitzcoa,

or "men of the rocks," on the north-west, and with other
Iberians on the south. We remained for more than two
months before any opportunity of escape occurred ; but at
last, during one of the forays, we were left behind in the
village, which was built upon piles at the mouth of a small
river. We got possession of a canoe, and having filled it
as far as we could with provisions, we ventured out to sea,
and contrived to reach the shores of the Celts, from whom,
in answer to many inquiries, I ascertained that some ships
had recently passed along their coast, and, from various

articles that they showed me, I had little doubt they were the
Ashtoreth, the *Dagon*, and the *Cabiros*. Making out from
the Celts that you had gone northwards, we left our canoe,
and took passage in one of their ships that was on the
point of sailing for Ar-Mor ; but upon our arrival we found
the people engaged in war with the Cymri of the Island of
Prydhayn, so that we could not get transported there. For
two months I sojourned in various parts of the islands of
Ar-Mor, and picked up some knowledge of Celtic ; but all
the time I was trying to devise some plan of following you

in the direction I felt sure you had taken. At length it chanced that I found a tribe of Cymri who were not at war with the people of Prydhayn, and embarked in one of their boats ; but a tremendous storm arose, and we were driven far away to the east."

"Talk of storms," said Jonah, putting in his word ; "was not that a storm ? I saw leviathans spouting water from their noses as high as your mast, and we were tossed about the waters like a log. For three days we had nothing to eat or to drink."

"Jonah is right," continued Hanno ; "the tempest was really frightful, and we were dashed upon the muddy swamps of the coast. The Cymri drowned themselves in sheer desperation, and we, more dead than alive, existed for more than a week upon roots and wild fruit from the wood."

"And what did you find to drink ?" asked Himilco.

"Nothing but muddy water."

The good pilot's sympathy was deeply moved, and he said :

"Sorry drink that, as I know by experience."

After this interruption, Hanno went on :

"Jonah persisted in blowing his trumpet perpetually, resolved if possible to attract attention, and at length succeeded in making himself heard by a troop of Suomi who were migrating eastwards in consequence of the aggressions of the Cymri and the Germani, who were appropriating territory after territory to themselves. Not only did Jonah's enormous trumpet excite the wonder of the Suomi, but I could observe at once that his huge and imposing stature, and his abundant growth of shaggy hair impressed this diminutive, smooth-faced people with superstitious awe, a sentiment which I resolved to encourage, with the object of turning it to our own advantage. We accompanied them in their migration to their new settlement, where we witnessed the erection of the village in which you found us, and my representations prevailed so com-

BLOWING HIS TRUMPET.

To face page 354

pletely that they recognised Jonah—Jono, as they called him—as their presiding deity, regarding me as his high priest. For some time, then, you see we have been in the lap of luxury; but nothing has ever led me for a moment to forget you or your ships, or to cease to long for the Great Sea and our noble Sidon."

"And Sidon ere long you shall see!" said I, when he had finished his narrative; "we are now on our way back; it is impossible to penetrate farther, and we are homeward bound."

"Sidon for ever! and long live the King!" shouted Chamai; "we shall see the sun again."

"And get some wine!" cried Himilco, tossing his cap in the air.

"And some new clothes!" chimed in Hannibal; "beggars in rags are our soldiers now."

In the midst of the general hilarity Jonah sat silent and full of thought.

"What ails you, trumpeter?" I asked; "cannot you quite make up your mind to go back?"

"It is no good my going back," he half blubbered out; "they will never believe me; they will only laugh when I tell them I have been to Nergal's kitchen and seen behemoths by dozens; and if I were to say I have been worshipped for a god, and had dinners brought me every day, big enough for a month, they will declare I'm stark mad."

"Never mind, old fellow," said Chamai; "we'll back you up; we will testify to the truth of your stories; and what's more, you shall be presented to the King, and he shall hear you blow your trumpet."

Overcome by Chamai's good-natured encouragement, and his own prospective honours, he fairly burst into tears.

"Do you really mean it? and will the King see Gebal too?"

"Aye, that he will; and we must teach old Gebal to act the courtier, and to make a bow."

Hannibal declared that he thought Jonah ought to be court-trumpeter, and to wear a scarlet tunic; and I pledged myself to use any influence I could to secure him the appointment, promising that if I succeeded I would make him a present of his first uniform.

Jonah chuckled aloud with delight.

"And shall I wear a scarlet tunic? and shall I play before the King? What will they say at Eltekeh? Happy day that made me come to Tarshish! Long live the King!"

With ejaculations such as these he withdrew to the extreme limit of the prow, and relapsing into silence, mused in solitude upon the dignity that awaited him.

From that day forward, Jonah was another man.

CHAPTER XIX.

BODMILCAR AGAIN.

SOME easy sailing carried us past both the eastern and western limits of Prydhayn and the Tin Islands, and brought us off the rocky shores of the archipelago o Ar-Mor, with its islands all perforated and undermined by the action of the waves. Hanno recognised nearly every locality.

"There," he said, pointing out one spot after another, "there is the island where I learnt to croak my little bit of Celtic; and that is the rock from which Jonah and I used to fish with bone-hooks; and over there is the island where the priestesses paint their faces blue and black for their religious mysteries. Whilst we were with them they wanted us to shave all our hair off our faces, with razors made of shells."

"They gave the same advice," said Himilco, "on the Tin Islands to Hannibal and Chamai, who came back to us one day with their beards gone and their chins as smooth as pebbles."

" I only wish," remarked Hannibal, "that they would do for Bodmilcar what we did for ourselves; only instead of a shell I should like to have a good sharp sword put across his throat."

The mention of Bodmilcar's name led Hanno to inquire whether we knew anything of him ; and this led Hannibal to tell him how on the day of the ambush he had given him a thrust in his side, which had been, no doubt, severely wounded, but his people had succeeded in carrying him off

"Never mind," exclaimed Chamai; "we are sure to have another chance."

"And then I trust," said Hanno, "it will fall to my lot to deal with him after his deserts."

"Unless I am beforehand with an arrow from my good bow," said a voice from the yard-arm high up in the air. Bichri and Dionysos were up there, playing with the monkey. Hanno laughed, and said that Bichri had been associated so long with the monkey that he was becoming a monkey himself, and was making Dionysos just as volatile. Without leaving his perch Bichri asked:

"Why should I not teach the boy the use of his limbs? and why should I not drill him to use a bow?"

"And why," added Hanno, "should you not teach him to read?"

"How can I," he said, "when I have never learnt myself? besides, reading will not help him to climb mountains, hunt wild goats, or put an arrow in a mark."

"You may learn some day," rejoined the scribe, "that a pen may be a surer and a sharper weapon than an arrow. Would you and Dionysos like to learn to read?"

Startled by the suggestion, the archer caught hold of a rope, and in an instant had slid down to Hanno's feet. Dionysos followed. The monkey flew up to the mast-head.

"To learn to read, did you say?"

"Yes," replied Hanno. "Let us make a compact; you shall teach me to shoot, and I will teach you both to read."

"Agreed!" cried Bichri, enthusiastically; "and I'll warrant that in a month you shall hit a mark no bigger than my hand at the ship's length."

And so the days passed on. Hanno taught Bichri and the young Phocian the alphabet. Himilco, as he piloted the vessel, kept up a perpetual howling over his compulsory abstinence; Chamai and Hannibal, when they were not yawning in idle listlessness, were generally playing at knuckle-bones ; the two women gossipped contentedly in their cabin ; and Jonah confided to Judge Gebal his dreams of future greatness.

In something more than six weeks we sighted the pillars of Melkarth, and shortly afterwards entered the harbour of Gades. The suffect, Ziba, and all our acquaintances had imagined that we had long since been drowned, and were loud in their congratulations on seeing us back again safe and well, and were full of surprise when I exhibited my magnificent cargo of tin and amber.

I inquired eagerly about Bodmilcar, but could only gather from the suffect's account that fragments of what were supposed to be his vessels had been picked up at the mouth of the Illiturgis, but that nothing whatever had been seen of his gaoul, so that the most probable conjecture I could form was that the scoundrel had been massacred in the interior of the country.

It cannot be denied that we had all been looking forward with much impatience for the opportunity of obtaining some decent food and drink. Himilco was really getting exhausted with his subsistence for so many months on a water diet ; so that on reaching land I took the very earliest chance of allowing my men to go ashore, where, doubtless, they directed their steps only too quickly to the wine-shops. Before Jonah left the ship I observed that he had some shekels in his hand, and asked him if he would not put them in his purse.

" No," he said ; " they will never be quite safe until I have changed them for wine, and put them into my inside."

Hanno, Chamai, and their sweethearts went with me to dinner at Ziba's house ; Bichri and Dionysos wandered about the streets and gardens of the city ; while Hannibal, who said that now that we had come to a civilised country he should wish his trumpeter to be a credit to his troop, carried off Jonah to buy him a proper tunic.

We had given up two days to recreation when, returning to the *Ashtoreth*, I met Himilco and Gisgo, both extremely

U

excited, in company with a Phœnician sailor who was a stranger to me.

"Good news, captain!" shouted Himilco, as soon as he was within hearing; "good news! tidings of Bodmilcar!"

"Tell me, quick!" I answered impatiently.

"Well, you must know," said Himilco, who was anything but steady upon his legs, "we met this good man; he was thirsty and we were thirsty, and I treated him to a cup at a tavern, where he told us that he had escaped from Bodmilcar's ship."

"Leave your plagued thirst," I said; "go on, tell me what you know."

"Leave my thirst? no, no; it's my thirst will not leave me."

"Curse you!" I said, half-frantic with irritation; "tell me at once!"

"Give me time and I will tell you all that he told us in the tavern."

"Where's Bodmilcar? you drunken fool!" I roared, stamping with rage; and turning in despair to the sailor, said: "Tell me, my good man, where have you come from?"

"Come from?" echoed the irrepressible pilot; "why he has come with us; he has come from where we have been drinking."

My patience was exhausted, and I struck him a sharpish blow across the mouth, a hint that he took that he had better keep quiet.

According to what I could make out from the sailor's version of things, he had come from an unfrequented bay some 150 stadia to the south-east; that Bodmilcar had been there, at first with one gaoul, the *Melkarth*, but afterwards he had three galleys besides; that he had forced a number of the natives of Tarshish into his service; and that by some means he had collected a great body of criminals and deserters. He had himself, he said, been kidnapped by Bodmilcar, but had contrived to escape, and having made his way on foot along the coast, was now going to make his deposition before the naval suffect at Gades.

I inquired how long it was since he had run away from Bodmilcar, and whether he knew anything of Bodmilcar's movements. He replied that it was a week since he effected his escape, and that he knew that it was the Tyrian's intention to make for the country of the Rasennæ, and thence to proceed to Ionia.

Telling the man that I was returning to Tyre, I offered him a passage with me, if he liked, as one of my crew, to which he agreed with apparent pleasure ; he not only assured me of his fidelity, but declared that nothing would gratify him more than to be able to avenge himself upon Bodmilcar.

On the third day after this, having thoroughly revictualled the ships, we set sail with our hearts all elated at the prospect of seeing our native shores. We sighted Calpe and Abyla, but the wind having freshened, we were obliged to beat to windward to enter the strait. Next evening I noticed a large galley sailing in the direction opposite to ourselves, and tried to hail her ; but as the weather did not permit us to get near, I made Himilco take half-a-dozen sailors in one of the boats and row towards her ; a circumstance that struck me was the extreme readiness with which the new sailor volunteered to take an oar.

The boat had not long pushed off before one of the crew rushed up to me with consternation written in his face, and exclaimed :

" Captain, we have sprung a leak ! "

I lit a lamp, and in a minute was making my way down into the hold. Two sailors and one of the helmsmen followed. My heart sunk within me at what I saw. The water had not only got into the hold, but it was already knee-deep ; worst of all, it was still rising rapidly. The sea was rough, and the ship was labouring hard against the wind. Unless the evil could be remedied, another quarter of an hour would see us at the bottom. Almost beside myself with agitation, I caught hold of a handspike and plunged it wildly about in every direction; the ill-tidings soon ran through the ship, and there was a general rush towards the hold, but I drove every one back, and suffered nobody to remain except the three men who had first come down with me, and young Dionysos, who had slipped in unobserved, and was paddling about in the water, which was up to his shoulders.

In the midst of my frantic endeavours to ascertain the position of the leak, my attention was arrested by voices above speaking hurriedly in a tone that indicated alarm, and I distinctly caught the names of Bodmilcar and the *Melkarth*. Almost at the same moment the man standing on the ladder to hold the lamp moved on one side to allow by-way for some one who flew, rather than ran, into the hold. The light was not so dim but that I recognised Himilco, his head bare, his hair dishevelled, and his cutlass in his hand. Before I had time to speak to him a trumpet was sounding overhead, and Hannibal's stentorian voice was shouting :

"Make ready the scorpions! Archers, to your ranks!"

"Good gods!" I exclaimed at last, "what does this mean ?"

"Soon told," said Himilco; "the man we took on board was Bodmilcar's agent, bent on mischief. I have managed to get my boat back, but the *Melkarth* and her galleys will be upon us in a moment."

He had hardly time to finish speaking, when the commotion above made it manifest that the struggle was already beginning.

"Then we are lost," I cried, in absolute despair at our twofold peril : "that infernal rascal has scuttled the ship."

Himilco groaned aloud in dismay.

A shrill cry of distress at this very moment rose from Dionysos, calling for help :

"Save me! save me! I am in a hole; I am sinking!"

The lad's head had already disappeared, when Himilco,

THE CHILD HAD FOUND THE LEAK.

To fa., page 213.

sticking his cutlass into the ladder, and shouting that the
child had found the leak, made a dive and brought him
back half-fainting from the water, and delivered him to the
sailors, who carried him on deck.   Not a moment was lost.
Carpenters and sailors were summoned to the task, and a
heavy wave making the ship lurch so that the leak was
actually seen, we put forth all our energies, and notwithstanding the combat that was being waged above our
heads, succeeded—all praise to our gracious Ashtoreth!—
in temporarily stopping the hole.

Meanwhile the clamour of the fighting had given place
to silence.   On remounting the deck I found several dead
bodies, and pools of blood in various places ; I saw that
the *Adonibal* and the *Cabiros* were lying alongside right
and left, but Bodmilcar's vessels had vanished in the
twilight.

Hannibal and Chamai were furious at their escape, and
could hardly find words strong enough to express their
contempt of a cowardice that had shirked a fair fight.
Hanno, with his bow still in his hand, avowed that
nothing else than the gathering gloom of night had saved
Bodmilcar; if he could have recognised him, he would
have been a dead man.

" When I was attacked in the boat," said Himilco, " I
recognised the villain who took my eye out of my head ;
and if there had not been some thousand of them
peppering away at us all at once——"

" How many, do you say ?" asked Hannibal, with a
smile.

" Well, then, I am sure there were six or eight ; but
never mind, many or few, there was one man I knew only
too well, and while I was down there looking after that
leak, no one knows how my heart was burning for a chance
of getting him by the throat."

All this time the wind was rising, and after a while it
blew a hurricane.   There was every cause for apprehension ; the leak was stopped so insufficiently that it might

break open again at any moment, and the waves were playing with our ship like a ball.

There was no sleep that night. The men, in relays, had to toil with all their might at scooping out the water; and after that had been reduced below the level of the leakage, it took more than five hours to strengthen and caulk the fresh planking that had repaired the gap. All danger, however, from that source was averted.

Daylight came, but the tempest was more violent than ever. I hardly recollect so furious a wind; the pigeons that I let loose were unable to withstand the hurricane, and fluttered back helplessly on to the deck. All control over the ship was lost, and there was no alternative but to allow her to drift we knew not whither.

CHAPTER XX.

THE WORLD UPSIDE DOWN.

FOR eight days did the tempest rage, when, at the end of that time, the wind dropped and the sky cleared, I found that we were quite close to the shore, and off a headland beyond which the coast stretched away indefinitely to the south. Continuing our course in that direction, we came in sight of a mountainous island, richly wooded and extremely picturesque. The glowing sun and the genial temperature reminded us of our beloved Phœnicia; and so tempting was the aspect of the place, that I resolved to disembark, not merely as a matter of pleasure, but to look to the ships, which, after their strain, required some examination.

We anchored in a charming bay, and were soon surrounded by canoes full of savages, of whom the first characteristic that I noticed was their low foreheads and yet elongated skulls. To my surprise, they addressed us in the Libyan tongue, and proved to be the true Garamantine or red Libyans. We were the first Orientals they had ever seen on their shores; but one of their old men stated that he had been to Rusadir, and had seen Phœnicians there. They received us very kindly, and told us that their island was one of a group that was situated to the west of Libya. Ignorant of navigation, they could give me no information about distance; and all that I could make out was that the coast of Libya extended far to the south, and was inhabited by people of the same race as

themselves ; and that still farther south there was a region
where the men were like animals, and perfectly black.

"That's a country worth seeing ; I should like to catch a
black man," said Bichri.

The residents, I observed, wore bracelets, necklaces, and
earrings, which were, I found, made of gold ; and in reply
to my inquiry whether the gold was found in the island,
they told me that they obtained it both in nuggets and
in dust from the Garamantines of the mainland, who collected it by means of fleeces at the mouths of their
rivers.

The people did not attach any great value to their gold,
and were quite ready to barter it away very freely for
many things we had to offer them ; for instance, for some
glass trinkets they gave me as much gold dust as I could
hold in the hollow of my hand, while for such things as
knives, lance-heads, or swords, they would give an equal
weight in gold.   The delight of my people was unbounded, and I had the utmost difficulty in preventing
them from bartering away all their weapons.   Hannibal
sold his helmet, crest and all ; and Jonah even parted with
his trumpet, boasting that he could now have one of pure
gold, with which to play before the King ; but so enchanted
was he with the country, that if the inhabitants would have
accepted him for their god he would have been quite ready
to reside permanently amongst them.

I spent a fortnight in purchasing gold and repairing the
ships, and an interesting period we all found it.   The
fertile soil was productive of some of the finest fruits I had
ever seen ; one fruit in particular with a scaly covering was
very delicious.   The valleys were full of orange-trees of
the growth of centuries, and the mountains were clothed
with magnificent woods, in which beautiful little birds
with yellow plumage were fluttering about, and singing
exquisitely.   Bichri, who did not care about purchasing
more than just enough gold to ornament his belt and
quiver, spent several whole days in these woods with

Dionysos, and succeeded in catching some of the bright little songsters, which he secured in a cage ; but his trouble was of little avail, as they all died upon their passage.

As for Judge Gebal, he manifested such a keen appreciation of the charms of the scenery that we had to keep him tied up to prevent his running away ; but the time for our departure necessarily arrived, and, after the repairs were all completed, we reluctantly bade farewell to the lovely archipelago, upon which I bestowed the name of the Fortunate Islands.

Once more at sea, I had no difficulty in determining my course. All my party were eager to visit the wonderful gold-countries, and Bichri persisted in saying that he should like to catch sight of the black men ; Himilco just at first protested against going in a direction where wine would not be forthcoming, but his objection was soon overruled, and he was contented with our resolution to sail southward. What caused us much bewilderment as we advanced, was, that not only did the sun rise higher over our heads, but the Cabiri descended lower towards the

horizon. Himilco complained that we were sailing out of
reach of the protection of the gods ; I pondered the matter,
but kept my thoughts to myself.

After running some distance to the east, the coast
resumed its southerly direction ; and then it was that the
sun, which day by day had gradually risen higher in the
heavens, stood vertically over our heads, and then began to
change its position, shining at last upon my left hand
instead of upon my right. Evening after evening, too,
brought into view constellations that were quite unknown
to us ; and so great was the amazement of all on board,
that I resolved upon holding a general consultation of
officers and pilots, and the more intelligent of the sailors,
in order to discover a solution of the mystery.

Hamilcar gave it as his opinion that the gods must have
been making some alterations in the face of the heavens ;
Hasdrubal suggested that perhaps we had passed the
bounds of our own world and entered upon another; whilst
Himilco avowed his suspicion that unless something of
that kind had occurred, the world must be round, and we
were on the other side of it. Absurd and outrageous
as Himilco's conjecture appeared to every one else, I
confess it chimed in to a certain degree with my own
speculations, and set me reflecting that if it were so it
must be the sun and the stars that were standing still, and
the world that was moving round them. But, after all,
Himilco was much more inclined to believe in a prodigy
than to entertain any of these fanciful theories.

Pressed with inquiries as to what I intended to do, I
announced my resolution of continuing my course to the
south ; if ultimately the coast should incline to the west
(or what I presumed to be the west), I should return to the
Fortunate Islands ; but if, as I anticipated, it turned to
the east, I should go on following it, under the expectation
of getting to the north at last, and reaching Egypt by
way of the Sea of Reeds. This scheme of circumnavigating
the entire land of Libya commended itself entirely to the

judgment of my pilots, but it quite baffled the comprehension of Hannibal and all the landsmen.

When I spoke to Hannibal about arriving at Egypt, he looked quite aghast, and exclaimed:

"Egypt! here are we sailing farther and farther away from the Straits of Gades; and yet you talk about getting this way to Egypt. Impossible!"

"Patience!" I said; "perhaps we may find you a short cut even yet!"

He shook his head dubiously; and even Hanno observed that the mysteries of navigation were very abstruse, and that the studies which he had pursued at Sidon did not enable him to solve these enigmas.

"Ah! you should have travelled more, young man," said Himilco; "and you should have learned to know the stars."

"I should think this voyage is travelling enough for any one," replied Hanno.

Chamai merely remarked that he was quite sure that they might all rely with perfect confidence in my judgment. And thus the consultation was brought to a close.

Many times did we approach the coast with the intention of landing; but either it was utterly desolate, or it was so crowded with black men, who yelled and assumed such a threatening attitude, that we always postponed any attempt to go ashore. One night in particular, as we were passing under a promontory that I had named "the chariot of the gods," the noises we heard seemed of so threatening a character that I deemed it prudent to put out a little further to sea; but at length our provisions began to run short, and there was nothing to be done but to venture on land. Bichri, patient and enduring as he ever was, complained of living on salt fish; Jonah murmured that there was short allowance for ourselves, and no fruit for Gebal; and Hannibal regretted that we were losing our chance of picking up gold. I was accordingly induced to lay to as soon as I found a convenient opportunity.

Our anchorage was the estuary of a river apparently as large as the Egyptian Nile; its banks were covered with thick woods; numbers of crocodiles and hippopotamuses were visible in the water by its shore; and great birds, uttering shrill and piercing cries, whirled around above our heads.

For four days we wandered about without finding any sign of human being; we obtained, however, an abundance of wild fruit, and shot several buffaloes and antelopes, of which a great portion of the flesh was carried on board and salted. On returning from one of the foraging excursions, Bichri came running to me, looking utterly woebegone; he was followed by Dionysos, weeping bitterly, and Jonah, gesticulating vehemently, and apparently as much agitated as himself.

"What's the matter, Bichri?" I asked.

"Gebal has gone!" he exclaimed; "he has been carried off by Bodmilcar's monkeys."

I burst out laughing. In his indignation he looked as if he could have annihilated me.

"I am sure they were Bodmilcar's!" he insisted; "creatures with long tails; they took him away; he never would have gone with them of his own accord."

Nothing I could do served to calm him; he would not be pacified until I allowed him to take some men and go out again in search of his lost favourite; but in the evening they all returned worn out with fatigue, only to announce, as might have been expected, that their search had been fruitless. There was no doubt the monkey had been delighted to join the troop of his own tribe that was gambolling in the woods. Bichri was very inadequately consoled for his loss by bringing back a great black monster, which, after he had wounded it, the men that were with him, in spite of the huge brute's desperate defence, had succeeded in despatching with their pikes. It certainly was a most formidable-looking creature, and I subsequently had it stuffed, and it may now be seen in the

IT SNAPPED A PIKE STAFF IN TWO.

To face page 301

temple of Ashtoreth in Sidon. Bichri told us that after it had six or seven arrows in its body it snapped a pike-staff in two as easily as if it had been a reed ; upon which Hannibal remarked that the strength that could break asunder a pike-handle made of oak of Bashan must be prodigious.

We were obliged to depart without finding any vestige of Gebal. After sailing on for about a fortnight, our supplies again ran short, and as we were discussing what steps we should take in consequence, Hannibal interrupted us by shouting :

"A gaoul ahead !"

Every eye was bent in the direction to which we were pointed, and sure enough there was a gaoul of Phœnician build ; but on farther scrutiny it was evident that it was all dismantled, and drifting at the mercy of the waves.

" May be a ruse of Bodmilcar's," suggested Himilco.

Taking his hint, we approached very cautiously, and it was not until we had thoroughly satisfied ourselves that there was no one on board to answer our signals that we ventured close alongside. It was perfectly deserted.

Gisgo said that he remembered having once abandoned his ship off the Pityusai Islands, and that probably this was a similar case ; but he could not understand what current could have borne the gaoul to this distant shore.

" Never mind where she comes from," I answered ; " let us hope she may prove a godsend."

Hannibal and Himilco, who went on board, brought back the welcome intelligence that the hold was well freighted with corn and wine, the whole of which we joyfully transferred to our own vessels, leaving the empty hull again to the wind and waves. In the evening I caused an offering to be made to Ashtoreth in acknowledgment of her manifest interference on our behalf.

Next day we hove in sight of a lofty promontory, the top of which was as flat as a table. A strong gale was springing up.

" Never mind the wind," cried Jonah. " What do I care

for the wind now? I've a purse full of gold; plenty to
to eat; plenty to drink; and a red tunic before long
Tempests be hanged! Long live the King!"

The gale for some days increased in violence, and all
attempts at steering were quite useless. When, after eight
days, the sea became calmer, I could make out that the
land was lying to our left. This was according to my
prognostications, and I followed the coast to the north
with renewed confidence, day by day becoming more and
more convinced that the sun was again rising in the
heavens; and one lovely night, about a fortnight afterwards, Himilco suddenly seized my arm, and making
me point to the northern horizon, exclaimed in a voice
trembling with excitement:

"See, the Cabiri!"

"Yes; true enough; there are the Cabiri," I answered,
as full of delight as he was himself. "We have accomplished an unheard-of thing," I added; "we have circumnavigated Libya."

"And to-morrow," he said, "we shall have the sun once
more on our right; we are on our way to the Sea of
Reeds."

"Aye, to the Sea of Reeds! and to Sidon, our own
Sidon! Sidon the glorious, Sidon the incomparable!"

There was none to witness; the crew were sleeping in
their berths; and in the fervour of our enthusiasm we
threw ourselves into each other's arms.

A month later, as we were taking in fresh water at the
mouth of a river, we fell in with some black men, who bore
a marked resemblance to the Ethiopians, who are often
seen in Egypt. One of them could speak a little Egyptian;
he told me he had learnt it in Ethiopia, which is subject to
Pharaoh. His own country, he stated, was six months'
journey below the southernmost limit of Ethiopia; but he
could give no information whatever about its distance by
sea. These negroes called themselves Kouch, and having
never seen any Phœnicians, took us for Egyptians; but as

soon as we explained that so far from being subjects of
Pharaoh we were enemies of the Misraim, they welcomed
us as friends, and treated us with the utmost cordiality.
They had evidently a great abhorrence of the Egyptians
on account of the cruel ravages that had been committed
on their northern boundaries.

For the next three months we never found a favourable
wind to speed us on our way. We employed our time
in transacting business with the Kouch, and in making
hunting-expeditions into the interior of the country. In
the way of exchanges we procured gold, ivory, pearls, and
skins; and an immense success attended our hunting-
excursions in a region that was found to abound in
elephants, rhinoceros, and giraffes, as well as in smaller
game. There was not one of us who had not some trophy
of our good fortune or our skill to exhibit. Bichri killed a
lion, with the skin of which he made himself a mantle, and
even little Dionysos brought down a panther.

At length the opportunity for which we had watched so
eagerly arrived, and we set sail once more. Ten days
after our departure, while a stiffish breeze was blowing
from the north-east, I noticed not very far ahead of us
a large Phœnician gaoul, which appeared to have sustained some damage, and to be drifting along under the
action of the wind. In answer to my signals, she gave me
to understand that she had lost some oars and her yard-
arm, and that she was in need of help. Always anxious
to render assistance to a vessel in distress, but yet fearful
of treachery I immediately ordered out my men, but
meanwhile instructed Hannibal to have the catapults in
readiness; and thus prepared, the *Ashtoreth* approached
the gaoul on one side, and the *Adonibal* on the other, the
Cabiros following in the rear.

There was no need for any apprehension on my part.
As soon as we were fairly within view of each other, the
captain, standing on the stern, raised his arms and shouted:

" By Baal Chamaim! it's Mago!"

" By Ashtoreth and all that's holy !" I exclaimed ; " it is my cousin Ethbaal !"

The recognition was a mutual pleasure ; our ships were soon alongside, and we were grasping each other's hands.

" How rejoiced I am to see you, Mago !" he repeated over and over again ; " Phœnicia has given you up in despair ; every one mourned you as lost. By Ashtoreth ! you must have been saved by a miracle !"

And he put his hands upon my shoulders and long and keenly scrutinised my face.

" Tell me two things," I said ; " where am I ? and what has brought you here ?"

Ethbaal seemed full of surprise ; but said :

" Come, come ; you are laughing at me. You must know well enough where you are."

I assured him that I was in earnest in what I said, and repeated my assertion that I was by no means aware of where I was ; and when Himilco informed him that we had come from a place where the Cabiri could not be seen at all, and where the sun shone on the wrong side of us, he looked as if he thought we had taken leave of our senses. Nor did he appear to understand much better when Himilco went on to expatiate upon having once drunk fish-oil, and having had no wine for many months together.

" Mysterious !" muttered Ethbaal to himself ; " here is Mago, close to the entrance of the Sea of Reeds, only six days' voyage from Ophir, and yet he comes from the south, after sailing four years ago westward to Tarshish ! Strange !"

He pondered awhile, and then addressed himself to me

" Yes ; you are close to the Sea of Reeds."

I uttered an exclamation of delight, and turning to my people cried triumphantly :

" Was I not right ? Did I not tell you that we were on our way to Egypt ? Lucky we did not not turn back from the Fortunate Islands :

Ethbaal appeared to be confirmed in his suspicion that I

must be mad, and declared his total ignorance of the Fortunate Islands :

"I have never heard of them!"

"No, nor yet of the Tin Islands ; nor yet of Prydhayn ; nor yet of the river of the Suomi ; nor yet of the chariot of the gods," exclaimed Himilco. "Compared with us you are mere coasters, loafing about in cockle-shells."

Genuine Sidonian as he was, my cousin could not brook any insinuation against his seamanship, and colouring deeply at the slight which he conceived was offered to him, he said in a tone of anger :

"Out upon your insolence! do you call a man a coaster who has made the voyage to Ophir ? do you call my gaoul a cockle-shell ? Are you mad, or are you drunk, you one-eyed fool ?"

Himilco, recalled to a sense of propriety, changed his banter into cajolery :

"Now then, my dear fellow, you can do a great deal better than bully me. Haven't you a little wine on board ? It would be a great boon to give us a skin ; we haven't tasted a drop this two months."

I interceded with Ethbaal, asking him to overlook what might seem to be rudeness on the part of Himilco, and assured him that our adventures had been so extraordinary that he must really pardon a little bragging. He not only took my mediation in a good spirit, but sent for a goat-skin of wine, which he himself handed to Himilco, in token of forgiveness. Saying that he should make an offering with it to the Cabiri, the pilot emptied so large a share of the contents down his throat that his companions began to wonder when his draught was coming to an end, and almost despaired of the wine lasting out till it should come to their turn to partake of it.

"Glorious wine! wine of Arvad, Hannibal," he said, smacking his lips as he removed the goatskin from his mouth, and passed it to the rest.

X

Gisgo and Hannibal clutched at the bottle together.

"Nay, nay, my friends," cried Ethbaal; "do not be fighting for the wine. I have plenty more. My cargo is all wine which I am carrying to Ophir."

"Could you not take me with you?" asked Himilco, eagerly; "my services are quite at your disposal."

As soon as the wind dropped, we submitted ourselves to Ethbaal's instructions as to the direction in which we ought to steer, and taking his gaoul into tow, we proceeded on our course to Ophir.

When evening came we found that by Ethbaal's orders a true Phœnician banquet had been prepared on the stern of the *Ashtoreth* : cheese, olives, figs, raisins, and a double allowance of wine were served out to the men ; and we ourselves took our seats upon brilliant carpets that had replaced the worn-out rags with which we had been so long familiar, and for the first time for months, nay, years, enjoyed the viands of Tyre and Sidon, and quaffed the wines of Byblos and Arvad.

Our spirits rose to the occasion, and I should hesitate to say how many times I filled and re-filled my wine-cup before I began to recount the adventures which Ethbaal was anxious to hear.

My story lasted far on into the night.

When I had finished, Ethbaal, who had never flagged for one moment in his attention, raised his hands to the stars in the heavens above, and swore by all the gods that my chronicle ought to be registered in letters of gold. He went on to tell me that the cargo I had sent from Gades and all my messages had been duly received at Tyre ; that everyone had come to the conclusion we must all have been drowned in the ocean ; and that nothing had been heard about Bodmilcar, who, it was taken for granted, had been punished for his treachery by the direct visitation of the gods.

I offered Ethbaal a present of some very fine pearls ; he at first refused to take any acknowledgment at all of his attention to us, but I induced him ultimately to accept the gift. The damages to his gaoul were only to the rigging, and did not affect the hull ; and as we had taken it into tow, there was nothing to cause us any anxiety, or to prevent us from retiring to rest.

Next morning, in the course of conversation with Ethbaal, Himilco asked :

" Have you had any fighting, captain, since you have been out ? "

" Fighting ? no, why ? " he replied.

" Because if you continue in our company you will soon find that fighting is our destiny. We are always fighting ; if we are not fighting men,—and that we are doing pretty frequently,—we are fighting the beasts of the earth ; and if we are not fighting beasts, we are fighting against wind and waves. Go where we will we attract the fightings, just like a headland attracts the storms. Fighting is our luck ; so I just warn you, you had better be on the look-out."

Ethbaal laughed. He said he hoped that we had come to the end of our adventures in that way, and that we should have a prosperous voyage to Ophir ; then turning to me, he asked what I expected to procure at Ophir, as I had already a large supply of gold, which was the commodity ordinarily obtained there.

I reminded him that I had a much larger quantity of amber than I really wanted, and that in return for a portion of it I intended to lay in a stock of sandal-wood and spices, peacocks and apes, and anything else that the country could offer.

The Arabian coast was rocky, but we sailed along it without difficulty for six days, at the end of which we

arrived at Havilah, the principal city of the kingdom of
Ophir and Sheba.   Unlike the Phœnician seaports, it has
no quays, fortresses, nor arsenals, but it is well-sheltered,
and forms a commodious trade-harbour; the town rises
like an amphitheatre upon the surrounding heights, and
the white terraces, with their brown and red domes, broken
by clusters of palm-trees, stand out in pleasing contrast to
the deep-blue sky, while the domes of the temples are of
gilded bronze, and glitter with dazzling brightness in the
sunlight.   Although the people are indifferent seamen, yet
it is to the sea that they owe their prosperity, their city
forming the mart between our own country and the distant
Indies.

The Queen herself takes a keen interest in all matters
connected with navigation, and her palace is situated close
to the sea-shore.   It is built of cedar, and ornamented with
trellis-work and open balconies; the walls are all adorned
with paintings, inlaid with precious stones, or hung with
curtains of variegated stuffs.

I was very anxious to secure the Queen's favour, and to
make her an offering worthy of her acceptance.   With
this object, I placed some of my finest pieces of amber in
a casket made of Tarshish silver, and carrying my gift
in my hand, I presented myself with Ethbaal and most of
my officers at the entrance of the palace, and sounded the
great drum by which it is the custom to demand admit-
tance to the royal presence.

Ordinarily the Queen occupies a tapestried tent that
overlooks the sea; she had consequently been aware of
our entrance into the harbour, and when we presented ourselves at the gateway of the palace she gave immediate
orders that we should be conducted before her.   We were
taken to her pavilion across a garden of surpassing beauty.
There were countless plants, wonderful alike in their blos-
soms and their foliage, grouped in exquisite order around
sparkling fountains; there were sumptuous tents of every
hue pitched amongst the rare and graceful trees, to the

boughs of which monkeys were attached by golden
chains ; Indian birds with gayest plumage fluttered overhead ; and peacocks, displaying their gorgeous tails, were
strutting along the avenues. Every thing we saw seemed
worthy of the stateliest empire in the world.

We prostrated ourselves before the Queen, who at once
bade us rise. She was young and very fascinating ; and
although she was surrounded by ladies in waiting and
maids of honour, she was conspicuous among them all for
grace and beauty. Her attire, redolent of perfume, was
alike sumptuous and elegant ; in her hair and round her
neck were jewels valuable enough not only to equip a
fleet, but to maintain it as well ; a long robe, embroidered
in gold with figures of men, beasts, and birds, was thrown
over her, but opened to display the richness of the dress
below ; her sleeves were loose to the elbows, and on
her wrists were bracelets that must have been all but
priceless.

We were dazzled into silence as we first gazed upon
her beauty and magnificence ; but Hanno almost immediately advanced, and ventured to recite some verses of
an Arab ode :

> " Fairer than moons are thy beaming eyes,
> Nay, they are radiant suns :
> Forth from the bow of thine arched brow
> Shoot the arrows that pierce man's heart :
> Be it thy justice prevails far and wide,
> The universe yields to thy charms.
> What are thy favours ? Say I not true !
> Fetters they are that bind the soul ;
> What are thy fingers ? What do I kiss?
> Keys of a heavenly joy."

The language spoken in Ophir is very similar to our
own, and the Queen, who understands Phœnician well,
expressed herself as being highly gratified at Hanno's
courtier-like address. She then deigned to examine the
presents I had brought, and requested me to give her a
brief outline of my travels and adventures ; then rising

from her seat, and bidding us follow her, she went out, acompanied by her retinue, into the garden, and moving with all the grace and dignity of a goddess, herself conducted us to every point of interest in her paradise. Before we took leave of her she desired me to visit her again on the eve of our departure, that I might receive some instructions that she wished to give me.

The same evening the munificent lady sent us a store of provisions for our ships, and various presents for ourselves, amongst which I should especially note several embroidered robes for the women, and a scarlet tunic, a hyacinth-coloured girdle, and a gold-embroidered shoulder-belt for Hanno.

We remained a week at Havilah, making exchanges, and inspecting all that was worth seeing in the place. Representatives of nearly every nation seemed to be congregated in the town; men from India and Taprobane, from Ethiopia, and the mouth of the Euphrates. The people of Sheba themselves bear a strong resemblance to the Jews, Phœnicians, and Arabians, the principal difference being that they are of smaller stature and darker

complexion. The queen, however, is remarkably fair
The gold and the tin that we procured here, as well as
the peacocks, tortoise-shell, and ivory, are all imported
from India ; but the spices, stuffs, and vases of opaque
glass, are brought through India from a still more distant
land, to which hitherto no one has ever sailed, and which
could not be reached in less than a two years' voyage.

On the day of my departure I presented myself again
before the Queen.

" I have to inform you, Captain Mago," she said, " that
the old King David who sent you to Tarshish died a year
and a half ago, and has been succeeded by his son
Solomon, of whose power, but especially of whose wisdom,
I hear a wonderful report. His dominions extend as far
as the Gulf of Elam on the Sea of Reeds, where he holds
the port of Ezion-Geber. I am eager to enter into a treaty
with him, and I commission you, on my behalf, to convey
to this august monarch a present that shall be worthy of
himself and me."

" Your will, O Queen, is my law," I replied, as I made
my obeisance.

"But first of all, captain," she continued, "tell me whether you and your companions in toil are too worn out with the fatigues that you have already endured to undertake another voyage in my service. Information has reached me that the King of Babylon, Assur, and Accad is on his way, with a powerful army, to the mouth of the Euphrates to put down an insurrection. No one so well as yourself can fulfil what I desire. I want you, if you will, to convey him some messages from me, and to be the bearer of presents that I shall send."

I did not hesitate to comply ; not only did I express my willingness to go, but assured her that the voyage would be neither difficult nor long.

"Go then, brave mariner," said the Queen, with a beaming smile, "and I shall not fail to recompense you royally."

I prostrated myself once again before her, and withdrew.

An hour later I had taken leave of Ethbaal, who was returning to Sidon by way of Ezion-Geber and the canal of Pharaoh, and, with all my people, I was embarking for yet another voyage.

CHAPTER XXII.

BELESYS FINDS BICHRI SOMEWHAT HEAVY.

IT did not take us much more than a month to sail to the mouth of the Euphrates, although during the time we made one sojourn with the Arabians, and another with the fish-eating Gedrosians on the opposite coast.

On receiving the announcement from me of the aged King David's death, Chamai and his fellow-countrymen observed a week's mourning, fasted, rent their clothes, and combed neither their hair nor their beards ; but at the end of the week they made plentiful ablutions, and held a festival in honour of Solomon, the King's son and successor.

It was early in the morning that we reached the river-mouth, and having entered it, proceeded till we came to a little town dedicated to the god Oannes.   There is no stone found in the country, and the place, like all the other towns on the Euphrates, is built entirely of bricks, the fortifications being circular walls constructed of bricks, baked and unbaked, cemented with layers of bitumen.   On the right were the remains of vast forests, which, according to the statements of the learned, were, three hundred years ago, the haunts of the elephant.   On the other side, extending as far as the eye could reach, was a long stretch of meadow-lands and corn-fields.   Looking up the river, we could count some hundreds of tents pitched among the crops or sheltered by the forest, the fires of the encampment sending up columns of smoke, and groups of horses

being picketed everywhere amongst them A few boats
and two large ships of Phœnician build were moored to
the shore ; but what struck us most of all was the swarms
of soldiers, many of them with swords drawn and lance in
hand, who were posted everywhere alike on the river-bank,
in the pastures, among the crops, and along the skirts of
the forest.

" The army of the Assyrians !" cried Himilco.

"The gods be praised !" said Hannibal, in an ecstasy of
delight ; "now shall I set eyes upon something like an
army once again. See, how admirable their position ! how
skilful their groupings ! I must make the acquaintance of
their officers."

He was stopped short in his panegyric by the shouts of
a troop of horsemen who were galloping towards us, and
ordering us, in Chaldean, to bring our ships immediately
to a stand-still, and to tell them who we were. From the
stern of my ship I answered the officer in command as
courteously as I could, and he, in reply, ordered me to
remain where I was whilst he reported my statement to
his superior. In about a quarter of an hour he returned
from the camp whither he had gone, and brought with
him a troop of cavalry, at the head of which rode a burly
fellow armed in a complete suit of mail, and carrying a
lance.

Hannibal again began to praise the order and accoutre-
ments of the troop and their leader to Chamai, who, while
admitting the superiority of Assyrian cavalry, contended
that the infantry of Judah was second to none ; but before
they had finished their military discussion, the Chaldean
had halted just opposite our ships, and was calling out
that our principal officers must come ashore and state our
demands in the presence of Belesys, the King's commander-
in-chief.

Hanno knew enough of Chaldean to remember that the
word "belesys" in that language signified "terrible," and
muttered that it was a formidable name for a man to have.

Taking the Queen of Sheba's letters, and followed by eight sailors carrying her presents to the King, and escorted by my own officers, I went on shore. The Chaldean was tall and stout ; he had a wide face, with a strong jaw and great deep-set eyes ; his beard was thick and frizzled like the rest of his company, and his manners were extremely coarse and insolent.

"Come, now, you sailor fellows, stir yourselves a little briskly, will you?" he cried ; "I'm not fond of walking my horse."

He conducted us first of all through an enclosure filled with war-chariots, and then past an encampment of infantry, composed of Mesopotamians armed with maces and spears, and in physiognomy bearing a striking likeness to the people of Judæa. A little removed from us was a regiment of Medes, the representatives of a nation recently subjugated, but whose ancestors had given Nineveh her line of kings. They were thickset, and had round heads, scanty beards, and obliquely-set eyes. Their fierce expression of countenance attracted our notice, and armed with their swords and short, strong bows, they must be very formidable in battle. As we passed, we were near enough to hear that they were making coarse jokes upon us in their own tongue. A noisy band of half-naked Arabs next caught our attention. These, with their camels, always form part of the contingent of the King of Assyria, and mingling with them I recognised some Midianite slave-dealers and some Phœnician merchants, who act as purveyors to the army, but make their chief profits by purchasing slaves and plunder from the soldiers.

We proceeded to the cavalry encampment, and when we were about in the middle of it, we were ordered to halt. We found ourselves in front of a large circular tent made of rich hangings, the entrance of which was guarded by Kardook infantry carrying maces, and equipped with breastplates, greaves, crested helmets, and round shields. This was the tent of Belesys, the terrible.

"Enter," said the officer who had been conducting us, adding in a jeering tone : "I hope the general will give you a handsome reception ; perhaps he will put on a good temper for the occasion."

He burst into a roar of laughter and galloped off.

"Stop!" cried Chamai, wrathfully; "is that the way you speak to a Phœnician captain ?"

But his words were wasted. The Chaldean was out of hearing, far away.

The Kardook guards scrutinised us narrowly, and consulted each other in an undertone. They appeared especially attracted by the dress of Hanno, who had arrayed himself in the costly presents of the Queen of Sheba. Turning to him, one of them said :

"Are you captain ?"

"No," replied Hanno, pointing to me; "there is our captain."

The Kardooks stared in astonishment.

I was dressed in my ordinary naval attire ; but as the Assyrians always associate dignity of place with costliness of apparel, they could only account for my appearance by conjecturing that I was in disguise.

"You wish to see Belesys ?" said the guard ; and having entered the tent, returned again immediately with permission for us to be admitted.

The Assyrian commander-in-chief was at the farther extremity of the tent, surrounded by a number of officers and slaves, and was reclining, or rather lolling, upon a luxurious couch ; he was superbly dressed, but wore no armour. Armed men stood on both sides of him, and two cupbearers were in attendance holding goblets of wine, of which, however, he was in no need, as he was already very drunk.

With the exception of Bichri, we all made a low bow on entering the tent ; but the young archer, who was not always in a conciliating mood, did not feel disposed on this occasion to exhibit any sign of courtesy.

Pushing aside one of the cup-bearers who was obstructing his view, Belesys stared straight at us. He was a tall man, with a great frizzled beard, thick lips, and a heavy jaw, and his hair was glossy with perfumed ointment. A heavy mace which lay by his side was surmounted by the figure of a bull's head. As he gazed at us, he shook his head, screwed up his eyes, and, indeed, distorted all his features; while his attendants, as if to flatter him by imitation, did precisely the same. We waited some time for him to speak, and at last, in a tone that quite confirmed our suspicion that he was intoxicated, he roared out:

"You see those two big fellows? and you see that youngster with the bow? Take them, and give them five-and-twenty lashes apiece; and then put them amongst my archers. I don't dislike the look of them."

Utterly astounded, I held my tongue. Taking no notice of Hanno's clenched fist and gleaming eye, he went on, hiccupping as he spoke:

"That young man with the gold shoulder-belt, strip him to the skin, and pack him off to the slaves. I don't care for the other old scarecrows; do as you like with them; there's an ugly one-eyed rascal among them; hang him or behead him as you please, the sooner the better."

"What?" shrieked Himilco, in ungovernable rage; "what? do you call me a one-eyed rascal? and our captain, a Phœnician admiral, do you call him a scarecrow? By all the gods!"——

Belesys burst into a roar of laughter, repeated his orders that we should be put under arrest, and taking a cup from the nearest cup-bearer, drained it at a gulp and flung it back into the man's face.

"Handcuff them, I say!" he bawled again.

Several of his men approached to execute his bidding, but I shook off the hands of the Chaldean who ventured near me; Hannibal floored the man who was about to assail him, by planting his fist heavily in the fellow's eyes after the Cymri fashion in Prydhayn; Chamai, in genuine

Celtic style, knocked down another by butting at him with his head in the middle of the stomach; but Bichri, the most agile of us all, took a much more determined measure. Bounding like a cat upon the couch, he fixed his knee firmly upon the general's breast, and with one hand caught hold of his beard, while with the other he held the point of his knife close enough to his throat to be felt.

"Capital, Bichri! well done!" shouted Hannibal, drawing his sword.

"Keep your hold, Bichri, and long live the King!" cried Chamai, following Hannibal's example.

Hanno and myself, resolved to act on the defensive, also drew our swords; Himilco tripped up another of the Chaldeans by one of those adroit turns of the hand with which a sailor knows so well how to take a landsman by surprise; and all my own sailors, seeing the aspect of affairs, in a moment set down their packages and unsheathed their cutlasses.

"Shall I cut his throat?" asked Bichri, coolly, appealing to me.

"No; wait a little," I answered; "let me talk to him a bit first."

Approaching near enough for him to hear me distinctly, I said:

"Belesys, you have only to cry out or make the least resistance, and in one instant that knife severs your head from your body."

"Soldiers," I continued, turning myself to his guard, "the moment you call for assistance or lift up your hands to attack us, that moment, mark me, your general is a dead man."

The proximity of Bichri's knife to the general's gullet seemed to have a sobering influence upon him, and in a voice very much subdued, he implored his soldiers and slaves to keep perfectly quiet, and at his wish they retreated to the sides of the tent.

Bichri began to whistle one of his Benjamite airs, and deliberately brought up his other knee on to the general's chest.

"You are stifling me, young man ; let me breathe, let me breathe."

"O nonsense, I know better than that," replied Bichri, without stirring an inch ; "I am a very light weight."

"Let me go," gasped Belesys. "Believe me, I was only joking ; let me free, and I will recompense you liberally."

"As to letting you free, that's not my concern ; that depends upon Captain Mago ; no one but the captain gives orders ; you should sue to him."

At a hint from me that he should allow the Assyrian room to breathe, Bichri removed his feet to the ground, but without relaxing his hold upon his beard or lifting the knife from his throat. Belesys was breathing heavily ; his face was pale ; his forehead moist with a cold sweat ; there was no doubt about his being sober now ; and he piteously asked for our captain to speak to him. Without waiting for me, Himilco began to jeer him.

"Ah! you would like to see the old scarecrow, would you ? and here am I, too, the one-eyed rascal ; it is a long way to come, all round Libya, to cut your throat, but it is quite worth the trouble if it teaches you that you shouldn't get drunk all by yourself."

And snatching the goblet from one of the cup-bearers he drained it off, and pitched the empty cup at the nose of the general.

"Gently," I said, and laid my hand upon the irascible pilot. "Belesys is mistaken altogether ; he did not understand that we were conveying presents to his King."

The Assyrian gave so violent a start that his neck was actually grazed by Bichri's knife. He was beginning to bawl out something about his illustrious sovereign Belochus II., when I admonished him that he had better not speak so loud, a warning that Bichri enforced by tightening his grasp upon his throat.

"I was but jesting ; you should take a joke," he gasped "Only tell your young man to loose his hold upon my throat, and I swear by the almighty Nisroch, I will not hurt a hair of your heads. Can you not trust me now ?"

"Not quite," I answered, smiling.

It was now my turn to assume the tone of irony, and with mock reverence I turned to him and said :

"And now, most valiant Belesys, servant of the mighty Belochus, will you condescend to do me the favour of visiting our ships ?"

"By all means. I am ready ; I will come at once."

"We will take our time," I continued. "Just attend to me : you must have, you know, every proper mark of respect ; on your way to the vessels you shall walk between Hannibal and Chamai ; they shall show their respect by drawing their swords, and Bichri shall walk close behind you ; that will be another sign of respect : and when you get on board you shall remain on board until I have had an interview with the King. On board ship, you have heard, it is the captain who gives orders."

'I think I understand your terms," he replied. "I am to go with you ; if I cry out you will murder me ; and when I am on your ship I am to be kept as a hostage."

"Precisely so," I said.

The incorrigible Himilco renewed his jeering, and asked whether he could not produce a little more wine, but the general made no reply, and closed his eyes as if he were in deep thought. Bichri took his seat upon the breast of his prisoner, who, in spite of the indignity he was receiving, seemed to be so much struck with admiration for the young man, that he promised to make his fortune if he would enter his service.

"But get up, get up, I entreat you," he begged him, in an imploring tone. "I assure you that you are a great deal heavier than you seem to imagine."

Bichri made no answer, but whistled an air, and jolted himself up and down upon his seat.

Y

Himilco, meanwhile, filched a flask of wine from one of the cupbearers, whom he rewarded by some good hard knocks, and then professed that he was enjoying himself extremely.

"Come now, general," I said at length ; "we can't spend all day waiting here ; we shall have some one coming in. Is your mind made up ?"

He made an ambiguous movement. Bichri frowned, and jerked his knife.

"Yes, I will come," he said, abruptly. "After all, I was in fault."

We now arranged our party as I had proposed. Assuming all the appearance of respect, Hannibal and Chamai placed themselves one on each side of Belesys, and Bichri, still whistling gently to himself, followed alone behind. I followed with Hanno and Himilco, and the sailors, taking up their packages, brought up the rear.

As we passed along the ranks, the soldiers all prostrated themselves in honour of their general, and I could scarcely suppress a smile at their ignorance of the true state of things. Belesys did not utter a word or make a sign, and in half an hour's time he was on board the *Ashtoreth*, witnessing the respectful salute with which my own people always acknowledged my return.

"To your posts, men !" I cried, cheerily ; "here is the noble commander-in-chief of the Assyrian army ; he does us the honour to inspect our ships."

"And he intends," said Himilco, "to treat you to a double ration of wine."

"Long live the King of Assyria ! long live his illustrious general !" rose in acclamation from a chorus of voices.

Belesys, who was still rather pale, smiled uneasily, but with a forced hilarity professed himself ready not only to give my brave men the double allowance of wine, but to provide them with some sheep and oxen besides. Once again a general cheer was raised, and Hannibal made him a military salute. Chamai merely shrugged his shoulders

IN HONOUR OF THEIR GENERAL.

and Bichri could not help confiding to Dionysos that the
man before them was nothing but a drunken coward, who
ruled the 50,000 men under his command by blows and
lashes.

"They are not Hellenes, then," said the young Phocian,
proudly ; "no Hellenes submit to blows !"

Belesys bit his lip ; he had overheard what was said,
and it mortified him ; he tried to conceal his annoyance,
and remarked to me that he had thought Phœnicians were
too much engrossed by commerce to have any concern in
the affairs of states. Hannibal was on the point of quoting
the case of Adonibal, the naval suffect of Utica, as an
instance to the contrary, when our attention was arrested
by the transit of a section of the Assyrian army from one
bank of the river to the other. The water was covered
with boats and with large rafts, on which were placed all
the war-chariots, and at the stern of every one of them was
a group of men holding the heads of the horses that were
swimming behind. The passage of the infantry was made
on inflated goatskins. The utmost confusion prevailed ;
several poor fellows were drowned, but that seemed a
matter of utter indifference to the officers that stood upon
the bank lashing the men with whips to make them
quicken their movements. At one place we observed that
a large bevy of prisoners was being conducted before an
official who was seated on a kind of open air tribunal, surrounded by guards. Some town had evidently been lately
captured. All the gods, and a quantity of booty, were
first laid at the officer's feet, and then the prisoners—men,
women, and children—were brought before him. They were
a wretched, dejected set, many of the men fettered with
heavy bronze chains, and nearly all with their hands bound
behind their backs, the whole of them being compelled
to prostrate themselves in turn before the officer, who placed
his foot upon their necks. In a few cases a respite was
granted and life was spared ; but as a general rule the
captives were forthwith hanged or beheaded in the pre-

sence of their fellow-sufferers. I observed that out of the number of miserable objects, four were selected and sent off to be tied to stakes that were driven into the ground on an adjacent eminence.

It was truly a heartrending spectacle. Chamai and Hannibal had seen something of the kind before in the course of the warfare in their own land; but to Aminocles and his countrymen, with their Hellenic ideal of liberty, the sight was intolerably shocking, and they were loud in their asseverations that they would die before they would incur the risk of any such utter degradation.

While we were looking on at this humiliating exhibition, a messenger arrived from the King to ascertain the object of my coming. I stated it as briefly as possible, and in another hour the man came again to summon us into the presence of Belochus. I took no one with me except Hanno, and the sailors to carry the Queen's gifts. As we walked along Hanno was silent, evidently preparing some graceful compliment; but his painstaking in this way was of no avail, as we were only permitted to view the splendour of the Assyrian sovereign from a distance. At about a hundred paces from the throne we were commanded to halt, and prostrate ourselves to the ground.

Belochus II. was seated beneath a group of trees, surrounded so closely by guards, cupbearers, attendants with fans and parasols, and slaves with fly-whisks, that for a long time I could see nothing of him except his tiara, which was very dazzling, his robes, which were very elaborate, and his unshod feet sparkling with gems. But at last the mass of gorgeous pomp seemed to open, and I could plainly distinguish the majestic countenance of the King, encircled with long hair, and conspicuous with a thick frizzled beard.

An avenue of soldiers was formed; some officers were sent to receive whatever documents and presents we had brought; we were bidden a second time to prostrate ourselves to the earth, and were then escorted back to our

WE WERE COMMANDED TO HALT.

see page 324.

ships. I found Belesys very impatient to be released from his imprisonment, and he looked much chagrined when I told him that it was necessary for me to detain him a while longer as a hostage for my own safety.

In about an hour afterwards some letters, enclosed in a casket of gold, arrived from King Belochus for the Queen of Sheba ; the present for the Queen was accompanied by a meagre gift of provisions and stuffs for myself and my people.

My mission was now accomplished, and I prepared again to set sail.

"You may go," I said to my prisoner ; "let us part friends."

Belesys gave a sigh of relief.

" I am glad you are a man of your word," he said.

I laughed heartily.

" Did you suppose I should keep you ? What good could you do me ? "

" Revenge is sweet," he answered. " I feared you would not let my injustice go unpunished."

" Ah, you mean that would have been your course."

Belesys smiled.

"The hand that cannot be cut off must be caressed," he said.

I took good care that before he left he should see the scorpions filled with missiles and put ready for action, and then I dismissed him with the most punctilious observance of outward respect.

Before quitting the ship he made another attempt to induce Bichri to join his service, an honour which was coolly and firmly declined.

HIMILCO AND GISGO IN ANIMATED CONVERSATION WITH THE CHALDEAN SOLDIERS. *To face page 127.*

CHAPTER XXIII.

WE SETTLE OUR ACCOUNTS WITH BODMILCAR.

IT was quite late in the evening before we reached the bar of the river, and as I was fearful of crossing it in the dark, I gave orders to lay to for the night. A small Chaldean camp was within sight, but I took every precaution to guard against any act of treachery on the part of Belesys.

A number of booths made of branches of trees had been erected on the shore, and some Phœnician dealers were purchasing plunder from the soldiers, and supplying them with wine in return. Himilco, Gisgo, and several others expressed a great wish to go ashore, and although I knew that they would only be drinking and bragging of their adventures, I could not find it in my heart to refuse them. I only stipulated that they should not go out of hearing. A couple of hours later, being curious to know what was going on in the little mart that looked so bright with its many lamps, I took Bichri and Jonah, and rowed to land. Just as I stepped on shore, I observed two galleys pass down stream, as if about to anchor below us; they were followed by a gaoul, which kept very close to the opposite bank; but as the river was very wide, and it was quite dusk, I could not distinguish its form. Knowing, moreover, that there was a great deal of slave-trafficking going on with the Assyrians, I did not give the circumstance more than a casual attention.

I found Himilco and Gisgo in animated conversation with the Chaldean soldiers, who evidently regarded all their tales about enormous stags, stinking fish-oil, and the sun shining on the wrong side, as mere romances, if not downright lies. One of them avowed that no power on earth would ever make him believe that any people could accept Jonah for their god, a mere human being like themselves. To this Bichri replied, somewhat contemptuously, that he could not see but that Jonah was every whit as good as Nisroch; and Gisgo added that he could believe anything after seeing how the Assyrians allowed themselves to be bullied by Belochus and his general Belesys.

Furious at the insults offered alike to his god and to his rulers, the Chaldean threatened to break every bone in Gisgo's skin; whereupon Gisgo replied that he was quite ready to accept a challenge, and that he would fight it out in any way he pleased; like the people of Prydhayn or Ar-Mor, if he chose.

"You had better not be fighting with us," said Himilco; "we conquer wherever we go; Sicilians, Garamantines, Suomi, Germani, we have thrashed them all. We have been to the river Illiturgis, and to the Pyrenees, and to the Chariot of the Gods, and to the Fortunate Islands, where we got as much gold as we liked. Everything succeeds with us ; and the best thing you can do is to leave us alone."

The man looked aghast at the string of names which Himilco repeated out so volubly, and, in a half-apologetic tone, replied :

"You Sidonians are wonderful travellers. I am a Kardook, and thought I had done something marvellous in coming here from my far-off mountains. The world is much larger than I reckoned."

Another Chaldean now put in his word, and said that though he had not been to Tarshish, he had just seen a man of Tarshish.

"Just seen one ! where ?" asked Himilco.

"In the royal camp. He was along with the Phœnician captain who has taken service under King Belochus."

A thrill ran through me. In an instant I recollected the gaoul and the two galleys, and the truth flashed upon my mind.

"His name ?" I cried. "Tell me his name, and I will give you a shekel."

"Make it two, and I will tell you."

I threw him the money, which he picked up and put in his purse. He was walking off, saying that he did not see why he need tell me the captain's name now that he was already paid. In my rage at the cool effrontery of the rascal I was about to knock him down, when one of the Phœnician dealers interposed :

"Never mind that fellow's nonsense. I will tell you what you want. The captain's name is Bodmilcar ; he is a Tyrian."

The very sound of the name was enough. My men caught it, and in an instant we were all on our way back to the ships. Once on board, I held a consultation with the officers, and put them in possession of the fact that Bodmilcar was lying in wait a few cables' length below us ;

that he was in connection with the army ; and that it was extremely likely that Belesys would attack us in the rear. How melancholy would it be, I urged, if our enterprise, hitherto so successful, should be marred by our hateful foe at last !

Animated by a general enthusiasm, my people declared that not a moment should be lost, the hour for action was come, and the attack must be made at once.

Chamai and Hanno began to contend for the right to kill Bodmilcar.

"Let me only get within reach of him !" cried Chamai.

" No, no," said Hanno, flushing with excitement ; " he is my rival, and by my hand must he fall."

" Don't be simpletons, young men !" I interposed ; " there is something better than wrangling for you to do now. Look to your duties.   We will make for the sea."

Using every possible caution, we proceeded towards the river-mouth. The *Ashtoreth* took the middle of the channel, with the *Adonibal* on her right, and the *Cabiros* on her left. Every light had been extinguished, and it was with throbbing pulses that the men on board stood, ready armed, peering out into the darkness. Bichri had spread out his arrows within reach upon the deck, and was crouching down, his bow full strung ; he was between Dionysos and Jonah. The trumpeter was armed with a huge hatchet in his girdle, and the little Phocian was provided with his bow and arrow ready for immediate use. Himilco, holding his cutlass and shield, took his post at the stern, directing the helmsman ; Hannibal and Chamai placed themselves at the head of their own companies, and stood almost on tiptoe in their eagerness to get the first glimpse of the enemy.

Before the hour of sunrise we could hear the rushing of the water at the river-bar, and in the faint dawn could make out Bodmilcar's three ships blockading our exit The *Melkarth* was in the middle ; the decks of all three being perfectly thronged by men in helmets. The shore was quite deserted.

"The stream is in our favour," I observed; "let us commence action with the fire-ships."

A number of planks loaded with combustibles was soon set afloat.

I did not wait long before ordering Jonah to sound the signal for attack : it was answered promptly by a challenge from the enemy ; a volley of lances fell upon our deck ; we discharged another volley in reply ; and the battle had fairly commenced.

As I had myself superintended the construction of the *Melkarth*, I was well aware that her flanks were far too substantial to be injured by any blow from our prows ; I knew, moreover, that her height was so great that it gave her an immense advantage in overwhelming us with missiles, and rendered every thought of boarding her untenable. But I also knew her weak points. I had myself experienced that her enormous weight made her difficult to move ; and I resolved in my own mind that, if possible, I would take advantage of this defect. After ascertaining from Himilco, who knew enough of the channel to form a reliable opinion, that the *Melkarth* drew too much water to be able to move a cable's length to the right of where she was, I ordered our boats to be laden with all the combustibles they could carry. I next signalled to the *Cabiros* to come alongside, and telling Himilco to follow me, I went on board her, Hamilcar being left in charge of the *Ashtoreth*. All this time the arrows from the enemy's ships were falling fast about us, and Bodmilcar, evidently expecting assistance from Belesys behind us, was fighting as if sure of victory.

Gisgo joined Himilco at the helm of the *Cabiros*, and I stood between them to give my orders. Never, I can confidently say, was a vessel more skilfully piloted. After taking the two boats in tow, and effectually setting light to their cargo of combustibles, we bore straight down upon the *Melkarth* ; and when we were within half a bow-shot, we were descried by Bodmilcar, who began to jeer us.

"All hail, Mago! you are right welcome; there are some old scores to settle between us,—that little affair in Egypt, and that other matter in Tarshish, and that piece of business in the Straits of Gades; we may as well wipe them all off to-day. I hope to have the pleasure of seeing you swing from that yard-arm before night. Most happy to meet you now."

An arrow struck him as he finished speaking; he started back.

"Hit! he's hit!" shouted Bichri, in a voice that rang out high above the general tumult.

"No!" roared Bodmilcar, "my cuirass is arrow-proof."

"Let us see whether your ship is fire-proof!" I bellowed in reply.

The *Cabiros* now dashed between the *Melkarth* and the galley on her right, and in endeavouring to avoid us, the gaoul became wedged between the burning boats. In the midst of a shower of arrows, one of which wounded my cheek, I cut asunder the towing-ropes; the flames broke forth, and a long jet of smoke rose high into the air. Gisgo was wounded in the thigh, and could not stand, but he continued bravely to steer upon his knees. So rapidly had we darted by, that the volley of missiles intended for our deck went splashing and crashing down upon the water in our wake; and as we retraced our course on the other side just as rapidly, I called out to Bodmilcar that I meant to serve his ship as I had served the Egyptian galley at Tanis. Himilco, too, did not spare him some cutting jokes upon his dilemma.

Having returned to my own ship, I ordered the *Adonibal* and the *Cabiros* to make a joint attack with me upon one of the two galleys, and then to get right ahead of the other. We made the assault with the very utmost of our strength; the galley made a desperate effort to escape us, but it was too late; before she could move I had stove in one of her sides, and driven her, by the violence of the shock, against the *Melkarth* and the two burning boats. In the midst of

the smoke I could see that the *Melkarth's* men were frantically making their way on board the *Adonibal*, which had
got between her and the other galley, and that the whole
of the six ships were thus brought together into a compact
mass, at one end of which the flames were raging furiously,
and at the other hatchets, swords, and cutlasses were being
wielded with relentless desperation.

"To the *Adonibal!*" I shouted; "board her! we shall
have them now!"

Simultaneously my own people and the crew of the
Cabiros made their way on to her deck. Bodmilcar was
already there. Hanno rushed towards him and cried:

"Now then, Bodmilcar, come on, and show yourself a
man for once!"

"Come on, young milksop! I am quite ready! As soon
as I have settled your business, I shall have time to attend
to the rest."

Their swords clashed as they closed in one upon the
other, but the throng around them was so dense that they
were quite lost to my view.

All at once Himilco, who had never left my side, made a
dash forward, and shouted:

"Ah! you monster, scoundrel, wretch, I have you now!"

He had recognised the man for whom he had been looking for the last fourteen years, and had knocked him
down: the two were rolling together on the deck.

"Well done, Himilco! hold him tight!" said Bichri,
who was passing, his sword all covered with blood.

"The brute is biting my arm; cannot you help me?"

Bichri, quick as lightning, slipped a knife into the hand
of Himilco, who plunged it deep into his adversary's side:
he rolled back; the death-rattle was already in his throat.

"Revenge is sweet," sighed the pilot; "this death of a
dog is too good for you!"

Meanwhile Jonah, backed up courageously by Aminocles,
was performing feats of wonder with his cutlass; Hannibal
and Chamai, with their armour all battered in, were on the

prow, pushing man after man back overboard into the water; Hamilcar was reported to be killed; Hasdrubal was badly wounded, but still clinging to his helm; I went to his assistance, and by our joint effort we succeeded in bringing the ship round so as to be out of the reach of the threatening flames; the *Ashtoreth* and *Cabiros* had sheered off a little, and were waiting my summons to come again alongside; and the other galley of the enemy, although it escaped the fire, had gone adrift.

Such was the condition of affairs, when as I was rallying my men for another onslaught, Hanno, his sword broken, and his clothes all stained with blood, rushed to my side.

"He has escaped!" he gasped. "I have lost him in the crowd."

"Patience!" I answered; "he is not far off."

I now resolved to fall back myself towards my two other ships, and as soon as I saw the opportunity, I shouted to my men:

"Back to the *Ashtoreth!*"

As we retreated, we left the prow of the *Adonibal* in complete possession of Bodmilcar's troops, and then by drawing up two lines of men made an avenue for our own escape at the stern.

Bodmilcar, perfectly helpless, was thus left in a trap, on board the *Adonibal*, which was exposed to the full fury of our arrows and catapults; his own ship was burning like a furnace; one of the galleys was sunk, and the other, as I have said, had gone adrift.

For more than half an hour, Bodmilcar endured our projectiles; but at length I came to the determination of again facing him on board the *Adonibal*. We found him standing on the bow, surrounded by a scanty remnant of hardly more than thirty men. His face was covered with blood.

"Shall I shoot him?" asked Bichri.

"By no means," I answered, laying my hand upon the archer's arm; "he must die a more ignominious death than that."

MY ACCOUNT WAS SETTLED WITH BODMILCAR.

To face page 335.

Desperate, but short, was the last effort of the Tyrian's body-guard. He was about to make a frantic rush upon myself, when Jonah seized him with a powerful grasp.

" Here's your man, captain !"

Bodmilcar struggled to get free.

" Attempt to escape," said the trumpeter, " and I'll shake the life out of your body !"

Foaming with supprsesed rage, the captured man submitted to his fate.

He was motionless and silent. Nothing could induce him to open his lips ; sullenly he heard my questions ; obstinately he refused to reply. He was tied to a rope's-end, and was soon swinging at the end of the yard-arm of the *Adonibal.*

My account was settled with Bodmilcar.

We were soon upon our homeward way.

After reporting our experiences to the Queen of Sheba, we proceeded to Tyre along the canal of Pharaoh, stopping only to pay our devoirs to King Solomon.

A triumphal reception awaited us. Throngs of our countrymen assembled to welcome our return ; and King Hiram, in our honour, gave a sumptuous banquet, at which he invited me publicly to narrate the history of our protracted and adventurous voyage.

The King munificently gave me the three vessels which I had brought safely home, and the people unanimously elected me naval suffect at Sidon.

I appointed Hannibal captain of my men-at-arms, and retained Himilco, Gisgo, and Hasdrubal in my service in various posts of good emolument. The report of Hamilcar being killed in action had proved too true.

I have little more to tell

All Phœnicia knows how I superintended the floating of

the cedar-wood and all the materials which King Solomon required for the magnificent temple he was rearing at Jerusalem. Chamai is a captain in King Solomon's army, and is invariably recognised with every token of respect when he comes with Abigail, his wife, to visit me at the Admiralty palace. Every one, too, knows Bichri, the rich vinedresser, who periodically comes to Sidon to sell his barrels and skins of sparkling wine, always inviting Himilco to the first taste of the produce of his vineyards ;

whilst every year a vessel is sent with all due pomp to Paphos to bring Hanno, the high priest of Ashtoreth, with the lovely Chryseis, her priestess and his wife, to sacrifice in the temple of their great metropolis. Dionysos, who has become a distinguished instructor of his countrymen in navigation, and Aminocles, his proud and aged father, generally accompany them.

On these occasions the *Cabiros*, adorned with embroidered hangings, puts out to sea in honour of my guests, and brings them to my private quay, where they are always hailed with acclamation as my former companions in the discovery of the Cassiterides, the Amber-coast, and the Fortunate Islands.

During the period of our festivities it is generally observed that Himilco does not walk home particularly straight, a circumstance that Bichri notifies by whistling some Benjamite or Cymrian air; and when finally the guests depart, Jonah is never missing, as he always insists on preceding them to their ship with a magnificent flourish of his trumpet.

NOTES.

CHAPTER I.

Phœnicians.—It is for simplicity's sake that throughout the preceding fiction I have adopted the classical name Phœnicians, which may be interpreted either as "the red men" or "men of the date-lands." Amongst themselves they were designated "Canaanites," or "people of the lowlands," in contradistinction to "Aramites," or "people of the highlands."

It would be out of place here to enter into any critical dissertation upon the words Khna and Aram, from which Canaanites and Aramites derive their appellation.—*Page 1.*

Shekel.—This word (which, in the Hebrew tongue, signifies a weight) is applied both to coined money, the use of which originated with the Phœnicians, and to a certain standard of ordinary weight.—*Page 2.*

Tariff of the Sacrifices.—The ritual or tariff of sacrifices is extracted from the work of the Abbé Bargès on the Phœnician inscription discovered at Marseilles.—*Page 5.*

Gaoul.—Originally this word signified any round hollow object. The Phœnicians designated the island of Gozo "Gaulo Melitta," Malta the Round, and it may easily be understood how the term came to be applied to their circular merchant ships, which were of a type essentially Tyrian. "*Onerariam navem Hippus Tyrius invenit.*" (Pliny, 'Nat. Hist.')

My authorities for the description of the Phœnician vessels are:

1. Two engravings in Layard.
2. Ezekiel's prophecy against Tyre. (Chap. xxvii. 7.)

Z 2

3. Xenophon's description in the ' Œconomia ' of the great **Phœnician** ship that came every year to the Piræus.

4. The engravings in Wilkinson.

I have likewise ventured to draw some inferences by analogy from the accounts of Genevan, Pisan, and Venetian ships of the thirteenth century, given by Col. Yule, in his edition of ' Marco Polo.'—*Page* 8.

Sheathed with Copper.—Although this may seem an anachronism, it may with some degree of certainty be alleged that the Phœnicians had an idea of using copper for this purpose. It would seem to be implied by Vegetius (' Rei militaris,' iv. 24) and by Athenæus (v. 40). An ancient legend attributes the invention to Melkarth, the Tyrian Hercules : *Hercules . . . n ive æned navigavit . . . navem æneam habuit* (Servius).

The other materials employed in the building of the ships are men-tioned by the prophet Ezekiel.

Besides the gaoul, I have introduced the barque, the fast ship, and the long ship, or fifty-oared war-galley.

Without entering into minute details, it may be said that the barque is essentially Phœnician. Barek, in Hebrew, signifies to bend or curve anything, as a plank. *Barca est quæ cuncta navis commercia ad littus portat* (Isidorus, Origines). In the modern Berber dialect it is called "ibarka."

The fast ship was called ἵππος, a horse, by the Greeks, either on account of its speed, or from the figure ordinarily found at its prow : Strabo distinctly asserts the latter reason. The vessel described in the text being of the type most frequently used in the Phœnician colony of Gades, has, on that account, been designated ' the *Gadita.*' Several Phœnician coins, apparently current on the coast of Africa, bear the impression of a horse's head ; and the legend of a horse's head being discovered in the foundation of Carthage, probably originated in the national symbol affixed to the Phœnician ships.

The true Sidonian war-ship is the fifty-oared galley :

ναῦν πεντηκόντορον Σιδόνιαν.

EURIP. *Hel.* 1141.

What was the tonnage of such a vessel, or how it could be worked by only fifty oars, or carry 400 men, are matters on which I give no opinion ; it is not my province to enter upon any technical argu-ments.

If an analogy be required, it may be suggested by the huge Chinese junks which were seen by the Arabian, Ibn Batuta, in the fourteenth century, and which carried 600 men, and had fifty or sixty immense oars, each oar being worked by eight men, by means of ropes pulled in opposite directions. Those seen by Marco Polo had four men to each oar. It is not improbable that the Phœnician vessels were worked by some similar method.—*Page* 9.

Purple sail.—My description of the parade-boats is not imaginary ; pictures of them are given in Wilkinson (vol. iii.), and all the ancient writers, from Herodotus to Plutarch, enter into details concerning them. Herodotus describes the Sidonian vessel, from which Xerxes reviewed his fleet, as being adorned with golden hangings, meaning Babylonian materials wrought with gold.—*Page* 16.

CHAPTER II.

Pigeons. Ravens.—The custom of taking birds on a voyage, to in-dicate by their flight the direction of land, is mentioned repeatedly in the annals of antiquity. As an instance of more modern time and of semi-barbarous races, it may be incidentally quoted that the sea-king, Ingolf, or Floke Vilgedarson, in 868 took with him three ravens when he set out for the discovery of Iceland.—*Page* 23.

Fleur-de-lys.—The tiara with this device may be seen amongst the engravings at the end of Botta's work.—*Page* 31.

CHAPTER V.

Pharaoh.—The blank which exists in the records of Egypt at the end of the eleventh and beginning of the tenth centuries B.C., renders me unable to give the name of the Pharaoh reigning at this period.

The war-chariots of the Egyptians were mounted by Libyans, i.e., by Perbers of the Tamachek race, of which the Kabyles and Touaregs are the modern representatives. These chariots and cavalry, also Libyan, formed the great strength of the Egyptian army.—*Page* 79.

CHAPTER VI.

Cydonians. Pelasgians.—Without entering upon any dissertation on this topic, I content myself with mentioning the existence throughout Europe of races distinct both in type and language from the Aryan races whom they preceded. Two of these may be especially remarked : one with round skulls of Mongolian type, commonly called Turanians ; the other with elongated skulls, classified as Australoids. These races have everywhere left traces alike of their presence and of their inferior civilisation In the island of Crete, the Greeks preserved the memory of the Cydonians by the few words which I have introduced into the text.—*Page* 100.

CHAPTER VII.

Homer.—My introduction of the name of Homer undoubtedly demands an apology. I can only plead that the temptation to uplift the veil of mystery, and to reveal the mighty poet in connection with my fiction, was very great. Even after Schliemann's researches, the date of the Trojan war is so uncertain that I feel quite at liberty to regard it as an open question.—*Page* 129.

CHAPTER IX.

Tyrrhenian Privateers.—The description of these vessels is based upon a figure found upon a vase in the Campana Museum.—*Page* 158.

Scylla. Charybdis.—The romances interwoven into my tale are strictly Phœnician ; and I have felt quite justified in introducing an allusion to the way in which the Tyrian sailors delighted to mystify strangers upon whom they could impose. I may adduce the passage in Herodotus, where he speaks of the young girls fishing for gold in the island of Cyraunis, and calls it a fine Phœnician story. "Tell it to the Greeks !" has passed into a proverb, and the Phœnician tar was only too glad to amuse himself and to enhance the price of his wares by giving a highly-coloured version of his adventures.—*Page* 164.

Nergal.—The superstition about the gigantic cock is borrowed from a Rabbinical legend quoted by Movers.—*Page* 164.

CHAPTER XI.

Adonibal.—I had already completed my fiction before I learnt from the researches of M. Sainte-Marie that Adonibal was the name usually borne by the naval suffects at Utica, or that it is at least established that a long line of magistrates were so called. It was a mere coincidence that I chose it as being the first appropriate Phœnician name that occurred to my mind.

I may observe here that I have throughout the preceding pages written proper names in the way in which they are most familiar. It would be mere pedantry to put Hanna-baal (cherished by the gods) instead of Hannibal, or Bod-melkarth (the face of Melkarth) instead of Bodmilcar ; and it will suffice for any reader who has not studied the Semitic dialects to know that any ancient Phœnician or Jewish name may be dissected like most modern Arab names ; for example, Hamilcar is Abd-Melkarth (the servant of Melkarth), like Abd-Allah (the servant of God). The student of the Semitic dialects will have no need to come to my book for instruction.

With regard to the names of places, I have felt considerable difficulty. My reasons for not writing them in Semitic are threefold :—

1. They are not all known to us under this form.

2. If known, they are unfamiliar to the general reader.

3. The identity, orthography, and pronunciation could not be substantiated without entering into minute arguments, which would be out of place.

I have accordingly, with few exceptions, used the most familiar forms, and have, at the risk of criticism, written Crete, for Caphtorim ; Egypt, for Mizraim ; Libyans, for Mashowiah, &c.—*Page* 177.

CHAPTER XII.

I have represented Mago as sacrificing in a dolmen in the form of a covered avenue below a tumulus. The details are drawn from Bourguignat's *Monuments mégalithiques du nord de l'Afrique.* M. Daux also gives a description of a similar temple. I profess, however, that I am very far from accepting Bourguignat's theory about rude stone monuments being arranged in the form of serpents, scorpions, and other figures ; I am altogether mistrustful of the accounts of prehistoric temples, and am quite of Fergusson's opinion, that these monuments are comparatively modern.—*Page* 202.

Atlantides.—To my mind there is nothing improbable in the idea of the existence of an inland sea in Algeria which is suggested by the text. I cannot, however, say so much for the existence of Atlantis, but while speaking of the migrations of the Libyans, it seemed consistent to mention all the ancient traditions that relate to them.—*Page* 203.

CHAPTER XVI.

Ar-Mor.—I entertain considerable doubt whether at the period of which I write the Celts had penetrated so far as the west coast of France; but at any rate they were already in the east, and upon the Rhone. I have ascertained the existence of anterior races, such as the Mongoloids and Australoids, and both here and in a subsequent chapter have referred to them. I plead guilty to an anachronism of four whole centuries, but I felt that to the general reader it would seem strange that I should depict my Phoenicians landing in Gaul without meeting with some well known Gallic people ; all that I can say in extenuation is that I have endeavoured to construct my story so as to make the anachronism not too flagrant —*Page* 244.

CHAPTER XVII.

Suomi.—There is no reason to doubt the existence of Finns at this date at the mouth of the Elbe. For want of an ancient Finnish name, I have invented an appellation from the modern Finnish word Suomi. —*Page* 261.

CHAPTER XX.

Circumnavigation of Libya.—Some adverse criticism may probably be aroused by my resorting to this expedient for the prosecuting of my story. That the Phœnicians might have accomplished it, cannot be disputed ; and although the *Periplus* of *Hanno* has recently been proved to be apocryphal, and the work of some scientific Greek romance writer, I have not hesitated to incorporate the prominent feature of it into these imaginary adventures.—*Page* 302.

CHAPTER XXI.

Sheba. Ophir.—The identity of this locality with the southern coast of Arabia is beyond a doubt.—*Page* 309.

" *Fairer, etc.*"—These verses are translated from some later Arabian poetry. Oriental taste has altered so little, that I may claim to be pardoned for putting into the mouth of a Phœnician, a thousand years before the Christian era, some poetry belonging to a period a thousand years after.—*Page* 310.